I0636010

LOVEBORNE

AURECIE MACBETH

RIPTIDE
PUBLISHING

Riptide Publishing
PO Box 1537
Burnsville, NC 28714
www.riptidepublishing.com

This is a work of fiction. Names, characters, places, and incidents are either the product of the author's imagination or are used fictitiously. Any resemblance to actual persons living or dead, business establishments, events, or locales is entirely coincidental. All person(s) depicted on the cover are model(s) used for illustrative purposes only.

Loveborne
Copyright © 2023 by Aurecie Macbeth

Cover art: Simoné
Editor: Kelly Miller
Layout: L.C. Chase, lcchase.com

All rights reserved. No part of this book may be reproduced or transmitted in any form or by any means, electronic or mechanical, including photocopying, recording, or by any information storage and retrieval system without the written permission of the publisher, and where permitted by law. Reviewers may quote brief passages in a review. To request permission and all other inquiries, contact Riptide Publishing at the mailing address above, at Riptidepublishing.com, or at marketing@riptidepublishing.com.

ISBN: 978-1-62649-977-5

First edition
May, 2023

Also available in ebook:
ISBN: 978-1-62649-976-8

LOVEBORNE

AURECIE MACBETH

To this incredible and terrifying feeling—love.

TABLE OF
CONTENTS

CHAPTER ONE
RISK AND OPPORTUNITY

The star-shaped Mortella General Hospital loomed above Alias, its five branches casting more darkness than the clouds gathering overhead. His stomach tightened. He glanced away from the two black-and-white-uniformed NID officers guarding the main doors and hurried toward the crowded lift, eyes cast down. Strangers may be deemed safe even for the unlucky souls who couldn't afford Avida—and Alias had been on antivirals his whole life—but there were exceptions to the rules.

Always.

The ride lasted eight seconds, and it was eight seconds too long. He rushed out of the lift and shuddered when a man dressed in a doctor's white coat brushed his shoulder.

Don't look. Don't feel a thing.

But he didn't need to look at the man to overhear him on his watchphone.

"We just lost her." The doctor sounded angry. "She was only four. Avida shouldn't have failed a child . . . I really hope it's an isolated case again . . ."

Alias stopped abruptly in front of a tall window that offered a view of New York City. He was looking straight at the black towers owned by McCarthy Ltd., but with the doctor's words gnawing at him, he saw the traditional family unit—a child holding their two parents' hands via the curved bridges linking the three uneven towers. A social structure of a bygone era: the promise of affection that became an open door to the most lethal virus humanity had ever known. The Loveborne virus had killed more than four billion people during the initial outbreak fifty years ago. In 2145, that had meant half the population.

Avida was supposed to keep the survivors and their descendants safe.

Alias slammed a fist against the pristine glass, startling the woman beside him. He apologized in a half-whisper. Visiting his mother always made him feel so sad he ended up angry. Mad at the virus and at the doctors who offered his mother less and less support, but mostly at himself.

But there was still hope, wasn't there? Despite the worsening symptoms over the years at Mortella General, his mother hadn't fallen into a coma. The doctors had no scientific explanation as to why she'd survived for so long, only the usual triteness: love was too complex to understand fully, and the virus was unpredictable.

Alias had meant to come sooner this month, but with two jobs and yet nowhere near enough money, he'd postponed until he started feeling guilty for a whole new set of reasons. Did Lyra McCarthy, the woman at the top of the pharmaceutical company manufacturing and distributing Avida, also have trouble sleeping at night, crafting worst-case scenarios?

He shook himself and headed for room E-8986. To get there, he first had to go through Wing A, where people who showed minor LBV-typical symptoms were grouped together. A man whose partner had just tested negative let out a joyous shout. Alias couldn't stop a pang of envy any more than he could quell his profound dislike of hospitals.

Wing B, next to it, catered to patients who'd been officially diagnosed with the virus. Some of these patients insisted on going back to their life for as long as they could. When the worst symptoms kicked in—crippling migraines, respiratory distress, fever, and extreme fatigue—they inevitably returned here. Alias almost tiptoed through Wing C and D, depressed once more by the aura of inevitable death that clung to them. Wing C was reserved for terminally ill patients who needed around-the-clock care, and Wing D for those who'd reached the last stage before death: coma.

Those who couldn't pay the astronomical price tag of Wing C or D ended up in Wing E, with mediocre care and overpopulated rooms.

Alias pushed the door marked *E-8986*, a comforting smile popping into place. "Hello, Mother."

"Alias!"

Kira Novar, 46 years old, AB, the small screen at the foot of the bed read.

The woman covered in white sheets appeared at least ten years older. Her blond hair was cut just under her ears, straight and pale like straw left outside under a blazing sun. Her jaw and cheekbones had become prominent lately. She'd always been delicate, but with so little fat left on her tiny frame and chalk-white skin even a blush failed to color, she had more in common with a ghost than with the only child she'd borne.

Alias worked a chair between his mother's bed and the one of a middle-aged man who often complained of hunger. "How are you feeling today, Mother?"

"Very good," she said, which was obviously a lie.

Her brown eyes were a perfect mirror of Alias's own. Although tentative smiles played on two pairs of lips, one was wan and honest, while the other was forced but nonetheless fond.

"Don't worry about me, my dear boy."

Alias couldn't help it. He worried about her every day, about what she could and couldn't do. His mother shouldn't talk too much, the doctors said. She shouldn't walk, shouldn't do anything that might strain her frail body and failing immune system. As a matter of fact, she shouldn't see anyone, but most patients didn't care about that rule.

And no one seemed to care about his mother, least of all the doctors, whose only interactions with her were limited to tests. For them, she was a mystery to solve, having been one of the few that lived for so long despite viral reactivation.

His mother never said anything, but he knew how seldom she got treated with gentleness or was offered a hearty meal, how often she went without a shower because she needed help and didn't get it, how little she saw the sun because this room had no window. She used to have a better room she'd shared with fewer people and much better care beyond occasional rounds of symptom-alleviating medication, but she'd been downgraded a year ago after Alias had lost the only well-paying job he'd ever had.

When his mother tried to sit up, Alias forgot all about his bitterness. He rushed to arrange the pillows at her back and held out the sheet she was trying to grab. Tremors ran through her hand. Alias pressed his own atop hers, rubbing aimless patterns over her knuckles. The tremors were nothing new, but every time the symptom showed, his chest tightened. The condition of hospitalized LBV patients tended to worsen unpredictably, as did his mother's episodes of respiratory distress.

He didn't cry. In front of her, he never did.

His morning run was a sacred ritual and a special kind of relief after brushing elbows with so many doctors. Focusing on the light strides of a casual jog helped dim his awareness of others. Under the vast, unthreatening sky, he got to be the cause of his quickening heartbeat. His mind became a simple extension of his body, and his body an enabler of his will.

Fortunately, only a few people were visiting the park this early on a Tuesday morning. Alias slowed to a walk as he neared the forty-feet-tall statue, finding immediate comfort in the familiar, striking mix of copper and steel. The woman gleamed brightly under the sun, the rain droplets weaving a shimmery gown on her naked form. Her long hair flowed around her shoulders, the strands weaved with cogs and other watchmaking mechanisms of extraordinary craftsmanship.

She reminded him of his mother a long time ago.

He dropped to one knee in front of the pedestal. October had already collected its debt, undressing poplars, birches, and linden. He felt equally stripped of his strength. The hospital bill was due in a few days, and he wasn't sure any amount of self-imposed starvation would make a difference this time.

His hands started shaking. They were fine-boned, like the rest of him, and for a moment, he felt so dizzy from the lack of sleep that he saw leaves instead, their five blades a rare skin color. He looked up at the sculpted woman's hands, willing his own to stop shaking. She had one outstretched like a shield, and the other splayed over her round belly. Lady Love, bearing hope. She was more than a reminder that love could kill—she was a beacon of fortitude, and a homage to the people who'd borne children despite the risks.

People like his mother.

A flying gardening bot, small compared to the others tending the various flower beds and gathering the fallen leaves, whirred past him. Sparks flared under its left wing. As tempted as he was to fix it and prove to himself that he was good at *something*, he knew better. One unregistered bot was enough.

He got up. The digits on his watchphone told him he had plenty of time to cover the last two miles, take a shower, and even have breakfast before he was due for his next dose, but he had more than one reason to hurry today. He breezed through the final stretch of his run, barely slowing down on the stairs inside his apartment building. When he reached the dark, narrow hallway leading to his shoebox of an apartment in Lower New York, his humanoid robot was already opening the door.

"Welcome home, Alias. Did you have a nice run?" Ben inquired. "You were very agitated when you left."

"I wish I could be paid to run." Alias toed off his shoes and shed his shirt, which he used to wipe off the sweat dripping in his eyes. "My wages barely cover Avida, rent, food, and my mother's hospitalization, and that's before Mortella decided to increase the fee for the third time this year. I have . . ." He grabbed his bottle of antivirals on the kitchen counter and popped a pill into his mouth, washing it down with what was left of his water from the run, trying very hard not to think about what that doctor had said about the little girl. "Ben, I have two jobs and it's not enough."

"I am certain you will find another well-paying job again, Alias." Ben did the head-cocking motion Alias had taught it.

Alias tossed his shirt to the floor and got rid of his shorts and underwear, his movements slow and defeated. "Yeah, well, I'm good with numbers and computers, but who isn't? There's a reason I haven't gotten lucky twice."

"I am searching for an opportunity nonetheless as we speak."

Being wirelessly connected to the internet, the hubot was always a flicker of processor away from the global network. Alias left Ben to its futile search. His run hadn't energized him, and the pang of hunger just made the nausea worse as he recalled the tremors in his mother's hand. The kitchen seemed to shrink, and it was quite small to begin with. Alias sagged against the counter, his white-knuckled grip on the chipped dark melamine the only thing keeping him up. Everything was gray or black in this windowless space he could barely afford, with only specks of white in the bathroom, where a crack ran down the one mirror he owned.

Staring at his wild-eyed reflection and wondering when he'd ended up in the bathroom, Alias witnessed how the unease within splashed outward, tightening the delicate features he'd inherited from his mother. He wasn't happy. Every day, he worried about triggering the dormant virus, and what the virus was already doing to his mother. There was also this emptiness within him that he couldn't explain, something missing, a whole dimension of his life lacking.

His pounding heart missed a beat as Ben came up behind him and squeezed his shoulder with the five fingers of its right hand. Its lipless mouth didn't move when it spoke, but its voice cut through the ringing in his ears. "I will find a solution for you and Kira. For now, focus on me."

Alias did, pressing his sweaty palm on top of the cool metal hand. Ben was a good two heads shorter than him but seemed taller and sturdier than its dented, flat torso and toeless feet implied.

"You are doing well, Alias."

From an actual human being, these words would have elicited unease rather than comfort. Fortunately, there was really nothing human about a humanoid robot. All hubots looked like machines—a mandatory design requirement—to prevent an emotional reaction strong enough to trigger the virus.

So Alias allowed himself to be comforted. He breathed through his nose, slow and methodical, as he listened to Ben count down from one hundred. The hubot's mechanical voice conveyed little in the way of intent, but the color shifting in its eyes, twice as big as a human's and reminiscent of manga aesthetics, more than made up for it. They were blue now, the color of approval.

". . . three, two, one."

Ben's index finger twitched. Somehow, the glitch was what finally allowed Alias's mind to settle. He picked up the hubot's hand and frowned at the misbehaving digit. He'd meant to fix it for ages, but something always came up. He traced the metallic articulation back and forth until the knot in his gut didn't make him want to throw up. Ben remained quiet. While any hubot could mimic and learn, even take initiative, there were still situations where they didn't know how to react. Ben used to "draw a blank" a lot more often, but it had gotten better at handling Alias. Not that Alias expected anything. He barely knew how to deal with himself some days.

He cracked a weary smile. "Thank you, Ben."

"I am here to help."

After a quick shower, Alias put on his most comfortable clothes—threadbare pants and a shirt two sizes too big—and set up his round-the-clock-office in his tiny bedroom, putting the single bed away to make room for the table and chair. Ben retrieved his laptop for him, perfectly able to multitask.

Alias cracked his neck and got to work. Time rolled by swiftly, the tapping of his fingertips on the keyboard the loudest sound in the room while he coded. At some point, Ben got him a meal bar. It tasted foul, but Alias needed the calories and couldn't keep skipping meals, or he wouldn't be able to earn any credit at all. Several hours later, he clocked out of his first job and started on the second one. There was little challenge in his work, and he missed the good mental stimulation his old job offered.

When he next glanced at the time on the screen, it was past 10 p.m. He put the desk away into the wall to get his bed back and flopped down on the hard mattress with a yawn. His body was tired, his mind was too, but sleep refused to come. Ben was standing nearby, completely immobile—still searching. Alias rolled onto his side and stared at the blank wall. Someday, he would liven it up. Put up a picture of the Grand Canyon, perhaps, or reproduce the live feed of that geyser in the Yellowstone National Park . . .

He stiffened. What was he doing indulging in wishful thinking when the base of his Maslow's pyramid was crippled?

Alias pushed himself into a sitting position and brought up his finances on his laptop. The third time he sighed, Ben perched on the edge of the small bed and twisted its torso in Alias's direction. It could do a whole three sixty with half of its body if the fancy struck.

"Were you not promised a raise?"

"At my two jobs, yes, but any extra credit won't help much if the hospital increases its fees again. And let's not forget that, unlike my employers, my landlord never mentioned rewarding me for thinking outside the box. Just last month, the rent went up again. I have no idea how I'll pay the bill. It's not that cold yet, is it? I could cut down on the heating. Do more overtime . . ."

"I am sure your mother would prefer you to be healthier than—"

"We're not discussing this." Alias glared at the digits, glaring harder as an ad popped up at the corner of his screen. *Exotic dancer.* Sweat beaded at his brow as he pictured himself on stage, rock-hard for the show and shriveling inside while strangers' hands reached for his swaying hips. Interactions of a sexual nature, or repeated nonsexual interactions involving attraction, were considered a limited risk, but a risk nonetheless, even on Avida. Only risk-seekers, or "riskeers" as they called themselves, indulged in promiscuity without a second thought.

"Alias? I believe you should watch the news."

The data on screen morphed into the figure of a man in his midthirties with short, dusty-blond hair and a suit that probably cost more than what Alias earned in a year. His white shirt stood out against his black pants and jacket, the buttons gleaming like obsidian under the sun. Snug at his neck, the red tie drew attention to his face. And what a face it was: a masterpiece of decisive lines, the nose straight and sharp, the cheeks well-defined, the jaw rough and masculine, the lips full and sinfully red, curled up into a confident smile. He had this air about him, as though he owned the keys to a safe most people didn't suspect existed.

Even though Alias had only seen the man in tutorials on robotics, he recognized him immediately: Deon Dehive, CEO of Dehive Inc.

But it wasn't the nature of Mr. Dehive's innovative work in robotics that held Alias's attention right now. He could deny the attraction all he wanted, but it was there in the dryness in his throat, in the clenching of his belly. His palms were clammy too, but this had more to do with the fact that Mr. Dehive stood in a very familiar park with an equally familiar statue in the background. He pressed his palm to the screen, focusing on the distance. There was no contact, like this. He was safe. Technically, he could look all he wanted.

Technically, his mother never should have ended up in the hospital.

Breathe, he told himself sternly, pretending it was Ben's voice keeping his thoughts in line. Between two of his fingers, the three towers of McCarthy Ltd. jutted out like claws behind Deon Dehive's smiling face. The superposition reminded him of an article he'd read last month. Did Mr. Dehive really dislike his former employer, Lyra McCarthy, as much as the rumors said he did?

"It's been a few months since Dehive announced an upgrade or a new product, and you are usually eager to share your plans for the company," a woman's voice said. "You've had the public intrigued by the creation of a virology department three years ago. Dehive belongs to the ten top sellers of hubots in the world, so why spread out your resources?"

"Because I could. And I was curious."

"What about the public's curiosity? You haven't issued a single statement about your virology department since its opening."

"I couldn't very well spoil the surprise, you see. And besides, I'm a perfectionist."

Alias dropped his hand. The close-up of Mr. Dehive turned into a forest and what lay within: Dehive's main offices. From above, the structure brought to mind the word *fractal*—a hexagonal shape formed from smaller versions of the same geometrical figure. It was three-stories high, although many said it spread deep underground in a maze-like fashion. The architectural marvel was well-known as "the Hive," a play on the CEO's last name more than a reference to bees, although rumor had it that actual beehives could be found in the building.

The journalist painted a portrait of Dehive's accomplishments over the last couple of years while showing the Hive and its surroundings under various angles. Alias took in the fall foliage as he considered Mr. Dehive's cryptic words. He wasn't well versed in business matters, but the secret surrounding Dehive's virology department stuck him as odd for a man otherwise so . . . open.

"Are you ready to reveal to the world what you've been up to in the shadows, Mr. Dehive?" the journalist asked, echoing Alias's musing.

The feed shifted back to the park. A few passersby had stopped, no more than seven, but that kind of attention would have put Alias on edge, even if the onlookers kept their distances. Of course, Mr. Dehive showed no sign of being bothered by his in-person public, and nodded at those he could see.

"Not quite just yet. However . . ." Mr. Dehive consulted his watchphone. "As of right now, thirteen new positions are open at Dehive Inc., including personal assistant to my very busy person."

"Is that the reason you are here today, talking to the world?"

His gaze returned to the journalist, or rather, to the bot she controlled remotely.

"Yes and no. I'm also here to remind anyone who's watching that we do things differently at Dehive," Mr. Dehive said. "These social work openings, so to speak, are opportunities for you to find out that spending time with your fellow human beings on a daily basis can change your life for the better."

"Are you actively encouraging citizens to have more of a social life than is recommended?"

"Humans are social creatures," Mr. Dehive replied at once, seemingly unbothered by the journalist's aggressive tone. "There is a reason Dehive is flourishing, Ms. Lopez. We need one another. And we need our common dream to become reality."

"And what dream would that be, Mr. Dehive?" the journalist prompted, not quite as aggressive now.

Mr. Dehive cocked an eyebrow. "Why, to change the world, of course."

"Is that what the creation of a virology department was about? The concretization of an old dream?"

"I believe we all have the same dream. We all want a world without LBV."

"Avida—"

"Avida is a good shield against the Loveborne virus, but it's an incomplete solution."

"An incomplete solution it may be," Ms. Lopez argued, "yet it has worked well for more than fifty years. And you, Mr. Dehive, disregard the consensus and encourage your employees to work in close quarters with one another. Is that how you plan to change the world? Or do you know something that the rest of the world doesn't? Are you still denying that your sickness one year ago is unrelated to your promiscuous tendencies?"

The barrage of questions made Alias dizzy, but Mr. Dehive remained perfectly composed and articulate, his poise one of complete confidence.

"I never lie to the public," Mr. Dehive said. "Or to my employees, present or future. And I want each and every one of you to feel safe, because humanity as a whole has lost that, and it's a loss I mean to address. As the head of Dehive Inc., I may take risks to get there, but that's not what I'm asking of you."

The camera zoomed in on his face. Blue eyes filled the screen.

"Trust me. That's the only risk I'm asking you to take."

Alias blinked at the screen. He couldn't shake the sense that Mr. Dehive had been looking at *him*, asking *him* if he was willing to that the risk. Challenging him.

"Trust me."

Alias pursed his lips together. Deon Dehive slept around right and left, cultivating lovers in his own workplace. The riskiest of all riskeers, according to the tales about him. But he was also filthy rich, and maybe, just maybe, one of those job offers could help Alias secure the care his mother needed.

He propped himself against the wall and set the laptop on his thighs. The thirteen job offers were easy to find. Unfortunately, he didn't have the qualifications for any of them.

"Not even this one?" Ben prompted, putting the first offer back on the screen.

> Job title: Personal assistant
> Employer: Dehive
> Salary: Starting at 350K credits/year, based on experience, meals and accommodations included.
> Schedule: 50 hours+/week
> Note: The PA has to be available on short notice for day, evening, night, and weekend work ranging from three- to eighteen-hour shifts. Must show efficiency, discipline, versatility, good interpersonal skills, and resistance to stress. Will work in close contact with other people.

"I can't do that." Alias looked between the screen and Ben, trying to convey his disbelief—and ignore the nauseous mix of hope and fear in his belly. "I can't be an *in-person* personal assistant."

"You could. You think outside the box and you are adaptable, which you proved more than once in your previous job as a personal assistant."

"*Remote* and *occasional* assistant," Alias corrected. "And unofficial to boot. I only ended up organizing a couple of things for my boss because I wrapped up my work early."

"Which shows efficiency and discipline."

"I really don't have the experience, Ben."

"It costs nothing to apply."

Alias buried his head in his hands. Three hundred fifty thousand credits a year. Three hundred fifty *thousand*. That was a fortune. Oh, what he could do with all that credit . . . and what he would risk, too, working for and with a man who thought nothing of close contact. With a screen between them, he'd felt relatively safe from his attraction. If he were to work with Deon Dehive in person . . . His antivirals might do their job, but they could fail him, too, just like they'd failed his mother.

"This is a once-in-a-lifetime opportunity, Alias."

Three hundred fifty thousand credits a year. Working as an *in-person* assistant. Being constantly *in close contact* with *people*.

He would never need to worry about his mother not getting the care she deserved ever again.

He would never be hungry again.

He might be able to have a place with windows.

Alias drew in a ragged breath. "Mr. Dehive never answered the question about what's going on in his virology department. Perhaps they're experimenting on the employees. That must be why there's so much money offered."

"This is your fear speaking. You are safe with your Avida."

"As safe as anyone can be, and that seems to be less and less the case." Alias stared at his hands. "Still, it doesn't . . . It can't change . . ." He felt thirsty and tired, his mind running in all kinds of directions, and he just wanted . . . He wasn't sure what he wanted. "People have been taking antivirals for decades and are still reluctant to work social jobs because a risk remains. Except the lunatics. Do I look like I'm as crazy as Mr. Dehive clearly is?"

Ben's metallic mitten-shaped left hand landed on his shoulder. Alias hugged his knees to his chest and let his head rest against Ben's arm. With all that complex circuitry running under its metallic veneer, Ben really was well attuned to humans. Alias glanced up. Ben's big eyes had gone yellow—the color of doubt. Because of Alias's resistance or the position itself?

He got to his feet using the wall for support. No matter where he stood in his apartment, a wall was always close by.

"I'll be in the shower."

A headache was building at his temples. For the second time that day, he stepped into the minuscule shower under the single flickering light and started rubbing his torso hastily under the lukewarm water. In his pulsating skull, the same word echoed over and over: *riskeer*. Deon Dehive was such a person. The riskiest of all, if the tales had any truth to them.

He reached for his feet, which required some gymnastics. The water ran cold now, but his body didn't get the memo. His eyelids fell shut. Solitude was a price he paid willingly to increase his chances of staying alive, but it wouldn't be enough for his mother. And Alias wasn't about to lose the one person it was safe for him to care for and love.

He pictured Deon Dehive's face—the easy smile, the confidence his whole being radiated. What if he was telling the truth?

When Alias returned to the bedroom, his computer was still on his bed. He sat down gingerly and clicked open the appropriate window. Ben opened the lid of the multi-vitaminized protein jelly that was the main part of his diet and handed it to him with a spoon. Alias dug in, but the taste was lost on him.

In-person personal assistant.

"That's the only risk I'm asking you to take."

He started filling out the application form. There were many, many questions, and his confidence wavered as he stumbled upon sections titled "Previous Experiences" and "Recommendations." Ever logical, Ben gave him advice based on similar applications found on the internet. Alias inserted the suggestions within his answers.

"Sent," he whispered. It sounded like a challenge. "What do you think, Ben?"

The robot picked up the empty bowl, eyes shining blue. "The included meals would take care of your huge appetite, at any rate."

Alias glanced down at his belly. Its flatness had little to do with muscle definition. That he'd managed a growth spurt in his teens and reached five foot seven was a miracle.

He flung the wet towel across the chair bolted in the wall and stretched on the bed, eyelids growing heavy.

"I hope I didn't just make a huge mistake."

CHAPTER TWO
THE HIVE

The call from Dehive on Friday had been unexpected, to say the least. Alias wasn't the most likely candidate, no matter how often Ben listed his strengths for him. A personal assistant was a social job, and Alias Novar had never been good with people *on purpose*. He was adept with a computer and well-organized, but surely such skill sets were commonplace in the twenty-second century? He truly was no one special.

Or so he'd thought.

The identity of the caller had been as surprising as the call itself: Jaden Angelius, Deon Dehive's current personal assistant until a replacement was found. Alias had stuttered through the whole conversation and expected Ms. Angelius to hang up on him in annoyance.

He still wasn't sure why that hadn't happened.

"What am I even doing here?" he whispered aloud Saturday morning. The address he'd been given was close to Upper New York, and he could have jogged there, but first impressions were very important, so he'd taken the tram instead. Rubbing elbows with people hadn't exactly helped with his stress level.

Was this even the right place? The unassuming two-story building showed no outright sign of its owner, and the wide windows and modern style weren't exactly unique in the area. There was no number on the door, holographic or otherwise. For the third time, Alias checked the GPS location. Yes, this was undoubtedly it. He just had to cross the street and open the door.

Never before had a door looked so imposing.

He wiped his hands on his best trousers and was immediately reassured by the familiar bulge of his vial of Avida pills in his right pocket. His next dose was in the evening, but feeling the bottle was doing wonders for his anxiety. Most people carried theirs on their person at all times. It wasn't just him or his all-encompassing paranoia.

What about Mr. Dehive's claims, then?

Alias gripped the bottle through the fabric and exhaled through his nose.

He had to stop overthinking this . . . opportunity.

The sudden appearance of a shuttle startled him. It had private transportation written all over it, despite the lack of any distinctive sign or logo. Did it belong to Dehive? Two women exited it. Despite himself, Alias found himself staring wide-eyed at the duo. Those women were talking and laughing together, hands brushing as they walked away from the shuttle.

Probably employees from Dehive.

Alias rushed inside the building, as if speed could make up for sheer stupidity. The door hissed closed at his back. Alias slowed to a tentative walk, befuddled by the bare white walls and the lack of, well, everything he associated with wealth. He hadn't expected anything like the Hive, but still, Dehive's name should be somewhere. Unless this was merely a rented space? With all the secrecy surrounding Dehive and his work, it would make sense that interviews would be conducted somewhere bland and unassuming that couldn't hint at corporate mysteries.

The place smelled faintly of fresh paint and something flowery. The only furniture amounted to a handful of chairs and an imposing desk behind which stood a hubot. Alias breathed a sigh of relief. After Mr. Dehive's speech about his employees' habits, he'd dreaded a human receptionist.

"Mr. Novar? Alias Novar?" the hubot asked.

"That's me."

"Welcome." When the hubot gestured behind itself, the sun hit the dark triangle fashioned with a twin *D* between its glowing eyes. "Mr. Novar, if you'll follow me."

Alias tucked his hands into the cheap polyester pants he'd bought only yesterday after skipping a few meals. At least the tie, which he'd found at one of the many all-hubot-staffed thrift stores in his neighborhood, matched his brown eyes.

The hubot led him through a door in the back. Alias matched its pace, pretending that clutching his Avida bottle wasn't a feeble attempt to find his bearings. Was he going to interview through a screen or in person? He tried to turn his focus to his surroundings, but the narrow corridor offered no distractions. His feet made hardly any noise on the tiled floor, and the hubot made none at all. A more pronounced note of sweetness wafted to his nostrils as they reached a nondescript door.

"Good luck," the hubot told him by way of a farewell.

The door chimed open. For a second, Alias was tempted to follow the hubot back to reception, but a human's voice—a more melodious voice—froze him in place.

"Good morning, Mr. Novar."

The voice hadn't come from a sound system. There was an actual person in this room.

Even though he'd never seen her, Alias had heard this melodious voice once before, and could only assume he was standing in front of Jaden Angelius. As the former personal assistant of one of the most powerful businessmen in the country, and one of few people to have done this job in person, she must be taking the matter of her replacement seriously.

Alias knew he ought to look at her face. There might be no screen between them, but it was relatively safe still. He wasn't familiar with her.

He hardly knew Mr. Dehive either, but that would change if he got hired, wouldn't it?

The polite words he'd rehearsed with his mother died in his throat.

"It's a pleasure to meet you in person, Mr. Novar."

Alias willed himself to speak up, but his tongue seemed to have doubled in volume, and the only thing he could convince his body to do was lift his chin and look at his interlocutor.

Ms. Angelius stood from behind a large black desk, hands clasped in front of her. The matching chairs on opposite sides of the desk were probably the fancy kind that would fit a body's shape. Nothing further decorated the room. The bright white lights embedded in the ceiling matched the impersonal walls.

The woman wasn't nearly as color-shy. Her red hair flew in wavy flames down her delicate shoulders, with a few strands braided together. She wore a combination of red and brown fabrics in complex superposition that couldn't quite be called a dress, but Alias couldn't put any other name to it. She wore no makeup, but she didn't need any, with the vivid pink of her lips and the warm chocolate brown of her eyes.

"Mr. Novar?"

Patience and understanding laced her tone, implying that she hadn't taken any offense by his staring. Maybe she suspected he didn't get out much.

"T-thank you for considering my application," he managed to say at last.

Inwardly, he cringed, but a smile flashed on Ms. Angelius's lips. His sigh of relief was cut short when she extended her hand.

Alias didn't step back, but it was a close thing. He understood what a handshake was, of course. He'd read about them. Alias told himself that touching someone he felt nothing toward was way down the risk scale. Barely higher than engaging someone in conversation.

Alias took a fortifying breath and grasped the offered hand gingerly. Ms. Angelius's hand, the first human hand he'd touched in years that wasn't his mother's, was dry but smooth. The handshake barely lasted a couple of seconds, but Alias held his breath the whole time.

"Please have a seat."

He waited for her to sit down before sinking into the other chair. Burying his hands under his thighs didn't stop him from squirming, but at least it kept him from fiddling with his clothes.

"May I ask why Dehive is hiring when he already has you?" he blurted out.

"I am not being replaced, not exactly," Ms. Angelius said before Alias could make even more a fool of himself by asking questions at random. "I will continue working for Mr. Dehive directly, but I will be more . . . independent. Mr. Dehive needs someone who'll follow him around, and I am not suited for that role anymore."

Alias frowned but kept his mouth shut.

"Let's say I have done enough mothering for a lifetime," Ms. Angelius added, correctly interpreting his confusion. "Deon Dehive is a great man, but he needs someone at his side at all times, and I have other projects . . . You're not used to conversing with actual people."

It wasn't a question, so Alias didn't reply. Ms. Angelius's expression was indecipherable, except for a flash of pity. Alias blushed, shame and rightful anger warring inside of him.

"You will need to work on that, if you want the position."

"I-I understand." He needed the credit. He really did. "I can do better," he said more firmly.

"Good." The pity was gone. "Your application says that you work two jobs currently. Could you explain to me what you do?"

"I-I develop software for a think tank overseas, and I help manage the sales of a local import-export company."

"Which is unrelated to the job you are applying for," Ms. Angelius replied, not unkindly. "You are a hard worker, but so are plenty of other people. What makes you a good fit for Dehive?"

"I'm adaptable and well-organized, and I learn fast, which was crucial in my previous job as an occasional personal assistant."

Ms. Angelius didn't seem to mind the use of *occasional*. "Could you expand on that?"

Alias had worked on his answer to this particular question with Ben for so long he almost sounded confident listing off everything he'd done for his previous employer, which had gone far beyond the scope of his employment contract.

"Sometimes I would handle his emails and help him work out the kinks in his busy schedule. He also requested my input on some financial aspects of his business, as I'm good with numbers.

I was told I see solutions in unexpected places, which made me invaluable for him."

"You only worked there—" Ms. Angelius scanned her computer screen. "—six months."

"My employer died." Alias bit his lip. "From LBV."

He tried hard not to think about his suspicions that his former employer's death had stemmed from his tendency to forget his Avida doses, despite the reminders Alias had set for him.

"An irregular schedule does not intimidate you?" Ms. Angelius asked.

"That's the only schedule I've ever known." A smile tugged at the corner of his lips despite the sweat gathering at his nape. "I've always worked at odds hours with strict deadlines, and that's— I'm all right with that. I'm not . . . unfamiliar with stress either."

More questions followed. Alias pretended he was talking to a screen, and after a while, the unfamiliarity of chatting with someone in the flesh turned from an instant danger to a low-key threat. He managed a couple of smiles while he outlined his assets and motivations as best as he could. Ms. Angelius smiled back at his use of the word *autodidact*.

"Why do you want this job?"

Alias had expected this question, but the answer he'd carefully crafted earlier had left his mind. Possibilities bounced around in his head.

"I—" Despite the coolness of the office, sweat trailed down his back. He shifted in his seat. "Because I need it."

"How so?"

Alias's gut instinct was to mention his mother, but he wasn't sure that was what Ms. Angelius was after. He wasn't quite clear on how he knew that either.

"I don't really have a life," he said, cheeks reddening. Oh, that had come out wrong, even if it was true. He shook himself. "I think . . . I'd like to do something useful that doesn't just involve numbers. Help—" *My mother.* "—p-people. And . . ."

Ms. Angelius hummed in what might be approval. "And the salary is interesting, isn't it?"

"It really is," Alias hurried to agree before he could think better of it. His face heated up further, but thankfully, Ms. Angelius only seemed . . . amused? "I mean, it is a lot of credit. But I-I'm also interested in the company's innovations in robotics. The facial recognition software developed at Dehive is incredible. Just last week . . ."

To his own surprise, he managed not to stutter over the next several sentences and even kept it simple—there was no need to gush about nanites, a technology still in its infancy despite nanobots having been in development for almost two centuries. His enthusiasm probably showed, if Ms. Angelius's quirked lips were anything to go by.

"I believe that concludes our interview, then," she said when Alias decided he'd talked enough about his passion. "Do you have any questions?"

Of course Alias had questions. Many, many questions. What was Dehive aiming to accomplish through his *other* department? Research on LBV? Would his mother be awarded some form of insurance credit if Avida stopped protecting Alias and he was too sick to work? Did he have to spend time in Mr. Dehive's presence every day? Would he need to up his bidaily dose of Avida, even though his maximum dosage was two pills per day? Was Mr. Dehive really sleeping around with his staff?

The thing was, those were not questions he could ask.

"No," he said, and almost tripped on his own feet as he stood up. Stretching out his hand wore away what little was left of his courage, but the approving smile it earned him was worth it.

"Thank you for your time, Mr. Novar." There was a new softness to Ms. Angelius's expression that Alias didn't know how to interpret. "I'll be in touch."

Alias didn't think that would happen.

A week later, on the last day of October, Alias almost accepted a third job. He hadn't applied for it, but someone at the software firm must have liked his work, because he got a call. He was tempted to accept because it meant more money.

"You have not had a full night of sleep in weeks," Ben reminded him quietly while Alias struggled to form a coherent answer.

He really was at the end of his rope, but he couldn't say that, so he thanked the caller and burst into tears as soon as the line cut.

"Sleep," Ben encouraged him.

But Alias didn't find sleep that night and spent Sunday juggling his two jobs in a daze, barely able to function. When his watchphone rang in the evening, he was half-asleep at his desk.

"Alias Novar speaking," he said in a wobbly voice.

"Good morning, Mr. Novar. This is Jaden Angelius, from Dehive Inc. We met for an interview."

Alias's mind went blank. If the interview on the Saturday before last had been unexpected, it was nothing compared to this call. He stared at Ben as the hubot did its best imitation of a thumbs-up.

"Mr. Novar?"

"Y-yes." Alias sat straighter in his chair. "Did you . . . Did you have other questions?"

"Actually, I have an answer for you, Mr. Novar. If you are still interested, the job is yours."

"It is?" Alias winced at the note of disbelief in his voice. "I— Of course, I'm still interested."

"When are you available to start?"

Alias opened his mouth and closed it again. After paying the last hospital bill, he'd eaten less than usual, and he couldn't imagine going through several days of fasting.

"I wish I could start tomorrow, but . . ."

"It's customary to give a two-week notice? I'm fairly certain that my employer and yours can come to an arrangement."

"That . . ." Alias quickly wiped away the single tear of relief trailing down his cheek. "That would be great," he croaked.

"Then I will see you tomorrow, Mr. Novar. You will find the details enclosed in the email I'm about to send you."

Alias thanked her, twice, and didn't even stutter. Ms. Angelius's chuckle as she hung up sounded amused rather than mocking, but Alias couldn't be sure. He didn't spend enough time with people.

That was about to change.

He spent the rest of that day distracted during working hours—and outside them too—because of the hope burning inside him, the kind he hadn't felt in much too long. He would be able to take care of his mother and himself. The prospect of dealing with people all day, and with Mr. Dehive on a regular basis, terrified him, but fear was nothing new in his life. He would handle it.

On Monday morning at five o'clock sharp, he met Ms. Angelius in the lobby of the unnamed building from his interview. She leaned back against the desk, typing away at her tablet. Her red hair had been made into a single, thick braid that rested on one shoulder. The complex dress-thing had led way to a black blouse and dark red pants.

Meeting her gaze was still hard, and Alias hoped he managed to appear less uncomfortable this time around.

"G-good morning, Ms. Angelius."

"Good morning, Mr. Novar. I hope you slept well."

Alias hadn't slept at all, but he wasn't about to expose himself further. Thankfully, Ms. Angelius didn't insist, and she didn't comment on his choice of clothes, not that he had a choice. Together, they stepped outside under a clouded sky.

The black shuttle from last time was waiting. To Alias's profound relief, the vehicle was empty and self-driven. He followed Ms. Angelius's example and set his trembling palm on the biometric scanner. It blinked green.

"You have your pick of seats. There's usually a dozen other Dehive employees boarding at this hour, but I've arranged for an extra ride."

They sat on opposite sides near the middle. Alias barely had time to register how comfortable and plush the seat was, how easily he could have fallen asleep in it had he been any less nervous, before the shuttle took off. He watched the tall towers of McCarthy Ltd. shrink in the distance with a sense of foreboding.

"There are several departures every day," Ms. Angelius said. "Your schedule isn't going to be set in stone, because it will follow Mr. Dehive's, but I recommend the five o'clock shuttle as your default morning ride. The last shuttle to depart from the Hive leaves at two in the morning, so rest assured that you will have a way home no matter what. The ride takes around forty minutes. I sometimes sleep on the way. You may too . . . Just not today."

Alias wished he could share her amusement. "That's convenient," he offered, and tried to sound grateful even though his insides churned at the prospect of spending that much time surrounded by people, asleep or otherwise.

"As I mentioned on the phone," Ms. Angelius continued, "you will first go through a test period. If afterward Mr. Dehive still believes you are a good fit for the company, you will stay. No matter what the final decision turns out to be, you will be paid for the duration of this period. Later today, you will also sign your first nondisclosure agreement. I'm sure you understand that Dehive can't have his employees disclosing sensitive information to the general public."

Sensitive information probably revolved around the virology department more than the robotic one, considering how open Dehive Inc. was about the latter. But there would be time to embrace his curiosity when he wasn't toeing the line of a panic attack.

"I-I understand."

"What do you do in your spare time, Mr. Novar?"

Alias noticed he'd been twisting his hands together and forced them apart with a heavy exhale. "I, er, jog."

"Do you jog every day?"

The memory of Deon Dehive standing in the park came back to him. "Yes."

Ms. Angelius kept the conversation going for the rest of the ride. Alias assimilated the information and did his best to come up with intelligent questions. It took some concentration. He hadn't slept, and this was the first time he'd left the city center, and the first time he'd engaged in a lengthy conversation with someone who wasn't his mother. And what about the firsts yet to come?

Forty minutes or so after the shuttle left the city, they were dropped at a path leading into dense woods.

"There's about half a mile to the entrance," Ms. Angelius said.

She moved with a confident grace, unbothered by the uneven ground despite the challenges presented by four-inch heels. The path must be very familiar to her. Would it become like that for him? The prospect both terrified and intrigued him.

They walked side by side, with a comfortable five feet between them. Alias tucked his hands into his pockets. Willing his fists to unclench a little more with every step, he took in his surroundings. There were trees in the parks he ran through, but this was a forest, a microcosm of sights and scents, a world of its own. Some of the tree species he recognized from his morning runs, and a ridiculous sense of pride stirred in his chest.

Alias braced himself for an encounter with other Dehive employees, but the road remained empty. The wind rustled through the leaves, a constant hissing jazzed up by the stridulation of locusts and the chirping of birds. Tilting his head back, Alias took in the delicate lines of sky branching out in between the colored treetops high above. To avoid the spread of leaf-eating larvae, some fully stocked trees kept their crowns from growing into each other's space. The phenomenon even had a name: crown shyness.

Alias could certainly relate.

All thoughts of trees left his mind as his place of work appeared before him. The Hive was more magnificent than video had conveyed, the black and gold of the metallic hexagonal structure shining brightly. He slowed down. He'd walked the whole time, and yet he felt like he'd just completed his usual jogging circuit—if such a circuit had consisted of uphill sections only. Had Ms. Angelius not kept a close watch on him, he might have braced himself against his knees.

"How about we start with a tour, Mr. Novar?"

"G-good idea."

The main doors were twice as wide as they were tall, and Alias could have jumped and not brushed the top. Voices filtered through the tinted glass, and some of the shadows—definitely people—went still.

A press of Ms. Angelius's palm parted the doors for them. Alias spotted four people and an equal number of hubots. He startled as the doors closed at his back, and tried to school his features into something he wasn't feeling while every pair of eyes seemed to zero in on him. Conversation stopped. Alias didn't know how to react, but he was sure of one thing: skipping breakfast had been the right decision.

"There's nothing to see here."

The calm authority in Ms. Angelius's voice sent people scurrying back to their work. Alias silently berated himself for being nervous. It could be so much worse. He wasn't required to touch anyone, to make friends with the other employees.

"Look around, Mr. Novar."

Alias forced himself not to startle again as Ms. Angelius's heels clicked loudly in the sudden quiet. His heavy breathing was embarrassingly loud in the lobby.

And what a lobby this was. The boring white from the building in New York was nowhere to be seen. Gold, yellow, beige, brown, and black occupied the space in perfect proportions, granting the vast hexagon a sense of warmth. The irregularly shaped bench to his right was made of wood, and the main counter appeared to have been crafted by the same artist. A candelabra of vines hung from the ceiling and spread in wide hoops around golden fixtures that allowed them to spill even lower, halfway down from the twenty-ish-foot-tall ceiling.

"Are you ready?"

Alias nodded. The coziness and the sheer beauty of the space had helped drain some of his nervousness, and it was with renewed determination that he followed Ms. Angelius down the first corridor.

True to the rumors, the Hive was a maze. The building spanned close to two million square feet split on five floors, two of which were underground. Ms. Angelius also told him that the meeting rooms, offices, laboratories, and factories were connected by a network of vertical and horizontal lifts. The latter bemused Alias, but he supposed that not everyone was used to reaching their destination on foot. Every corridor branched out in two or three duplicates. The intersections were hexagons, and so were a lot of the decorations—abstract wooden and metallic structures arranged at random.

If the idea was to get a stranger lost, it worked splendidly.

His guide never hesitated, gesturing right and left, painting a general picture of the place with ease. Given that everything else was meticulously labeled, Alias wished Ms. Angelius would explain the occasional unmarked door or sector, but he reined in his curiosity.

He did ask about the bees, though.

"Oh, yes," Ms. Angelius replied, and waved at two men passing by. "There are certainly bees around."

The men returned her wave. One of them nodded at him, but by the time he gathered the courage to do the same, the duo was long gone. Ms. Angelius retrieved her tablet from the pouch at her hip and tilted the screen to show Alias what looked like a map of the Hive.

"That's your office. It's very close to Mr. Dehive's office, for practical reasons."

Alias's eyes zeroed in on the labeled box in between the two rooms Ms. Angelius had just indicated with one polished nail.

"And is that . . . a daycare center?"

"Don't worry, the walls are soundproof. It's actually on a different level too."

"I'm not concerned about the noise. I . . . think it's great that Dehive has a daycare center." Alias ran a finger over the daycare label.

"The Hive is a very interesting place to get lost in, but I recommend you familiarize yourself with the layout as soon as possible." With two fingers, Ms. Angelius zoomed out. "Your current security clearance gives you basic access to all main areas. A tablet including a generic map will be provided later today.

Both your security clearance and the map may be upgraded in time should you retain the position."

She traced a circle over an area in the far-right corner. "Robotics is around here. You'll hear the staff refer to our main department as 'the BotHouse,' for obvious reasons." Her lips twitched in a half smile. "You'll learn more about the virology department in due time." *Or not at all*, was left unsaid. "Any questions so far?"

If not for the timely interruption of three other employees, a man and two women talking in hushed voices, Alias might have answered with actual words. Their expressions were pleased, a fact Alias couldn't begin to comprehend, given that there was barely a foot of space between them.

"I ought to remind you that this much human contact is nothing compared to what you will be experiencing as a PA," Ms. Angelius remarked.

"I know," Alias said, perhaps a little too harshly. He'd been in a constant state of unrest since he'd stepped into the shuttle, but that was no excuse—not for the fierce redhead staring him down, anyway. "I-I'll get used to it," he said, not quite convinced.

Ms. Angelius sighed. "Mr. Dehive has only the barest concept of personal space. *He*'s the one you'll need to get used to."

"I'm . . . I'll do my best." He had to stop his hands from fidgeting. His shirt was creased enough as it was. "You mentioned my office?"

Ms. Angelius handed him the tablet. "Find it for us."

The distraction of finding his way through the maze worked like a charm. He didn't notice the change at first, but as they closed in on his office, he found it easier to breathe. His initial panic at the beginning of the tour had dimmed to a prick of unease, and the few people crossing his path registered as obstacles he had to get around rather than threats. He should probably be proud. Or worried that carelessness had led to pride.

When he reached his destination, he turned toward Ms. Angelius.

"Go on."

Alias placed his right hand on the smooth metal of the scanner. The door slid open, letting him into the most beautiful room he'd ever seen.

"This is where you'll be working, when Mr. Dehive has no need of you elsewhere."

Alias stood rooted to the spot. The walls were painted a pale blue and slightly darker green, with wide stripes of textured brown weaving in between large windows like supple tree trunks. Small branches spread upward alongside vines to frame a domed ceiling made of stained glass, each panel depicting a landscape. The sun lit up the colored glass, and the sheer beauty of it all struck a chord deep in Alias's chest.

"Wow."

Ms. Angelius's heels clicked on the floor. Alias followed her farther into the circular room, unable to fix his gaze anywhere for long.

"Your job will be easy enough," Ms. Angelius said in a tone that claimed the exact opposite, leading him to a desk displaying three computer screens set in front of a tall column. "As Dehive CEO's personal assistant, you'll handle every call directed to Mr. Dehive personally. There will be managers, high-level employees, representatives from other companies, business partners, politicians: all strangers, some of which will become quite familiar to you in a very short time. There will be files on 99.9 percent of them in the main database, notes detailing their affiliations with Dehive, how to address them, and if, at all, you should transfer them to Mr. Dehive. *Never* transfer a call to Mr. Dehive just because the person on the phone insists you should. Most of your callers will."

Alias gulped. Was he supposed to argue with people now? He leaned into his workstation for support, trying not to appear as overwhelmed as he felt. The desk was made of a golden metal matching the twenty-inch statue standing with its back to the column. The soothing sight of Lady Love gave him strength.

"Is there any call I should transfer to you?" he asked in his best attempt at a level tone.

"It'll be in the notes, but I can tell you the gist of it: the calls that Mr. Dehive should take but doesn't."

"That . . . happens?"

"Quite often, I'm afraid. It'll be your role to keep track of those, and mine to smooth things over."

"I understand." At least, he understood the general principle.

She gave him an encouraging nod. "Very few people will visit you in person. The bulk of your visitors will be other employees, and they should be easier to handle than your average call."

Was that supposed to reassure him? Alias's legs wobbled. When Ms. Angelius nudged his shoulder, he bit back a squeal.

"How about you sit down? I'll show you the ropes, and then you can sign the contract."

He did as he was told and sighed in relief when the chair conformed to his body. An option for massages caught his attention just below his right thigh. At least he would be comfortable while he panicked.

"Let's start with the various communication systems."

There was nothing too alien about the software Ms. Angelius showed him, and he followed her explanations with ease, focusing on the zeros and the ones instead of the unknown number of people he'd be expected to deal with tomorrow morning. Afterward, Ms. Angelius practiced several scenarios with him, detailing the various dos and don'ts. Alias's previous experience as an occasional and temporary personal assistant didn't give him much of an edge, but he could be creative, which Ms. Angelius seemed to appreciate as much as the employer he'd lost.

After training all morning, they took a break and ate in his office. Alias tried not to make too many noises around his mouthfuls of hearty stew, but it proved difficult: the meal had to be the best he'd ever eaten. Unless it was merely the fact that, for once, he got to eat as much as he needed.

The afternoon was spent going over more scenarios.

"You're quite the quick study," she complimented as she brought the contract on screen at last. "Certainly more than I was on my first day. You'll do fine."

"You have more confidence in me than I do," Alias said without thinking.

The admission startled a laugh from her. Alias found himself smiling as he read the contract. There was a lot to it, and quite a few unfamiliar turns of phrase, but Ms. Angelius didn't seem to mind the slow reading, or the occasional question. Alias had to go through the nondisclosure agreement twice before he felt confident in his understanding of the finer points. It all boiled down to one thing: what happened at the Hive stayed at the Hive. Alias could only talk about his work to Ms. Angelius and, of course, Mr. Dehive. Considering how little Alias wanted to interact with anyone, that wasn't going to be a problem.

When he was done reading, he signed everywhere required. He was disappointed, though not surprised, that the contract contained no hints about the work being done in the virology department.

"That concludes the first step of your hiring," Ms. Angelius announced, and stood up with much more grace than Alias to shake his hand again. "Welcome to Dehive Inc., Mr. Novar."

His first week as Mr. Dehive's personal assistant was overwhelming, and he hadn't even met Mr. Dehive. The more he took calls, the more it became glaringly obvious that he lacked the quiet confidence that Ms. Angelius radiated effortlessly. At least he did fine on the technical front, juggling a growing array of tasks, including answering questions over the phone, organizing Mr. Dehive's calendar, and typing emails. Sometimes, especially during the last leg of his shift, it seemed as though he were watching his crazy day unfold from outside of his body.

He got to eat proper meals on the regular for the first time in a very long time. He downright cried over his first slice of apple pie. The coffee—rich, dark, and bitter—became an addiction after the second cup. He ate whenever he could, darting in and out of the cafeteria like a ghost. There were often other employees in the well-lit room, sometimes as many as twenty, and they invariably stared.

At least, they didn't try to talk to him.

The employees who visited his office in person, he couldn't ignore. He hid behind his messy bangs and tried not to stutter too much as he answered their questions to the best of his abilities. He still dreaded angry callers, but any rant in his ear was a lot easier to handle than a polite human being standing at his desk.

Strangely enough, the man he was supposedly working for didn't contact him once. Alias got no visit, no call, and the few high-profile people he patched through hit voice mail. According to Ms. Angelius, who was acting as a stand-in for Mr. Dehive, the CEO was dealing with the expansion of the virology department. Evidently, he didn't require Alias to follow him around.

"One step at a time, Alias," Ben reminded him while Alias stared at the ceiling, heart thundering after yet another nightmare where Avida had failed him, just as it had failed that four-year-old girl at Mortella. "Those people are not dangerous to you. You can even have friends. Most studies show that love, in that form, is mostly safe . . ."

"Most studies, mostly safe," Alias whispered. He was all too aware that he'd talked to more people in five days than he had in twenty-four years. "That's not enough."

"Even if this isn't enough, you take Avida regularly."

"And when Avida stops working? Humanity as a whole has been very lucky that an antiviral has been found, but there are still cases of people dying without warning, of the virus being extremely aggressive—"

"Isolated cases," Ben argued, but his eyes were glowing yellow in the darkness of the room.

Alias didn't throw in the towel. He thought about it constantly, though: At his desk at the Hive, fiddling with his bottle of Avida whenever he wasn't typing. In the bathroom he locked himself in to deal with a panic attack. Curled onto himself in the shuttle, surrounded by other employees, overwhelmed by them. Running in the morning before sunrise. In his bed in the dead of night.

Whatever sleep he got was nowhere close to enough, and by the time Friday rolled around, he was running on coffee and disbelief. He didn't have a minute for himself before 1 p.m., and his stomach was grumbling as he dropped by the cafeteria. He refilled his coffee mug and grabbed two sandwiches. The half dozen other employees kept their distance. Alias managed a croaked hi—his first—in their general direction. He got several waves and nods, and returned to his office with a strange mixture of anxiety and pride. He was so out of his depth it was ridiculous, but he was making an effort. A very, very big one.

The phone rang nonstop the whole afternoon. Around five, the door opened. Juggling three different lines, Alias threw up a hand for the newcomer to wait. He'd already decided to patch Person 1 through to the robotics department and transfer Person 2 to human resources, and he was considering two options for Person 3 when a fourth call rang. He'd been nursing a headache for the better part of an hour, and he still didn't know how to fit three appointments in the same time slot for next Monday, which was when Mr. Dehive would be done with whatever he was doing that required his presence full-time in the virology department. A tear burned down his cheek. Alias blamed frustration as he reconnected Person 2.

"Thank you, sir. One moment, and I will trans—" He cringed as the man's voice rose to a scream. "I'm s-sorry, sir," he stammered, "but I can't do this. Mr. Dehive is not available at the—"

The fully formed sentence he'd already built in his head crumbled to pieces as he gazed upon his latest visitor.

Deon Dehive was even more entrancing in person. He was about Alias's height, but built stronger, and muscular in all the right places, a fact made painfully obvious by his tailored suit. The first three buttons of the beige shirt under his cerulean jacket were undone, exposing a hint of tanned chest. Alias's eyes jerked up, which only made it worse because now he got to see how that carefully sculpted facial hair showcased the hard line of a well-defined jaw. Mr. Dehive's amused smile brought a flush to Alias's cheeks. This was the mouth of a thousand tales, infamous for its searing kisses and thrills.

Devastatingly handsome—that was the kind of man Deon Dehive was. And his charm went beyond aesthetics. This man exuded power. Should he walk into a room, he became the north to all compasses. They could have been alone in the world, for all Alias cared about the angry voice in his ear. He should stop staring, even though Mr. Dehive clearly wasn't shy in giving him a lengthy once-over.

Don't look.

Don't feel a thing.

"Is it Mr. Arvin again?"

Alias checked the screen before squeaking a breathless "Yes."

"Transfer him to my private line, will you?"

Mr. Dehive leaned an elbow on the desk and propped his chin on his fist, a gesture that brought them closer. A strand of hair fell across his brow, the blond hair brushing against an arched eyebrow. Somehow, both ice and fire raced through Alias's veins. Every cell in his body urged him to reel back, but those blue eyes pinned him in place.

"B-but Ms. Angelius told me never to transfer people not on your list . . ."

"Because I can only be bothered by so many questions in any given day. Dear PA," Mr. Dehive said in a soft tone that turned Alias's inner turmoil up a few notches, "I'm asking for it now."

With trembling fingers, Alias did as instructed. If he mixed up Person 2, 3, and 4 after that, well, it was only to be expected. Mr. Dehive spent less than one minute with Mr. Arvin, pacing in front of the desk while he spoke rapid-fire about deadlines. Alias's mind had turned into mush, and every word out of Mr. Dehive's mouth sounded like a foreign language.

"There you go," Mr. Dehive said casually, hanging up. "This one shouldn't bother you anymore. How about that?"

Alias nodded jerkily. Mr. Dehive didn't seem bothered by his lack of a verbal answer—or by the white-knuckled grip he had on the desk.

"Have you been sleeping in those clothes, Mr. Novar?"

Alias stiffened. Of course he hadn't, but it was the second day in a row he'd worn this outfit. What few clothes he owned were fit for running, not meant for a prestigious in-person job, and a good portion of them showed signs of wear.

"I . . ." A blush crept up his cheeks. "No, I-I didn't sleep in these clothes, but e-everything else is, er . . ."

Mr. Dehive dismissed the nonexplanation with a flick of his hand. He had big hands, and his fingers looked strong. The nails were short and dark, as though he'd played with soil or grease. An unexpected sight: in this day and age, hubots tended to do the manual labor.

The silence lasted long enough for Alias to wonder if he was going to be fired. His heart raced.

"I c-can purchase more appropriate clothes."

"Don't beat yourself up for such a trivial thing. Hardworking is a good look on you."

Alias meant to focus back on the screen flashing urgent messages at him, but his muscles were locked into place.

"You know you're an open book, right?" Mr. Dehive dragged a finger across his chin, scratching at the finely trimmed blond hair lining his lower lip. His blue eyes appeared both dark and light, as if the mind beneath leaked paradoxical hints of its complexity for others to decipher. "You'll have to work on that, if you don't want to be eaten alive around here."

Alias couldn't place the tone. Was there a question in there?

Mr. Dehive straightened, his silence encouraging Alias to finish handling the current calls. Alias stammered more than usual, but Mr. Dehive didn't comment, only waited until Alias was done, then gestured toward the door.

"Let's walk a bit."

Alias hadn't had time to explore the woods before, and he followed Mr. Dehive outside, both dreading their time together and anticipating seeing the grounds. Birds chirped at each other from all directions, and one dared to come out from its hiding spot, its blue plumage quite fetching among the warmer tones of the forest. Movement in the bushes sent it away. A squirrel? A beaver? A fox? Something bigger?

They exited the carefully marked path early on. The CEO navigated the woods with ease, as though he could make out a road beyond human senses. Alias wouldn't mind getting lost. The prospect was certainly less frightening than his guide.

At least he wasn't required to talk. He could look his fill, and look he did, eyes wide in wonder as he took in the majesty of his surroundings. The sheer density of the vegetation boggled him. There was so much of everything: here a pine that loomed tall, its trunk askew toward the top; there a maple tree with its roots meandering above ground . . . Colorful leaves and dried pine needles covered the wet soil, muffling his steps where the moss grew sparse.

When he tripped over a root, a hand caught him.

Alias froze. The grip on his elbow was firm, a steady pressure that kept him upright—and set his whole being on high alert. For several seconds, he couldn't get his body to move or his brain to function. The last time someone who wasn't his mother had touched him so casually was . . . He truly had no idea.

With a gasp that encompassed too many emotions, he yanked his arm away.

Mr. Dehive dropped his hand to his side with a faint frown. "Didn't want you to face-plant," he explained. "You were . . . quite engrossed by the surroundings. Not that I blame you. Do you like it here?"

Alias wrapped his arms around his middle, feeling as though he'd tripped on something a lot more dangerous than a root. Did he like it here? He doubted Mr. Dehive meant the woods. What was he supposed to say, then? The truth—*of course not*—wouldn't do him any favors, and the simple *yes* Mr. Dehive must be after refused to get past his lips.

"I-it's . . . interesting."

"Not as much as it will become, I'm sure."

Was he referring to the work being done in the virology department? This time, there was no root to explain Alias's stumbling. Mr. Dehive chuckled as he caught his arm again. He made it seem natural to touch another human being.

"You okay, there?"

The hand on Alias's bicep felt warm and calloused, so different from his own. Goose bumps exploded all around that point of contact, and a spark of heat sizzled up his shoulder and zinged down his spine. The intense scrutiny only added to his inner turmoil. Every smell permeating the forest faded behind Mr. Dehive's scent—an expensive cologne layered with musk, masculine and intriguing.

Appealing.

"I . . ."

Mr. Dehive released his arm. Alias clutched the nearest branch, a pine that smeared his fingers with sap. He knew he was red in the face, but he couldn't stop blushing as long as Mr. Dehive stared at him so intently—or at all, really. The hand at his side turned into a fist. The strangest urge to reach out and *touch* formed unbidden in his mind. How would it feel to card his fingers through that golden hair and learn its texture? To map out such handsome features, to lean in close enough to count the eyelashes fanning over striking sapphire eyes?

He dug his nails into his palm. He'd never wanted to touch someone besides his mother and Ben. Why should he want to break his own rules twenty-four years in the making? His heart leaped into his throat. This ache blooming inside him wasn't nausea, and it was all kinds of wrong.

Mr. Dehive's voice hacked straight through the rising tide of panic.

"I've been told you were shy, but that's . . . You're not touched often, are you?"

The fine hairs on the back of Alias's neck stood on end. "It's not safe," he whispered.

Alias checked the time: one hour left before his next dose. Relief surged through him, turning the anxiety down a notch. The wind shifted, and a pine sap scent replaced Mr. Dehive's. He was okay. They'd just touched hands. Arms. He was fine.

"I won't try to change your mind yet, Mr. Novar, although it saddens me to meet someone so . . . touch-starved as yourself. And starved, period." A note of disapproval crept into Mr. Dehive's voice. "You're aware you can eat as much as you like from the cafeteria free of charge, right?"

"Yes." Alias had been rubbing his arm where Mr. Dehive had touched him but couldn't bring himself to stop. It burned in a not-quite-bad way. Which was bad. "T-thank you for that, sir."

The corner of Mr. Dehive's lip quirked up. "Are you only so polite when you're afraid?"

Perhaps it was the fear, perhaps it was the lack of sleep, perhaps it was the twinkle of amusement in those blue eyes, but to Alias's surprise, the teasing words brought a quip to his lips. "I don't know. Are you always so bored by social conventions?"

Mr. Dehive's face went blank . . . and then he burst out laughing. It was a rather pleasing sound, much to Alias's dismay.

"Good. You should never hesitate to speak your mind, not to me."

For a moment, it looked like Mr. Dehive was about to touch his shoulder for no reason, but he merely brushed a strand of brown hair away from Alias's brow. "Your test period is over. Would you like to stay and become my PA officially? I think you'll be a good fit, in time."

Alias wondered if Mr. Dehive knew how little of a choice Alias had.

"Yes—I mean, do you not need to . . ." He winced at his awkwardness but kept going. "We've not exactly worked—" He took a deep breath. "—t-together."

"And?"

Alias wished he'd stopped at yes. "And . . . you just met me."

"That I have. But Jaden—Ms. Angelius, that is—assured me you will do well as her replacement. I've been incredibly busy this week, like she told you, but I also wanted to give you some time to get acquainted with the work outside of my orbit first. And you've done great. Look at you . . ."

Alias watched with growing confusion—and a lot of confusing sensations—as Mr. Dehive held out his hand between them, as if to touch him anew. He almost did, too, but he seemed to rethink his action and stepped back. The back-and-forth was getting more and more unnerving, and yet there was something dangerously tempting about Mr. Dehive's reflex to touch him, in the way death's mechanisms were tempting to unravel.

"You're still trembling, you've been trembling the whole time I've been in your presence, but you've been fighting your fear. That's no easy thing to do, not for anyone."

Alias's eyes burned with unshed tears, and he didn't know why. "I . . . Okay. Thank you. F-for the job, I mean." He gritted his teeth and forced the words out: "I'd like to stay."

"Great! You look like you really need sleep, so how about I walk you back to the shuttle, and we sign the final contract on Monday?"

"Great," Alias echoed back.

"And after you've read all that fine print, I'll give you the proper grand tour myself. That okay with you?"

"Yes," Alias replied in a strangled voice.

The sun dipped below the colorful treetops. The sky had turned a violent shade of purple, and a buzzing sound came from the distance, faint beyond the thumping of Alias's heart. Incomprehensibly, the knots in his stomach loosened one after the other under Mr. Dehive's unrelenting scrutiny. The urge to run away from an invisible danger was fading, buried beneath several layers of other emotions begging for his attention. Anger. Fear. Arousal. Impatience.

Alias had never felt more alive.

CHAPTER THREE
THE LAB

According to Ms. Angelius, Mr. Dehive wasn't a morning person. Alias had been told that if the CEO emerged from his living quarters at the Hive before ten, it would be with a long face and an abrasive temper. Consequently, when Mr. Dehive burst through the door of Alias's office at nine the following Monday, Alias assumed the worst.

"M-Mister Dehive?"

With his grease-stained linen pants, a lab coat buttoned over a skin-tight shirt, and a careless mess of sweaty hair falling around protective glasses hooked on top of his head, he resembled more a mad scientist than a businessman. His usual confidence bled through in his gait and the proprietary way he held himself, as if he owned everything in that room, including Alias.

The sudden pang of hunger in Alias's belly had nothing to do with food.

"Don't mind me, Alias," Mr. Dehive drawled.

Cheeks hot, ears ringing with the two syllables of his first name so casually used, Alias had to ask the lady on the phone to repeat herself, but at least he managed to end the conversation without making too much of a fool of himself. It was nothing short of a miracle, considering that Mr. Dehive had watched him the whole time, eyes alit with curiosity, as though Alias were not his PA but an exotic bird whose every gesture fascinated the man who had everything. At least, he wasn't touching him. Alias had spent the weekend turning over in his head their walk in the forest, and there were times when the arm Mr. Dehive had touched itched all over.

Times like right now.

"A-am I in trouble?"

Mr. Dehive sounded genuinely perplexed. "Not to my knowledge. Unless you've suddenly decided to hunt down corporate secrets and leak them to the press."

Alias had received email requests for interviews. Several. When he'd brought it up with Ms. Angelius last week, she'd helped him craft a polite refusal, and recommended he use it systematically. Which he had.

He'd started to do his morning run in the woods surrounding the Hive, but surely that wasn't grounds for suspicion?

"I have no intention of betraying your trust," he said in as firm a voice as he could manage.

"I thought your contract included accommodations?"

"'Accommodations,'" Alias parroted, in a feeble attempt to think past the static brought about by the non sequitur. "Er. There was a clause about that? I think?"

"Then there's something of a mystery you must solve for me."

"What mystery?"

"Well, that of your current residence. You still live on the fourth floor of that apartment building on Fifty-Eighth Street, right?"

"Yes?" Alias rolled his chair back as Mr. Dehive cocked a hip against the desk and crossed his arms. A week of working with people was nowhere near enough to get used to anyone's proximity, let alone Mr. Dehive's. He suspected he'd always be tense in the CEO's presence. "W-what of it?"

"You could afford better by far."

Alias frowned, part annoyed, part mystified. How was his place of residence Mr. Dehive's business? Yes, he could afford better, and yes, moving was part of his long-term plans, but he was used to very little. The credit he was earning went into ensuring optimal care conditions for his mother for the first time in her life, but again, that wasn't anyone's business but his own. "I'm happy where I live," he said at last.

"Are you really?"

The shield of affront made it easier for Alias to meet Mr. Dehive's eyes. "I am," he said firmly. "I don't need . . ." His fingers spasmed over the keyboard. "Is there something I can help you with?"

"Actually, yes."

The tension thickening the air vanished. Mr. Dehive stepped away with a brilliant smile. "Remember my offer of a private grand tour?"

"I do." Alias had been looking forward to it, even if it meant extra time with someone he definitely should avoid. "When would be a good time?"

"As soon as you're done reviewing your final contract and the wordy NDA attached to it. Check your emails."

Alias found the attached document in his inbox and started reading despite the distraction of mounting work. At least Mr. Dehive was giving him a semblance of space and privacy, walking through pools of colored glass-filtered light with a tablet in hand while Alias worked his way through the document. There were a lot of stipulations in his favor. Standard for the Hive, presumably?

"I'm done," he announced after the retinal signature, mind swirling with legalese—and most importantly, with the confirmation of a theory: Dehive's virology department was focused on LBV.

Mr. Dehive pocketed his tablet with a bright smile. "No questions?"

Alias had so many questions, most of them linked to the answer that had just been sprung on him, but where would he start? What was he allowed to ask? He shook his head and started to stand, only to sink back into his chair at the thought of all those names and dates waiting to be arranged.

Two calls came in. He went to pick up the first out of reflex, but the motion was aborted.

He stared at the hand covering his and forgot to breathe.

"Let it bounce back to reception."

Alias opened his mouth, but no words came out.

"Do you work for that person on the line?"

"N-no?"

"Then let's move the show elsewhere," Mr. Dehive suggested in a low voice.

His thumb brushed the side of Alias's wrist, slow and steady, at counterpoint to his frantic heartbeat. Alias should do something about this. Why wasn't he doing something about this?

Mr. Dehive pulled back with a strange expression Alias couldn't decipher. "Ready to learn some of those secrets the journalists are after?"

Alias stumbled to his feet. He felt like a puppet with his strings uneven and tangled. The fact that he missed Mr. Dehive's touch—perhaps more than he dreaded it—didn't sit well with him.

Don't feel a thing.

The words he'd clung to all his life didn't offer such comfort anymore. He added a note to a file before logging out of his session. After all his hard work, he wasn't going to call it quits because Mr. Dehive seemed to discard any notion of personal space, be it by stopping him from tripping or touching his hand. He suspected there was no malice on the CEO's part, merely a lack of concern justified by years of a riskeer's lifestyle.

"A penny for your thoughts?"

"I'm sorry, what?"

"Never mind. Is that an outfit from your care package?"

Alias tugged at the bottom of his beige long-sleeved shirt. When Ms. Angelius had informed him that all new employees at Dehive got a welcome care package, Alias hadn't known what to expect. The delivery bot that had shown up at his door with a bundle of new clothes had delighted him. The fabric of the clothes was so soft, unlike anything he'd ever owned. And the sweet and salty snacks at the bottom of the box had been the cherry on top.

"Y-yes," he said at last. "I like these clothes very much."

Despite his words, Alias regretted having put his new clothes on now. The positive comments he'd received in the cafeteria this morning had made him nervous, but not nearly as nervous as under Mr. Dehive's gaze. The distinct approval warmed him up inside.

"The tour!" he exclaimed with exaggerated enthusiasm. At least he wasn't stuttering. "Where do we start?"

"The BotHouse."

Getting there took all of five minutes. Alias stared at the double doors. They were twice as tall and three times wider than the already-massive main doors. The biometric scanner to the side was also bigger and more complex. Alias had considered exploring the robotic department on his own—it was marked on his map, after all—but he'd doubted a level-three security clearance would do the trick.

"Here, put your hand on the scanner and wait a minute," Mr. Dehive instructed.

Alias complied, more curious than uneasy. He couldn't see what Mr. Dehive was doing on his tablet, but within moments, the thick doors swung open on the biggest room Alias had ever seen. The ceiling stretched a good sixty feet above his head. Everywhere he turned, there were hubots on displays, rows upon rows of them stored on top of each other. Generic bots drove modified forklifts to add to or remove from those rows.

Partitioned workstations in various states of disarray occupied the remaining free space. Employees in relaxed outfits tinkered around, assisted by robots as small as a hand. Most of them called Mr. Dehive by name and gave a nod that seemed to encompass Alias too. Alias practiced his smile. It came to him more easily now, especially in a vast space dedicated to robotics. He gave a timid wave to a passing coworker and did the same when he came across a very tall hubot. He kept the smile pasted on when Mr. Dehive glanced at him with a smile of his own.

Curiosity kept his head high, and he followed Mr. Dehive's hands as they moved right and left to underline a point. The CEO led him past a row of alcoves where hubots in pieces lay on workstations. Just like Ben, all these models possessed fingers out of practicality rather than humanity's tendency to anthropomorphize, and their paint was of a non-skin color. Even their name reflected their function: long strings of numbers and letters inked their nape, meaningful only to a computer.

Ben3min's original name had been B3-M2-I6-N9-1354690909.

Alias pushed away the bittersweet memory. The familiar tools lined up near a robot arm helped cheer him up. Without thinking, he reached for the closest one.

"You've got experience with any of this?" Mr. Dehive inquired. "I mean, you did mention an interest in bots during your interview."

Alias's smile faltered, although the question had sounded casual enough. He pulled his hand back. He was well aware that he was skittering the edge of legality as the unregistered owner of Ben. Technically, a discarded hubot belonged to the state. By fixing Ben, Alias could declare ownership, but it would mean a mandatory check of the AI core by a specialist, and this cost a lot of credit. While Mr. Dehive might not be the most law-abiding citizen around, he could decide that Alias was in the habit of stealing hubots and couldn't be trusted—and fire his new PA.

"Okay, I get it, the assembly lines are boring," Mr. Dehive declared, and frowned. "How about we—"

"No! I mean, no, it's n-not boring." Alias scuffed his feet. "I like . . . It's interesting."

"Great. Still no questions?"

Alias grew alarmed. "Should I have any?"

"Only if you're confused about something, I suppose."

Oh, Alias was confused all right, but it had nothing to do with their current location. The air was distinctly warmer in the BotHouse, and Mr. Dehive had taken off his lab coat a while ago and tied it at his waist, revealing a sleeveless shirt that exposed strong arms and muscled shoulders. Alias pretended not to be affected by the sight. If he could smile long enough to convince himself that he was happy, he could probably become immune to Mr. Dehive's appearance. If only it was just the man's physique that made him all wound up and fidgety . . .

"Ready to continue?"

Alias squeezed the bottle in his pocket and nodded with relief.

They resumed the tour at a more sedate pace. Alias tried to blend in with the shadows, lost in his thoughts, swinging between enthusiasm and fear. In his distraction, he almost crashed into a roboticist. The man mumbled his apologies without looking up from his tablet, a dozen bots the size of butterflies trailing after him.

"And Jaden says I'm obsessed with my job," Mr. Dehive said, raising his voice to be heard over a machine. "Oh, here we go. Look over here, Alias."

The smell of grease and melting ore was stronger in this area. Sharp blades sent a fountain of light spilling at his feet. Movement at the back caught his eye as the tallest robot he'd ever seen stood up. His jaw dropped. This robot had to be fifty feet in height, and its unique eye shone bright white under the brow of Dehive's logo.

"What is this one's purpose? It's much bigger than a crowd-containing hubot!"

The clattering and hammering were so loud that they had to shout at each other. Mr. Dehive didn't seem to mind.

"It was supposed to be a transportable tinkering lab. For building bots within a bot, you see? But it was just as impractical as I was told, and it's been repurposed to accomplish basic tasks and impress newcomers. Is it working?"

Alias was very impressed, but the teasing glint in Mr. Dehive's eyes encouraged him to tone down his reaction. "I . . . suppose?"

Each robot they came across seemed to have a history, and Alias found himself enraptured by every and all explanations.

"This one," Mr. Dehive said, waving at a three-foot ball-shaped bot with three hands struggling to push a cart full of parts, "is one of the company's most notorious flops, at least for those who know of its existence. We keep it around as a reminder that there are limits to creativity."

Mr. Dehive sounded fond. Alias didn't know how to feel about this and squeezed the bottle of Avida in his pocket while his employer told him of a chocolate egg treasure hunt organized by the hubots at reception last year. He had no idea if these stories were made up, but it mattered little. He was . . . smiling.

Not quite relaxed, but a lot less stressed, even though hearing himself referred to as "Alias" still felt strange.

"Careful, there!"

They stepped away in perfect synchrony to let through a smaller vehicle loaded with octopus-like bots. Mr. Dehive resumed the tour, listing off machines and detailing their functions as if he'd built the whole place from scratch by himself, gesturing with a wild kind of enthusiasm all the while.

They paused at the end of a row.

"Your interest is certainly refreshing. Not everyone appreciates my work the way you do."

Alias's hands twitched at his sides. There was something about the mess of Mr. Dehive's sweaty blond hair that called to him. He wanted to run his fingers through it, feel the wet strands part for him, and he shouldn't. Want. That. At all.

"Don't worry. You won't be quizzed about this tomorrow."

Alias smiled weakly, pretending that he'd been worried about that. Mr. Dehive appeared unconvinced and like he might pursue the issue, but a middle-aged woman chose that moment to shout a question to a colleague operating a gigantic robotic arm, and the CEO took it upon himself to reply. The woman startled, then burst into laughter. Mr. Dehive grinned at her.

"Keep up the good work! The BotHouse really wouldn't be the same without you."

Even from afar, Alias could see the woman blush. He wished he couldn't relate.

"Deon!"

The voice belonged to a man around sixty. The volume of white and black curls on top of his head more than made up for the lack of facial hair.

"Deon!" he called out again in a surprisingly deep and strong voice for a man so small. He was at most five six and looked closer in musculature to Alias than Mr. Dehive. "I feared yet again that I wouldn't get you down here in time to see my new project."

A wide grin split across Mr. Dehive's face. "Dario!"

He strode toward the workstation, a mess of wires and tools Alias didn't have the first inkling at, and pulled Dario to his chest.

The employees nearby should have done a double take, but no one seemed to bat an eye, as if their CEO walked into robotics every day to hug this man. Perhaps he did.

"Don't break all of my bones," Dario protested, but his tone hinted at amusement. He pushed his protective glasses from his eyes to his brow. "I've got a good twenty years of employment left in this beehive of yours."

"At the very least, old man."

Dario chuckled. A pat to Mr. Dehive's shoulder was all it took to free himself. "My artificial arm is bound to become obsolete at some point," he remarked, wiggling his metallic fingers.

Most people tended to go for a prosthesis that blended in, but Dario hadn't bothered: his arm was a soft metallic gray with visible joints a shade paler. Alias tried in vain not to stare as the men bantered.

"Dario, this is my new PA, Alias Novar, selected amongst the *crème de la crème* by Jaden. Alias, this is my chief engineer and roboticist, Dario Quint."

Mr. Quint extended his right hand—the human one. Alias would have very much preferred the other, but he had practice now and went for the handshake with what could be construed as casual ease.

Mr. Dehive's watchphone flashed with an incoming call. "I had a GUT feeling she would call," he said, and burst out laughing. He was still chuckling as he reached for his earpiece and stepped to the side. "Hello, dear . . ."

Alias blinked. His confusion must have been obvious, because Mr. Quint took pity on him.

"The joke is a very nerdy one. Mr. Dehive meant 'G-U-T,' all capitals, as in Grand Unified Theory." Mr. Quint grabbed a thin white tube off of his workstation. "It's a joint effort in the scientific community to bring together the rules of quantum physics and gravity."

"Oh," Alias said faintly. The notion rang a bell, albeit a distant one. He wiped away the sweat clutching to his eyelashes and tugged at the collar of his shirt. He could really use a glass of water.

"So, what do you think?" Mr. Dehive chimed in, expression much more serious than before.

What did he think of what? Alias assumed he wasn't being asked about his opinion on this theory, or the call Mr. Dehive had wrapped up so quickly. The BotHouse, then? He stepped aside to give way to a small bot on wheels. "It's . . . fascinating."

Mr. Dehive checked his watchphone and frowned. "You think you can keep being fascinated for the next twenty minutes? There are a few calls I've got to make, and the reception down here is spotty, so just distract Dario here."

"You're a menace," Mr. Quint said, but he beckoned to Alias. "Why don't you sit down and tell me what you think of the arm?" He laid it down on the desk between them.

"It looks incredible," Alias complimented shyly. "I'm not familiar with prosthesis, but I've been teaching myself the basics of robotics."

"Ah yes? What sparked the interest?"

Alias bit his lip, his mood darkening briefly as he recalled his first encounter with Ben3min. The sixty-foot fall into the factory dumpster would have killed a human being.

"Ben-three-min," he said, annunciating each syllable. "Ben, for short. It's a hubot I found and fixed." Ben almost hadn't made it. Its circuits and artificial limbs had been so badly damaged that Alias had seriously doubted his ability to get the hubot back online. Carrying the broken body back to his place had been a spur-of-the-moment decision fueled by a longing for company. "I knew nothing about robotics back then," he admitted, convinced that he still didn't know enough, "but I've learned a lot in the years since, and I hope—"

He cut himself off in panic. He'd never told anyone about Ben, for obvious reasons, and here he was, confessing to what was technically theft.

"Which model is it? What kind of processor does your hubot have?"

Alias blinked at Mr. Quint. If his coworker was more interested in Ben's specs than in its history of ownership, Alias was certainly not going to argue with him. He answered every question with enthusiasm, and asked plenty of his own. Robotics had been a favorite subject of his for years, and there was only so much he could learn on his own without hands-on practice.

Alias could hardly believe he was having such a good time engaging in casual conversation.

"You taught yourself a lot more than the rudiments." Mr. Quint gave him an appraising look, expression serious for a moment, and then he smiled again. "You've been staring at the arm a lot."

Alias's stomach sank. "I'm sorry." He shot to his feet.

"Don't you dare apologize for being curious. I so seldom get to have a nice conversation with a fellow roboticist."

Alias blushed. "I'm, er— I'm not a roboticist."

"Not professionally, perhaps, but you certainly have the spirit."

Encouraged by the engineer's open expression, Alias settled back on the chair and began asking questions about the arm. He even prodded the limb at Mr. Quint's invitation, a little shy at first, but too used to having a hubot at home to feel too awkward about touching the prosthesis.

"How did it happen?"

Mr. Quint shrugged. "A moment of inattention in this very factory." He picked up the handle of a small electronic blade that could be turned on and off with a code. "It was my own fault. I was working too late fixing the newest series of bots at the time, and I made a mistake that cost me a limb. It didn't kill my love for engineering or robotics," he added with an affectionate pat to his artificial limb and a reassuring smile. "I seriously doubt anything could."

"You guys are bonding over my bots?"

Alias startled. Mr. Dehive had reappeared. He pushed bot parts aside with unexpected care and hopped on the desk, ignoring Mr. Quint's eye roll. Alias tried not to smile and failed. He couldn't stop smiling. And it wasn't a polite smile either— it was the kind of joy blooming outward from deep within, the exultation that came with a good run, or when Ben said something funny or clever.

Or when he spent some time discussing robotics with a like-minded man, apparently.

"Mr. Novar here is quite the knowledgeable fellow," Mr. Quint remarked. "Did you know he fixed a discarded hubot all by himself?"

Mr. Dehive didn't spare a glance to Mr. Quint, who was nudging him toward the edge of his desk to give the parts more room. "Really?"

Alias paled. He thought of Ben being taken away because of his failure to properly claim the hubot and considered the empty space it would leave in his apartment. Ben had a few glitches, but it wasn't faulty in Alias's eyes. It was his friend and deserved protection. "S-sir, I—"

Mr. Dehive waved a hand. "I'm not the NID, Alias. If anything, I'm even more impressed by you now. Is it one of my models?"

Alias shook his head.

"It doesn't matter, does it, Deon?" Mr. Quint said as he stood.

"Of course it doesn't. I like my employees with initiative." Mr. Dehive caught Alias's eyes. "Don't worry about your little friend. I have more than enough of my own here."

A giant weight lifted off Alias's shoulders.

"Not that I wouldn't like to avoid all my responsibilities, but Jaden will skin me alive if I hide in here much longer."

"Wait until this one learns to do it all by himself," Mr. Quint quipped.

Me? Alias mouthed the word in disbelief. He would never skin anyone alive, no matter how metaphorically. Or push his boss gently but firmly off his desk, like Mr. Quint was doing.

Mr. Dehive hooked his thumbs in the lab coat tied around his hips. "We have to go. See you around, old man."

Mr. Quint smiled at Alias as he offered his hand—the artificial one, this time. "It was a pleasure meeting you."

Alias shook the prosthesis and returned a wobbly smile. "The pleasure is all mine."

The CEO led him out of the factory at a swifter pace, one at odds with the tour so far. Alias wasn't sure what to make of it, or rather, he was beginning to dread the next step on the tour. Mr. Dehive kept quiet. Alias barely dared to breathe. The air was getting cooler with every twist and turn of the "shortcut" between the BotHouse and their destination, but sweat still beaded at his brow.

"Here we are."

Mr. Dehive scanned his hand, retina, and voice in front of another huge door that looked strong enough to withstand an explosion.

"Welcome to the virology department, or the Lab, as we call it," he announced proudly.

Alias didn't budge, stomach sinking far below ground level at the sight revealed to him.

The Lab was irregular in shape, far away from the hexagonal design paramount in the Hive or the oval of his office. The ceiling was a good forty feet tall, but unlike in the robotic factory, the workstations encroached on one another. The bots were few and far between, almost invisible with so many scientists whispering to themselves and each other.

"Alias?"

If not for Mr. Dehive beckoning him from the bottom of the ramp, Alias might have stepped backward instead of forward. His legs shouldn't threaten to give under him. These scientists weren't about to experiment on him, unlike the doctors who'd stuck his mother with countless needles and pumped her full of experimental products before her transfer to Mortella. These people seemed perfectly content to ignore him.

He took a deep breath and another step forward. There was a distinctly organic quality to the Lab. The walls evoked bark, if bark were wet and had a heartbeat. At sporadic intervals, different spots would turn green, or blue, or something in between. Alias suspected an illusion, but he could swear that the walls, the ceiling, and the floor were adjusting to the coral-like furniture and the complex-looking machines spread around the airy space, evolving around it all.

Fascinated but still freaked out by the proximity of that many people in white coats and the reminder of the virus, Alias joined Mr. Dehive at the bottom of the ramp. A strange smell permeated the air, a mix of disinfectant, herbs, and something sharp and unidentifiable. His gaze landed on a door branded with the biological hazard symbol and famous block letters—AUTHORIZED PERSONNEL ONLY. He tried to find comfort in his bottle of Avida. There was nothing to fear here. Nothing more than usual, that was. LBV samples posed no threat to him. Why would they? He already carried the virus, just like everyone else. The danger lay within himself . . . in the feelings other people elicited in him.

Feelings like desire.

"What's your first impression? Weird? Sublime? A dream or a nightmare?"

"It's, uh, very . . . pretty," he said weakly, tasting bile at the back of his throat.

Mr. Dehive chuckled, and his breath brushed Alias's nape. Warm. Too close. "That's what happens when I give carte blanche to an architect who thinks only outside the box. Not everyone likes outside-the-box thinking, but I'm a huge fan."

Mr. Dehive stepped further into the room before Alias had a chance to move away.

"It's also a state-of-the-art laboratory, which is why we've got the best scientists working around the clock on LBV."

Alias's hand spasmed around the bottle in his pocket. He nodded sharply and fell into step beside his employer. The number of scientists in the Lab was impressive. Alias's shoulders tightened when a woman with a vial dashed past him, and then slumped. How was it again that he'd ended up working as an assistant to one of the most powerful men in the world? He was aware of his skills, but was it really enough? Last week, he'd kept expecting Ms. Angelius to come to her senses and realize she'd hired the wrong applicant. The feeling of inadequacy grew stronger as Mr. Dehive led him to what looked like the only unoccupied workstation, glancing back as if expecting questions and Alias was failing him by staying quiet.

As uncomfortable as inadequacy felt, it was better than anxiety, so Alias clung to the distraction.

"Are you afraid right now?"

Alias hopped onto the blue stool in front of the desk at Mr. Dehive's invitation and tucked his shaking hands between his thighs. "N-no."

Mr. Dehive claimed the stool beside him. "If you want me to believe you, you'll have to lie better than that."

The lump in his throat expanded as the panic threatened to rob him of speech. "I d-don't know what you want me to say, sir."

"You're on Avida."

Alias nodded, although it hadn't been a question. Was Mr. Dehive . . . trying to help him curb the anxiety? There'd been no judgment in his statement.

"And I'm sure you never forget a dose," Mr. Dehive added gently.

"Antivirals are fallible."

"Yes, that's true. Viruses can always mutate, but Avida has kept you safe for a very long time, hasn't it? There's no cause for concern."

"Yes, but—"

"And this 'but' is why Dehive has been developing an alternative to Avida over the past few years."

Alias was glad he was already sitting. "A *what*?"

"An antiviral alternative. I've had this project for a very long time, but I didn't want to give the world false hopes, which is why this is a well-kept secret." Mr. Dehive rested his elbows on his knees, leaning forward. His intent expression was not unlike the one he'd had during his interview in the park, when he'd told the journalist that they all wanted the same thing. "There has been lots of testing. The rigorous kind. The World Health Organization is very strict, and it's not the only entity Dehive has to please to get this product on the market."

Alias's mind spun. "So, it's not ready yet?"

"Oh, the LX has been working for a while now, but there were some final . . . tweaks, so to speak. I'll make a public announcement in the next few days."

"Is that . . ." Alias was nonplussed. "Is that why you're showing this to me?"

"The Lab? Why, yes. I wanted it to be part of the tour because my assistant should have more context about LX than mere words on digital documents. I also believe that sharing the news that LBV is building resistance to Avida faster than anticipated—which we've confirmed right here—might be less of a shock with the distraction of an unfamiliar environment."

Hysterical laughter tickled the back of Alias's throat. The eccentricity of the layout, and the limited distraction it offered, had worn off. "I already know that cases of spontaneous failure with Avida are more common now. Avida has never been foolproof, and it's only getting worse." Too agitated to keep still, Alias gripped both sides of his stool. "And then there's the fact that Avida just doesn't work well for some people."

If Alias had lost his cool, Mr. Dehive appeared more serene than before. "Panic has never helped anyone, Alias, and yes, it is horrible that the virus still kills, but we're talking about isolated cases of mutation."

"So far. You say that there's no cause for concern, but children are supposed to be the safest age group, and yet just the other day, a girl of four died because Avida couldn't protect her!"

Mr. Dehive's expression darkened so briefly Alias wasn't sure if he'd imagined it. "LBV may be mostly triggered by desire and romantic feelings these days, but there are exceptions to exceptions. LX should take care of those."

Alias's fingers clenched and unclenched on the metal of his chair. He'd heard claims of alternatives before. Every now and then, a company would even announce they'd found the key to eradicating LBV. Alias remembered all too well those supposed cures, and how they'd made his mother sicker every single time.

There was no cure.

"LX is no more a cure than Avida is," Mr. Dehive said, inserting himself into Alias's thought process with disturbing accuracy. "But it offers better protection against viral reactivation . . . You know how this all works, don't you?"

Finger by finger, Alias released the edge of his seat. He might not know as much as he'd like about being a personal assistant, but LBV? The virus and its inner workings shadowed his every thought.

"LBV is dormant in the vast majority of the population nowadays. In this state, it's harmless." The word sounded weird spoken alongside *LBV*. "The virus gets activated—well, reactivated, that is, because technically it first becomes active in all of us when we catch it during infancy—when certain . . . feelings, roughly based on the same group of hormones and neurotransmitters, are experienced to a certain level. That level is different for everyone." Alias swallowed hard. "Avida has no bearing on the feelings themselves." A shiver crept up his spine when he recalled his reading on the earliest attempts to lower the death rate. There had been neuro-suppressants then, too strong, and people had become numb and died anyway. "Avida keeps LBV from reactivating by inhibiting a specific viral enzyme."

"LX is a different type of antiviral." Mr. Dehive drummed his fingers on the desk, careful not to touch anything, unlike in the BotHouse. "LX doesn't inhibit enzymes: it straight up damages the latent virus contained in the body's infected cells, which eliminates the possibility of it ever being reactivated. Humanity's strongest bolt yet to our anti-LBV crossbow, if you will."

"Are you . . ." Alias trailed off, torn between two distinct kinds of fears. Or rather, fear and hope. "Are you quite sure that there's no more, er, 'tweaking' to be done?"

"Absolutely," the CEO said briskly, shadows gathering in his eyes. He hopped off the stool and waved in clear irritation. "Would I be risking lives if it wasn't ready? My own employees' lives? Some members of the staff and their children have already received LX, and every single one of them is in perfect health. Which scenario is more likely? That they're all lucky, or that I waited until my team perfected the injection before I considered offering it to other people and making it public?"

For the first time, Alias could feel Mr. Dehive's anger aimed straight at him. His stomach did the strangest flip, and the back of his neck started to burn.

That was when he figured it out.

"Oh."

"'Oh'?" Mr. Dehive echoed.

He still sounded angry. Alias almost apologized, and he would have had he not just pieced together what his subconscious had been trying to tell him.

"Was it the side effects of a more experimental version?" he ventured.

"I'm sorry?"

His resolve began to waver, but Mr. Dehive's anger seemed to be fading in favor of curiosity. Alias twisted his hands in his lap. "I read . . . I read that you were sick one year ago . . . That's because you tried the LX on yourself, didn't you? A-and . . ." His eyes widened as the last piece slotted into place. "The side effects made you ill."

Mr. Dehive's lips curved into a smile. "Being able to read between the lines is a very good skill in a personal assistant, Alias."

That bit of praise was so unexpected after the show of anger that Alias forgot how to breathe. A delicious warmth sizzled through his body, from the roots of his hair to the tips of his toes. He had no idea what he was projecting, but Mr. Dehive was watching him with clear interest.

"You're right: this is exactly why I waited. I am the first, and only, test subject to experience any side effects from the LX injection."

"Oh, that's . . ." Alias frowned. "Wait. You said . . . injection, singular?"

"That's the beauty of it." Mr. Dehive stretched out both arms as if to say, *Voilà.* "One injection, and it's done. It makes LX an appealing alternative, which is just as well considering that LX and Avida can't be taken together."

Alias tensed. One injection sounded too good to be true . . . but then so did this job. If he waited too long and Avida stopped working for *him*, perhaps the injection wouldn't help at all. But what if he switched to LX immediately and got an allergic reaction? What about the long-term effects, which couldn't be known yet because this alternative hadn't existed long enough? If Avida didn't work for some people, surely it was the same for LX? Surely further mutations down the road would make LX ineffective too? What if this was just like one of the promised cures they'd tried on his mother?

A hand landed on his shoulder. "Hey."

Alias gasped. He pulled back, but the moment the contact was lost, regret uncoiled in his chest. It didn't last, though, not when terror was gripping him. And rightfully so.

"I'm sorry."

"'S okay." It really wasn't. The urge to take his dose early was almost unbearable. "Are you going to fire me?"

"Why would I do that? You're efficient, not prone to gossip, and you make for a good conversation partner for old Dario. Your fear of the virus doesn't get in the way of your job."

Alias was about to argue that point, but Mr. Dehive wasn't done.

"Not as much as it could, anyway. You impress me. Listen." There came a soft chime from his watchphone, but Mr. Dehive ignored it, just like he seemed to ignore the curious scientists who kept glancing their way. A strand of blond hair fell across his brow as he leaned back in his chair. "You can receive the injection early, but you don't have to. You don't have to do anything you don't want to."

Mr. Dehive's expression was blank, but his eyes were not. Alias couldn't say why, but he knew, he just did, that Mr. Dehive wasn't merely talking about the injection.

CHAPTER FOUR
A SLEIGHT OF HANDS

D eon Dehive scheduled the announcement three days later, on Thursday. By then, all employees, except the three who weren't done with their test period, had been told of LX, and discussions about the injection were had in hushed murmurs that never left the Hive.

As personal assistant, Alias had distributed the updated NDA regarding the injection. So far, every other employee who'd been made aware of the antiviral alternative had requested the injection. Alias kept the alphabetical chart created by Ms. Angelius up-to-date, ticking one box after another whenever an employee got their injection from Mr. Arvin, the assistant to the head of Virology, Dr. Lentz. *Novar* was halfway down the list, and every time Alias saw the unchecked box on his NDA, doubts plagued him.

On the morning of the announcement, he rose before the sun. Ben expressed confusion at his wish to leave so early after a midnight run, eyes flashing yellow as it pointed out Alias's recent bouts of insomnia.

Alias undid all the mismatched buttons of his shirt and started over, careful not to skip the first one on the left side this time. "I'll be okay, Ben."

He didn't feel okay as he boarded the shuttle. Thankfully, there were only three other employees riding this early, and they gathered at the back, matching coffee mugs in hand with the Dehive *D* embossed on them. In the subdued space, Alias could make out the subject of their conversation rather easily. He was tempted to cover his ears with his hands, except that wouldn't help with the anxious thoughts bouncing around in his head.

He was so, so tired . . .

"Hi, Alias."

Alias pressed a hand to his chest with a gasp. The woman with the short blond hair sitting in the seat across from him didn't look familiar, but then, few employees did. Her eyes, though . . . That blue hue reminded him of someone.

"I apologize. I didn't mean to startle you."

Alias pasted on his professional smile. "H-hi." He was getting better at this, but the prospect of the day ahead didn't exactly help his nerves.

"I'm just curious." The woman cocked her head at him. Her lab coat was decorated in stripes of gold and black, quite unlike the standard uniform favored by employees of the Lab. "Did you take it?"

Even in his state of overall exhaustion, Alias grasped her meaning. "I . . ." Did he have to answer? He picked at invisible specks of dust on his pants. They were an old pair of his that he put on to exercise. Why hadn't he put on an outfit from his welcome care package?

"So, did you take it?"

Alias recoiled. Suddenly, the woman was gone, and Deon Dehive smirked at him. But that wasn't the only reason for Alias's shock: the CEO was holding out one hand, and as he waited for an answer, he began stroking the vein at the crook of Alias's elbow.

"Trust me."

Alias reared back. Pain exploded in his head as his skull smashed into the window. Eyes flashing open, he stared uncomprehendingly at the empty seat across from him. Mr. Dehive was gone. The only people on the bus were the three women at the back.

He twisted around in his seat and pressed his temple into the window, rubbing at the welt. Of course he'd get a vivid nightmare about work at the start of a particularly stressful day.

"You're very subtle," he mumbled, addressing his subconscious.

The shuttle came to a stop. Still chatting among themselves, the other employees didn't pay him any attention as they exited. With one last glance at his troubled reflection in the window, Alias followed them out.

Everything was colored red and black in the sunrise. Hidden in the branches that stretched like snakes toward the sky, early birds sang. Alias started at a slow jog on the gravel path and quickly passed his colleagues, eyes forward and breath steady. The moment the Hive came into view, he darted to the left and followed the marked path.

This maze, at least, was a lot easier to navigate than his head. The road was large and clearly defined, an oval that looped around the Hive. Another path, thinner and a lot longer, wove through the trees in an irregular shape farther in the woods. Alias seldom met other runners on this one, and at this hour, he was the only one around, cocooned by noises that weren't voices.

Such as the buzzing of bees.

He'd made the discovery two days ago on an evening run. The little insects had been so loud that he could have foregone light and found them by sound alone. There were hundreds upon hundreds of them, flying around or grouped in large patches on the hives built for them. The cabin nearby, a wooden structure the size of his tiny apartment, only added to the mystery. Alias would have gotten closer if not for the suited-up individual bent over one of the numerous hives. What if he was trespassing?

Trespassing was the least of his concerns this morning with LX's announcement and Deon Dehive on his mind. With a punched-out gasp, he sank to the ground a few feet from the circle of beehives. Bees could be dangerous, but he didn't recoil, not even when they started to circle him. Was his ease toward a visible threat the result of dreading for too long a danger he could neither see nor touch?

Don't feel a thing.

It was a little late for that.

He looped his arms around his legs and propped his chin on his knees.

The attraction wasn't fading, no matter how often Alias wished it would. Despite himself, he recalled Mr. Dehive's easy smile, the warmth in it—the heat of his hands on him. Alias hadn't said anything. After watching Mr. Dehive interact with other staff members, he'd come to suspect that the teasing, the casual touch, and the compliments were simply how Mr. Dehive was with everyone. Alias wanted to be angry at him, but that wasn't how things worked. Mr. Dehive's actions were harmless on their own.

It was Alias's reaction to them that posed a threat. His failure to summon indifference.

The tears came as a relief.

Just a couple more minutes, he told himself.

The red slowly bled out of the sky as the sun rose.

Freshly showered and sweating nonetheless, Alias showed up at the hangar. The biometric scanner let him through without a hitch. He gave the screen a double take as he spotted the authorization level listed under his name: eight. He'd assumed he was still at level five, the one he'd been granted in order to access the BotHouse during his tour with Mr. Dehive. Level 8 . . . Wasn't that the highest one, the one that . . . He checked his tablet, and yes, there it was: the Lab, newly indexed in his personal map.

He might have fretted at what the upgrade implied if he were not faced with the jet that would take him and Mr. Dehive to Washington, DC, in ten minutes. It was a little late to wish he better understood the mechanics of flight. Or would a more acute comprehension make him more nervous? His only consolation was that he couldn't waste too much energy on his usual source of stress as long as he came up with scenarios of plane crashes.

He dragged his feet inside the jet and got an eyeful of lavish design. He wasn't sure why he'd expected a utilitarian space rather than a vast array of comfortable seating options. His skin crawled as he spotted a bed at one end of the cabin. It was big enough to accommodate at least three people, and as it happened, there were three people on the plane right now.

The owner of the jet straightened from his lounging sprawl with a yawn. "Hey, there."

He'd put on a black-and-white three-piece suit that was perfectly tailored, like all of his clothes. The shirt's top two buttons were undone, and the tie was askew as usual.

He gave Alias a critical once-over. "You look like hell."

Alias stiffened. "Thanks, I guess."

His word choice, or perhaps the annoyance in his tone, earned him a chuckle.

"Be nice, Deon." Ms. Angelius reached for the blue tie and adjusted it, giving the fabric a sharp tug. "God, you're hopeless." When she spoke next, she sounded much more amiable. "Good morning, Alias."

"Good morning, Ms. Angelius."

The red-haired woman was dressed in dark blue today, the hue an exact match to the tie still in her grip. The sleeves of her blouse flared at her elbows, highlighting the airy quality of the fabric, and tightened again at her wrists, the cuffs adorned with small silver buttons. Two silver lines ran down the sides of her mid-length skirt, and a silver clip with small blue flowers decorated the bun atop her head. She was stunning. Even her eyes were riveting, of a brown far more fetching than Alias's own.

Mr. Dehive rested his head against her hip. According to the Hive's rumor grapevine, they had been in a relationship for years. While Alias hesitated to apply the label *riskeer* to Ms. Angelius, he couldn't deny that these two made quite the pair. They both had wits, beauty, and charisma, and then there was the ease with which they shared each other's personal space.

"Where's my good morning?" Mr. Dehive complained.

Alias's mouth went dry. Ms. Angelius was running her manicured fingers through the mess of blond hair, coaxing pleased noises. A tablet lay on a glass table, but they didn't pay it any attention, although they'd both been leaning over it when Alias had stepped into the jet.

A strange sensation overcame him. He couldn't tell what it was, but it twisted his gut in an unpleasant way. Like anger, it burned. He also felt strung up, as though he were expecting to fight at a moment's notice, to . . . to what exactly? He wasn't the belligerent type, and the growing unrest only added to his confusion.

Remembering his manners, Alias cleared his throat. "Good morning. Will you be coming with us, Ms. Angelius?"

He had no idea what expression he was wearing, but Ms. Angelius's brow furrowed in apparent bemusement.

"No, I have much to do here." She scowled as she tried to put order in Mr. Dehive's hair. "Please make sure he doesn't go off script, all right?"

If that wasn't a concern Alias had had last night, it certainly was now. He blanched. "Er . . . How do I do that?"

Ms. Angelius tugged on the strand of blond hair curled around her forefinger. "Just remind him to behave. He knows the word, even if he pretends ignorance."

Mr. Dehive waved her away with a scowl. "Don't be so dramatic."

"This is not dramatic at all. I can be a lot meaner than that, and you know it." She turned her full focus to Alias. "Don't worry. Mr. Dehive here is going to behave himself, isn't he?"

"Mr. Dehive is going to have so much fun," drawled the concerned party.

Ms. Angelius's expression hardened. "Good."

Alias tried to make sense of this confusing interaction—and his unexplainable reaction to it—as Mr. Dehive and Ms. Angelius bid each other goodbye. He made his way toward the seat farthest from the duo and kept his chin down, hoping that the knot in his belly would loosen. But the longer he stared at the speech on his tablet, the more the words blurred. The urge to lash out refused to go away, and it scared him. Perhaps it was the prospect of flying and being exposed? This must be it.

A hubot appeared in front of him.

"Take off is in five minutes, Mr. Novar. Would you like something to drink?"

"Just water, please."

Why did he feel so hot inside? Mr. Dehive was staring, but that was hardly new. Alias tilted his head back, pressing his nape into the comfortable headrest, and began counting the silver and golden circles decorating the ceiling. When the ground started vibrating under his feet, he called it quits and gripped the armrests. Inhale. Exhale. The usual drill.

"Your water, sir."

"Thank you."

Mr. Dehive let out a faint sound akin to a chuckle. Alias drained his water in three large gulps, hand white-knuckled on the glass. Was the CEO . . . mocking him? A few moments later, however, he caught Mr. Dehive thanking the hubot that handed him his drink.

Their eyes locked, and Alias was too torn between contradictory feelings to look away.

"Do you know how to put on the seat belt?" Mr. Dehive asked.

The correct answer was *no*, but Alias would rather figure it out on his own. "I'm fine, thank you," he snapped, tightening the seat belt a little too much in an attempt to distract himself from the burning sensation in his chest.

"Maiden flight?"

"E-excuse me?"

Mr. Dehive stood and crossed the space between them, seemingly unbothered by the rocking motion of the floor. "It's an expression," he said, not even watching his hands as he buckled in next to Alias. "First time flying, right?"

They were close. Too close. Alias fisted both hands on top of his work tablet, trapping it in his lap. "Is that not in my file as well?"

"What do you mean, 'as well'?"

Alias had no desire to justify his choice in residence again. "Can we speak of something else?"

"Of course."

As Mr. Dehive set his glass aside, Alias caught a whiff of something sweet he couldn't identify. The list of things he failed to name was growing by the minute.

"Are you still worried about the injection?"

Alias pressed his lips together. He'd asked for it, he supposed. Before he could think of an evasion, though, Mr. Dehive changed subjects.

"You should call me Deon, you know. 'Dehive' makes me feel ten years older, and I'm closing in on forty already."

Alias jumped at the roar of the engines. It said a lot about the effect Mr. Dehive had on him that the swift run of the plane on asphalt came as a reassuring alternative to their continued conversation. But then again, plane accidents were much rarer than LBV casualties.

Alias's stomach still rolled when the jet lifted off the ground. He shot a glance through the small window and promptly regretted it. They were moving *fast*. A thumping sound registered, but by the time he realized it was his tablet hitting the ground, it was already out of reach.

"Relax, Alias." Mr. Dehive stopped the tablet from sliding farther away with the tip of his shoe and dragged it back, then loosened his seat belt just enough to pick it up. "You're safe here. You're safe with me."

Alias willed himself to reach for the tablet, but his hands refused to budge from the armrests. The stinging sensation on his tongue told him he must have bitten it. He exhaled sharply. "You must . . . tell that to everybody."

"To use my given name?"

Alias could picture only too well the teasing smile that went with that tone, and it did nothing to calm his speeding heart. He could almost feel it in his throat, blocking his airway.

"Don't—"

The plane tilted back, racing through the clouds. The next thing he knew, he'd captured the closest hand and squeezed hard. A pained grunt filled the air.

He was touching Mr. Dehive. Of his own volition. And the contact gave him comfort.

"S-sorry," he stuttered. He tried to relax his grip, but the signals must have gotten tangled up somewhere, because he held on even tighter.

"I was nervous on my first flight too," Mr. Dehive confessed, tone gentle. "Squeeze all you want."

Outside, the ground dropped away at incredible speed. Soon, the clouds were blanketing the city far below in a layer of fluffy white, like a wintery landscape. The sun was so bright it hurt his eyes. His stomach dropped, but there was no nausea, only the fast-building tension of excitement, a heat in his chest that didn't burn.

"Pretty, right?"

With a start, Alias realized he was still holding on to Mr. Dehive's hand. He pulled back with a reluctance that unsettled him all over again and mumbled an apology. *Pretty* was an apt descriptor, he supposed. This word must apply to many aspects of Mr. Dehive's life.

It certainly applied to the persons in it.

He wasn't sure where that thought came from, and he sought a distraction from the puzzling tightness in his chest.

"I . . ." He cleared his throat. "Would it be impolite to ask h-how the two of you met?"

"Me and Jaden?"

Alias nodded, surprised at his own audacity. He tried not to squirm as Mr. Dehive considered his answer.

"Jaden is a business manager, like me and . . . McCarthy. We studied together, so I knew what to expect when I asked her to fill the position of PA. And I was very lucky she agreed, because I'm not exactly easy management."

Not for the first time, Alias wondered about the fallout between Mr. Dehive and his former employer turned business adversary, Avida creator Lyra McCarthy. He'd overheard conversations at work about "the Ice Lady," and had watched enough videos of her rare speeches to understand how she'd earned the nickname: she never smiled when she advertised her antivirals, nor did she look angry when she spoke about Mr. Dehive's "bad habits." She'd certainly gone from cold to icy after a two-month vacation she'd taken just before her and Mr. Dehive's fallout. Watching her, it was easy to believe she'd never feared anything.

Ms. Angelius didn't look like she feared much either, but she could never earn such a nickname with a kind smile like hers.

"Why did you replace her?" Alias asked.

"Because she can help the company better in a different way," Mr. Dehive replied, his answer just as vague as Ms. Angelius's had been the day of his interview. "Alias, is something the matter?"

The change in pressure made Alias's ears pop, but that wasn't why he stared in horror at the bright blue sky.

Oh no.

Someone with more experience in human interactions—a riskeer—would have realized at once the reason for his strange reaction earlier and been able to name that feeling so close to anger. Alias had no such experience. He'd never spent any length of time with a person he found attractive, and he'd been spending a lot of time with that person.

The moment he thought the word *jealousy*, his body went limp. Attraction, jealousy, and then what? He turned his focus inward, questioning the way he breathed, the tension deep within, terrified that such emotional upheaval might have triggered the virus.

"Alias?"

"First time on a plane," he choked out.

"It's a good thing the flight isn't long, then. Are you about to throw up?"

If only that would help. "Need . . . I need a distraction."

"Name it, and you'll have it."

Alias curled up into himself as much as the belt allowed it. What he needed was for Mr. Dehive to be mean to him. Such kindness only doubled the attraction and worsened the jealousy. "How . . ." He swallowed thickly. "How d-did you come about your company? I've heard—read—about your career, but . . ."

"There are holes in the tale?"

Alias nodded.

"Isn't it intriguing, how a nobody from Lower New York rose to worldwide fame in less than five years? I suppose that by Lower New York's standards, we were middle class, my mother and I.

But the moment I enrolled into e-college, our lifestyle became quite frugal."

The sweet scent from earlier filled his nostrils as Mr. Dehive sipped at his drink.

"What happened next was part luck, part timing. I started a program in robotics, but abandoned it after three semesters. It was interesting, but it wasn't getting me where I wanted to be." Mr. Dehive gave the golden content of his glass a contemplative look as though it reflected his past. "Anyway, I'm more a people-person, which is kind of a rarity these days. This ease I have in society is one of the reasons I got hired by McCarthy after I finished my studies in management." His voice grew somber. "I worked there for a while, learned the ropes, got— It doesn't matter now. We had our disagreements, and she couldn't see past them. That was seven years ago."

Alias knew most of that, but he didn't point it out. He was getting a distraction, and that was the point of this exercise.

"I'd heard about a robotics company on the brink of collapse, and I had the means by then, and the interest, to help it stay afloat. That's how Dehive was born. The virology department came later, when I realized I could explore this old dream of mine, a dream that we all share."

"The dream of a world without LBV," Alias finished for him, echoing the words from the interview in the park.

Mr. Dehive's little finger brushed against his own. He didn't seem to notice the contact, but Alias could swear he was free-falling. Warmth shot up his arm. His mind raced as he shoved both hands between his thighs, away from Mr. Dehive.

"We should go over the speech," he said in a thin voice, holding out his hand for the tablet.

"Let's address the quiet panic in your eyes first."

"I'm not afraid."

Mr. Dehive just looked at him.

Alias hated that he couldn't hide.

"Your antivirals are still working. I might have my issues with McCarthy, but there's nothing wrong with Avida itself: the problem lies with the virus." Mr. Dehive cocked his head to the side. "From your expression, I can safely assume that you still haven't made up your mind about LX."

Mr. Dehive didn't sound angry, but Alias recoiled all the same. He'd discussed the matter at length with Ben. Avida was still protecting him, but for how long? It had failed his mother abruptly during his childhood like it had been the 2140s, when parent-child affection triggered the virus as often as romantic feelings and lust. Avida had also failed that little girl at the hospital. Really, what assurance did Alias have that Avida would prevail for him, especially now that Mr. Dehive was so often on his mind? Surely LX was worth trying if the World Health Organization was backing it, unlike all those suspicious substances his mother had been injected with.

But the more Alias considered it, the more he felt unworthy.

"What if it doesn't work for me?" he said at last, gut churning. "Antivirals don't work on some people."

Some people spend too much time thinking about other people to deserve a shot at what might be a better antiviral.

He half expected a burst of anger like the other day in the Lab, even if he'd managed to keep the last part to himself, but Mr. Dehive's calm demeanor didn't change.

"There are always exceptions, but we both know that you're overthinking things."

The floor of clouds parted, revealing another plane farther down.

Alias huffed. "Why aren't *you* afraid all the time?"

"Because I refuse to live shackled to fear. I know that I can have friends, even feel attraction, and I won't deny myself the very act of enjoying life, of being human." Mr. Dehive handed his empty glass to the waiting hubot. "I used to feel like you do, just after my mother died. She is among the very unlucky, very rare ones who got sick out of the blue and died within days of the virus reactivating."

"I'm sorry," Alias said in a strangled voice.

He was looking at Mr. Dehive, but it was his own mother he saw, the frail body lying still in a hospital bed. The room was dark, the air heavy with illness. Mr. Dehive spoke of his own mother's death like it was nothing, and yet Alias reacted to a pain that must exist, reaching for the other man's hand and covering it with his own.

"Alias?"

Mr. Dehive's voice held a hint of disbelief, and Alias couldn't blame him. He jerked back, breathing ragged. He hadn't felt such compassion in years, and he'd never, *ever*, acted on the urge to comfort another human being who wasn't his mother.

More importantly, this was the second time today he'd initiated contact with Mr. Dehive.

Outside, the clouds were coalescing into a vast gray sea. Lightning slashed his reflection, fracturing his pale face in two. He felt equally divided inside—an uneasy state of being that was becoming uncomfortably familiar.

By the time Mr. Dehive joined the World Health Organization representative on stage at the WHO's headquarters several thousand feet below the cloud cover, Alias was crawling out of his skin with nerves. At least he got to keep to the shadows, scribbling notes while Mr. Dehive and his colleague shared the limelight.

"So Avida failing is to become the norm rather than the exception," a woman's voice chimed from the speakers of her remotely controlled bot.

"Viruses have mutated and built resistance through history. LBV is the same. Avida has offered very good protection through the decades despite a few cases of very aggressive reactivation," the WHO representative hurried to say, not quite looking at the bot hovering in the air three feet from her face. "Nevertheless, alternatives—"

"Are you finally going to reveal what your highly secretive virology department has been up to, Mr. Dehive?" another journalist piped in.

"An alternative antiviral?" a man's voice boomed from a bot farther back.

"How do you think your former employer will react to your attempt to take over a market she's controlled for years?"

Mr. Dehive frowned, and his jaw tightened for the world to see, but when he replied, he was all smiles once more.

"Dehive Inc. wishes to offer the world a safe, thoroughly tested and approved alternative against LBV. It isn't a perfect solution any more than Avida is, but the LX injection provides better protection because—"

"How better a protection are we talking about here?"

"How does it work exactly?"

Mr. Dehive and the tall ebony-skinned woman representing the WHO answered the flurry of questions, seemingly unfazed by the swarm of bots hovering much closer to their faces now. They were all dragonbots, the model favored by journalists. About ten inches long and two wide, they were either gray or black, and an articulated double lens protruded from one end. Their four wings, a cosmetic design meant to hide the propellers allowing for stationary flight, further enhanced the similarity to a dragonfly—or rather, to its long-extinct ancestor, the *Meganeura*.

"No, LX cannot be taken together with Avida," Mr. Dehive said, replying to several versions of the same question.

"How thoroughly tested was this injection? Avida may not offer as good of a protection anymore, but for those of us who remember the dark days before it hit the market . . ."

Alias hadn't been born then, but he knew what the journalist was getting at: hastily conceived antivirals that seemed to help, right until the virus mutated just enough for the experimental products to become harmful without warning.

The supposed cures overeager doctors had tried to give his mother weren't any better.

"The testing process has been supervised by the World Health Organization during more than a year and will soon become a matter of public records," the representative from the WHO explained. "While LBV has mutated more over the past twelve months, the LX injection provides just as much protection now as it did one year ago because of the way it works."

"Will it help those already sick with LBV?"

"It was our hope when we developed it, but unfortunately, no," Mr. Dehive said somberly.

Alias's heart squeezed. He'd already known the answer, but he couldn't help wishing for a different one. A chuckle of disbelief escaped him when yet another question related to McCarthy's reaction was asked. How could these people be curious about their relationship at a moment like this?

The bottle of Avida in his pocket seemed to weigh a ton while more questions about LX were raised.

"So all your staff have received the injection?" inquired the journalist who'd asked about LX testing.

Mr. Dehive's eyes met Alias's for barely a second—long enough for a handful of dragonbots to pay closer attention to the man trying to fade into the background.

"All my employees are welcome to it if they so wish."

"What about the rest of the world?"

"Nationwide distribution will happen very soon," the WHO representative assured. "In the meantime, Avida remains the number one defense against the Loveborne virus."

The swarm of journalists buzzed louder than ever with questions.

Word spread like wildfire. Specialists on the internet dissected every word of Mr. Dehive's speech. The video of his interview was quickly becoming one of the most viewed feeds all over the world.

And it had only been five hours since the announcement.

Alias had been back to his office for an hour, and in that time he'd received as many calls as he usually did in several days. Emails flooded his inbox so fast he could only filter them while he answered as many calls as possible. His main screen was split in two, the top half dedicated to his inbox and the lower one to a growing list of contact information. Ms. Angelius filled in the blanks in real time as he added the names of specialists, CEOs, and government officials who wanted a slice of Mr. Dehive's time.

The rightmost screen showed Mr. Dehive's calendar, in which new appointments and meetings were added by Ms. Angelius, Alias, and Mr. Dehive. The three communicated in a vertical thread beside the calendar.

On the third screen, to his left, the video of Mr. Dehive's speech ran in a loop, with new comments popping up several times a second, ranging from grateful to hateful, and several million of doubtful inquiries in between. Alias had it on mute, but everything Mr. Dehive had revealed in that wide conference room in Washington still played in the back of his mind.

"Dehive offices, how may I help you?"

He typed another entry into the calendar, sent a quick update in the chat window, and dealt with another three calls before he managed to take a cold sip of what was left of his drink. Smile, cajole, answer, type, repeat. His smile, even forced, helped him end arguments before they started. He was becoming quite good at the whole cajoling business.

Besides the constant beeping of the phone and the gentle whisper of Lady Love's water fountain at his back, the office was quiet. Things were much more heated at Dehive's remote offices where he'd been interviewed. Hundreds of hubots surrounded the building, and more flying bots swarmed above. People wandered close by in small clusters, evidently curious.

Alias exited the window he'd just opened. His third cup of coffee was making him jittery enough already—watching that feed just made things worse.

The next email to hit his inbox was titled: *THE MIRACLE PROMISED FOR DECADES? ALL ABOUT THE NEW INJECTION THAT WILL CURE LBV.*

The link below read: *LBV GIVES HOPE TO TERMINAL PATIENTS.*

"Idiots," Alias mumbled to himself. "That's not at all what he said."

His stomach growled, but he ignored it and picked up one of four simultaneous calls. "Dehive offices," he said, and promptly stifled a yawn.

The video stopped looping. After typing an answer to Ms. Angelius's most recent query and being hung up on by all four callers, Alias refreshed the page. As the announcement started to play anew, a thread next to it suggested related videos, including interviews with Mr. Dehive. One such video was titled *The Man of a Million Fantasies*.

Alias clicked on the link without meaning to.

Deon Dehive jumped on screen—clad in swimwear and nothing else.

Alias swallowed hard. The CEO was emerging from a vast expanse of water and looked straight ahead with a challenging expression. His blond hair was plastered to his head, dripping wet, and Alias's face burned as he dared to look down, past the sharp symmetry of collarbones, and farther down still, to toned pectorals and a mouth-watering taut belly. Distantly, he was aware of the work piling up, of just how long he'd been staring, but the performance of Deon Dehive walking out of the ocean kept his hands still.

Alias's heart pounded. How could a person feel so unbearably hot all over and yet cold to the bone? The alarm bells at the back of his mind urged him to exit the page, but he couldn't make himself close the window into Mr. Dehive's past—into his own risky present. Not when he was enthralled by the water rivulets gathering at the faint line of blond hair below Mr. Dehive's belly button.

Alias bit back a helpless whimper as the cold of dread and anxiety within him melted under the ever-increasing tide of a desire he didn't know how to control. He willed himself to look away, only to continue drinking in the sight of Mr. Dehive's groin framed quite clearly by the thin swimwear. And those legs . . . While the CEO wasn't tall, he had solid, thick thighs. A fantasy unlike any Alias had ever had unfolded in his confused mind: his hands on Mr. Dehive's wet legs and his mouth following suit, tasting the salt left by the waves, licking at—

"Shouldn't you have left by now?"

Alias almost toppled over as he rushed to clear the screen with trembling fingers.

"Hey, are you okay?"

A fully clothed Mr. Dehive surveyed him from the other side of his desk. Alias's eyes zeroed in on the exposed collarbones before dropping to his own lap.

Oh God, he was hard.

He gripped the bottle of antiviral in his pocket, willing his erection away, but neither the embarrassment nor the panic steadily crushing his chest helped. He wasn't safe, despite what Mr. Dehive kept saying. How could he be when he reacted so strongly to simple fantasies? He should take the injection. He really should. Before the virus mutated further or Avida stopped working for him, before he did something incredibly stupid like throwing himself at Mr. Dehive. After all, he'd been crazy enough to initiate contact twice.

And that was exactly why he didn't deserve the injection.

"Alias, what's going on?"

"L-lot of work."

"I can relate."

Mr. Dehive's eyes narrowed, but his tone was friendly enough. A nervous laugh bubbled in Alias's chest. Mr. Dehive kept talking, but Alias couldn't make sense of the words, not when he was busy questioning his sanity. What if he'd crossed the line? What if the virus was now duplicating beneath his skin, hungry for the biological manifestations of his passion and attraction—

"Alias?"

"I-I have work to do. More work." He waved at his desk. The stress of failing at his job did the trick, and he relaxed as his arousal deflated. "Calls. Your . . . schedule." It was so hard to think, and Mr. Dehive was still too close, because Alias could smell his cologne, and the musk of his skin, and it was too much, and too little, and his eyes stung with unshed tears. "Just— I just . . ." *Need.* "Want to work."

"You're beginning to sound like Jaden, and it's not even been one month. You've slaved all day; don't you think you deserve some rest?" Humor was shining in Mr. Dehive's blue eyes, making the handsome face, with its neatly trimmed facial hair and square jaw, even more seductive. "You should go home now." He jerked his head toward the door. "Even the fountain has been shut down for the night."

"But the work . . ."

"The work can wait, Alias. You deserve so much more than a good night's rest after today."

"You deserve so much more."

Alias had to get out of here. Now.

"Y-You're right. Good night, sir."

He walked at a brisk pace, struggling with his bottle of Avida. He almost dropped the whole contents when he picked up the sound of footsteps behind him. He whipped around.

"Are you following me?"

"I am," Mr. Dehive replied, unfazed. "I was going to offer you a ride home."

"I . . ." Alias swallowed his dose too quickly and coughed. He fidgeted with the bottle for a few more seconds, and then pocketed it. "Isn't that out of your way? I mean, you live here, sir, and you need your sleep too."

"I told you to call me Deon. And I don't mind giving you a lift, even though I wish you would move to a better neighborhood."

"I-I can take care of myself."

"Perhaps I should mention that there are still journalists lying in wait for a comment, and while I'm sure you can ignore the dragonbots, surely you'd appreciate spending that time sleeping instead?"

Mr. Dehive—*not Deon*—waited with a keen stare.

Alias hesitated. He shouldn't hesitate. On the one hand, waiting half an hour for the next shuttle wasn't so bad, and neither was a couple of dragonbots. On the other hand, he really could use the extra sleep, or the extra time for jogging, and more to the point . . . wasn't he already spending his days with Mr. Dehive? Weren't they only a couple of feet apart, right now?

He just had to keep his reactions in check.

"O-okay."

A smile lit up Mr. Dehive's face. "Splendid."

Alias followed him to the underground garage, which he'd never visited before. The air was cool, but Alias sweated as though the dimly lit space were a furnace.

Mr. Dehive pointed out vehicle options.

"Take your pick."

Alias fumbled for a polite answer. Mr. Dehive owned one car, and twice as many . . . were those *motorcycles*? Not only had Alias never seen one before, but he'd been convinced such vehicles were prohibited. He eyed a sleek black motorcycle, trying to understand how anyone would willingly pick such an unsafe means of transportation when alternatives existed. And then there was the proximity between driver and passenger to consider. So many risks packed together.

Goose bumps broke out all over Alias's neck.

"Not the motorcycle," he said firmly.

"Let's take the car, then."

Alias kept his chin down as he climbed into the luxury car. The interior was spacious enough to grant plenty of personal space, and the seat was the form-adaptive kind that shifted to better fit the back and thighs. This kind of comfort reminded him of the jet, and so did the scent. A crisp, interesting smell that he tentatively identified as leather—and something that was all Mr. Dehive, much more intense here.

Fear gripped Alias's throat as saliva flooded his mouth. His most recent wet dream from two nights ago—the first one he'd had in years, which he'd worked hard to forget the morning after—came back to him in a flash: a warm chest pressed against his own, hands inching toward his groin, a mouth, *Mr. Dehive's* mouth, gliding alongside his jaw . . .

"You look awfully distracted."

Mr. Dehive wound his arm around the back of Alias's seat, reversed out of the parking space, and headed for an underground tunnel. Alias braced himself as Mr. Dehive slammed the gas pedal.

"You okay?"

Alias's hands were balled on the belt. "Yes." *No.*

"You're not sleeping enough." The car took a sharp turn exiting the tunnel, wheels screeching ominously on the gravel road leading away from the woods. Mr. Dehive glanced at him, one hand on the gear shifter, the other on the wheel. His eyes were sharp but underlined with purple bags. It would seem that Alias wasn't the only who had trouble sleeping.

Mr. Dehive didn't wait for a reply. "I'm one to talk, you might say. But I've been doing this a long time, and you just started. Wouldn't want you to burn the candle at both ends."

Alias hummed in acknowledgment. The intimate quality of Mr. Dehive's tone melted his spine in all the right ways . . . and all the wrong ones too.

On the highway, Mr. Dehive kept up a monologue of trivial tidbits as he zigzagged between cars and trucks with an ease fortunately equal to his driving abilities. Alias tried to focus on the scenery rather than the potential collisions, but the deep bass of Mr. Dehive's voice thwarted his attempt to relax. He regretted not having taken the shuttle. Mr. Dehive appeared to pick up on his unease halfway to the city and stopped talking. Considering that he never had more than one hand on the wheel and kept checking on his passenger, it really was for the best.

"You can relax," Mr. Dehive said. He sped past another sports car and took the next exit. "I'm insulted, you know. I've been driving for twenty years, and I could do so with my eyes closed . . . I'm kidding, Alias, don't— Alias?"

Mr. Dehive's voice was coming from far, far away. Every muscle in Alias's body was taut, every nerve ending about to blow into a thousand sparks. There wasn't enough space in the car. And there wasn't enough skin on his bones to contain the trepidation within, the overwhelming contradiction of fear and curiosity. He was ready to throw up. Or throw himself out of the moving car.

"Alias."

Alias squirmed, thoughts of LBV and car crashes and promiscuity and danger, danger, danger, bouncing against the walls of his skull.

"Alias, it's okay. We're here."

The car was indeed parked in front of his apartment building. Mr. Dehive reached for his hand but stopped short. Where was the relief Alias should feel? He tried to undo the belt buckle, but his hands refused to cooperate.

"I should have driven slower. Was it your first time in a car?"

Alias snarled at the belt. One sharp tug and he was freed. "Doesn't matter."

"What you feel matters."

The door handle was right there. Alias just had to grab it.

He didn't. He could, and he should, but he found himself pinned to his seat the moment his gaze met Mr. Dehive's. The scent permeating the car seemed to become stronger, and he breathed it in, nostrils flaring in greed. Warmth bloomed in his belly. He wetted his lips, words of denial trapped in his throat. Electricity crackled in the air as the silence stretched on. His emotions didn't matter, because he shouldn't feel such emotions right now.

Curiosity and desire, both so potent, showcased by distress.

"You're doing so well, despite being scared."

Mr. Dehive's eyes appeared black in the dim light, with barely a ring of blue around the pupils. And that darkness expanded as Alias kept staring, transfixed by Mr. Dehive's expression of awe and wonder, as though *Alias* was the one with magnetic appeal and not the other way around.

"You should be proud of yourself."

Unbidden, a moan tumbled from Alias's lips. For the third time that day, and for the worst reason yet, he reached for Mr. Dehive's hand. And Mr. Dehive allowed it. He turned his hand around to return Alias's grip, slow and careful, a match to the question swimming in his eyes. Alias wished he could find relief in the semi-darkness that softened the sharp features of Mr. Dehive's handsome face.

All he felt was *want*.

Feeling like he'd lost control of his body, he brought Mr. Dehive's hand to his own face. The sound he made upon contact was something pained and wild that he barely recognized as his own. He flushed to the tip of his ears as he rubbed his cheek against Mr. Dehive's palm, soaking up the warmth of such forbidden touch. Dread mangled with desire until he couldn't tell them apart anymore. He released Mr. Dehive's hand.

The hand stayed where it was. The heat in Alias's belly flared and spread to his whole chest as he leaned toward Mr. Dehive, knocking aside those fragile inches of propriety until only a sliver of air remained.

Mr. Dehive exhaled sharply. "Alias."

Alias's eyelids fluttered open. When had he closed his eyes? He tilted his chin up at the hint of pressure and shivered at the brief caress of a thumb along his jaw. Every inch of explored skin felt hypersensitive, like it had never been touched before. And it hadn't. Not this way.

"Do you have any idea how you look right now?"

Alias couldn't speak. The thumb returned, the touch firmer. Pleasure zinged down his spine as the digit dug into his cheek.

"You look like the ground opened under your feet." Mr. Dehive's voice came out rough and low at the edges. "But mostly, you look like you're longing for something you don't even know how to ask for."

Alias licked his lips and felt a thrill as Mr. Dehive's eyes zeroed in on his mouth. He wanted the warm palm on his mouth, and on his chest too, right over his thundering heart. That word, *longing*, tugged at his loins, unlocking snippets of dreams he thought he'd forgotten.

Get out, he thought at himself. A reflexive thought that prompted no motion.

"W-what is it you think I want?" he rasped.

"For someone to touch you."

Mr. Dehive's hand traveled down the expanse of his throat, all textured warmth and ghosting pressure. Such a touch felt so good yet so wrong, and it was gone too soon and not soon enough. Alias reached for the hand, but his fingers closed on empty air.

"You should go."

Alias couldn't decide which direction to move. The want pulsating under his skin was so much more potent than jealousy. His hands were clenching and unclenching on his thighs, seeking something, as unable to settle as his mind. He'd never been struck by lightning, but somehow he imagined this must be how one felt in the aftermath.

Words he'd never thought he'd say left his mouth in a rush.

"Touch me again."

Mr. Dehive pressed a finger to Alias's mouth. Alias parted his lips on a shaky exhale. Desire pooled in his gut, thicker by the second, burning down every last reasonable course of action. He tilted his head back, awaiting something, anything.

Mr. Dehive wrenched his hand back with a curse. "Fuck. I'm sorry, that wasn't— Alias, you need to— You have to rest."

Alias pressed his hands to Mr. Dehive's chest. One of his fingers caught a button. The alarm bells were ringing louder in his head. He forgot what they meant, with the smooth fabric of Mr. Dehive's shirt barely trapping the warmth beneath.

"Why are you shaking?" he asked.

Mr. Dehive took hold of the wandering hands. "You're the one who's shaking, Alias."

Hypnotized by the strong heartbeat at his fingertips, Alias became aware that yes, he was the one doing all the shaking.

"Go, Alias."

Alias recoiled. Hurt. Confused. Angry to be both.

Mr. Dehive removed Alias's hands from his chest and then gripped the wheel, eyes on the windshield. "You might want to look up the words 'power imbalance.'"

Alias didn't move.

"Please, Alias."

It was the first time Alias had heard that word from Mr. Dehive.

"You really should leave now."

As soon as Alias stumbled out onto the sidewalk, Mr. Dehive sped north. The car was gone in a matter of seconds. Alias gripped the cold metal of a lamppost. It blinked on. When Alias failed to move, darkness returned. He remained there until his hand was numb.

Until the fire in his veins died out.

CHAPTER FIVE
IRRESISTIBLE

D eon Dehive had Alias backed up against his desk and was dropping equations in his ear, mouthing at his earlobe in between numbers. The condensed calculus lesson shouldn't affect him, but the minuses and pluses, the endless string of variables, translated into bursts of heat in his gut.

Mr. Dehive's thumbs dug into his sides, an anchor and a claim. Alias didn't panic when blood started oozing around the digits, perhaps because the blood flowed *into* Mr. Dehive's thumbs. And the more his life force transferred to Mr. Dehive's, the more the mathematics gained power over his body and mind.

". . . square root of ten . . . two by thirty thousand is not equal the variation of . . ."

Mr. Dehive kissed him. Alias tried to push him away, but when he thought *push*, his hands *pulled*. Mr. Dehive chuckled as he nipped at Alias's lower lip, prying out moans of arousal and shame. Alias's hips bucked on their own accord as an eager tongue delved into his mouth. He couldn't think. He *was* the calculus lesson.

"So eager for my touch, Alias. One, one, two, three, I'm going to blow your mind . . . five, eight, thirteen, twenty-one, come for me now, that's it . . ."

Alias woke up hard and aching, one hand already wrapped around his cock, the Fibonacci sequence branded in red in his mind. A sticky trail of pre-come was drying on his wrist. He planted his feet on the mattress and gave his erection a few sharp pulls, gasping in surprised pleasure. It'd been years since he'd last touched himself. Technically, masturbation wasn't risky as long as the feelings motivating the act weren't too intense or frequent, but the occasional article about people masturbating to death had kept Alias from indulging. Besides, it was all too easy to ignore the urges.

Not anymore. Alias fucked his fist in quick, desperate thrusts. He didn't think about the fine line between lust and longing when he rolled onto his belly and rutted into his only pillow, desire swelling inside him with each stroke. He pressed his face into the mattress, and the lack of oxygen, instead of turning him off, drove him to an even more frantic pace. Never before had his cheap pillow felt so good between his thighs.

"So eager for my touch, Alias."

He slipped his free hand between the mattress and his mouth and pressed two fingers between his lips. He sucked on them like they were someone else's, and he so wanted this to be real that he started sobbing around his mouthful. How would it feel to be touched by someone else? To share pleasure? Would Mr. Dehive take him in hand and purr words of praise in his ear until Alias exploded all over his fist, or would he drape across Alias's back and press his fingers in *there*? Light-headed and delirious with need, Alias felt his hole twitch. He gagged on his fingers.

"Come for me now."

All the nerve endings in his body seemed to come to life at once as his orgasm slammed through him. Alias let go of his spent cock with a hiss and rolled onto his back, blissed out. There was come on his belly and on his hand, and now there was some sticking to his back as well. He grinned at the ceiling of his minuscule bedroom. Why would anyone fight this?

Fear surged through him a moment later. He scrambled to a sitting position, one hand curled into a fist over his quickening heart, smearing come onto his chest. It took him all of ten seconds to find his pants and empty the front pocket.

The bottle wasn't there.

Alias's stomach sank. Had he dropped it on his way home? In Mr. Dehive's car, when he'd—

Focus.

He shook his pants, as if the missing content might reappear by sheer force of will.

"What is going on, Alias?"

Ben stood at his side, eyes glowing yellow. Alias flung his pants to the ground. "I . . . My bottle of Avida. I lost it." His voice was too loud in the small space. He clambered to his feet and wiped up the drying come with harsh, angry gestures before putting on some clothes. He'd never, *ever* lost his antivirals.

"Your next dose is in several more hours." Ben tapped his shoulder with a metallic finger, the one that twitched. "You have more than enough time to procure more Avida."

Alias wanted to hug Ben. Instead, he hurried out of his apartment and leaned back against the brick wall. The gravity he bore so effortlessly on a normal day seemed to crush him now, compressing his lungs until he thought he'd collapse right there on the pavement, a two-dimensional human-shaped sheet of condensed anxiety. He couldn't get enough air.

The bricks were cold at his back, and so was the wind blowing into his face.

Air. More than enough to breathe.

He drew one long gulp of air into his lungs, and then another, and one more, until the night stopped swirling around him. Who was he supposed to ask for help? Even if his mother could magically summon a bottle of Avida, the last thing he wanted was to add to her concerns. His mother was sick because of him, because of her love for him. She was his responsibility, not the other way around. Only Ben was allowed to witness his breakdowns.

But Ben couldn't help him right now. No one could, except, maybe—

He called a taxi before he could change his mind.

Even in the dead of night, the Hive was staffed, and familiar shapes taunted him at the edge of his vision. He braced himself for an interaction, but the few human beings amongst the more numerous hubots steered clear of him. Their avoidance probably had something to do with the wild look in his eyes or the bed head he'd made no effort to tame. Unless it was the strange ensemble he was wearing. He'd put on the first clothes he could find, which were probably not suited for work. He hadn't bothered with a shower, and if he could sense the sweat drying in layers on his back, no doubt other people could smell it.

Anxiety was riding him hard, sharpening his focus to the point where he could orient himself without a map despite the corridors being nearly identical. He walked fast, as fast as he could without running, more worried about taking a wrong turn than he was about appearances.

He had no idea where to find Mr. Dehive, and more than once, he almost walked right out of the Hive. What if he'd lost the pills somewhere else than in the car? What if Mr. Dehive had no backup pills to share? He didn't take them, so he might not have any. There was also the matter of what Deon's presence meant for him. How it made him feel. Seeing his boss right now might just make matters worse . . .

But what other option was there? Pharmacies were closed at this time of night.

He selected Mr. Dehive's number on his watchphone and tried again. The first three calls he'd made had bounced to voice mail, and he was growing increasingly concerned that the CEO had left the Hive for some reason. He didn't care if he woke him up and got fired. Not when he didn't have any more pills.

The large doors leading to the BotHouse came into view. Alias hurried to the scanner and slammed his hand down. He had to speak his name three times before the recognition software agreed that yes, he was Alias Novar.

He stumbled and caught the wall before he could face-plant. The noise and warmth hit him like a slap to the face. He had no certainty that Mr. Dehive would be here. His meager hope was based on Mr. Quint once saying that their CEO enjoyed napping in the BotHouse and his knowledge that watchphones tended to misbehave in this part of the Hive.

Alias ventured down an alley, trying to orient himself despite the tears blurring his vision.

"Mr. Dehive!"

His voice was drowned in the racket of machines, but a hubot's hearing was sharper than a human's and several metallic heads swirled in his direction. Alias's skin prickled with goose bumps, and his eyes landed on his watchphone. He couldn't tell if the shortness of breath he was experiencing was because of the virus or the panic, and it drove him crazy. Every time he spotted a human silhouette, his heart jumped into his throat, but it was never *him*. The lights blinded him. What if he was turning in circles?

What if he was becoming a riskeer too?

What the hell had he been thinking? It was one thing to be attracted to someone he'd never met, but quite another to touch the person and entertain fantasies of intimacy. He knew that physical contact made it much easier for the virus to be reactivated. He hadn't forgotten in the car, he just hadn't cared.

Mr. Dehive was right: Alias was terrified. Of himself.

He veered so fast around a corner he almost knocked a small cylindrical bot over.

The automatic apology died on his tongue.

The man he was searching for was bent over a small desk mere feet away, navigating the information spread on a holographic screen.

"M-mister—"

"Alias?" Mr. Dehive said, spinning around. "Are you okay?" He banished the holographic screen and hurried toward him. "What's going on?"

Fresh tears sprang to Alias's eyes.

"Alias." Mr. Dehive's voice was pitched low with worry. "Breathe."

Had Alias stopped breathing? He definitely held his breath when two strong arms closed around him. Mr. Dehive smelled like sweat and grease, and a warm musk that made his head spin. Alias jerked back. Just as his knees decided to give, Mr. Dehive directed him to a chair.

"You're okay."

The room was spinning and narrowing down—to the man in front of him, to the intoxicating smell already seared into his memory, and to that firm voice in his ear.

"Breathe."

Alias breathed. It hurt, and he wrapped his arms around his torso and clawed at his sides as his lungs burned. Mr. Dehive was talking to him. Eventually, the words broke through the haze of his anxiety.

"Tell me what's going on."

Alias inhaled. Exhaled. He pretended Ben was there, guiding him as he counted down from ten. "I-I lost my bottle of Avida. In your car, I mean. I think . . ." No, that wasn't right: he had *not* been thinking.

Mr. Dehive gave him a long stare. Alias could hear the question he wasn't asking and tensed further: *Why don't you take the injection?*

"Well, I haven't found your bottle." A note of impatience laced the words. "But I can get you Avida if that's what you want. Why didn't you try calling me?"

"I tried calling you," Alias snapped. "You didn't answer. That's fine. I'll just—"

"I just told you I would get you Avida!"

Alias clenched his fists. "It wouldn't help!"

"And why not?"

"Because it's too late!" Taking advantage of Mr. Dehive's shock, Alias scrambled to his feet, knocking the chair to the floor. "I dreamed of you!"

Get out!

This time, he listened to the alarm bells. He flew down a row of what he thought were robot torsos. How ironic, that he worked for a company that built things, whereas he kept breaking down.

"Alias, wait!"

A hand landed on his shoulder. Alias spun around with a snarl.

"I just saw your calls. I wasn't ignoring you." Mr. Dehive squeezed his shoulder before letting go. "The reception's really bad in here."

For all that Alias had hated the initial contact, he missed the touch immediately. A stabilizing touch, like that day in the woods. Or in the plane.

"You look like you're longing for something you don't even know how to ask for," Mr. Dehive had told him in the car, cupping his cheek, touching his mouth. That kind of intimate touch had been anything but comforting, and yet Alias yearned for a repeat as much as he dreaded the consequences.

"Alias."

How could a near stranger know Alias better than Alias knew himself? He wiped the tears with his sleeve.

"Alias."

His muscles locked up as Mr. Dehive's hands took hold of his shoulders.

"It's going to be all right. I'm going to take care of it," Mr. Dehive promised. "Of you."

His hands traveled down Alias's shoulders to rest above his elbows. Alias bit his lip through a full-body shiver.

"It's all y-your fault," he hiccuped.

"What is?"

Alias's belly clenched. He was making a fool of himself. He *was* a fool, accusing the one person who was willing to help him. But the words wanted out. "The dream," he rasped.

"What was the dream about?"

"You kissed me."

"That sounds like something I try very hard not to do."

Alias's mind went blank. A helpless noise tumbled from his lips when Mr. Dehive's thumbs dug in on either side of his skull. He'd tried to massage the area before, but he could never get the angle right. Mr. Dehive had no such problem. As he rubbed his thumbs in small, concentric circles up and down his nape, and then at the junction of neck and shoulders, Alias's chest expanded. Breathing didn't hurt anymore. His fists unclenched at his sides. Sweat dripped down his brow, but the heat didn't come from within anymore. To his amazement, he was relaxing under Mr. Dehive's touch.

Forming words proved harder than it should.

"The . . . pills."

"Yes, the pills." Mr. Dehive dropped his hands. "Come, I'll get you a replacement bottle."

For a moment, Alias could only stare at Mr. Dehive through heavy-lidded eyes.

"Ah." Mr. Dehive's eyes sparkled with a mix of sadness and amusement. "That good, uh?"

Alias recoiled into himself. "I'm s-sorry."

"Whatever for?"

"I shouldn't have . . . disturbed you. At work. In your home. And then I lost my calm and . . ." He took a step back, as if apologies were better accepted with space. "It isn't fair—"

"Alias."

"Yes?"

"You didn't disturb me. I like taking care of my employees, and you need . . ." Mr. Dehive mumbled something. "Come. Let's go find some peace of mind, shall we?"

Alias lost track of time. He kept his eyes down as he followed Mr. Dehive, not as interested in their destination as he was in what awaited him there.

He expected to be led to the Lab or an office. Instead, he followed Mr. Dehive into a set of rooms that didn't feature on the map he'd learned by heart.

"Sit down." A glass of water was pressed into his hand. "I'll be right back."

Alias took a sip, gaze drifting to the pond in front of him. It was an actual pond, with water lilies, lotuses and colorful fish that he'd never seen outside of digital picture books. Slowly, so as not to frighten the shy inhabitants, he took a seat on the edge of the veined marble basin and dipped a finger into the water. It was lukewarm, in contrast to the cold content of the glass. Alias set it aside. A strange serenity descended upon him. He felt . . .

Safe.

Such a concept was ludicrous, of course.

Alias pulled his finger from the water and dried it on his shirt. Mr. Dehive was nowhere to be seen, but Alias was too busy looking around to fret. He'd thought his office beautiful, with the branches climbing up the walls and the plants granting life to the circular space, but it didn't hold a candle to this room.

The walls and the ceiling showed the woods and the night sky so clearly that he could have sworn he was sitting under the stars.

The place was huge and lavish and by far the most personalized space of the Hive. There were plush-looking carpets that must work magic for tired feet, a lounging chair littered with discarded clothes, and three-dimensional art pieces located between tall bookcases filled with actual books.

Alias's eyes jumped from one piece of furniture to the next, cataloging the electronics, tools, and mementos distributed over the surfaces. He did a double take at the bed, and not because of its colossal dimensions or the carved wooden canopy. Somehow, he'd completely failed to recognize the rooms for what they were: Mr. Dehive's personal quarters.

A story his mother used to read when he was a boy came back to him, something about a princess unable to sleep because of a small vegetable trapped in between the layers of her bed. A pea, maybe. As he stared at the forest of green pillows propped haphazardly against the headboard, an unbidden fantasy spun the story into a decidedly less innocent fairy tale.

Approaching footsteps brought a flush to his cheeks. He tore his eyes from the bed and almost tumbled into the pond as he tried to sit straighter.

"I've been told it's quite a nice view," Mr. Dehive said, either not taking notice of Alias's state or merciful enough to pretend he hadn't. "You get the full experience of a night in the woods, without the mosquitoes. And if you grow bored of the darkness . . ."

The woods vanished, leaving behind not the array of windows Alias had expected, but a mosaic of high-quality display screen panels. A heartbeat later, algae splashed over the walls, and Alias found himself at sea bottom, surrounded by fish of all colors and sizes. Exotic creatures he couldn't name surfed the underwater currents.

Mr. Dehive held out his tablet. "There are several more options to choose from. Feel free to shuffle through them while we wait for your taxi."

Alias's attention drifted to Mr. Dehive's other hand. "Is that—"

"Yes. Avida, your dose for a month."

It took Alias two tries to uncap the bottle. He couldn't help but notice Mr. Dehive's frown as he set not one but two pills on his tongue, but he wasn't here to make someone else happy.

And, as it turned out, neither was Mr. Dehive.

"You're under no obligation to take the injection, but you really should, for your own peace of mind. In case this happens again, and I'm not available. There really are no risks, Alias."

Alias snorted. It came out weak and half-hearted, but at least humor helped keep the anxiety at bay. He wiggled the bottle. "Except I'd have to stop taking these first."

"Considering that LBV's resistance to Avida is increasing—"

"Isn't that what is bound to happen for the LX injection too?"

"Are you a virologist?" Mr. Dehive arched a brow. "Or for that matter, a pharmacologist? No? And yet you swallow your pills without questions, even risk a double dose."

Alias dropped his chin. In the pond, one particularly daring fish breached the surface with its bright orange fin. Alias followed it with his eyes, until he spotted his distorted reflection in the water.

You could take it, but you don't deserve it.

"I should go." He pressed the fist containing the bottle against his heart. He barely deserved these. "Thank you for your help, sir."

"What's wrong with 'Deon'?"

Alias stiffened.

"I don't mean to push," Mr. Dehive hurried to clarify. "Your taxi will be here soon." He lapsed into silence and shifted on his feet. Not closer, but not farther away either.

Alias spent the next fifteen minutes on Mr. Dehive's tablet, perusing the various landscapes and asking questions. It seemed to be the right thing to do, because Mr. Dehive granted him more space as he began putting away the discarded clothes, and Alias grew increasingly more excited as he tried out the landscapes. What could it hurt to admire some colors before going back to his depressingly gray apartment?

When Alias put the woods back on display, Mr. Dehive confirmed that it was the forest outside. Some tweaking turned on the mics of hidden cameras. Alias jumped as an owl hooted from afar, ears perking up for the next sound of night life. The forest, sadly, remained silent.

The beach wasn't so quiet. Alias hurried to change it and breathed a little easier at the sight of sea bottom.

"Having fun?"

Mr. Dehive was no longer folding clothes. He stood with his back to the reef, one knee up with his foot resting against the wall, his arms crossed. Alias willed his expression not to change, but he wasn't that good of an actor, and he blushed—suddenly, vividly— as he recalled the scantily dressed man from the video.

"The outside is solid rock."

"Rock?"

Alias felt lost, and alarmingly warm all over.

"The outside of the Hive is either metal or windows," Mr. Dehive explained, his tone neutral, as though he were giving another tour. "Except for this room and the en suite bathroom. The part above ground level is carved inside natural rock."

"There's a rock formation in the forest," Alias said, unsure if he should know this considering how far off the path it was. He forged on, encouraged by Mr. Dehive's silence. "I mean, that place in the forest a quarter mile north of the trail, where there are, uh, actual beehives."

When nothing was said, Alias obeyed the illogical impulse to look up.

Mr. Dehive was smiling. Alias had never been on the receiving end of such a smile before. It hinted at secrets, but also of approval. The mix had heat sizzling up his spine. He tried to ignore the sensation, replace it with indifference—in vain.

"Do you keep bees for the honey?" he blurted out.

That smile widened.

Something in Alias's snapped. He rose to his feet, movement slow, as though Mr. Dehive was the one bound to take flight. His palms were clammy and his heart slammed into his throat, but it wasn't fear that drove him, it was *want*.

Perhaps he'd run out of fear.

Mr. Dehive held perfectly still. Except for his mouth.

"Alias."

The name contained a warning, but also a plea. It echoed Alias's own state of being. Part of him hoped this was still a dream, where desire had limited bearing. But he doubted it. And the closer he got to Mr. Dehive, the more he wished for this, whatever it was, to be real.

Mr. Dehive's shirt felt soft against his palms, the texture distinct from the fabric he'd touched last night, but the heat underneath was just as intoxicating. He let his hands wander higher. The shoulders he cupped were strong, and the muscles tensed as Alias tightened his grip. Mr. Dehive's hands landed on his hips, a delicate touch at odds with the tight lines of his handsome face.

Confidence bolstered by the double dose of antiviral he'd taken, Alias let one hand wander toward Mr. Dehive's throat and stopped where the blue shirt gave way to tanned skin. He rubbed his thumb back and forth over cotton and skin, marveling at the contrast and at his own folly. Back and forth, back and forth . . .

Mr. Dehive pulled him into his arms with a low groan. "Alias," he said again, without the warning from before.

The scent of him, musky and masculine, filled Alias's head with white noise. He rose to the tip of his toes, nails digging into skin and fabric. He wanted to press his ear to Mr. Dehive's throat and check if the pulse there matched the frantic pace of his own. Would it beat faster if he covered it with his palm?

If he captured it with his mouth?

The caressing hands on his sides caused his breath to hitch. How would it feel to have them touch him without clothes? No one had ever—

Mr. Dehive's breath fanned over his cheek.

"What are you thinking about?"

Alias gripped two fistfuls of shirt. "You," he confessed, because lying wouldn't change the truth of how he felt, against all reason.

Their eyes met, brown and blue, a match of earth and sea.

Their lips crashed together. The kiss could have been chaste, but the man leading it was anything but. Alias had dreamt of it just a few hours ago and woken up more aroused than he'd had any right to be. He'd wondered how the press of a foreign mouth might feel, if partaking in such intimacy would disgust him, terrify him, or blindside him with need.

Now, he knew.

He shut his eyes with a trembling sigh to better savor the warm glide of Mr. Dehive's mouth against his own. He couldn't breathe, but he didn't mind. He should pull back, but the longer the kiss lasted, the less he could remember why. His body was turning into a live wire, and every shift of Mr. Dehive's mouth against his pushed a current of pure electricity through his body. He wanted this: the smooth caress of Mr. Dehive's lips, the scratch of facial hair against his jaw, the twin burn spreading like a wildfire under his skin. And when the tip of Mr. Dehive's tongue traced his bottom lip, Alias longed for more.

"You taste exactly like I thought you would, and I try really hard not to think about you this way at all," Mr. Dehive whispered against his lips, hands gliding down his sides, close but not close enough.

When he pulled back, Alias captured Mr. Dehive's hands in his own. "L-like what?"

Mr. Dehive licked at the string of saliva connecting their mouths. "You taste like sin. Divine."

There was an obvious contradiction in there, but Alias was too busy trying to stop his hips from moving to point it out. He failed.

Mr. Dehive didn't seem to mind.

"That's it. Take what you need."

Goose bumps broke out all over Alias's nape. These words were not equations Mr. Dehive groaned in his ear, but the echo of his dream broke the last of Alias's self-control. He ground against Mr. Dehive firm thigh in earnest, too taken by the sounds he caused to slow down, too turned on to even consider it. Acting on an earlier fantasy, his only guide in such matters, he dove in and pressed his lips to Mr. Dehive's throat. The skin was velvety there, softer than the hands digging into his hips. The taste was a revelation, explored through eager licks of tongue.

"Fuck, you're hot."

Alias's hips bucked at the strain in Mr. Dehive's voice, and then again when something hard dug into his stomach. He mouthed at the offered throat with increasing fervor, egged on by the grunts in his ear. He'd never considered himself greedy, but that was before his senses had been set aflame. His kisses turned sloppy as he dared slip a couple of fingers past the hem of Mr. Dehive's shirt.

"You going to come like that?"

Alias made a pained noise, and then another one as Mr. Dehive's hands ventured further down to grab his buttocks. His cock was so hard he was surprised he hadn't spilled in his underwear already. He caressed the vast expanse of Mr. Dehive's broad back, delirious with need. He ached to touch the older man everywhere, to have Mr. Dehive touch *him* everywhere. He'd never thought he would do this, any of it, but now he dared, now he wanted. His clothes had to come off. Right now.

The push that came wasn't hard, but it was so unexpected that Alias stumbled, eyes widening in shock, breathing ragged.

Mr. Dehive scrambled backward until he bumped into a low table. "Shit." He rubbed a hand over his face and laughed. The strangled sound hinted at frustration more than anything else. "I'm sorry. That was— I shouldn't have done that."

Alias's hands tingled. He rubbed them together, but it didn't help. "You keep saying that," he whispered, neck burning not with desire, but shame. "But you didn't— It is I who . . . I'm sorry."

Mr. Dehive waved the apology away. His face was white, his features taut. "You haven't searched the words yet, have you?"

It struck Alias as odd that, of the two of them, Mr. Dehive was the one on the verge of panic. The man was a riskeer. He shouldn't care. "Why do you care, if LBV isn't a danger to you?"

Mr. Dehive's lips thinned to a faint line. "I care because it's unfair of me, and unfair *to* you. Because you're my assistant."

"That's not important." Alias spoke a little louder. "It has no bearing compared to—"

"Stop."

In a flash, Mr. Dehive was back in his personal space. He shushed him with a finger, just like he'd done in the car. "You don't understand." Forefinger switched to thumb, the digit a languid caress on the wet skin, at odds with the frustration in his voice. "You work for me." He pulled back abruptly. "Sit down. You're going to keel over."

Alias did, mostly because his legs refused to support him anymore. The constant back and forth had left him reeling. If what they did was so wrong, and it *was*, why did Mr. Dehive keep doing it? Why did Alias?

Mr. Dehive returned with two glasses and an opaque brown bottle, which he uncorked in one smooth gesture. He sat down on the floor, following Alias's example, but left a polite distance between them.

"Here. Give it a try."

Alias wrapped his fingers around the stem of the tall glass. It felt entirely too breakable in his unsteady hand, but Mr. Dehive appeared unconcerned as he sipped at his own glass. Frowning, Alias tilted the delicate piece to the side. The liquid swirled sluggishly, thicker than juice. Its solid amber color conjured up the hives outside. A deep inhale brought forth pictures of tall grass and wildflowers. The first drop tasted like their kisses.

"Honey?" He took a larger sip and grimaced. "With alcohol?"

Mr. Dehive just stared at him.

"Did I say something wrong?"

"Oh, no." Mr. Dehive showed him the bottle, the look of consternation wiped from his face. "This is a honey wine, but the alcohol content is pretty low. It's called mead." He tapped at the hand-written label with his thumb. "Homemade and everything."

Alias reverted to smaller sips. While he didn't exactly like it, he wasn't actively repelled either. "Hence the hives," he said.

"Precisely." Mr. Dehive was already pouring himself a second glass. His every gesture was smooth and precise. "The little cabin nearby is where we make it. Would you like more?"

"No, thank you." He really should leave now. Go somewhere safe. Home was safe. So was Ben. He set the glass on the floor after one last sip and stood up.

He made the mistake of looking at Mr. Dehive. His breath stuttered.

Mr. Dehive was dragging his palm over his clothed erection, his glass of mead held loosely in one hand. A shiver ran down Alias's spine. So many words strained against his lips, words that didn't belong together.

Mr. Dehive yanked his hand away from his crotch and drank more mead. Alias picked up the bottle of Avida. He should thank the man. After all, these pills were the reason he'd come all the way to the Hive.

"Hey." Mr. Dehive sought his gaze. "You're fine, Alias. You took your dose."

Alias hugged himself. The fact that Mr. Dehive wasn't touching himself anymore didn't make the tent in his pants any less obscene. Or appealing.

"You're okay," Mr. Dehive insisted. "You're not at risk here. There are no feelings involved, just plain old desire. You're safe. Get some sleep, okay?" He climbed to his feet with a wince. "Come in later today. How does midday sound?"

Alias agreed in a thin voice.

The notes of honey on his tongue tasted like poison.

CHAPTER SIX
COLD SHOWER

Alias pressed his brow against the cheap plastic toilet seat. Ben hovered nearby, its multifunctional appendices clinking and rattling as its neuronal networks sought the appropriate response to its owner's disarray.

"My scans show no fever, Alias, and the two pills you took earlier that morning should have ensured your safety. I believe you are having a strong panic attack. It can be terrifying, but you are in no immediate danger."

Alias dry-heaved one last time before flushing the toilet. "No," he agreed, although a little voice at the back of his head kept screaming yes. He knew what he had. Or rather, what he didn't have. Having grown up with a mother suffering from LBV, he knew the symptoms intimately and had been watching out for them all his life.

"This is . . . was . . . a panic attack," he agreed. He generally stuck to the recommended bidaily dosage, but he'd taken two pills at the same time on occasion in a vain attempt to calm himself. As far as he knew, it had had no additional effect—good or bad. "I . . . I'll be fine."

"Would you like something to drink?"

Alias heard a watery laugh and pressed his lips together. The acrid taste on his tongue had long drowned any lingering sweetness. "Please," he croaked.

After downing the content of the glass Ben brought him, Alias dragged his feet into the shower. Despite the hot water, he had goose bumps all over. The soap slipped from his trembling hand, and when he bent to pick it up, he almost cracked his skull on the tile. He started crying, quiet little sobs of exhaustion mingled with frustration.

He'd thought he'd understood it before. Temptation. He'd taken comfort in the belief that, whatever shape it took, fear would protect him. And yet here he was, a fool who lusted after a man he'd touched.

He gave his cock the quickest wash possible.

Ben helped him into bed and even pulled the blanket up for him, its eyes switching back and forth between blue and yellow at dizzying speed. It was four in the morning though, and Alias was too exhausted to worry about a possible new malfunction.

"You are safe here." Ben's voice conveyed a reassuring neutrality only robots could display. "I am watching over you."

Alias gripped the sheet under his chin.

"Would it help to talk about what triggered this attack, Alias?"

A reasonable question, considering the amount of time Alias had spent on the bathroom floor.

"I . . ."

His body ached to rest, but his mind was spinning. He rolled onto his side and curled into a ball. "I have . . ." His hands shook around his legs. *Breathe in. Breathe out.* It occurred to him that the words weren't his own thoughts but calm orders delivered by Ben. He exhaled through his nostrils and counted down with the hubot.

"I engaged in sexual promiscuity." Saying it out loud felt like ripping off a Band-Aid. Painful. Freeing. "With Mr. Dehive."

"I thought you went out to get Avida?"

"So did I. I figured that Mr. Dehive might have found my bottle or have extra pills. After all, LX hasn't always worked." His ragged breathing echoed in the room. It was such a small space compared to Deon's lavish bedroom. There were no stars, no colors beside the electric blue of Ben's big eyes. Blue eyes, just like Deon's. "I'm not sure what happened," he admitted, biting back a giggle. It would sound hysterical. "He gave me the pills, and the next thing I know we're kissing. Again."

Ben remained quiet for several seconds. "You are not sick, Alias," it offered at last. "I can only conclude that you regret what happened. Did Mr. Dehive pressure you?"

"Actually, he stopped me . . ." He raked both hands through his sweat-messed hair and tugged at a few strands hard enough for the pain to flare and the ache to dim. The ache to be touched again. "I think I'm going mad. Am I going mad?"

Ben whirred reassuringly. "It is normal for a human at their sexual peak to crave the touch of a partner. Avida protects you."

But for how long? Alias wanted to scream.

Or run.

He left the bed and opened drawers at random, picking clothes that didn't fit and hardly matched. Ben filled his water bottle and handed it to him.

"Thank you, Ben." Alias pressed the bottle to his chest. "I know I should sleep, but I . . . I can't stay still."

"It is alright. You like to run. It helps you." Ben's eyes settled on blue. "Good run!"

Alias barreled down the stairs and through the front door. The first gulp of fresh air felt ridiculously good in his lungs. Cold puffs came out of his mouth as his feet led him from one street to the next, the pattern familiar, automatic. A hubot's journey. A procession of cars flashed past him, so many that Alias paused to watch them imitate that disconcerting thing called "traffic" that had been so problematic at the end of the twenty-first century. Back then, public transit hadn't rendered most cars obsolete.

And the population hadn't been cut in half just yet.

It was a stroke of luck for humankind that the virus wasn't triggered by proximity alone. The problems didn't even start when attraction or affection became part of the equation . . . only when those feelings got out of control.

And there were as many points of no-return as there were people.

Alias shook off that thought and slowed to a walk as he entered the park. A few bots were busy fighting the entropy of vegetation growth around Lady Love, but there was no one else around so early on a Friday.

Just Alias, sitting with his back to the statue, head tilted back to admire the gears in her static hair fracturing the morning sunlight.

He rested his elbows on his knees and sighed. He felt drained to the marrow of his bones. He hadn't had so many panic attacks in so short a time in years. This was bad. This job. No, not the job. It was neither the job's fault nor Mr. Dehive's.

Alias wiped away the drying tears on his cheeks. He would go back home now. Shower, try to sleep a little before going for work. He needed to rest.

Beset with correspondences and calls all afternoon, he had little time to question his sanity or Mr. Dehive's decision to spend the day locked up in the Lab. In the evening, he jogged in the woods until exhaustion took its toll. He managed to sleep soundly at last that night and felt confident enough the next morning to call his mother. She seemed to buy his reassurances and rejoiced at the news that he'd visit soon.

Monday morning, Alias was braced to see Mr. Dehive at their meeting with the WHO, but Ms. Angelius showed up at his desk with a cup of freshly brewed coffee to tell him that she would attend that session in his stead. She mentioned something about cornering Mr. Dehive for another kind of serious discussion afterward, but Alias was so relieved at the opportunity to continue avoiding Mr. Dehive that he didn't ask questions.

Around ten that night, he was finally able to shut down his computer. Going for a run was the last item on his list before boarding the shuttle, but he ran into Mr. Quint in the employee lounge, which led to them going to the BotHouse. As tended to happen whenever the two engaged in conversation, Alias lost track of time. When he reached the bottom of his mug and let out a loud yawn, Mr. Quint grinned, white teeth lit up by the sparks of his shaping tool.

"I shouldn't have dragged you down into the BotHouse so late."

"Oh, I enjoy being here talking to you." Alias eyed the usual organized mess on the desk with interest while Mr. Quint turned the metal arm around to work on the shoulder joint. "I just . . ."

"Forget that sleep is a thing? It's a common issue around here."

Alias opened his mouth. Closed it.

Mr. Quint looked up at him. "What's on your mind, Mr. Novar?"

"It's about"—Alias dropped his voice to a whisper—"my hubot, Ben3min."

And just like that, the arm and tool were pushed aside. Alias sat in the only chair that wasn't piled up with material and told Mr. Quint about the various issues Ben had been having.

"I fixed some myself, but there's a new kink with its eyes. They're supposed to shift, it's the model's design, but sometimes they just flash back and forth endlessly between—"

"Oh, like this?"

Mr. Quint plucked a hubot head out of a pile on the floor and pressed the command button at the base of its nape. The bulging eyes turned on, bright white. Then black. White. Black.

"Similar," Alias agreed. "Except Ben's eyes are multichromatic."

Mr. Quint was the first person Alias had met who spoke his language. Alias listened in awe as he offered various explanations as to why Ben's eyes were malfunctioning. Having worked for more than fifty years for various engineering companies, Dario Quint had a wealth of experience. He expressed himself with a great deal of enthusiasm, using his hand aplenty, much like Mr. Dehive. As his friend and the company's oldest employee, it made sense the two men would trade habits.

"Any more issues—big or small—you'd like to talk about?"

Alias hesitated. "Surely you have more important—"

"More important? Not at this hour. More interesting? I doubt that." Mr. Quint grinned. "Go on."

Time passed swiftly as Mr. Quint worked him through a list of Ben's specific features and problems, listing solutions on the metallic fingers of his right arm. Loud machinery started nearby, but he just spoke louder. He talked a mile a minute, and Alias was on the edge of his chair, drinking it in.

"You know what? If you'd like, you could bring it here, let me have a look at it."

Alias watched him sip at his now-cold mug of tea. "You . . . wouldn't mind?"

"You're indulging an old man's enthusiasm, that's what you're doing. And no, I won't accept any credit from you, young man."

Alias closed his mouth and pursed his lips, to Mr. Quint's apparent amusement.

"Don't be so stubborn about such things. You remind me of our common boss, and in that particular instance, it's not a compliment."

That comment distracted Alias from the idea of payment. He glanced at his watchphone. It was well past his bedtime—and the shuttle's last ride to the city. He could call a taxi, but the unseasonably warm day gave him a more appealing idea.

He bade Mr. Quint good night and went back to his office to grab a jacket.

The chirping of the morning birds pulled him out of a deep slumber. He tried to fall back asleep, but a skunk scurried past him, and a black bird landed a foot away and croaked quite enthusiastically into his ear.

Alias rubbed his eyes. The lack of a mattress hadn't kept him awake long last night. The ground was hard but the grass soft, and the gorgeous display of stars had lulled him to sleep in a matter of minutes. He didn't even feel stiff. He rolled his head to the left.

"Someone's in need of attention?"

The bird cocked its head to the side and croaked again. With a sigh, Alias sat up and reached for his chatty companion. It took off in a scurry of feathers. Alias watched it fly away and huffed, torn between irritation and amusement.

The latter won over.

Alias unrolled the jacket he'd been using as a makeshift pillow and tied it at his waist. His stomach growled and went ignored. He'd eat after his jog.

The path to the cabin proved easy to remember despite the lack of clear signage. In less than twenty minutes, the sky lost what little remained of its red taint, and the beehives appeared around a pine tree.

The black and yellow insects parted around him as he stepped closer to the biggest, busiest hive. Slowly, he leaned down to study the neat little rows where the bees stored their extra honey—the so-called "honey spurs." On one of the nights he couldn't sleep, he'd researched bees and honey culture extensively.

He knelt on the ground and twisted to study the underside of one hive. The bottom board was clear wood. One bee lay in the grass, unmoving. Heart clenching, Alias slid his palm under the dead bee. If not for its lack of reaction, the bee could have been asleep.

"Alias, are you okay?"

Alias almost dropped the bee. With a soft exhale, he put it back where he'd found it. "I'm fine, Mr. Dehive."

"You can't stay here. Stand up. Do not make any brusque movements."

Alias stood up not-so-slowly, his nostrils flaring. Was it too much to ask for a moment of peace? "I'm not afraid of them," he said primly, illogically insulted on the bees' behalf. "They never hurt me."

Mr. Dehive scoffed. "When you told me you've seen the hives, I thought . . . Wait, are you telling me you get close and personal with my bees *without a suit* on a regular basis?"

Resigned to a confrontation, Alias turned around.

Mr. Dehive had his arms crossed and a thunderous expression to match. His three-piece charcoal-gray suit and pointy black shoes were definitely not intended for a walk in the woods.

Alias willed his heart to slow down and tried to keep his tone even. "How did you know where to find me?"

Mr. Dehive's lips twitched. "A lucky guess."

In an effort to distract himself, Alias skimmed through Mr. Dehive's schedule of the week in his head, which he knew by heart despite it changing multiple times a day. He really should address the upcoming business, or the last meeting with WHO, before the conversation veered in the direction he dreaded.

Mr. Dehive beat him to it. "Step away from the hives, now. Don't make me come and get you."

Alias ventured further into the swarm of bees.

"Damn it, Alias."

Mr. Dehive stormed toward the cabin. Bemused, Alias watched him take the protective suit from its hook and put it on, swearing in his struggle with the fixation straps at the head. When the thinly woven net came down over the handsome face, Alias still wasn't sure if Mr. Dehive was the person he'd seen wearing the suit the other night. After all, they'd had their back to him.

"That's enough, now."

Before Alias could think up a rejoinder, Mr. Dehive grabbed him by the shoulder and pulled him out of the swarm, one careful step at a time.

"You still haven't taken the injection," he remarked. "And yet you come here and play with enough bees to risk getting seriously hurt."

Alias huffed. "It would take more than a thousand stings to kill me."

The gloved hand tightened before relaxing its grip. Alias shuddered. It was unfair how weak in the knees that simple touch made him feel, especially through so many layers. And unfairer still how soon he missed it.

"I will—I will take it," he heard himself say, heart pounding. "The injection. It's just that I . . ." *Don't deserve it.* "Need more time."

He wasn't talking only about the injection, but Mr. Dehive seemed to take the statement at face value. "I can give you time. All the time you want." He sighed. "And I appreciate that you've told the press you've taken it." He jerked his chin toward the hives. "What I appreciate a lot less is you spending time with the bees without protection."

"They won't attack you if you don't attack them."

"In theory."

Mr. Dehive turned around and began unfastening the suit, which he hung back up. His clothes didn't have the slightest wrinkle. Only his brow was furrowed. "Every time I think I have you figured out, you surprise me."

Alias licked his lips, nervous for the right and the wrong reasons. He wanted to touch. Embrace the madness within him. Despite many a night fighting the ache, it hadn't diminished.

"I looked it up over the weekend," he heard himself say, voice breathy.

"What?"

"The words you told me. 'Power imbalance.'"

The vinegary scent permeating the beehives had faded, replaced by that bewitching masculine scent. Mr. Dehive's facial hair looked as perfectly trimmed as it had last week, as if no time had elapsed since the fateful night that Alias had succumbed to temptation.

Alias stepped forward. Mr. Dehive raised one hand to stop him from moving closer. "Then you understand why this can't happen."

Yes, Alias meant to say.

"No," he said instead.

Mr. Dehive's eyes widened. "No?"

"Whatever hold you may have on me is nowhere near as strong as my fear of dying," Alias explained, which was as ridiculous as it was true. And stupid to boot: why was he even arguing? He should find relief in Mr. Dehive's reticence. "I—I apologize. You didn't ask for this . . ."

"Hey." The hand Mr. Dehive was holding up landed on Alias's shoulder. He gave it a squeeze before pulling back. "You have no reason to apologize. I may not have put it in so many words, but I did ask for this. I've been flirting with you and I shouldn't have. Do you think I've been giving you a wide berth since I got you home last Thursday because I didn't want to see you? If anyone should be apologizing, it's—"

"I flirted back," Alias cut in, knowing the words were true the moment he said them. "I did that. And I'm the one who initiated contact the other night, I . . ." He swallowed thickly. "It's not— I just. . ."

"You don't know what it is you want."

"You said I only didn't know how to ask for it."

"Well, I shouldn't have said that either."

Alias bit back a hysterical laugh. "Why does it matter if you're my employer?" He couldn't believe the words coming out of his mouth. He could hardly believe he was still standing here, *asking for it*. The words kept coming anyway. "You can't fire me yourself. The list of my rights takes one and a half page in the final contract."

"That list wasn't there originally."

That gave Alias pause. "What do you mean?"

"All those clauses protecting you." Mr. Dehive began pacing. "After our little walk outside, I went to see Jaden and had her amend the final contract. It was remiss of me not to consider how much—"

Alias shook his head. "It's not your fault if I . . ." His throat locked up. Those words he'd been about to say, he'd never spoken them out loud. Would it make any difference for the virus?

Mr. Dehive stopped pacing. "If you?"

"It's not your fault if I want you," Alias confessed in a half whisper.

Mr. Dehive sucked in a breath.

"You're not pressuring me." Despite having spent the weekend discussing the issue with Ben, he hadn't known what he was going to say or do until now—until Mr. Dehive stood in front of him. "I don't believe you're manipulating me. You're just . . . reckless, and apparently, so am I." He meant to step back, but he walked toward Mr. Dehive instead. This time, he wasn't stopped. "I wish I didn't need to be afraid all the time. That I could enjoy touch, and . . ."

Mr. Dehive's face fell. "Oh, Alias. You can."

"Can I?"

"You can," Mr. Dehive insisted, his eyebrows pinched. It resembled pain, but that made no sense. "You can interact with people, have friends. It's safe to do so. To enjoy it. Human beings are not meant to be solitary creatures. We need touch to remain sane. But it's not— It doesn't have to be me that provides, it should *not* be me. You shouldn't . . ." He racked a hand through his hair. "No matter what you think you want, no matter all the precautions I've taken . . ." His jaw tightened. "You're new to this, Alias. Sometimes, people say yes but they mean no."

"You're right."

Mr. Dehive looked crestfallen. Pain lanced Alias's chest with the need to explain himself and wipe that expression off that handsome face.

"You're right to say that this is"—*dangerous*—"new for me. I know this. I know that I shouldn't want anyone at all—"

"That's not what I said."

"But this is what I believe, and I take offense that you doubt my ability to know my own mind, as full of contradictions as it may be."

"I see." The words came out strangled.

Mr. Dehive's fists clenched at his sides. Was he fighting the urge to reach out and touch him? Alias's throat went dry at the possibility. It was hardly the first time this had happened. There were moments—a lot of them—when Mr. Dehive halted himself, and Alias was usually grateful for the show of restraint.

Not now.

"There's no need for such . . ." The word "restraint" caught in Alias's throat. He glanced up and bit back a moan. The hungry gleam in those blue eyes reminded him of Thursday night, in the lavish car. To swirling landscapes, when he'd traveled in more ways than one. The all-encompassing want had returned, and Mr. Dehive had barely dared touch him yet. He shouldn't ache for it so badly, but the dam was already broken. Was this the way so many people had died? Because, just like him, they couldn't help themselves?

What was the point of switching antivirals when none of them might keep him safe *now*?

"Deon," he whispered, the name foreign on his tongue.

Mr. Dehive's nostrils flared. The only things Alias could hear was his own heartbeat and the bees. Their ambient buzzing was so loud it seemed to originate from his own head. He couldn't feel his face.

"Please."

Alias wasn't sure who kissed whom. It didn't matter. As soon as their mouths met, Mr. Dehive's hands were on him, warm and firm and everything Alias wanted. He moaned into their kiss, tilting his head to the side to better feel the scratch of facial hair against his jaw. If the kiss became awkward as a result, Mr. Dehive didn't give any sign of being bothered, lips gliding against Alias's own without pause. The hungry noises he made matched the intention in his gaze, and Alias welcomed them all. He wanted to be devoured.

"D-Deon."

He could feel the hard ridge of Mr. Dehive's erection against his belly, and he wanted . . . He wanted more. Everywhere Mr. Dehive touched him, sparks leaped, feeding the heat gathering in his loins. God, it felt so good to be touched, and Mr. Dehive's hands were still rubbing against clothing. To have them slip under his clothes, roam over his chest in warm patterns he couldn't predict, up and down his sides before slipping into his pants, touching him in ways no one had ever touched him before . . .

He darted out his tongue to dip past Mr. Dehive's lips. Empowered by the groan of approval, he pressed in deeper, licking boldly into Mr. Dehive's mouth, parsing the taste for individual notes. The tang of coffee. A hint of sweetness reminiscent of honey. Growing more adventurous by the second, too eager to feel self-conscious about his lack of experience, he wrapped his lips around Mr. Dehive's tongue and sucked.

A savage groan rewarded him. Desire flooded him, blazing further with each brush of Mr. Dehive's thumb across the thin line of exposed skin between his pants and shirt. *At last*, his mind chanted, the want unstoppable, crashing through his defenses, reinforced through decades of solitude. *More!*

He was gripping the front of Mr. Dehive's shirt as though he couldn't stand otherwise, and that might very well have been true. After a last sloppy suck, he pulled back with a moan and buried his face in the crook of Mr. Dehive's neck. The hand at his shoulder blades migrated to his nape and stayed there, a pressure that both grounded and unsettled him.

Had fear always felt so similar to desire, or was he merely losing his mind?

"Do you even know if you're after sex?" Mr. Dehive asked bluntly. He pulled back, brow furrowed. "You've been touch-starved for so long. Maybe a hug is all—"

"I'm not starved," Alias protested, and he took a step back, toward the bees, toward a danger he understood better. "But I want . . ." That word shouldn't roll off his tongue so easily, but it did. "I want this."

"A hug or a kiss?"

"Both."

Alias twisted his hands together. He kept having dreams. Fantasies where Mr. Dehive would redden the skin of his throat and inner thighs with the coarse stubble, where he'd bite and suck marks into his skin, establishing a claim, possessing him like no human being should ever be possessed.

Those dreams hadn't stopped because Alias willed them to, and they would hardly stop now, after . . .

He shook his head, trying to dislodge the thought. Another one took its place. "I meant to ask. Why . . . why was I chosen?"

"Chosen?" Mr. Dehive's confused expression might have been amusing under other circumstances.

"Hired," Alias clarified. "I know why I wanted this job, but I'm still unsure why you hired me. I'm not, er, bad at it, but you must have had your pick of candidates."

Mr. Dehive rubbed at his chin. The bags under his eyes had become darker since Alias had last seen him. Perhaps yesterday's meeting hadn't gone well. Perhaps it was the stress. A stress that was different from Alias's own, but not any less real. Mr. Dehive was fighting a world-threatening virus—Alias had just himself to battle.

"Well, you were selected for many reasons." Mr. Dehive's smile didn't reach his eyes. "The fear, right here, is one of them."

Alias's eyebrows jumped to his hairline. "So, I'm your PA because I'm *afraid*?"

"Because you push past it. I've met a lot of people over the years, and many are content to remain shackled to it, controlled by it. The applicants who belonged to the other category—those who had long emancipated themselves—just didn't have the right set of . . . motivations. But that's only one reason." Mr. Dehive's expression hardened in a peculiar, incomprehensible way. "You have experience in the field, as temporary and occasional as it may have been. You speak your mind when it's important. You're the hardest-working person I've ever met beside Jaden and myself, and you know when to lie and when to tell the truth. You like bots as much I as do, which was an unexpected bonus. More importantly . . . you share my vision." He smiled. "Deep down, you seek change."

Alias bit back the words that wanted out. He knew better than to express any doubts.

Nevertheless, Mr. Dehive seemed to read his thoughts.

"Jaden doesn't just hire anybody to handle me," he said, voice dripping with something resembling amusement, but also exasperation. "If she thought you could do the job after she'd kept a close eye on you for a week, then that fear is well within your abilities to tame."

The fear was familiar. Comforting.

But it wasn't the only emotion keeping him company anymore.

That night, Ms. Angelius dropped by his office with the sour expression of someone dealing with one problem too many. Alias, who'd been close to hanging up on one pesky journalist who kept twisting his words, assumed he gave off a similar vibe.

"You're taking tomorrow morning off," Ms. Angelius told him in a tone that brooked no argument.

Alias blinked at her. "But that's Wednesday. Mr. Dehive needs—"

"To catch up on sleep, and so do we. All those journalists hounding us for more information about the injection, and—" she scoffed "—the intrusive ones asking inappropriate questions about Mr. Dehive's dating life and his relationship with McCarthy are still going to be there at midday, trust me."

A groan of dismay escaped Alias. Ms. Angelius tapped her watchphone with a finger. "Midday. Not a minute before."

That was how Alias ended up visiting his mother bright and early the next morning.

"Hello, Mother."

The sole occupant of the room flashed him a brilliant smile. "Oh, Alias! I'm so glad to see you!"

Alias closed the door behind himself with a smile of his own. The large window, clean smell, and quietness of room C-7535 were vast improvements over the living conditions in Wing E. Alias brought a chair to his mother's bedside without having to navigate a maze of strangers' beds, for once.

"You look better," they said at the same time.

His mother laughed. Alias froze in his seat, the hope and happiness so strong he could have sworn his lungs were on fire. He couldn't recall the last time he'd heard his mother laugh. The fee for this room was astronomic, but he was more than willing to spend his paycheck on hospital bills if this was the result.

"So, tell me." His mother's voice was rough, but she seemed more energetic than the last time he'd seen her. "How is your new job, really?"

Alias chose his words carefully, working his way through what his protective instincts and the NDA allowed him to disclose. "I'm getting better at interacting with people," he said with a straight face. It was true. *Too* true. "I'm enjoying the multitasking. Reminds me of that job I had once, except there's more of everything . . . Nothing I can't handle, of course."

His mother stared, concern written over her features. His smile dimmed. She'd always been a little too talented at spotting the holes in his tales. The things better left unsaid. Alias had thought he'd gotten better at deception—after all, hadn't he been practicing *lying* as part of his job? He lied when he smiled, when he said how delighted he was to patch this or that important person through. Only Mr. Dehive's hands on him, and Alias's reaction to them, felt like the beginning of a truth too dangerous to contemplate.

"I'm physically weak, Alias, not brain-addled," she said, lips pursed in disapproval. "You make too much credit to just take calls and manage schedules. No insult indented."

"None taken." Alias leaned forward to grab a veined hand. It was much cooler than Mr. Dehive's.

Guilt struck. Could he really blame work, or even his dislike of doctors and hospitals, for how long he'd gone without visiting his mother? He should have come earlier.

He should do a lot of things differently.

Shifting this gaze to the full IV bag of symptom-alleviating medicine, he tried to find comfort in the fact that her hand wasn't shaking today, at least. She wasn't healing, of course—this was merely the consequences of better care. Nothing and no one could cure her.

But he could be there for her.

"Alias?"

He cleared his throat. "I do make a lot of credit, but there's a reason for that. Very few people wish to work as in-person assistants, so the credit offered for the position needs to be substantial," he explained, quoting Ben's explanation to him. "Besides, this job involves a lot more work than taking calls and managing a schedule. I deal with internal matters with the staff, keep myself up-to-date about virology so that I can handle rumors and speculations, I accompany Mr. Dehive on his trips—"

His mother's shrewd look stopped him.

"What?"

"Just to reassure your old mother: This boss of yours doesn't ask personal 'favors,' does he?"

"Mother!"

Alias didn't have to feign the outrage. While he was shocked at his own actions, he hadn't done any of it for credit, and would have said no had Mr. Dehive been that kind of person.

Is it really better if you do it for free? an insidious voice whispered at the back of his mind. *If you keep asking for it like a riskeer?*

His mother probably caught him blushing before he had the presence of mind to bury his face in his hands.

"I'm just doing my job," he muttered between his fingers. On the nightstand, a vase of fresh flowers added color to the white room. His cheeks must match the red roses.

"Then why are you blushing? You're full of potential and talent, my dear boy, but the fact remains that you have no experience as an in-person assistant, and Dehive Inc. is not exactly a small business. Tell me truly: Are you being coerced?"

"No. I am *not*."

"But something happened."

Alias cringed.

His mother let out a string of swear words that left her breathless.

"Calm down," he urged her, reaching for a glass of water and pressing it into her hand. "Please. There's no cause for concern. It's not— It's not what you think."

Their eyes met over the rim of the glass.

"Then what is it?"

Alias lifted his hands and kept his voice low, so as not to upset her. "I hadn't meant for any of this to happen; it's just that when we . . ." He cringed again, harder. "When I t-touch him, when he . . . t-touches me, I . . . I like it," he confessed. His stomach rolled, but at least the weight on his chest had lessened.

His mother pressed their brows together. "He's not asking this of you?"

Alias shook his head. He told her how much Mr. Dehive wasn't asking for it, how he'd given him several outs, how he'd also amended the contract to protect him before he started.

"I—I know I shouldn't—shouldn't pursue him, shouldn't do any of *this*, in case—"

His mother's expression softened. "I'm not concerned about you experiencing your first crush, merely about the extra difficulties stemming from your respective positions."

"I know the p-power imbalance makes it look bad." There were so many reasons why this was bad. Alias knew the whole list by heart. "But you should know that the contract I signed protects me very well. Almost more than it protects him."

"The power imbalance might be what concerns me, but it's not what concerns you, is it?" His mother heaved out a sigh. "You seem to forget that I'm a special case, Alias."

Avida failing isn't a special case anymore, Alias thought, but the last thing he wanted was to upset his mother with a comment about children dying again.

"I just— That's not— I don't have a crush, Mother." He slammed his hand onto his thigh to keep it from trembling, but his right foot kept bouncing with nerves. "We just . . . t-touch sometimes. K-kiss a little."

"Oh, Alias." His mother pulled him into a hug. "I wish you weren't so afraid."

"I—I don't know how," he stammered.

How true was that if there were times when he was nowhere near scared enough?

Alias took a deep breath. Mr. Dehive kept saying that relationships of all kinds were safe, but the parent-child bond was supposed to be the safest these days and yet here was his mother, face sickeningly pale and glistening with sweat. How could Alias accept that his foray into intimacy was anything but a death sentence carefully stretched over time, with the virus building more resistance than ever?

"This new injection, the LX, offers better protection than Avida, doesn't it? It destroys the virus rather than inhibiting its replication," his mother said, so gentle, always so gentle with him, so understanding. Her brow furrowed. "Didn't you get it?"

"I could have," Alias said in a strangled voice. "I want to. I'm going to take it. I just . . ."

She smiled sadly. "Your mother is a constant reminder that there are exceptions."

"No, Mother, this isn't because of you."

It was only half a lie. Whenever he considered LX, he thought of the experimental products that had been given to his mother before he got her to Mortella, and how all of them had made her worse . . . But also, if his mother couldn't take LX, how could he, when he was acting like a riskeer? He exhaled sharply. "If anything, Mother, I—"

When she tried to reach for his face, Alias lifted her hand and held it against his cheek. The electrocardiogram spiked, and Alias tensed, ready to call a nurse, but his mother was one resilient patient and only sank further into the pillows with a breathy exhale. The ECG returned to normal.

"You have to stop blaming and punishing yourself for my state, my dear boy. You are the best thing that's ever happened to me, and I have accepted a long time ago that this love I feel for you is also killing me. The virus has never changed how I see you, Alias. If anything, I love you a little more every day. If I could go back in time, I would just love you even more."

Alias felt like all the air had been punched from his lungs. "*Mother.*"

"The world is a dangerous place, always has been, even before the initial outbreak." She fussed with the pillows at her back and sat straighter with a hint of her former grace, snarling in jest at his offer to help. "Caution has kept us alive all this time, but it would never have been enough to guide us if not for the hope we thrived on. Right now, there's no hope for someone like me—"

"Mother—"

"You know it as well as I do, Alias," his mother continued, hoarse voice laced with determination. "But who knows when that might change? Change makes the world go round, my dear boy, and it's not necessarily a bad thing. You have to keep hoping for the best." She gave him a pleading look. "Please, don't allow fear or misplaced guilt to make such a claim on yourself."

"You speak like him."

"The man who shouldn't warm your bed?"

Alias choked on his saliva. "He doesn't— I don't—"

His mother shook her head with a faint smile. "I'm just teasing you." She glanced around. "I must thank you again for the room. And the flowers. You made a sacrifice—"

Alias squeezed her hand. "Taking care of you is no sacrifice, I assure you."

A scream rose and dissolved farther down the corridor. Hubots whirred past the door, exchanging information too fast for the human ear. Another scream, another wrong note in the harmonious melody of death hovering. Alias shivered.

"I'll refill your glass."

When he returned to the room, he entertained his mother with innocent tales from the Hive, and was relieved to hear her laugh—and be able to laugh with her—at some of them. Deep down, he knew that life could not be restricted to fear and guilt, or it was no life at all. Feeding his mother small pieces of chocolate brownies and pear-stuffed micro pies, he made a mental note to have deliveries of what she liked best.

A nurse came in half an hour later. By that time, his mother was sound asleep, exhausted by their interaction and the toll it had taken on her feeble body. Alias kissed her brow, biting back yet another apology. His feet led him to the colorful garden on the rooftop. It was quite the spectacular sight, even for a regular visitor such as himself.

From his position in between two neat rows of tulips, Alias found himself yearning for the woods of the Hive. He'd often suspected that Mortella's architect had meant to give the dying a last glimpse of beauty. If not for his dislike of hospitals and doctors, Alias might have spent more time here. Or maybe not. He changed his mind a little too often these days.

He himself had changed quite a bit in just a couple of weeks. Case in point: a man stood close by, a ragged-looking fellow who evidently didn't care much about personal space, and not only did Alias not startle, but he didn't move away to put some distance between them.

For a while, he sat on an empty bench and just drank in the sight below. A puzzle of still forms, gray and black, like someone had forgotten to add color. Out of the corner of his eye, he spotted a little boy sitting in a woman's lap, probably his mother. He gave the duo a covert look—and he wasn't the only one. When LBV had first struck, children had died in horrifyingly high numbers.

Even after an antiviral had been found and children became the best protected age group, the sight of one still stirred most people's protective instincts.

For Alias, it also brought back memories—happy ones, from before his mother got sick.

"Do you see that?"

The hushed conversations in the garden were growing in volume. More curious than worried, Alias drifted toward the trio who spoke the loudest and followed the finger pointing downward.

People filled the sidewalks. Dozens, no *hundreds*. Several hundreds of people split in two groups that were about to meet right there in the middle of the street. Alias's jaw dropped. People never got together on such a scale if they could avoid it. He leaned closer to the railing and spotted personalized digital signs. Huge ones, if he could tell what they were from so high up.

He frowned in puzzlement. Protests had been unheard of for more than a decade. People lodged complaints electronically or sent a hubot to deliver them. The last demonstration had been over a shortage of Avida in Texas. It had ended in a bloodbath— although not because of the virus itself.

Brow furrowing, Alias checked the date on his watchphone. November the eighteenth. A hundred thousand LX injections were being readied for a first large-scale release today or tomorrow, according to the ever-changing schedule set by the team of scientists at Dehive and the World Health Organization. Were these people demanding the injection?

What would they say if they knew that he'd said no when he'd had the chance?

His chest clenched. He couldn't breathe. How could he turn down what so many were begging for?

He dashed back inside and to the staircase. In the dimly lit space, he leaned against the heavy door, heart hammering, and pulled out his tablet to torture himself with the live feed of what was going on outside. Two masses of people in motion, angry waves expending in width and length, unstoppable, it seemed, as cars honked to get past only to get stuck between the two groups, which bore opposite messages.

Antivirals are dangerous! one sign read. *Don't trust LX!* said another.

We want the injection! read a sign from someone in the other group.

The woman holding the sign claiming that antivirals were dangerous was tripped by the man expressing his desire to get the injection. Fists started to fly, and someone dropped their sign in the ensuing chaos.

No privileged treatment for Dehive's staff! Alias read before several pairs of feet covered the shiny letters.

Officers of the NID rushed in to split the two groups before anyone could get hurt too badly. Alias pressed a fist to his mouth. *Privileged.* That was what he was, beneath the collar of multilayered guilt choking him. He might not see himself as worthy, or certain, but had Mr. Dehive expressed any uncertainty about LX? If it had been Alias's decision whether Mr. Dehive got the injection, would Alias have considered him unworthy?

Was anyone who wanted to live unworthy?

Sweat trailed down his brow. He felt for the bottle in his pocket and took a deep breath. Held it and released it after a count of three. He could probably take two pills. Even three. Go running.

Or try something else entirely. Change a little further. He could swallow all that fear and shame. Kissing Mr. Dehive and wanting to do it again shouldn't make him unworthy of safety.

"Change makes the world go round," his mother had said.

"Everything is temporary, except change," Ben had told him years ago, underscoring a dead poet's words with a digit that wasn't malfunctioning at the time.

He couldn't help the way he felt, but he got to decide what he *did.*

He pocketed his tablet and careened down the stairs. In his mind, something had flipped—a delicate yet crucial switch that had been there all this time. On the sidewalk in front of Mortella General, he darted aside to avoid getting knocked over by the people running away from the NID officers. From the earbud linked to his watchphone, he listened to the man announcing that the Dehive's remote offices were being stormed by a crowd two hundred people strong demanding the injection, making this protest larger than Alias had believed at first.

"And as some of you might already know, there have been thirteen new cases of Avida failure today in the state of New York," the announcer said gravely. "Of these thirteen people, the six who are romantically involved already show severe symptoms of LBV that usually appear after several weeks . . ."

A loud honking startled him out of his thoughts. With a yelp, Alias jumped back in time to avoid getting hit by a car. He'd been so caught up by the voice in his ear he'd almost died. From a road accident.

He didn't manage to hold in the hysterical laugh and got a few strange looks for it.

After checking both sides of the road, he crossed the street and tried a number he'd only ever called from his desk: Mr. Arvin, who assisted the head of Virology, notably by giving employees their LX injection.

A dragonbot appeared in front of him before the call could connect.

"Mr. Novar, how do you feel about being one of the few people who've received the LX injection?"

Alias blinked incredulously. It was one thing to answer questions over the phone, and quite another to be confronted outside of the Hive. All of his rehearsed lines flew from his mind as a second dragonbot approached.

"Mr. Novar, is it because the LX injection has serious side effects on children that Mr. Dehive hasn't been allowed to begin mass production?"

Alias shook himself, suddenly angry on Mr. Dehive's behalf. "The LX injection was trialed on children only after models reviewed by both Mr. Dehive's team and the World Health Organization indicated that it would be safe. All these children are in excellent health right now, and the general public should have access to the injection very soon," he said firmly.

"Mr. Novar, what do you have to say about the allegations that—"

Alias ducked under the two bots and hurried toward a taxi waiting by the curb.

The main doors of the Hive opened on Ms. Angelius, as resplendent as ever in matching blue and violet pants and a sleeveless blouse.

"I'll call you later, I'm sorry." She concluded her call and turned toward Alias. Golden rings flashed at her ears as she gestured him inside. "Thank you for coming in early, we really need you. Follow me."

She didn't comment on his dubious choice in clothing as they headed toward Mr. Dehive's favorite meeting room halfway between their two offices, and Alias didn't explain why he wasn't dressed the part, or argue that he'd actually come earlier to get the injection. He was needed.

Ms. Angelius pressed a hand to her brow. Her red hair fell in soft curves past her shoulders, bouncing with every step, with a small braid lost in the fire. "This is a shitstorm."

"All these people demanding or rejecting the injection?" Alias ventured, walking faster to keep up with her.

"That's only part of it."

They locked gazes, and for a moment there, Alias could have sworn he was under suspicion. But for what?

No other words were exchanged until they entered the windowless meeting room a few minutes later. Several employees wearing lab coats sat in a half circle around a wide table, busy at their computers. Mr. Dehive stood in one corner, doubly isolated in what appeared to be an unpleasant phone conversation.

"Of course, LX hasn't always been ready, that's why it was in *development*, officer. There are no side effects beyond those already disclosed for the current iteration, unless my own employees keep lying to me, and I'd like to think I can still trust most of them. Who at the World Health Organization did you—" He hit the wall with his fist, but it was obvious he'd held back, perhaps in deference to the others present. "That's fine, I don't need to know who their mole is, I'm busy enough dealing with these employees of mine who dared . . . Listen, all the details of how LX was conceived and thoroughly tested were going to be made public . . . Of course McCarthy would claim the risk still exists! Surely you are aware that she has the most to gain from discrediting me after Avida started to— Why yes, sure, send someone over here; I'm always happy to cooperate with the NID," Mr. Dehive said in a distinctly unhappy tone.

The reason behind the strange look Alias had gotten from Ms. Angelius became clear.

"I never talked about any of this to anyone," he told her urgently.

"You weren't a suspect for long."

She still didn't appear happy. Alias tried not to take it personally. He was still there, wasn't he? Following Ms. Angelius's instructions, he claimed the remaining seat around the table and logged into his session, bringing up his usual work tools. With thirty people in the room, it wasn't long before he missed the solitude of his office, all the more so with the tension in the air. Perhaps that was the point. Perhaps Mr. Dehive aimed to find the mole this way.

Ms. Angelius held out her tablet.

"You did well, dodging these questions earlier."

Alias blinked at the screen showing him rushing toward the taxi. The knot in his belly loosened at her words.

"I should have expected they'd eventually approach me outside the Hive and been better prepared," he apologized.

Mr. Dehive pressed his hand over the earpiece and squeezed Alias's shoulder, the storm in his expression cleared. "We all should have done a lot more work on the expectation front, but let's not dwell on that, shall we? Damage control is all we can do now."

Alias nodded and got to work. As soon as he turned on his work line, calls started coming—and didn't stop. There was indeed plenty of damage control to do. Half his callers wanted to know when LX would become available; the other half were concerned about those supposedly severe side effects. Alias had realized during the first week that his job went well beyond the scope of what a personal assistant normally did, but he didn't mind supporting the call center in the Lab when they were overrun.

"No, the present iteration of the LX injection only has minor side effects comparable to Avida's," Alias told a stubborn journalist, resisting the habit to touch the bottle in his pocket.

The top article on his screen read: THE LX INJECTION: A DEADLY SOLUTION? He closed it with a grimace and answered the journalist's next question as politely as possible. "Yes, Mr. Dehive was planning on sharing all information pertaining to the development of this antiviral with the public." *But someone else beat him to it and spun it in the most alarming way possible.*

Mr. Dehive disappeared for a while when the party from the National Intervention Department showed up. At the computer next to Alias's, Ms. Angelius was amending Mr. Dehive's speech for the LX distribution.

"That's exactly what we wanted to avoid," she said in a half whisper, blowing at a wild strand of red hair. It wasn't clear if she spoke to Alias or herself. "We were supposed to control how that information got out."

Time flew. Alias kept track of it through his coffee consumption. Every time he drained his mug, it was refilled. The other scientists and staff members were similarly attended by hubots. Mr. Dehive's coffee mug was refilled the fastest. The two top buttons of the red shirt were undone, and his gray tie ended up on the back of his chair upon his return from his meeting with the NID. He kept rearranging—crumpling—the collar as he paced. His irritation worsened with every call he took, and it culminated around Alias's third cup of coffee. Should he succeed in standing still for more than a minute, he did so at Alias's shoulder, winnowing down the ever-growing list of meeting requests awaiting his input on Alias's computer screen.

In contrast, Jaden Angelius remained calm through the storm, a poised queen in a bustling hive. Alias wasn't sure how he himself pulled it off. He worked and worked and worked until it became his new state of being, adjusting and reorienting gears at the heart of the giant Dehive machine with a degree of competence he'd never expected to possess. He kept an ear open for instructions, and re-adjusted Mr. Dehive's schedule in between answering frantic calls and searching the web for journalists who wrote the least controversial articles about LX.

"You doing okay?"

It took a moment for Alias to realize that Mr. Dehive was talking to him. He nodded, distracted by the voice of the journalist in his ear and the schedule in front of his eyes. Mr. Dehive leaned closer to read Alias's collated notes on how the public perceived LX and the recommendations he and Ms. Angelius had come up with. The former PA was currently several seats over discussing with Mr. Arvin.

"Amazingly enough, I can't tell which part you wrote and which part Jaden did," Mr. Dehive murmured.

When he smiled for the first time in hours, Alias decided it must be a compliment.

It was seven past nine when Mr. Dehive was allowed to release the first distribution schedule for the LX injection with the WHO's seal of approval. The room erupted into cheers, and Mr. Arvin patted him on the shoulder.

"We've got this," Mr. Arvin announced cheerfully. "The Ice Lady may act like she's got the winning hand, but we all know that's a lie."

Alias turned around. "Can I . . ."

But Mr. Arvin was already heading for the door. Apparently, Mr. Dehive was also leaving—this time with Ms. Angelius, the two of them speaking in hushed tones as they crossed the threshold.

Alias kept his focus on the screen, still busy transposing Mr. Dehive's conversation with the president of the country into well-articulated notes. He entered the last word as unease stirred in his gut. He'd heard Ms. Angelius say the word *bee*, and he just couldn't fathom how the hives justified the CEO's disappearance in the middle of a war council—Mr. Dehive's words, not his. For the first time since he'd started this job, Alias resented being kept in the dark while the former PA was obviously kept in the loop. Was he still under suspicion, despite Ms. Angelius's reassurances earlier?

He dropped the mug he'd just picked up, eyes wide as he realized that losing his job wasn't the only thing he was afraid of.

He was afraid of losing whatever he had with Mr. Dehive—perhaps more than he'd ever been afraid of having it.

He startled at the sound of an incoming call and stared blearily at the familiar number on his watchphone.

"Mr. Dehive?"

"Hey, are you home yet?" His breathing came out harsh, as if he'd been running. "Sorry about that hasty retreat."

Alias's nerves had been jittery before his last cup of coffee and hearing Mr. Dehive's voice directly in his ear only made him more restless. He climbed to his feet, a flare of anger bursting through the panic he'd locked away all day. "Why am I not with you right now, dealing with . . . whatever it is you're dealing with? The NID came to investigate McCarthy's claims earlier. Is that resolved?"

"It will be, for I have nothing to hide, and all the paperwork to prove it," Mr. Dehive assured him. "As for what I'm dealing with right now, it's not something you ought to be concerned about," he added, but the words sounded insincere. Distracted. Rehearsed.

Alias made out Ms. Angelius's hushed voice in the background and crouched to pick up his mug, knuckles white on the handle. "Are you sure there's nothing else I can do? I'm still in the conference room. I could—"

"Alias, just go home and get some rest." Mr. Dehive's voice softened. "Please."

Alias glared at the schedule, at all those meetings and conferences that wouldn't fit. Those mismatching puzzle pieces were still a lot easier to understand than his contradictory feelings.

"Alias? You're still there?"

"Yes," Alias choked out.

"You did a great job today."

Ms. Angelius's voice got stronger in the background, snuffing out the delicate warmth surging within him from the praise.

"Okay," he whispered. "Have a good evening, sir."

"You too, Alias."

For a solid five minutes afterward, Alias remained rooted to the spot, trying to remember why he couldn't go back to his apartment just yet.

Then he recalled his earlier resolution.

His legs were wobbly despite his determination, but they supported him well enough. He kept a clammy hand on the wall as he made his ways toward the Lab and began walking faster as he closed in on his destination. Before he knew it, he was entering the uneasy organic space of the Lab.

Strangely, a small part of him relaxed.

"Mr. Novar?"

The sharp tone reached Alias through the daze. It took several tries, but eventually he got enough words strung together to express his purpose. He was led to a workstation and made to sit down. He obeyed, content to hand the reins to someone competent and look around him instead of within.

"Mr. Novar."

The worried-looking lab technician had fetched a stern, older person whose voice sounded familiar. The head of Virology himself.

"Dr. Lentz."

Alias tried his best not to let his dislike for doctors color his voice. Dr. Lentz was a colleague. They were also the person behind LX.

"Decided to get the injection at last, huh?" Dr. Lentz cocked their head, small eyes narrowing. Their bald skull gleamed under the sharp lights. "Nice way to wrap up a shit day. Pull up your sleeve, Mr. Novar. The decor freaks you out?"

Alias bunched his sleeve out of the way with trembling fingers, tensing despite his best efforts when Dr. Lentz stepped closer to position the needleless hypospray. The antiviral was delivered painlessly.

"You're good to go. At least until we get a fun variant that renders LX obsolete."

Alias rubbed the itchy spot on his shoulder while his stomach did its best to shrink several sizes. The virologist was already walking away muttering about mutation and variants and ridiculous overtime when Alias gathered the courage to discuss these ominous words. He hopped from his seat, scratching at his shoulder with increased aggressivity, and made a beeline for the exit. He was fine. LX would help. Dr. Lentz wouldn't be distributing the injection if they didn't think so.

Alias wasn't sure where to go next, but his feet kept moving, and that was all right. He didn't want to keep still. He felt wide-awake despite his body begging him to sleep. And nauseous, but he chose to blame that on his caffeine intake.

After a long shower in the Hive's facilities and very little success in the way of calming down, he ended up in front of a door he'd tried not to picture too often. He hadn't meant to come here. Or had he? He knocked. His stomach churned. He took a step back, but the door slid open before he could flee, revealing a handsome man wearing a pair of loose pants and nothing else.

"Alias?" Mr. Dehive's eyes widened. He turned off his razor after a little fumbling. "Is everything okay? I thought you'd gone home . . ."

"I'm fine." Alias could hardly blame the answering frown. "I just . . ." *Got the injection*, he meant to say, but the words stuck in his throat. He clasped his hands together, feeling silly. Mr. Dehive had enough on his plate without a surprise visit like this. "I shouldn't have come. I'm sorry—"

"Come in, please."

Mr. Dehive's expression was unreadable as he pocketed his razor. Alias's gaze darted between the clean golden tiles of the floor and the blue eyes trained on him. Despite the clear invitation, Mr. Dehive didn't budge from the doorway. A sharp intake of breath filled the air, and Alias swore he could sense the thinning of the finite thread of Mr. Dehive's patience. His nerves spiked.

He was standing at a crossroad.

On one side, security and familiarity, the road large and well-marked but gray, bleak. The safe thing would be to go home and forget about his infatuation.

On the other side, a path fraught with obstacles, a thrilling adventure that could end with the next misstep, despite the LX in his bloodstream.

The choice wasn't a choice at all.

Alias stepped forward but tripped in his haste. Mr. Dehive caught him without hesitation, his strong arms a blanket of heat wrapping around his thinner frame. Alias squeezed back, giving in to the urge he'd harbored all day. His eyes were burning. His heart threatened to burst out of his chest. He'd really had too much coffee. He—

"Hey, it's all right." Mr. Dehive held him tighter, one stubbly cheek pressed against Alias's temple. "Shh . . ."

"I'm s-sorry . . ." Alias hiccupped and fisted one hand in the waistband of Mr. Dehive's pants. "You had a very rough day, and you don't need t-to deal with—"

"Alias—"

"Someone here betrayed you and it's making your job *helping people* even more complicated," Alias babbled. "You've been forced into a position where you have to defend yourself, and I wish I could have done more to help. Perhaps if I hadn't run from those journalists earlier, if I'd found the right thing to say—"

"Hey, hey, listen to me." Strong hands framed his face. "That's not on you, none of this is. The NID is just being *very* thorough, as always when children are involved."

"Do you— Do you think I betrayed you?" Alias's voice broke. "Because—"

"No, I don't." Mr. Dehive let out a faint chuckle, his thumbs stroking the skin under Alias's eyes. "To be perfectly honest, I suspected everyone at some point this morning, but you're the second person I cleared after Jaden. You're fine. We're fine."

The room was warmer than anywhere else in the Hive, and the heat seemed to roll off its owner. To Alias's dismay, Mr. Dehive pulled back.

"I should let you rest," Alias said softly.

"I'm not planning on sleeping anytime soon, and I doubt you are either." Mr. Dehive gestured at his half-shaved lower jaw. "I was about to take a shower. Just . . . sit for a while or lie down.

Have something to drink, if you'd like, while you catch your breath. I'll be right back."

Alias was already taking a place on the floor near the pond, ignoring all the more comfortable sitting options. A few seconds later, there came the sound of a shower running. Calmer but still confused, Alias dipped a finger in the pond and twisted it around in senseless figures, watching the small waves lap at the marble edges of the basin. The screens shaping the walls of the room displayed a casual pattern of deep gold and dark red circles. It was soothing.

A bottle of mead rested not far away amongst robot parts on a low table. With Mr. Dehive's invitation in mind, Alias poured himself a glass, and ended up filling it to the brim. He drank in small sips, rolling the alcohol around in his mouth, reacquainting himself with the taste. The burning sensation down his throat and the warmth gathering in his belly brought along a sense of peace. He didn't mind that Mr. Dehive made a few calls, the shower stopping occasionally to be replaced with a muffled voice before resuming.

After his first glass, it occurred to him that he could drink straight from the bottle, and he did just that, tilting his head back and taking a hefty swig. The mead sat heavy in his stomach now, a weight that crushed the lingering knots of too many feelings trying to fit in a limited space. The room became progressively softer around the edges, blurry by patches. He drank more. A little voice in his head—his inner riskeer, he surmised—prompted him to lick around the rim to catch a belated kiss, in case Mr. Dehive had also had the brilliant idea of foregoing the glass.

His extremities began to tingle.

He set the bottle aside and unbuttoned the top of his shirt before rolling up his sleeves, the movements uncoordinated. The room felt too hot. That might have been the alcohol, or the side effects from the injection, or both. He immersed both hands in the pond and brought them to his face, rubbing water into his skin. Droplets trickled down his wrists. He started rubbing his thighs together as the tingling sensation moved down his spine.

His cock swelled under his questing palm and hardened fully on the first stroke.

What was he doing here again? Ah, yes, catching his breath while Mr. Dehive—no, *Deon*—worked from his shower. Alias stumbled to his feet, hand still moving over the bulge in his pants. Would Deon be willing to kiss him and share some of that fire he was harboring? He didn't feel like standing for too long, so perhaps Deon would let him sit in his lap and touch him where he'd wanted it the last time Alias had been here? His knees grew weak as the picture solidified, so much sharper than any detail in the room. He let go of his cock to catch himself against the back of a chair.

"Alias?"

Deon emerged from a cloud of steam. He wore clean linen pants, and his chest glistened. Alias wanted to lick every inch of him, especially what lay between those thick thighs, hinted at by the blond treasure trail. He let go of the chair with a groan that drew Deon's eyes to his groin.

"Well, I'll be damned." Deon's voice was rough. "Are you tipsy?"

Alias giggled. He never giggled. The reluctant amusement shining in Deon's eyes filled him with another shade of warmth he didn't bother cataloguing. "I think I got the injection."

"You *think*?"

Alias shrugged, unconcerned. "I realized I was holding on to my fear a little too hard, and I . . ." He frowned, trying to put some order to the mess of his thoughts. "I might have been trying to punish myself, too, for the moments I was *not* afraid. For taking risks. But it's okay. I should welcome change. It isn't all bad, is it?"

"You should be proud of yourself," Deon said softly. "I certainly am." He cleared his throat. "Proud of you."

The light brush of Deon's fingers on his wrist shot straight to his cock. Words tumbled out of Alias's mouth, bold words he'd only considered in fantasies.

"I like your hands on me." His breath caught as the grip on his wrist tightened. "It's like a dream I'd never been aware of, when you touch me." A moan squeezed out. "I think I was angry earlier, and anxious, because you left and didn't say anything, and I thought . . . I felt *useless*, and now . . ." He was so hard, *so hard*, and he used his free hand to try to get some friction again.

Another moan rose, but it wasn't his.

"All I can think of right now is how you make me feel better, and . . ." He licked his lips. His wrist was beginning to hurt, but he didn't care. It was contact. But it wasn't enough. "We should kiss again. I have too many clothes, haven't I? I should—"

Deon released him so suddenly Alias almost fell into the pond.

"Holy shit, Alias. You're not tipsy, you're fucking drunk."

"That's just a side effect of the injection."

Alias's next attempt to touch was stopped by a hand on his chest.

"I think not, Alias."

Alias tried to lift that hand to his mouth, but it was snatched out of his grasp before he could decide if he'd rather suck or lick the fingers. He whined in protest. "I feel good." He glanced down and smiled at the sight of an erection tenting Deon's pants. "You're hard."

"Alias—"

"You make me feel good, and I want you to feel good too. Don't you want to feel good after the day we've had?"

He stepped forward, but Deon was quicker.

"You're drunk," he repeated, voice strained. "And feverish."

"I feel great. I want you." Why did Deon fight this, after all the talking they'd done? "I want you on me." He let go of his cock and reached behind himself, pushing two fingers into the fabric and digging in his crack. A whole new need overwhelmed him. "Deon, I want you in me."

Deon looked like he'd been sucker punched. "Alias, stop this."

"But you want me, and I want you," Alias stated again, convinced that insistence would do the trick. "I told you it's okay, you can have—"

"That's enough!"

Alias recoiled, but Deon wasn't done.

"It's not about *want*," Deon said harshly, eyes blazing. "You're drunk, probably on what you just did, on top of my mead. Unfit to consent to *anything*."

"You keep complaining that I'm afraid all the time, and now that I'm not—"

"For fuck's sake, Alias, you're twisting my words around! You don't even know what you're saying right now. What you need is rest. My most recent PA has been most difficult to acquire, and I don't wish him to leave because I can't control myself." The anger bled from his tone. "I want us to keep trusting one another, and indulging in what you think you want right now will accomplish the exact opposite."

Alias was about to burst into tears all over again. He turned around, fully intending to leave and return to New York on foot if necessary, but a hand closed on his bicep and spun him around.

"You think you're going back to the city in that state? Yeah, I don't think so. Come here."

He didn't fight as Deon stripped him down to his underwear and helped him into bed. Sadly, getting him to join proved impossible. There was work to do and assholes to handle, or something along those lines. Alias tried to win him over with a kiss.

"Get some rest," Deon told him firmly.

Alias frowned, displeased by the growing distance between them. But the bed was so comfortable. Moreover, the forest was coming alive around him as the room dimmed. The song of locusts ebbed and flowed, melodious waves shifting with the current of the wind. Alias settled down among the pillows and pulled the sheets over his nose, drinking in Deon's scent.

He was out like a light.

CHAPTER SEVEN
HOT AND COLD

A lias drifted into wakefulness, humming contently as he rubbed his face against a pillow. The bed felt wonderful and smelled even better. There was another pillow snug between his knees, and the soft sheets covering him weighed just enough to lull him back to sleep.

The next time he stirred, he stretched out with a sigh. The bone-deep sensation of being well rested wasn't near familiar enough. He kicked back the covers and opened his eyes.

The reason why he'd slept so well struck him at last.

This was Deon's bed.

He'd spent the night here.

In his haste to leave the bed, he forgot how much higher it was than his own and almost face-planted on the floor. Wide-awake now, he picked up the first shirt he could find and put it on. It didn't stop the shivers, but it was a start.

The blue-and-golden bathroom matched the bedroom in terms of opulence. Alias took in the large marble tub with its golden faucets and the transparent shower stall that could easily accommodate three people. The blue floor tiles became purple as he stepped on them, the color always darker around his feet.

When he returned to bed, he was already combing through what he could remember of last night, which wasn't much. What had he done to end up here? The blinking light on his watchphone, charging on the bedside table, caught his attention. He pressed play and reached for his bottle of Avida.

"Good morning, Alias." It was Deon. Who else? "I gave you an anti-hangover last night, but you might want to take another one. They're in a blue bottle behind the first mirror to your left in the bathroom. Drink plenty of water. I arranged for you to start later today, so sleep in. By the way, congratulations on taking the injection."

The injection. Alias set the Avida bottle back on the bedside table, feeling numb. It was all coming back to him. Someone at Dehive had betrayed Deon's trust. Hopefully the NID was helping investigate that on top of McCarthy's allegations. There had been panic in the city, people demanding LX and other people raging against it. He'd taken the injection. The stern face floating in his mind was Dr. Lentz's, head of the virology department.

As wrong as it was, the bed registered more as a comfort than a threat, so he tucked his feet under the blankets, rubbing at his temples. He felt like one of those old light bulbs during a storm. On: arousal, hope, sweetness on his tongue. Off: disappointment, anger, confusion. The headache was more than manageable, no doubt because of Deon's help. He eyed the bottle of mead with a sense of betrayal. Getting drunk enough to warrant an anti-hangover was a change in his life he could have gone without.

"I was hoping you'd still be here."

Alias's hands dropped to his lap. The sight of Deon in a dark blue shirt, sleeves rolled up, thumbs hooked casually on the belt looped in black slacks, burned through the cobwebs in his brain like a gust of wildfire. More memories popped into place: him standing defiantly in front of Deon, his total lack of shame as he'd groped himself through his pants, his attempt to touch while begging to get touched back, a thousand and one ridiculous declarations he wished he couldn't remember.

"I'm s-sorry. What happened was . . . unbecoming of me." *Unbecoming* was certainly one word for it. "You kept saying no, and I—I didn't listen . . . Not that I should have ever . . ."

Thrown myself at you in the first place.

Embarrassment might have disintegrated him on the spot had Deon not turned away to pull off his tie, granting a brief respite from his all-too-seeing eyes.

"You drank quite a bit," Deon said with a teasing smile. "And don't take it the wrong way, but I can handle you just fine."

Alias unfolded the edge of the sheet he'd been twisting. "It doesn't make this ri—"

"Alias." Deon's tone turned chiding. "You throwing yourself at me can't hurt me, no matter how dedicated you are."

"Fuck you."

Deon spun toward him, a wicked smile tugging at the corners of his mouth. He reached to unbutton the top of his shirt as he strutted toward the bed. Alias yanked the sheet all the way up to his chin. He couldn't believe he'd just said that.

"As appealing as that sounds . . ." Deon gave the sheet a tug as he sat down on the bed. "I'm sure you didn't mean it quite like that."

Alias let go of the sheet. The fabric pooled in his lap, a soft caress down his torso. He opened his mouth, an apology for his latest outburst on the tip of his tongue.

Deon spoke first.

"Is that my shirt you're wearing?"

Alias went scarlet. The shirt felt a little too big and too smooth. "I was cold," he mumbled.

"I'm not complaining. Are you still cold now?"

Alias bit down on his tongue. The knowing look in Deon's eyes shifted to something more intense. "Alias?"

"N-no, I'm good."

"Have you taken another anti-hangover? They also help for the side effects of the injection."

"I don't . . . need . . ."

Deon was sitting as close to him as physics allowed. Alias's breath hitched as Deon leaned in to place an airy kiss at his temple. The scratch of facial hair, combined with the warm touch of lips, cranked the vague itch he felt into the precise need to touch and be touched.

"Should I leave you to rest some more? I'm afraid there's another long day ahead of us, but if you need more sleep . . ."

"No, no, you're right, there's work to do." Alias leaned around Deon to try to locate his clothes. Somehow, he grabbed Deon's arms instead. The purple bags under those sapphire eyes gave him pause. "*You* should rest. God, you've been up all night, and I just—"

"I don't hold it against you, Alias."

"But you need the bed." Alias would have hidden under a rock if there'd been any. What if Deon hadn't slept at all because someone else had been passed out in the bed? His own bed? "I'm so sorry. I . . . I'll just . . . get dressed . . ."

"You'd probably find your clothes faster if you let go of me."

Alias's fingers spasmed. "R-right. Sorry."

"Stop apologizing, damn it."

Deon surged, enveloping Alias in his arms. Alias returned the embrace readily, hands prompted into motion once more. He couldn't keep them still. There was so much of Deon to touch. So much heat to soak in, miles of skin to discover at his fingertips. The need blossoming inside him beat like a second heart, a distinct entity, and he didn't know how to ignore it.

"Should I go? I probably should."

"Go or stay: it's up to you."

There was something off about Deon's intonation. Alias pulled back and surveyed those bloodshot, heavy-lidded, magnificent blue eyes. Another part of last night came back to him.

"I trust you, Mister— Deon. And I . . ." He blushed fiercely. "All I said last night is true."

Deon pecked his cheek. A dry, brief press of lips that set half of Alias's face on fire.

"Are you lying to yourself right now?"

Alias debated with himself. It was no use. "Do you really want me to stay?" He whispered the words with as much indifference as he could muster. He probably failed. "Last night, you said . . ."

"You were drunk, then."

Alias's heart sped up. "I'm not drunk anymore."

Deon's eyes crinkled with amusement. "That you're not. You're blushing a lot more now that you're sober."

"Shut up."

Deon burst out into laugher. "Make me."

Alias had no idea what had changed Deon's worries about the power imbalance. Perhaps, like him, Deon had reached a point where he didn't care about the consequences.

Alias exploded into motion, climbing into Deon's lap and diving for his mouth with such fierceness that Deon ended up on his back. They kept kissing as Alias straddled those inviting hips, their lips moving in a sloppy mess, their tongues gliding against each other until they were both out of breath. Alias bit down on Deon's lip without meaning to—and did it again, on purpose, encouraged by a moan. His cock, already interested, filled out further at the brush of a knuckle over his nipple. When Deon gave the hard bud a pinch through his shirt, Alias's hips bucked.

"That okay?"

With a gasp, Alias nodded. "F-feels, *ah*, good."

"That's sort of the point," Deon purred, and tugged at an earlobe with his teeth before rolling on top of Alias. "Would you like to go back to hugging or—"

"No."

"All right, then."

The knuckles over his shirt—*Deon's* shirt—became fingers wandering beneath the fabric, teasing his nipples directly. Alias arched his back, welcoming more of those touches. Yes, it was an aberration to want this. To act on that want. But the rules no longer felt like a coat of protective armor, more like manacles. He struggled against their hold, grinding up against Deon's crotch with breathless little moans. How could he have allowed fear to control him for so long when such joy was within reach?

"Fuck, Alias."

In a burst of confidence, Alias took off the shirt he'd put on earlier. He wasn't cold anymore, and the flush on Deon's cheeks hinted at a similar state. The first button of the shirt Deon wore gave easily. The next one flew sideways, and the third one ended up hanging from a single thread.

Deon hummed. "So eager. Keep going."

As soon as the shirt was out of the way, Alias latched his mouth onto a collarbone, fingers twisting in the blond locks at the back of Deon's head. The sensation of a hard cock digging into his own crotch caused him to part his legs further. He wasn't sure what it was that he needed, how exactly he wanted to be touched, because he'd never done any of this, but he trusted Deon to show him. He moved his hands down Deon's chest in fascination. There was *hair* there. He'd known it from the video, but it was quite different to feel the soft trail by himself, to explore . . .

"Would you rather I don't touch you?"

Alias pulled back in confusion, only to spot the hand he'd apparently just trapped in his own. He frowned. He hadn't been aware of doing it. "I don't know why I did that."

Except that now, he did. Eyes locked on Deon's face, he lifted that hand to his mouth, darted out his tongue, and gave little kitten licks along the index finger, half-afraid he'd get laughed at, half-afraid he would die.

Deon didn't laugh.

Alias didn't stop breathing.

Tentatively, he sucked the tip inside his mouth. He might be new to all this, but he knew how he must look doing it, knew what Deon must think about when he drew another finger in and slurped around the two digits.

"Fuck, you're a vision."

Blushing at the praise, Alias released Deon's fingers and guided the hand that was teasing his belly button to the waistband of his underwear. "Can you . . ."

"Tell me what you want, sweetheart."

Alias lost the ability to speak upon hearing the last part, so he showed Deon instead, moving their linked hands down while their lips met for another kiss. The moment a calloused palm brushed against the bulge in his boxers, he let out a muffled whine.

"Delicious," Deon cooed.

He kept talking, complimenting Alias as he rubbed at the erection through stiff cotton.

"This feels good too?"

"N-nh." If Alias hadn't been running on pure, undiluted desire, all those helpless noises he kept making would have embarrassed the hell out of him. "Y-yes."

"Do you want me to keep caressing you like this, or should I touch you more directly?"

Alias had no idea what half of the words out of Deon's mouth even meant. This was real, but it still felt like a dream. Every little thing.

"More."

Deon's hand disappeared.

"D-did I . . .?" Alias wished his voice was steadier, but the disappointment was probably audible. He tried again. "Did I do something wrong?"

"Oh no, sweetheart. You're perfect."

Deon's thumb trailed down his chin and ended over his pulse point. Distantly, Alias registered the crazy-fast thumping of his heart.

"I'd like to go down on you," Deon continued. "Give you pleasure with my mouth. Is that something you'd enjoy?"

Anticipation uncoiled in Alias's chest, painful and electrifying. The wet patch on his underwear was impossible to ignore. He should say no, but that was the old fear talking.

He nodded.

Deon slid down his body and knelt on the floor. "You can change your mind at any time. You can leave whenever you want." He sounded entirely too calm about everything, but then this was hardly new to him. "Do you understand?"

Alias nodded again.

"I need you to say the word, Alias."

Yes. It was one word, one syllable. The simplest of words. But there was nothing simple about its use right now. It carried weight, expressed surrender. And Alias had only ever bowed to one master.

And where had that led him?

"Yes," he gasped.

He expected Deon to push down his underwear, but instead Deon pulled him to the edge of the mattress, pressed his face into Alias's crotch, and started to use his mouth just like he'd said.

"Oh God . . ."

Deon mouthed at Alias's cock through his underwear with wet, eager noises, soaking the fabric with saliva. It should have been uncomfortable at best, but Alias had not been more turned on in his life. Deon's hands on his belly, caressing the flexing muscles of his stomach before trailing lower to lock onto his hips, were the only thing keeping him still. What little remained of his rational thinking splintered as Deon pulled the underwear down—with his *teeth*. The kiss to Alias's cock was soft and reverent, a caress that coaxed a few more drops to his tip.

"Tell me to stop and I will," Deon said and went for the kill.

At least, that was how Alias felt at the first stroke of tongue across his tip: slowly dying from an overdose of pure excitation. Deon showed no hesitation in pulling the head of Alias's cock into his mouth, and his quiet confidence twisted the knots tighter in Alias's belly. His dark eyes remained set on Alias while he sucked, a burning promise in them. Alias reached for the blond head, unsure if he wanted to push or pull, and ended up grabbing fistfuls of silky strands in an instinctive compromise.

Deon pulled back and nuzzled his inner thigh. "You still okay?"

Alias blinked at the mess that was Deon's hair. A mess *he'd* made.

"Yes," he whispered, and it didn't exactly taste like a lie.

Deon pressed a kiss into the thatch of hair at his groin. "You can keep pulling my hair, if you want." He demonstrated, covering Alias's hand with his own and pulling. Hard.

Alias's breath left him in a rush. "You . . . like that?"

"I like a great many things."

Alias pulled, more out of curiosity than anything, and Deon darted out his tongue with a low moan. The sight of it twirling around his glans was hypnotic, so much so that Alias didn't have time to brace himself before his cock disappeared into warm, slick heat. His hips bucked without his permission, free to do so now that no hands held them. Deon neither stopped him nor relented, only let out a garbled sound akin to a laugh. His stubble dragged on Alias's thighs as he bobbed his head, the burning sensation sharpening Alias's focus even as it heightened the pleasure building in his loins.

"D-Deon . . ."

Alias clung to Deon's shoulders as his right leg spasmed. With those sharp blue eyes steady on him and that mouth stretched obscenely around his cock, he looked like all of Alias's dreams from the past few weeks put together.

"I-I'm— I think I . . ."

Deon swallowed abruptly, taut muscles spasming around Alias's cock, securing the head in luscious heat. A callused hand cupped his sack, and he was gone: he spilled down Deon's throat with a wheezing sound, curling onto himself with the force of his orgasm.

Deon swallowed, his eyes two pinpricks of darkness.

"Oh, God, that was . . . I'm sorry, it must . . . Everything went so fast and . . ." Alias couldn't stop babbling. He hid his face, spinning more nonsense through his fingers. "This was—"

"One hell of a turn-on?"

Alias lowered both hands, mouth gaping. "What? But I just—"

"You came in my mouth, and that's exactly what I was offering." Deon licked gently at the tip of Alias's softening cock. His touch remained soothing as he tucked Alias back into his underwear. "Now . . ."

He paused as Alias gestured to the erection in Deon's pants, obvious now that he was standing. "I could touch you too . . . Give you pleasure?"

Deon kissed his brow. "That's not why I did this. Making you feel good is its own reward."

They kissed again. Alias, because he couldn't help himself, and Deon, for reasons Alias couldn't begin to comprehend. His cock began to harden again, which made his face burn. He should leave. There was work to do. But Deon was so warm, the merest touch from him so exciting . . .

"Please," he gasped, not sure what he meant, exactly.

Deon glanced down between their bodies and made an amused sound at the back of his throat.

"Ah, to be young again."

"You're not that old."

"I have almost fifteen years on you, and that makes a difference in such matters," Deon argued. Thumb brushing Alias's chin, he asked, "You want more?"

Alias's will to fight became a stray thought buried under layers of curiosity and *need*.

"Y-yes."

"Do you trust me with your pleasure?" Deon's voice was gravelly, thick with lust. His thumb moved to Alias's lower lip and tugged, just a little bit.

Alias's lids dropped to half-mast. Every time he said the word, his conviction grew. "Yes."

"Can I trust you to tell me to stop if you don't like it, or it becomes too much?"

"Yes."

Deon stepped back. "Then lie down on your belly."

Torn between awkwardness and trepidation, Alias was nevertheless quick to comply. As soon as he was comfortable and said so, Deon climbed in bed and straddled the back of his thighs. Alias started panting as Deon's chest flattened against his back, the muscles in his buttocks and lower back tightening at the sensation of an erection digging through layers of fabric. Before Alias could feel trapped, Deon shifted, dragging his mouth down Alias's spine in a series of open-mouthed kissed. He squeezed one buttock, then the other. Alias bucked into every touch.

Deon pulled the boxers past his buttocks, one slow inch at a time. Alias gripped the sheets with a choked-out moan.

"Still okay?"

"Y-yeah."

"Good."

Alias forced his body to remain still.

Deon tossed the garment to the side. "It must have been difficult to stay still for me." He worked his way up Alias's calf with his lips and added, "You're doing so well."

They discovered that kisses at the crook of his left knee tickled, and his inner right thigh was sensitive and erogenous. Alias let Deon lay beacons on the under-explored flesh, mapping hills and valleys of aches and needs, playing the role of skillful cartographer to Alias's land. This was nothing like the first few times Deon had touched him, and yet it was the same.

The heat simmering on both sides of his skin. The hunger that food could never sate.

Deon's warmth disappeared. When he reappeared to straddle him, he was fully naked. Alias threw his head back with a strangled cry as a cock slid alongside his crack.

Deon pulled back with a chuckle. Confused but ridiculously aroused, Alias let the hand at his lower back guide him to being on all fours. The two pillows that went under his belly made the position more comfortable, if no less embarrassing. He felt exposed, with his ass on display. He wanted to hide, and yet he couldn't get his body to move past a few twitches and shivers.

"This won't hurt, I swear. I'm just going to use my mouth on you, if you're agreeable."

"On m-me?"

"Yes."

Alias tensed at the press of fingers near his rim, tugging gently at his ass cheeks, nudging them apart. Did people really do this? The warm breath blown over his entrance must have short-circuited his brain, because he tilted his hips back instinctually.

"S-sorry!"

Deon's reply to the startled apology was to flatten his tongue over Alias's rim and *lick*.

Alias jumped, both hands skidding on the sheets.

"Perfect." Deon uttered the word with his mouth against Alias's hole, tongue circling his entrance in a slow, bold caress. "Perfect boy."

Alias gave a full-body shiver and moaned, the sound half-choked and a little wet. Deon splayed both hands on his ass and flattened his tongue, lapping at his furled hole with hungry, animalistic noises. Alias buried his face into the mattress and clawed at the sheets. Saliva coated his rim, trickling inside and down his thighs, wet and warm. The scratch of Deon's stubble became more pronounced, intensifying the caresses of his lips and tongue. Alias smothered a shout into his fist.

"Don't hide. Let me hear you." Deon rubbed his nose into the cleft of Alias's ass, panting hard.

Reaching around Alias's hip, he gave his erection a couple of firm strokes. Alias's next whimper was loud and quickly followed by another. Deon released his cock and went back to his rim, blowing softly over his hole as he squeezed his buttocks.

"Fuck, you're a delight. So responsive."

He pushed his tongue inside.

Alias yelped and spread his thighs, eliciting a wanton grunt from Deon. God, he should feel ashamed. He should feel filthy. Urge Deon to stop. Instead, he rested more weight on his elbows, head hung low, and arched his back like one of those riskeer whores, babbling eager *pleases* and *yesses* in an endless loop. A sob racked his body when Deon tugged insistently at his rim with both thumbs, thrusting his tongue faster and deeper inside, lapping at his inner walls avidly. Deon was *fucking him with his tongue*, and Alias couldn't fathom how he hadn't come yet.

A coherent question came together in his head and remained mostly intact on delivery.

"Doesn't it bother you t-to use your mouth—*ah*—there?"

"Absolutely not." Deon nibbled at one buttock. "You taste clean, and I enjoy doing this. I'm so damn hard I could come just from eating you."

He pulled at Alias's hair, a painless request. Alias followed the motion and found himself sitting back on his heels, Deon's chest against his back. Saliva and sweat made everything sticky, and Alias couldn't care less. His body was a live wire. The delicate trail of fingertips along his jaw echoed in his toes, and the kiss pressed to the side of his neck shot straight to his groin.

"So sensitive. I suspect you've gone too long without giving your body the relief it needs." Lips tickled his ear as Deon whispered, "After a couple more orgasms, you won't feel so wound up, I promise."

"N-nh."

Deon gave a low chuckle. "You're just reconnecting with your sensuality." A hand disappeared from around him and a *click* sounded. "Do you feel it blooming, roused by your want for pleasure? For this?"

A knuckle teased his rim.

"D-Deon!"

"Just say the word and I'll stop. Do you want me to stop now?"

Alias sagged in Deon's embrace. "N-no."

The knuckle at his hole vanished, replaced by the tip of a finger. It dipped in, wet with something more than saliva. Alias grabbed the arm holding him, muscles locking up. The finger stilled. It felt . . . intrusive, but not exactly unpleasant.

"Does it hurt?"

Alias gasped as he released his grip on Deon's arm. He'd been digging in crescents and hadn't meant to. "No."

"Good. It never should."

Deon wriggled the slick finger a little. There truly was no pain, and the tension ebbed as a hot mouth found his nape. Alias wanted more, but he didn't know how to ask for it, wasn't even sure he should, but he trusted Deon—with his body's reactions and his pleasure. And the pleasure did return, a pressure building steadily in the pit of his gut through the double stimulation of mouth and finger.

"Never touched yourself there, have you?"

Half-blind with desire, Alias panted louder as the hand on his ribs moved to curl around his throat. The hold was no more coercive than the grip on his wrists earlier, but its meaning, the suggestion that Alias was trapped and about to be ravished, robbed him of what little self-consciousness he had left. He ground up, drawing that slick finger in.

"That's it, sweetheart, take what you need."

Alias shut his eyes, focusing on Deon's grunts in his ear and the squelchy sounds of the digit moving inside him.

"M-more."

Deon obliged. The second digit sank wetly alongside the first with a little resistance but no pain.

"Christ, you're tight."

Deon had to work to slide that second finger in all the way, but as soon as Alias managed to follow his counsel and relax, he rotated his wrist and pushed the two digits in opposite directions, stretching the taut channel.

"Feel . . . f-full," Alias confessed. His right leg seized. "And weird."

"Okay, that won't do."

Alias didn't have the faintest cue what Deon was on about, but he allowed himself to be maneuvered onto his back.

"The angle's wrong," Deon explained. "Here, let me . . ." He maneuvered one of Alias's legs over his shoulder. With his free hand, he reached for an opened bottle and poured liquid onto his finger, but he wasn't looking at what he was doing—his eyes were trained on Alias and remained fixed on him as he rubbed his fingers together.

"Let's try again," he purred, and reached between Alias's legs. The digits slid back inside his hole. He pumped them for several minutes, slow and careful, before quickening the pace a little. "How about—" He curled both fingers and pushed at an angle. "—there?"

Alias's mouth opened on a silent cry. The fingers were teasing a part of him he couldn't name, a secret spot he didn't know he had. Pleasure washed over him, intense and sharp, different from anything he'd felt before.

"That's better, right?"

Deon bent to kiss him, licking into his mouth as he kept dragging the pads of his fingers *right there*. Alias took over the kiss, tremors coursing through his body. When Deon withdrew, his features pulled taut with hunger, Alias chased after his mouth with a feral noise. The coppery tang of blood made his head spin.

"Want . . . more. P-please." A wrecked sob escaped him.

"Shh, I know." Moving down, Deon peppered the inside of his thigh with kisses as he quickened the pace. Alias bunched his hands in the sheets. Squelching noises filled the air as Deon added more wetness and a new pressure: a third finger, massaging the rim but not quite going in. With a strangled noise of need, Alias reached for his own ass cheeks and pulled them farther apart.

"Oh, sweetheart . . ." Deon let out a low groan and finally slipped in the tip of that third finger, working it in alongside the others. The stretch hurt, it actually hurt now, the burn slicing through the warm weight of pleasure, but Alias didn't want to stop. He focused on the bite of his nails in his buttocks and brought up his other leg, setting it over Deon's shoulder, grunting as he lifted his pelvis off the mattress. When the third finger slid in to the second knuckle, he dug both heels into Deon's shoulder blades.

Deon slammed his other hand down onto the mattress with a surprised groan. "Fuck."

The heat wrapped in that single word encouraged Alias to use his newfound leverage. Thankfully, years of running had given him solid thighs and calves, and he kept rocking his hips, working in that third finger until it was fully sheathed inside him.

"Yes, that's it, fuck." Deon braced himself over him, the muscles in his shoulders bulging under the strain of keeping up with Alias's jerky motions. "Can you come like this? Yes, of course you can, you beautiful boy."

Alias could sense the edge, so close, closer with every twist of those clever fingers, but he couldn't get there, not quite. Despair soured his pleasure. "P-please, please, I can't . . ."

"You can," Deon grunted, coaxing, encouraging him with his fingers, his eyes, the whole of his body language. "Come for me."

The order did the trick. Alias tipped over the edge with his cock untouched, tears of relief spilling over his cheeks as his body seized up. Deon pulled his fingers back one at a time, gently. Alias mourned the emptiness until he saw them wrapped around Deon's cock. Deon was fucking into his fist with abandon, and Alias could see the alternative all too clearly—Deon fucking into him, stretching him on every thrust. Deon's cock wasn't unlike his own, uncut and of a similar length. A little thicker, maybe. Incredibly appealing because, no matter how alike it appeared, it was *Deon's*. Alias reached for the glistening tip.

His fingers brushed Deon's cock, and wet heat spilled across his hand and wrist. Deon collapsed on top of him with a grunt.

"Fuck."

Alias's hand itched where Deon's come had landed. Or, maybe, he itched to do something about it.

Deon wiped it clean with a corner of the sheets before Alias could make up his mind, and rolled to the side. Alias stared at the ceiling, at the sky that wasn't there but existed beyond the illusion of screens buried under rocks. His limbs felt heavy, and his heart heavier. There was a new layer to the pleasure still lingering in his body, a rawness of sorts he couldn't explain. And he was on edge in a way that wasn't entirely bad, but not entirely good either.

"You all right?" Deon asked, glancing at Alias's arm.

"Yeah," he rasped. Evidently, he'd been rubbing at the injection site. He moved his hand away, taking a deep breath as he glanced up. Deon had propped himself on one elbow, expression earnest despite the flush of arousal. Gold hair stuck to his brow.

Alias found himself fighting the urge to touch, even now that he'd touched so much.

Deon didn't have such qualms and tucked a brown strand behind Alias's ear. When his watchphone beeped, he looked at it and scowled. "Work calls," he lamented.

Alias was out the door before Deon was fully dressed.

The rest of the day went by fast, but not because the dust was settling. If anything, the night had allowed for misinformation to spread. The claim he kept hearing—and denying—about how LX didn't work very well for children baffled him, but not as much as the hearsay that LX's efficacy rate was twice as low as Avida's. *Do I look sick to you?* he almost shouted at a doctor from the Philippines—who couldn't see him—and doubly thanked the hubot who kept him from losing his calm with a fresh mug of coffee.

Tracing the ridiculous rumors back to the source proved easy enough. Every major news channel was rehashing them, quoting a string of studies released overnight—studies funded by none other than Lyra McCarthy. Alias didn't forward the information to Deon. For one thing, he'd rather not distract the CEO while he was supervising the first largescale distribution of LX in Lower New York. For another, chances were high that Deon already knew. Wishing he could be more useful, Alias took as many calls as he could in between overseeing the nationwide distribution and triple-checking the numbers. He couldn't tell if the headache he'd started having around midday was one of the milder symptoms from the injection or the result of too much stress and people's naivety.

He supposed he was naïve too, but a lot less than he used to be.

When the door to his office opened on a fuming Deon, it was almost 11 p.m., and Alias's nerves were so frayed he almost flew right off his chair. Gripping the edge of the desk with one hand, he hastily thanked the thousandth frustrated—and frustrating—caller of the day, hoping he'd helped counter the tide of doubts looming over Dehive.

Deon stormed toward his desk, fury rolling off him in waves.

Alias hung up, clamping down the instinctive need to get out of the way.

"What's wrong?"

"Everything. Give me that."

"Give you . . ." Alias trailed off as Deon reached for his forgotten mug of lukewarm coffee and drained it in one gulp.

"Damn it. I hate cold coffee." Deon slammed the empty mug down, snapping off the handle. With a snarl, he picked up the broken mug and tossed it in the garbage can, missing it by several inches. Shattered porcelain flew across the floor. "Lying *bitch*."

Alias considered his next words carefully. "I assume you're talking about Lyra McCarthy."

"My contacts at the World Health Organization insist that there's no cause for concern because all the LX doses planned for the day have been given away, but what about tomorrow? There are already more than enough people showing uncertainty," Deon muttered. "The injection works better than Avida, it worked for everyone who took it at the Hive, and yet the public's focus seems to be on the much lower success rate of *her* study group." When he threw a handful of porcelain toward the bin and got it in this time, it was with a lot more force than strictly necessary. "The core of the problem is that her damn studies took place because one of my own employees is a turncoat who provided her with LX weeks ago." He hurled a few more pieces in the trash, each motion disdainful. "The results are completely fabricated, but there's just enough truth framing her lies that people eat up her bullshit, including the NID!"

He stalked toward the window with a curse and splayed both hands on the glass. "She's planting the word 'greed' in all the right ears, and yet she's the one who still sells Avida at four times the price of LX. I bet she's going to find a way to make this work to her advantage too. For all I know, she has people at the WHO and the NID on her payroll. I don't need the public to like me, but if everyone is too focused on dissecting my reputation to consider her motivations, if people are afraid of LX because they feel they can't trust me . . ." He trailed off with a choked sound. "What am I supposed to do?"

Hesitantly, Alias rose. At some point today, the old temptation had appeared—to listen to the panic he'd fed his whole life, to once more be in thrall of worst-case scenarios—but he'd resisted. The act of throwing his bottle of Avida into the trash had helped. He knew LX worked. He felt it. "I don't think everyone sides with her," he said softly. "Not everyone who called today was buying McCarthy's lies, and some of those who did changed their mind by the time they hung up." He inched closer. When had he become the one to offer comfort in their partnership? "I trust you," he insisted, "and I'm not alone in this. In time, the people you wish to help will come to see McCarthy's actions as those of someone desperate. And she is desperate."

"That she is, but then so I am, albeit for vastly different reasons." Deon's brow came to rest against the window with a soft *thud*. The sound he made, something small, muffled, and wounded, tugged at Alias's heartstrings. He didn't know what more to say. The urge to offer a hug and take some of Deon's strain away made him dither even more.

"You should get some rest," he said at last.

"I can't." Deon whipped around. The storm brewing in his bloodshot eyes had given way to something that Alias had so far only associated with himself: despair.

"I can't," Deon said again. "I keep thinking about— I still can't believe these rumors she spewed about children. As if my entire focus isn't devoted to . . ." Face crumpling, he let out a mirthless chuckle. "I suppose I shouldn't be surprised, though. Feelings don't get in her way, ever. She's always been an artful manipulator because of this; she's spent years chipping away at my reputation since— Need a lift?"

The non sequitur gave Alias whiplash. "What?"

"Do you want a lift home?"

This wasn't all that was on offer. Desire shimmered in Deon's tired eyes. They promised pleasure, and anticipation sizzled up Alias's spine. The word yes was on the tip of his tongue, but he swallowed it back. He couldn't accept Deon's offer—not because of the virus, which used to be a good enough justification, but because darkness lurked beneath the hunger.

As new as Alias was to this terrible, dangerous dance, he knew what this meant. If he couldn't consent to being touched when he was under the influence of mead, neither could Deon when he wasn't in his right mind, drunk on fatigue and rage.

"No, thank you."

Deon snorted. "Right. You'd prefer to wait half an hour for a taxi to pick you up.

Alias stiffened but didn't take the bait.

Deon threw his arms in the air. "Why do you have to make everything complicated?"

The sliding doors in the Hive couldn't be slammed, but Alias imagined that if they could, Deon would have left with a bang loud enough to shake the windows.

"You're one to talk," Alias mumbled to himself.

Deon sure had made *his* life more complicated. Alias tried to hang on to his anger on the way home, but his concern for Deon, his mother, his own future, and the anxiety that stemmed from it all, doused the flame that wasn't his to begin with. His inability to control his own feelings frustrated him.

It was past midnight when he exited the taxi a couple of miles from home. He'd been at his desk all day and most of the evening and itched to move. Too tired to run, he contented himself with walking despite the drizzle. Hopefully, some time outside would help clear his mind.

The spotlights at Lady Love's feet were malfunctioning, blinking on and off in unpredictable intervals. In contrast, the three towers of McCarthy Ltd. were well lit. Alias frowned at the sight. What was McCarthy's endgame? Discrediting Dehive Inc. would wreak havoc on a frightening scale, but it wouldn't help her—it wouldn't give Avida back its efficacy. Lies could fool people but not the virus. She couldn't possibly hope to win in the long run.

Unless Alias was missing something big and the hand she'd shown so far was merely the tip of the iceberg.

By the time Alias unlocked his door, it was well past one in the morning. Ben saluted him but didn't engage him in conversation, taking its cue from its owner's stiff body language. Alias shed his clothes and aimed to take the shortest shower in existence, a resolution helped by the persisting lack of hot water.

His shower was interrupted by a loud crash. He cut the water and hurried out of the stall. Voices came from the kitchen. He pulled on his boxers, adrenaline kicking in. He'd thought break-ins only happened in movies. What could thieves want from someone like him? The recent improvement of his living standards wasn't reflected in much beyond his wardrobe.

The lights flickered. He pressed his hand to the control on the wall, and the door slid open.

Three men were in his bedroom, all taller and bulkier than him. Ben moved in between them and Alias, its eyes flashing yellow as Alias stood in the doorway.

"I'm calling the NID," it said.

"Take care of that piece of shit."

The bald man who'd spoken pushed Ben to the side, a worrisome grin stretching his thin lips as he looked Alias up and down.

Alias stepped forward, not sparing a thought for the danger. Had he been alone, he might have frozen up. But he wasn't alone. "Leave my apartment at once!"

"You're that PA, right? Dehive's lying bitch?"

A hand slammed down on his shoulder, and he was dragged into the corridor outside of his apartment. Alias shot an elbow back and hit his aggressor in the side of the neck, startling him into losing his grip.

There were still three of them and only one of him.

Ben's eyes blazed red. "Remove your hands from him."

The largest man pulled Ben toward the fire exit at the end of the corridor. Alias didn't know what he could do to protect Ben, but he had to try. A hubot could not defend itself against a human.

"Don't touch him!" he called out, hands turning to fists.

"Now you're asking for it."

Alias was too slow, and the huge fist hit him squarely in the solar plexus, forcing the air out of his lungs. With a derisive snort, the intruder kicked him in the shin, sending him crashing against the wall. Alias scurried back, but there was nowhere to go. He curled onto himself to protect his face as a kick landed on his ribs. Pain flared up his side. In between his fingers, he watched Ben get dragged onto the rusty landing of the fire escape.

"Hey!" Alias wheezed.

Narrowly dodging a kick to the head, he shot to his feet and rushed after the bald man who was pushing Ben over the railing.

He was too late. Ben smacked into the cement below.

"No!"

Pain struck Alias deep inside, well past the reach of fists and boots. He stopped breathing, mouth hanging open, one hand outstretched. The world froze around him before it snapped back into place.

For the first time in his life, he felt the urge to hurt someone else.

He rushed the stranger with a scream of rage but tripped over something hard. The coppery taste of blood burst into his mouth as his chin slammed into the ground. He blinked up at the muscles towering above him: black clothing against the black sky, teeth flashing white. His chest clenched in panic.

"I hate repeating myself," the man grouched, and let his fist fly.

CHAPTER EIGHT
HURT

A lias lifted a hand to his left cheek, gingerly tracing the lump around his eye. Even this light of a touch stung. He looked away from the window of the taxi, blinded by the rising sun. His arm was shaking when he dropped it across the metallic torso taking up most of the bench. Ben's damaged body was a reminder that strangers weren't as harmless as he'd believed, even with the virus taken out of the equation. Its eyes were red—the color for disapproval, the warning of a nearby threat, or the sign of a mechanical malfunction.

The red hue had been the default color until Alias had managed to fix the head, and it had never reappeared.

Bile rose in Alias's throat. He swallowed, willing himself not to throw up again.

"ETA: six minutes," announced the mechanical voice of the self-driven car.

Alias couldn't stop petting Ben's scratched head. The first thing he'd done after waking up disoriented and soaked on his own doorstep had been to limp down four flights of rusty stairs to the sidewalk, where Ben had lain still on the concrete. Dragging the hubot back to his apartment would have been impossible had the lift not been miraculously functioning, for once.

The NID officer answering Ben's earlier distress call had taken several hours to arrive and hadn't seemed to care about Alias's roughened-up state or finding the culprits. With Avida failures going up and the controversy surrounding LX, people were growing restless and violent, the officer had told him. He'd concluded with a recommendation to get his wounds checked out and made some vague promise about keeping him posted.

Alias had watched him leave through the front door—or rather, the hole where the door had been. The apartment wasn't safe anymore. He'd thought about calling Deon, but had decided against it.

He hadn't gone to the hospital either.

The taxi hit a bump in the road, jolting the head in his lap. Alias held on to it reflexively, thinking back on all the hours he'd spent locked up in his bedroom warding off the double scourge of a concussion and a panic attack by trying to fix Ben. Sadly, the damage caused by the fall was too extensive. For all that he'd learned about robotics over the years, he still lacked the specific knowledge someone else working at Dehive possessed.

He called Mr. Quint, only to hit a cheerful voice mail.

The taxi dropped him off in front of the Hive's front doors, which was technically forbidden. Alias extracted himself from the back seat, pulling Ben with him, and propped the heavy metallic body against his side while the scanner read his palm.

He was as discreet as he could be, but he still got curious looks on his way to the BotHouse. He entered the loud warehouse with a sweaty brow and aching ribs. His watchphone alerted him to a call from Mr. Quint, which he accepted it with a raspy vocal command. "Mis–Mister Quint?"

"Good morning, Alias. Is everything all right?"

"I, er . . . D-Does . . ." Why was he back to stuttering? Mr. Quint wouldn't hurt him. He took a deep breath, or at least tried. His ribs really hurt, but this pain was the least he deserved for blowing off Deon's concern. "Does your offer to help fix my hubot still stand?"

"Of course! Do you have an idea when you'd stop by?"

"Er." Alias grunted with effort. "I'm already here."

Mr. Quint had already cleared his desk when Alias joined him. Another bot stepped in to help him carry Ben. Alias thanked it and grimaced when the bot dumped Ben onto the desk.

Mr. Quint's gaze flitted back and forth between his two visitors. "What happened?"

The concern wasn't for Ben. Alias tensed reflexively, guilt twisting his gut into knots. If only he'd heeded Deon's advice and moved to a better neighborhood, none of this would have happened.

"A bad fall," he said, and smiled his work smile as he tried to direct Mr. Quint's focus back toward Ben.

Mr. Quint stared at him, unwavering.

Alias squeezed his eyes shut. "Please. Ben fell off a fourth-story balcony and hit concrete. I tried to fix him, but I . . . I can't . . ."

"That's a lot of falls in one night," Mr. Quint muttered. "You sure you shouldn't be resting?"

"It's already a quarter past—" Alias glanced at his watchphone with its now-cracked screen. "—nine." A spasm of pain shot up his side. He ignored it, linking gazes with Mr. Quint. "I've got work to do."

Mr. Quint muttered something about workaholics but didn't insist further. Together, they managed to get Ben facedown across the table. Its feet hung over the edge; the scratches it'd collected gleamed under the sharp light. Alias couldn't hold back a whimper as his left side lanced him, the pain sharper than before. Thankfully, the ambient noise drowned it.

Mr. Quint unscrewed the discreet panel at the base of Ben's head with practiced motions. "You're sure you only got a black eye in that fall?" he asked nonchalantly, narrowing his eyes at the delicate electronic parts exposed. He set the panel aside. "Seems like you got it worse than poor Ben here."

The thieves had been brutal to them both, but Alias wasn't worried about himself.

He wrenched his hand away from his black eye and busied himself with Ben's mangled left arm. The limb was twisted backward, the paint stripped off near the joints.

"Just some bruises," he said dismissively.

Mr. Quint shrugged, but his jaw tightened as he began to pull wires out of Ben's head.

Alias skipped breakfast, only stopping by the lounge for a dose of much-needed caffeine. His office was how he'd left it: calm, dark, and devoid of human beings. He leaned back against the door, breathing in the scents of the various plants. Through the windows, the woods appeared gloomy, the trees warped lines bent out of shape. Little light filtered through the stained glass of the dome-shaped ceiling, but each step he took triggered another motion sensor, and soon enough the office was basking in artificial sunlight.

Mindful of his wounds, he took his time sitting at his desk. Thankfully, the caffeine was already doing wonders for his headache, and hopefully his aching muscles would soon become easier to ignore.

He stared blearily at the impressive list of emails and missed calls waiting for him on the leftmost screen. The center display showed news articles prioritized by an algorithm set in place by Ms. Angelius. The top one was McCarthy's first public appearance since the LX reveal one week ago.

The Ice Lady was doing credit to the name once more. She always dressed in blue, but today the paler hue granted her a new degree of coldness. It matched the remarkable blue of her eyes, hard and intent on the journalist bots as she replied to questions about LX as though she'd created it, reminding the viewers that Mr. Dehive was known to "take risks."

"He could do with a reminder that the world isn't his playground. Others before him have tried to release what they claimed to be the best antiviral possible, and we all know how that ended." She barely moved as she spoke, except to clutch her chest twice, just over her heart, and to brush the scar on her cheek. Neither gesture appeared to stem from nerves, even though they should. Her even tone never faltered. "The scale at which LX has been tested is not sufficient by far to justify those false hopes coming from the Hive. We need to be able to trust each other in these difficult times. And we need certainties that this injection is safe for our children."

A live feed at the top right of the screen showed throngs of people in front of Dehive's remote offices. One of McCarthy's supposed experts chimed in, analyzing the public's displeasure as bots zoomed in on aggressively worded holographic signs. Alias had to hand it to Lyra McCarthy: she was uniquely skilled in distorting truth to fit her own narrative . . . and feed people's paranoia.

He shut the window and dialed Deon's number.

"Alias." Ms. Angelius had answered on the first ring. "I was about to call you. Have you watched this ridiculous speech yet?"

Alias quashed a flicker of annoyance. It wasn't any business of his who else Deon slept with. Though it meant he wasn't going to stay with Deon tonight. Where would he sleep? The prospect of going back to his cold, doorless apartment filled him with dread.

"She should be ashamed of playing the children card like this," he said in as neutral a voice as he could manage. "Is Mr. Dehive available?"

"Not right now." She didn't sound happy about it. "But I've been tasked to address our local liar's latest speech with you. Should I drop by or do you prefer to do it remotely?"

Alias's chest tightened. "Remotely."

Ms. Angelius didn't seem to mind. And by the time they wrapped up the statement, Alias felt better. It was amazing what the satisfaction of a job well done could do for a person.

When the first visitor of the day walked through the door, glaring at his tablet, Alias jumped, his heart rate going through the roof. Although Mr. Arvin was a colleague, the fear, as irrational as it was, had returned with a vengeance. Alias drained his coffee to win some time while his guest launched into his latest problem.

"Mr. Novar, I need you to clear that up for me."

The word *need* helped Alias to ground himself. This was his purpose here. Helping. He thrived in this role. He actually thrived here, in the eye of the cyclone.

"Of course," he said with confidence, and reached for the proffered tablet while Mr. Arvin grumbled about the ever-growing cost of living, typing at his watchphone all the while. Mr. Arvin complained a lot.

When Alias handed back the tablet, the other man cut himself off with a gasp. "What happened to your eye?"

Alias didn't roll them, but only because it hurt. "A fall," he said flatly.

It remained his explanation through the day. Not that many people visited his office in person. A good portion of the Dehive staff was too busy dealing with the crisis to remember his existence, which suited him just fine. Deon's radio silence bothered him, though. Wasn't Alias's main purpose to assist him? He shelved the rancor alongside his concern for Ben.

It was still early by his new standards, a little after 6 p.m., when Deon barreled into the office. *You're safe*, Alias told himself, one hand clenched in his shirt over his hammering heart. Deon must not have shaved, for his stubble was more wild than stylish today. The top two buttons of his shirt were undone, revealing a burn that Alias was pretty sure hadn't marred his collarbone the last time they'd . . . spoken. Purple was still smudged under his eyes, and anger held his shoulders tight.

"Put that on hold, Alias."

"I—I'm almost d-done," Alias stuttered, trying to cover the mic and hide his unease at the same time. "Just give me—"

"Unless you want me to do it myself, you will put that fucking call on hold!"

Nerves caused Alias's fingers to slip, and he hung up instead.

"What's wrong with you?" he cried out.

"You'd better have a good explanation for being so fucking stubborn!"

Alias pushed away from the desk, shocked into silence. In the taxi, he'd tried to distract himself by considering Deon's angry hunger from last night under a new light. What if Deon had been seeking comfort in his own way, not unlike Alias had after getting the injection? Alias had been ready to overlook their uneasy exchange, but Deon's outlandish accusation changed things.

"I d-don't know what you're t-talking about."

"You should have said yes, damn it!"

Anger rushed through Alias like a balm, filling the hollowness left behind by the fear. He lifted his chin, nostrils flaring. "You should have told me that sex was mandatory to keep the job!"

"What the hell are you talking about?"

Deon appeared genuinely confused, but Alias had had enough. "I'm talking about the fact that apparently I can't say no to you, after all."

"What?"

"What *what*? You just said so. I didn't want sex, and we both know that was what you were offering."

Deon's jaw dropped. "You think I offered you a lift to have sex with you?" His face paled. "Is that what you . . . Fuck." He let out a brief chuckle, bitter and choked. "I wouldn't have been opposed to it, but that's not why I offered *a lift*, Alias." He jerked a finger at Alias's face, features tightening again. "My being really pissed off right now isn't about sex, believe me."

The skin around Alias's shiner tingled. His hands spasmed at his sides as he thought of that fist flying toward his face.

Deon's eyebrows furrowed in concern. "Dario told me you didn't seem too keen on seeing a doctor. Why didn't you call me last night? What kind of fall leaves you and your bot in such a state?"

Alias stiffened at such indiscretion. He supposed it had to be expected, given the long friendship between Mr. Quint and Deon. "An accident," he said defiantly.

"Don't lie to me. I read the NID report."

"That's a breach of privacy!" Alias slammed his hands down on the desk. "It's none of your business!"

"The hell it isn't!" Deon advanced on him, but the desk stopped him short. He raised his voice instead. "If you're attacked because of your association with Dehive, with me—"

"I was doing just fine until yesterday!"

"You have the means to live in a better neighborhood, surely the hospital bills for your mother—"

"Don't you dare bring my mother into this!"

"I'm just trying to help you, you stubborn idiot!"

Alias couldn't help it: the moment Deon charged around the desk, he jumped out of the way, his hands balling into fists. Rationally, he knew Deon wasn't about to hit him, but his nerves were still frayed, his fight-or-flight reflexes all tangled up.

His hands were shaking badly—that fourth cup of coffee might have been a mistake.

"Alias." Misery poured out of Deon. His voice became coaxing. Gentle and strained. "I won't touch you, but *please*. Look at me."

Alias didn't look up but compromised by not moving farther away.

"Who did that to you?"

"The report didn't say?"

Deon didn't answer.

"I don't know," Alias said, throat tight. "I've never met them before, but they recognized me as your PA, and they must really like what McCarthy is saying . . ." He trailed off. *They hurt Ben*, he thought, and gripped the edge of the desk. "It's nothing."

"It's not nothing."

Their eyes met. Alias could tell Deon wanted to touch him, and Deon wasn't even twitchy. It was just . . . that obvious. Alias's heart sped up. Not in fear. Not *only*.

"Can I—"

"Yes," Alias whispered, and leaned forward just enough for Deon to kiss his brow.

"It's not nothing," Deon repeated. "Fuck. I'm so sorry. About your hubot too but a lot more about you."

Alias cracked his first smile of the day. "It's not your fault."

"Not directly, but I should have insisted more that you move. That neighborhood really isn't safe."

"The world isn't safe."

The door opened. Alias heard the beginning of an inquiry, and then a quick apology. The door closed.

Deon pinched the bridge of his nose with a sigh. "I just wish you would be more careful."

"You're a hypocrite, Deon."

"Excuse me?"

Alias gestured at Deon's face. Three distinct bumps swelled at his throat. "You got stung."

"Oh, that? Well, at least *I* had the protective suit on." He dug a finger into the swelling above his collarbone and didn't so much as flinch, as if to prove a point. "If anything, you're the hypocrite, telling me to take care of myself while you obviously don't give a shit about your own safety."

"It's not like I asked to be punched in the face!"

"Tell me the rest."

Alias scowled. He'd been manipulated, hadn't he? He was tempted to leave the room, but the concern underlying the demand made him stay. And talk. The words spilled out his mouth like a secret begging to be shared. The NID officer had been indifferent, but Deon wasn't, and Alias found himself providing details he'd left off his statement.

Thankfully, Deon didn't give him an earful for putting himself between the men and a hubot. However, he did have many colorful things to say about how the situation was handled by the NID.

"That's it, we're going to Lentz."

"Dr. Lentz? Why?"

"They're my only scientist who also happens to be a medical doctor. Did it not occur to you that you might have a concussion and cracked ribs? Come with me."

Alias's instinct was to resist, but arguing further required energy he just didn't have. He still dragged his feet all the way down to the Lab, to Deon's bemused exasperation.

"Seriously, Alias, it's either the hospital or the Lab, and the latter is a lot closer."

"I just don't like doctors."

At last, Deon slowed down to match Alias's pace. "That . . . actually explains a lot. I'm even prouder of you."

Alias sure wasn't proud of himself. He entered the Lab with a pounding heart and sweaty hands, and tried not to bite his lip bloody while Deon fetched help. When Dr. Lentz came into view, they were scowling, Deon stone-faced by their side.

"You know I quit hospital work because I prefer research by far, Mr. Dehive."

With a smile, Deon encouraged Alias to sit, and glanced at Dr. Lentz with an arched brow. "Well, I pay you well enough to get reacquainted with your past every once in a while, don't I?"

"That you do," Dr. Lentz muttered before directing their attention toward Alias. "Follow that light with your eyes."

Alias willed himself to stay still when a hand flashed close to his face, but the memory of that punch was still too close to the surface—and that was without taking Dr. Lentz's lab coat and the medical setting into consideration. He recoiled so violently he almost toppled off his chair.

It helped that Dr. Lentz didn't snap at him. And somehow, their reluctance to conduct the examination in the first place helped even more. By the time they were done testing reaction time—while arguing with Deon about the necessity of getting imaging tests—Alias's grip on his stool wasn't so tight.

"Looks good to me," Dr. Lentz concluded with a scowl Deon's way. "If you insist that I be the unofficial doctor on retainer, you have to stop arguing with my prognoses." The scowl dimmed a fraction. "Get some rest, Mr. Novar."

By the time they left the Lab, Alias was wound up so tight he jumped at the hand brushing his back. Deon pulled away at once.

"S-sorry."

Deon's eyebrows shot to his hairline. "What are you apologizing for?"

"I know you're not trying to . . . hurt me," Alias explained, cheeks burning.

"You don't have to justify yourself."

Keeping a little more distance between them now, Deon led him to the bathroom of his quarters.

"I'll find out who did this to you. I swear it." He turned away from the various bottles he'd started gathering, probably ointments and healing salves of some kind, voice warmer when he spoke again. "Thank you for putting my mind at rest by allowing Lentz to do the examination. You did well. Would you like to take a shower? The heat might help you relax."

Alias accepted. The pressure of Deon's shower was heavenly, and the hot water soothed all the aches he'd known about and a few more that hadn't registered. Even his bruised eye wasn't bothering him anymore. He toweled himself perfunctorily and put on the clothes left for him. Steam had spread in the bathroom, swallowing the edge of counters and sinks, covering the ceiling in ephemeral clouds. Alias began to drift, his thoughts swirling in mist. He dragged his feet toward the door.

Deon waited for him by the bed and glanced up with a soft smile. Alias flopped down on the mattress with a yawn and dared resting his head on a familiar shoulder. The fact that Deon barely reacted encouraged him to relax further. There were no doctors here, and no one who might attack him.

"Will you stay the night?" Deon's voice was calm and soothing, barely above a whisper. "To sleep, I mean. Just so I know you're safe."

"Okay."

"Thank you. That's . . . I appreciate it."

Alias was rubbing the soft fabric of his shirt between two fingers. He was wearing Deon's clothes. Again. His chest fluttered. It wasn't a bad feeling.

"You're lucky you don't have a concussion," Deon whispered, resting a tentative hand on Alias's thigh. "How about we put those ointments to good use?"

At Deon's express invitation, Alias kept sleeping at the Hive. He could have had a room of his own, like Ms. Angelius, but he'd elected to share Deon's quarters.

He wasn't sure why. It definitely felt strange to put away the clothes he'd salvaged from his old apartment in Deon's immense walk-in. Less strange than falling into Deon's king-sized bed and cocooning himself in that comforting scent, but strange nonetheless. The knowledge that it was all temporary helped him adjust to his new situation.

The fact that he went to bed on his own and woke up by himself, Deon's side cold and untouched, for a whole week, both helped and didn't.

Was Deon crashing in one office or another, too tired to make his way back to bed? Or in the cabin, for some time alone? Alias meant to ask, but there was always an urgent matter requiring his attention. Truth be told, he enjoyed the solitude as much as he found it unsettling, and wasn't that a headache he didn't need?

The only upside of the mess unleashed by McCarthy was how it kept Alias's wandering thoughts to a minimum. There was always a meeting to attend or a trip to make, and Alias was right there, shadowing the most sought-after man in the world. His mind buzzed with arguments and counterarguments, statistics and statements.

On the nights he didn't have nightmares about the attack, he dreamed of work. McCarthy's string of carefully twisted truths was the subject of most conversations at the Hive. The Ice Lady kept parading supposed experts on the news with their most recent findings, such as how the flawed chemical structure of LX would inevitably cause problems when the virus mutated further and a more aggressive variant emerged. Alias dismissed those claims, but he was well aware that a concerning majority did not. People believed McCarthy because they'd rather face an enemy shaped like a man than a microscopic threat they didn't understand.

Men could be contained—or eliminated—a lot easier than viruses.

By Friday morning, he wasn't in the best mindset when he started taking calls. His uncomfortable conversation with his mother around midday didn't improve his mood. He wanted to shield her from his attack, and thus couldn't visit or tell her why, and getting off the phone without lying had been tricky. Toward the end of the afternoon, Alias watched the Indian president's speech. His work for the day was almost done, and what little he had left required the CEO's input. Which would have to wait, because Deon was down in the BotHouse getting some unexpected rest at Mr. Quint's station.

Alias slumped into his chair, an empty mug dangling from his right hand. At least the Indian president wasn't calling Deon Dehive a "loose cannon that needs to be brought in line." He even said that he'd much rather have LX available in his country than watch the death rate grow.

"I believe in facts," he stated, expression completely blank.

He walked away, leaving the vice president to step forward and address other matters that were of little interest to Alias.

"Mute."

The cacophony of inquiries was replaced by the welcome, faint sound of water trickling down to the feet of the miniature Lady Love. Alias set the empty mug aside and added *India?* to Deon's travel plan for the next month, linking the speech and a few articles about India's LBV and Avida statistics. After a quick message in the three-way conversation thread to keep Ms. Angelius and Deon appraised, he reviewed his boss's calendar one last time.

Next week was chock-full of holo-conferences and meetings with specialists, public debates, visits to LX distribution clinics because Deon enjoyed mingling with people . . . and two upcoming inspections from the NID.

The problem with the NID was that they valued protection of the American people against the Loveborne virus more than rational thinking and objectivity. And McCarthy knew exactly how to manipulate them and trigger the strongest response possible by using expressions like "vulnerable children" and "dangerous experimental drug." The WHO's seal of approval on the LX injection meant little if the NID wasn't satisfied with Dehive's work.

The rapidly degrading health of a child in the daycare center at Dehive had only made things easier for McCarthy, who made sure that the world focused on the fact that the five-year-old had gone off Avida to receive the LX injection, rather than the much more relevant fact that the little boy had been suffering from an autoimmune disease for years.

Alias's jaw tightened at the memory of Deon's crestfallen expression when he'd learned about this. At least the NID officers weren't accusing Deon outright, but merely discussing McCarthy's claims.

Alias turned off his computer, put on the change of clothes he kept in one drawer, and left the Hive for a much-needed run. He couldn't help Deon any more than he did, and getting all wound up about his helplessness wouldn't do anyone any good.

In the woods, the birds were barely chirping, and the wind, which had been fierce in the morning, had died down to an intermittent murmur in the background. He barely noticed it when he left the well-marked path behind. He'd come to know these woods intimately, so much so that he could navigate the intricate tapestry of roots and branches on instinct.

His heart leaped into his throat as he spotted a familiar silhouette in white, brilliant against the fiery line of the setting sun. It would seem that Deon wasn't napping in robotics anymore.

Alias slowed. A drop of rain hit his nose, and a second trailed down his temple. The woods awakened around him, small animals scurrying from under thick bushes and leaping over twisted roots. Under his foot, a branch creaked. Despite the poor lighting, Alias could tell the moment Deon registered his presence: he went stiff and turned around, exaggeratedly slow—which made sense, because he held a frame dripping with honey. Hit with the reminder of those beestings, Alias waited quietly while Deon returned the frame to the hive. The bees followed the figure in white, then dispersed and gathered anew in intriguing configurations.

"Good evening, Mr. Novar."

Jaden Angelius pulled the veil back.

Alias blinked. "Hi. I didn't—"

"Expect me?" Ms. Angelius stripped out of the protective gear in quick motions that spoke of habit. The drizzle had turned into a shower, but it didn't seem to bother her, even if the complex array of braids suggested time and effort. She hung the suit on the hook and gestured Alias inside the cabin.

"Have a drink with me?"

Alias didn't see a good reason to refuse. Ms. Angelius unlocked the front door with something Alias had only seen in old movies: a key. It looked heavy, and it turned in its matching physical lock with a grinding sound. Was it brass? Bronze?

"Have a seat. I'll pour you a glass. You like mead, right?"

"Sure," Alias replied absentmindedly.

For all that he'd spent whole evenings sitting with his back to the cabin, he'd never set a toe inside. To his surprise, the cabin displayed none of the luxury inherent to Deon's quarters. It shared more similarities with the BotHouse, if the BotHouse had been much, much smaller and smelled strongly of honey and earth. The furniture consisted of a chair, a small bed, complex machinery festooned with tubes and containers of all sizes, and overfilled shelves taking up one wall.

Still, it felt a lot homier than his apartment.

Ms. Angelius crouched in front of a small container and retrieved a bottle. The dark amber liquid gleamed under the dim light as she poured for them both. Whispering his thanks, Alias took the proffered glass and brought it to his lips. The scent lacked the usual sweetness. The bitterness slid over his tongue on the first sip. He tried to stifle a grimace, but the cough gave him away.

"This one hasn't quite had the time to mature," Ms. Angelius explained and drank, deep red lips curled in satisfaction.

Since Alias had taken the only chair, she opted for the bed, sinking down in the middle of it with casual familiarity. She was wearing beige pants and a matching sleeveless top, but she would have been stunning even in Alias's clothes. The rain hadn't made the slightest dent in her beauty. Deon would probably look just as handsome soaking wet, as well.

A minute of silence passed. Two. Ms. Angelius toed off her shoes and leaned against the wall at her back with a soft sigh. Even her naked feet were pretty and well-proportioned, the nails painted gold to match her fingernails. Alias tried not to consider his own feet while he fussed with the stem of his glass. In a flight back from Atlanta two days ago, Deon had fallen asleep with his head on Alias's shoulder. He'd mumbled something about bees and twitched and turned until Alias began running his fingers through his hair. Had it been Alias's presence that had brought Deon comfort or the gesture itself—one that Ms. Angelius did all too often?

Alias didn't know what to make of his feelings toward her. Ms. Angelius was a kind soul, competent and helpful. Any question he had, she could answer. Every problem found a solution in her capable hands. She accepted him for who he was, the wasp in their beehive.

She was also close to Deon. Not for the first time, Alias tried to decide if he should embrace this strange emotion called jealousy if only because it might dilute his attraction to Deon. But he had no wish to be angry at Ms. Angelius, and jealousy felt very much like it.

And he didn't want to complicate whatever it was he had with Deon any further. Not when Deon made him feel safe.

Good.

A shiver raced up his spine.

"Mr. Novar?"

Alias cast his gaze down. The floor was simple wood planks. Had Deon designed the place for himself? For Ms. Angelius? Was this where they met when they disappeared together and Ms. Angelius answered Deon's private number? Alias tilted his glass to the side and watched its content swirl, the little amber waves licking at the sides before the whole surface evened out at an angle. He'd once wished to be freed of his attraction toward the powerful man he'd come to call by his first name, but working at Dehive had revealed just how fine a line lay between safety and prison. Everything posed a risk.

LBV was just so omnipresent that he'd lost sight of the bigger picture.

"Sorry." Embarrassment and irritation tinted his cheeks red—it seemed that living in Deon's quarters, as temporary as the arrangement might be, worsened the mess in his head. "Thank you for the drink. I should go back to work."

"What you should do, Mr. Novar, is stop overthinking things." Ms. Angelius was fixing the end of one braid, but her gaze remained firm on him. "Overthinking might be a necessary part of your job, but do not let that habit spill over into your personal life. You'll become miserable, trust me."

The last part wasn't delivered in quite the same posed tone.

"I trust you," Alias said, gripping his glass so hard it hurt. "Both of you."

"I'm also asking you to trust yourself, and that includes your feelings."

Alias set his half-empty glass onto the floor. "Could we please not talk about this?"

Ms. Angelius ignored him. "The relationship between Mr. Dehive and myself shouldn't be relevant to the one blossoming between you."

Her tone was gentle, but Alias felt like he'd just been slapped. He stumbled to his feet, contradictory feelings he'd just been told to trust warring inside him. "That's not— There's nothing blossoming—"

"Please, Alias, do not insult either of us. You're an even worse liar than he is." She met his eyes as she stood, her shoes in one hand, the bottle in the other. "Do you know how many people possess level nine clearance, the highest security possible at the Hive? The one that grants access to our CEO's private quarters?"

Alias's heart hammered in his chest. He waited, but the question must have been rhetorical in nature. Had the offer of a drink been a disguised offer to talk? He tried to smile back at Ms. Angelius, but she left before he could manage it. There was a sour taste at the back of his mouth. He yanked the door open and stood in the rain, every drop hitting his face feeding his confusion.

Predictably, Deon's quarters were empty. Alias could afford to spend a long time in the shower, so he did, turning the water just shy of too hot. He was red from head to toe when he got out, but he felt better. Calmer, if still confused. He returned to the bedroom with a fluffy towel hanging at his waist. His plan to put on some boxer shorts and call it a night came apart as he approached the—once again—empty bed. He pulled on his underwear, followed by a shirt and pair of pants. The door opened as he was struggling with his socks.

"Hey." Deon shed his jacket and went to toss it on the tree-shaped coat rack but paused, staring at Alias. "You're leaving?"

"I thought . . ." Alias cocked his head to the side. "There were some files I needed to double-check, and while you're here, you could . . ."

He trailed off, unnerved by the angry set of Deon's mouth. And then he remained silent for a completely different reason.

There was a smudge of dark pink at the corner of Deon's mouth. No, not pink. Red. Like Ms. Angelius's lips.

Deon kicked off his shoes and hung his jacket, evidently oblivious to Alias's agitation. The bright light above the pond outlined the harmonious gray and black lines of his pants and gave the metallic black tie, now loosened at his neck, an even darker glint. In contrast, the white of his shirt skirted the edge of blinding.

"Hey there, pretty things. I bet you're hungry."

Deon retrieved a small bottle from a hidden compartment in the marble basin and tilted it, pouring a cloud of shimmery powder on the surface of the water. A strange feeling surged through him, increasing tenfold as Deon greeted each fish by name.

"You look feverish. Were you out in the woods?"

Stunned by the harsh edge to Deon's tone, Alias barely moved as Deon crowded him.

"You shouldn't be spending that much time in the woods in this temperature." With an aggravated sigh, Deon cupped Alias's face tenderly, angling it to get a better read. "We're almost into December, not the middle of summer."

Alias barely heard the words. Deon's hand felt so good. Just right, as though the contact straightened a thousand wrapped-up feelings inside him. Alias had missed his touch in a visceral way he couldn't begin to comprehend.

And he knew, with a certainty that should have frightened him, that having Deon close meant more to him than safety ever had.

Deon kissed his brow, and a thousand shivers raced down his spine.

"When was the last time you slept?"

"When was the last time you did?" Alias countered.

Deon sighed. "You should go to bed."

"I'm not tired," Alias lied. "I want to go see Ben."

"You and I *and* Dario know it's not responsive yet. Besides, your face says otherwise. You're barely standing on your feet, sweetheart."

Sweetheart.

Alias recoiled as if hit. "I . . ." The rest of the words got stuck in his throat as he zeroed in once more on the smudge of red at the corner of Deon's mouth. This time, he couldn't look away. Contradictory urges flooded him. Ms. Angelius's comment about overthinking things just added to the frustration bubbling up in his chest. How was he supposed to not overthink something so personal? Even without the taste of Deon in his mouth, even without these hands on him, he could sense the link between them growing taut like a tightrope.

He might not cower from the attraction now, but the implications sure were overwhelming.

"I—I'd like to see Ben all the same," he managed to say.

He reached for his shoes, but a hand stopped him.

"What's going on with you?" Deon's demeanor had shifted from concerned to . . . slightly less so. Wary, maybe. He balled his tie and threw it over his shoulder. It landed in the pond, causing the fish to scatter and abandon their food. Deon didn't pay it any mind. "When you're angry at me, you usually speak your mind, so tell me: What's going on?"

Alias undid the still-tied laces on the first shoe. "I'm not angry at you."

Deon's eyes bore holes in his nape. "Then it's damn close to that."

Deon's tone hinted at a growing impatience. Alias pulled too hard on one lace and had to thread it through the tiny hole again. A bit of red stood out on the left side of the shoe. Blood? Berry juice? Some more of Ms. Angelius's lipstick? It didn't matter. None of this mattered.

He set the shoe down and shoved his foot in it, definitely angry now: at himself. "I'm just confused about some things." He tied the laces too tight and put on his other shoe. "You can— Just get some rest, please," he said, verging on desperate. He shouldn't be greedy, shouldn't want to have Deon all to himself. This possessive person unfolding inside him . . . that wasn't him, was it? He should want to be in his own space, like he'd been most of his life. Part of him wanted to be, but apparently not a big enough one to warrant a dedicated search for a new apartment.

His attempt to leave was thwarted by Deon's hand on his shoulder. He spun, gearing up for a fight, the attack still too fresh. Deon letting him go stopped him short.

"Alias . . ."

Alias made the mistake of staring at the spot of color on Deon's mouth for the third time. A bemused expression settled on Deon's face.

"Are you jealous, Alias?"

Embarrassment clawed at Alias's chest. "I certainly am not."

"I thought we've established that you're a shitty liar."

Alias hadn't liked being told that earlier in the cabin, and he enjoyed it even less now. He jutted out his chin, doing his best not to blush and failing spectacularly. "I just— I told you I was confused," he said haltingly. "I'll just . . . go. Work and . . ." He felt like such a fool. LBV was building a dangerous resistance against the medication that had worked for decades, and the person manufacturing most of it was doing her best to keep Deon from giving the world a measure of hope. Nausea rose in Alias's throat. He was being so selfish. "I'm s-sorry. I don't know why I feel this way. You're right, and I'm . . . This is embarrassing. I'll just be out of your way—"

"Alias . . ."

"I know I should have been looking harder to find an apartment; it's just that every time I do, I . . ." *Think about how much I would miss you, and how terrified I am to be attacked again.* The words hurt in a way the fading bruises didn't, even with him pressing down on a yellow blotch on his shoulder. He didn't want Deon's pity, and he didn't deserve it either. "I'll find something this week. Tonight. Right now, I'll—"

"Take off your shoes."

Alias froze. "Why?"

"You aren't going back to work. We're both done for the day. Our injection supplies, the possibilities of me traveling to India— they'll still be there tomorrow. Just like the NID, who will still be breathing down my neck because of McCarthy."

He guided Alias to the chair. He had to make some room first, and several shirts, pants, and contraptions that were not clothes ended on the floor in a heap.

"You're apt at so many things I keep forgetting that you're new to this. There are parameters to every relationship. It is within your rights to express wishes and ask for clarification. While I can't fault you for making assumptions, considering my reputation, I can assure you my sexual life hasn't been as unbridled as the tabloids would have everyone think."

"I—I don't even know what I want," he choked out.

"You try to pretend you can do without what you want, which is not the same thing."

Heat crept up Alias's face. Thankfully, Deon wasn't looking at him anymore. At the wide bookcase Alias hadn't explored yet, Deon reached for what looked like a dark-red tome. Instead of pulling it off the shelf, though, he seemed to be fumbling with the cover. A soft *click* broke the silence. Deon didn't open the book—it opened for him.

"Not many people like the real me, Alias."

Alias stretched out his neck to try to confirm that the book was a safe in disguise, but Deon had shifted and blocked the view.

"What do you mean?"

Another *click* was heard. Deon turned away from the not-book with a furrowed brow. "I'm blunt. Very much so. I have my own way of handling things, and not many people accept that. I don't trust easily." He undid the last button of his shirt and shouldered it off, stopping halfway to take off the silver cufflinks. "I'm too exigent, too . . . passionate, in every aspect of my life. I used to be promiscuous too, but after a while even I got bored with impersonal encounters. Some masks are just . . . too heavy to bear."

"You shouldn't try to be someone you're not." Alias winced. Deon had just said the same about him. "You're an incredible man, Deon."

"You think so?"

"Did it sound like a lie?"

Alias tried to smile, but the ache in his chest wouldn't let him. Deon's intense scrutiny used to make him squirm, but right now, it felt strangely freeing. Deon walked up to him.

"Tell me what's on that mind of yours, Alias. Ask what you wish to know. Ask for what you want."

Alias stood up on shaky legs. Deon caught one of his hands, but it was Alias who intertwined their fingers and squeezed until he couldn't tell where his hand ended and Deon's began. It must hurt, but just like in the jet that day, Alias couldn't bring himself to let go, and Deon didn't offer a single word of protest.

"Are you . . . seeing other people?" Alias said at long last. "H-how many are you . . ." He took a deep breath, grateful for Deon's patience. ". . . having sex with?"

"Just the one."

Alias's heart sank. Of course. Ms. Angelius had a much stronger claim: she had known Deon for years before either of them had ever heard of Alias Novar. He couldn't possibly compete with that. "Oh. I see." The words were barely audible to his own ears.

"Just the one," Deon repeated. He shook his hand free and cupped Alias's cheek. With his other hand, he found the small of Alias's back and pulled him closer. The dual touch, light but firm, so welcome after days of uncertainty and solitude, brought a relieved moan to Alias's lips. "And that's *you*, sweetheart."

Deon's eyes held so much tenderness. Letting out a sharp exhale, Alias splayed both hands against Deon's chest, finding comfort in the solid muscle. His knees threatened to give.

"Ah," was all he could muster.

Deon chuckled. "I care a great deal about you, you know."

Alias buried his face in the crook of Deon's shoulder. God, the heat in that voice . . . Deon probably wasn't even trying, and yet here Alias was, face flushing, heart aflutter, all worked up over a simple string of words. The warmth from Deon's presence was beyond physical—it reached deep within, spreading wider every time they touched.

Was that the main reason he was tempted to spend the nights in Deon's quarters for just a little while longer?

Deon pulled back to rub at the corner of his own mouth, wiping away the confusing red. "I really like honey, but there's a case to be made about strawberry jam." He waggled his eyebrows playfully. "About a lot of sweet things around here."

Alias squirmed. *Sweet.* "Is that what you like about me?" he blurted out.

"Among other things, yes." The hand at his back drifted to his waist, careful over his healing side. "You're very likable, Alias. On so many levels. You're curious, hard-working, open-minded, loyal, generous, and one of the most caring persons I know. The fact that you're very pretty is just a nice bonus."

Kiss me, Alias wanted to say. What came out was: "Please."

The back of Alias's thighs hit the bed as Deon's mouth caught his. *Please* meant that the remaining space between their bodies vanished and that Deon's hips rolled against his own, granting Alias's erection the most delicious friction. *Please* meant that Deon worked his tongue inside Alias's mouth the instant Alias's lips parted to welcome him. Deon tasted of honey and strawberry, of coffee and alcohol, of confusion fading into certainty, and Alias let himself be devoured. *Please* also meant that Deon's hands remained on him. Goose bumps broke out under the pads of Deon's fingers, spreading a sense of urgency that blinded Alias to the obvious for several minutes.

Deon wasn't hard.

Alias broke the kiss with a gasp, worried and unsure. "D-Deon?"

"I'm sorry." A lopsided smile flashed on Deon's lips. "I must be more tired than I thought."

"You should be resting; what was I— I'm sorry."

"Never apologize for how you feel." Deon gave him one more kiss, tender but quick, before heading for the bathroom. "You warm the bed for me. I'm going to take a quick shower, and then I'll join you."

Alias stripped back to his underwear and slipped under the sheets. Not a minute later, the shower started. Deon hadn't closed the door, which soothed Alias's nerves a bit. He reached for the tablet on the bedside table and set the panel to act as a mirror, curious to see the lips Deon had just kissed, the cheeks he'd just caressed. They should look different, but they didn't. Only his eyes did, wide and glazed over.

Alias stared at his lips, which seemed to tingle. Deon's mouth caressed his body better than his own hands ever could . . . With a bitten-off moan, he pictured his legs spread wide, crying out in rapture while Deon plucked pleasure from his body. The man who yearned for such intimacy was him—the same man who stared back from the mirror.

Alias had changed. Was still changing. In his chest, he felt it. In his mind, he thought it. The change was growing over his bones, shaking loose the old skin of solitude. He'd changed so much in so little time he barely recognized himself some days. He didn't quite trust that new Alias just yet, but he could rely on Deon—a man with too much confidence and too many secrets.

Words his mother had told him years ago came back to him. *Change is dependable.*

Something was missing from the idiom, but he couldn't recall what it was, only that he used to ascribe a vastly different meaning to those three words. A flutter of anxiety cut through his self-reflection. The more he stared at his face, the more he felt keyed up, frantic. It was neither fear nor jealousy, but it evoked both. It took a moment to place it.

Longing. He *missed* Deon—even though Deon was one room away. They'd kissed minutes ago, but he felt cold already, his insides twisting into knots. What if this kiss had been their last?

Where was this coming from?

A door slammed shut at the back of his mind.

Heart pounding, Alias gripped Deon's pillow and buried his face into it. He couldn't stop thinking about that kiss being their last, about Deon vanishing from his life as easily as his scent was fading from the pillow. He had no idea why he felt so vulnerable, so untethered, but his heart refused to slow down. He tried to picture Deon's face, but the only thing he saw was that door, now bolted several times over. A giant weight in his mind that rattled.

Unless that was someone calling out his name? Yes, there were definitely words being said. Familiar words.

The voice was familiar too.

"... Alias? Alias, are you okay?"

He rolled over and blinked up. Deon's face was cast in shadows, his hair dark and dripping wet, brow furrowed in concern. Alias let go of the pillow and reached for any part of Deon he could touch. The naked thigh at his fingertips felt solid. Real.

Relief hit him like a ton of bricks. If he hadn't already been lying down, he would have collapsed.

"Alias."

"I'm— I'm fine," he said, voice a weak croak. "Just tired, I guess."

"What did we say about lying, uh?"

The bed dipped beside him. It took Deon wiping at his cheeks for Alias to realize he'd been crying. Whatever he was feeling seemed to pull at the very seams of his being, constricting his chest like a giant fist.

Deon's hand danced on his cheek, soft and undemanding. "Can I hold you?"

"You can," Alias said, the scratchiness in his voice hiding his surprise. If he didn't know better, he would have sworn that Deon felt . . . vulnerable.

"Thank you."

Deon guided Alias onto his side and settled at his back, slotting a thigh between his legs and throwing an arm across his hip. Alias stared at the wall until his eyes were dry once more.

I'm fine.

I'm fine.

I'm fine.

There is no immediate danger of any kind.

Deon's lips brushed his ear. "I just got a call . . . The men who attacked you? They're behind bars now. I told you I'd get them, and I have."

Alias whimpered softly, pain and relief mingled together. Deon held him tighter.

"You're safe here. You're always safe with me."

The remaining tension in Alias's body faded. "I know," he whispered, half-asleep.

It was the simple truth.

CHAPTER NINE
SHADES OF AFFECTION

D R. Lentz piled ginger cookies onto a plate like they were going out of fashion. Since it was late at night, they were the only other person in the lounge. Alias stared blearily at the coffee machine, trying to remember how it worked. After three tries—two more than usual—he got it started. Dr. Lentz crossed the room to get some tea, nodding at Alias in passing. Alias nodded back. For once, the head of Virology didn't have their lab coat on, but even the blue shirt with bright flowers didn't make a dent in their sullenness.

"Driving all of us into the ground," Dr. Lentz remarked gruffly, dropping four tea bags into their cup of hot water. "How's the head?"

Alias stiffened reflexively at the medical inquiry. "Head is fine," he said carefully after a moment.

Thankfully, that seemed to be the extent of Dr. Lentz's interest. Muttering about ridiculous deadlines and bot problems, they left the lounge, holding their mug of concentrated tea to their chest as though their one-time patient was about to steal it from them.

As Alias waited for the coffee to brew, he considered his own state of exhaustion. Work was becoming more and more demanding, it seemed. At least he didn't have a deadline to find a new apartment. Just three days ago, after sharing the news of his attackers' arrests, Deon had told him in no uncertain terms that his quarters were *theirs* for as long as Alias wanted, and Alias . . . didn't want to leave. Not yet.

He pressed the pad of a finger to the corner of his left eye. The bump was gone, and the skin hardly felt sensitive. As soon as he got a good night's sleep, he'd be able to visit his mother.

His watchphone beeped with an incoming call.

"Alias Novar speaking."

"I was pretty sure you'd still be up. You're almost as bad as he is."

The friendly concern in Mr. Quint's voice made him smile as he poured himself a cup of coffee. "Is he with you right now?"

"Yeah, but he's not the only one you'll want to see."

Alias didn't squeal in excitement, but it was a close thing. He rushed to the robotic department, coffee sloshing in his mug and optimism filling his veins despite the tiredness. LBV deaths were still on the rise, but LX was working, and more and more people were taking the injection. His mother missed him but was doing as well as could be expected. And now, Ben was back online. Mr. Quint must have been working overtime to have been able to bring Ben back so quickly.

Whatever life threw at him, Alias decided with his first sip of steaming hot coffee, he could handle it.

He stepped inside his favorite part of the Hive and made a beeline for the chief engineer's workstation. It was just as messy as always, except for the center of it, where a familiar torso and head were braced against a precariously tall pile of parts.

"Ben!"

The hubot twisted its head, following him with its wide blue eyes, but didn't reply. Alias set his coffee aside, delighted to see Ben awake, if not up and moving yet. He scanned the area, but Mr. Quint was nowhere to be seen. Instead, he found Deon, fast asleep in the chair usually claimed by Mr. Quint, head bent at an uncomfortable-looking angle.

Alias tiptoed toward Deon. An unnecessary precaution, considering the level of noise in this place. Did Deon need the ruckus to quieten his mind and fall asleep? Alias sank down to one knee and uncurled Deon's fingers from around his mug, spilling the dregs on the floor. Deon mumbled something incomprehensible, and his legs relaxed open as he slouched further into the chair. Alias smoothed Deon's furrowed brow and huffed in exasperation. How was it that Deon could tell him to rest, but Alias's own attempts to get him a few hours of shut-eye were met with iron resistance?

"Alias . . ."

Deon's voice was drowned in the local chaos, but Alias saw those sensual lips move and form his name. Warmth unfurled in his chest. He wanted to be able to take care of Deon, even more than he wanted to be cared for by him. Death lurked around every corner no matter what he did, and there was no defense against it, but he could do this much: take care of the people he held dear. Which he could do a lot better if he lived at the Hive.

If he'd been told that one month ago, he wouldn't have believed it.

"Here you are! I had to take a call, sorry about that."

"Mr. Quint, hi! It's—it's quite all right."

Alias stood so fast he almost tripped. His hand tingled where he'd touched Deon, and he shoved it into his pocket, heart hammering in his chest. Going by Mr. Quint's searching look, his attempt at casualness failed. After a small eternity, Mr. Quint's focus shifted to their employer. He shook his head, lips pinched in disapproval.

"I was awfully tempted to spike his coffee with a soporific, because he drinks that thing like water. He hadn't slept in more than thirty hours, you know."

Alias did know, and there was something in the engineer's tone suggesting that he knew Alias did. "So." With a concerned glance toward Deon, he changed the subject. "You made good progress on Ben?"

"That I did."

There was no small amount of pride in Mr. Quint's declaration. He encouraged Alias to come closer and showed him every part he'd fixed and all the small improvements he'd made. Alias had given him *carte blanche* because of his expertise and listened raptly, soaking in the knowledge this man offered freely. Mr. Quint's enthusiasm for this project was unmistakable and endearing.

"It still requires plenty of work, but it can see you." Amusement crept into Mr. Quint's voice. "Ah, and the left index finger doesn't twitch anymore. I've been working on its speech center too, and there are some strange bugs there that I've never seen."

Alias confessed that *this* must be his mistake, but Mr. Quint dismissed it, assuring him that Alias couldn't have inserted those glitches himself. Like always, Mr. Quint conveyed half of his explanations through wild gestures, and with his white hair tussled like he'd just laid a hand on a power outlet, he gave a strong "mad scientist" vibe.

"I don't know how I could possibly thank you, Mr. Quint . . ."

"Oh, I'm having fun."

"You're working long hours just like the rest of us," Alias pointed out. "It's not fair of me to add to your—"

"Are you going to tell me how to spend my spare time, then?" Mr. Quint's expression grew serious. "I'm lucky to have a nice project to relax with after a long day, and you're lucky to have me. How about that?"

"I guess . . . you have a point," Alias conceded with a smile. It was fantastic to see all the progress Mr. Quint had made with Ben, almost as nice as watching Deon getting rest. The urge to touch Deon was a physical ache.

"He cares a great deal about you, Alias," Mr. Quint said, startling him.

Alias had no idea what to reply to that, and his face heated up. The tingling from earlier returned to his hand, spreading to the rest of his arm lightning quick to end up wrapped around his heart. It was hard to breathe, and yet it didn't feel like a panic attack. He rubbed the back of his neck. "I c-care for him too."

Mr. Quint nodded once, flipped on his magnifying glasses, and selected the metal cutter hidden in his prosthetic hand. He often worked while they talked, but there was a tension in the air that hadn't been there before. When the cutter's fine point bit into a loose wire in Ben's mangled arm, Alias could swear it bore through his chest as well.

"I'm glad to hear this." Mr. Quint bent lower to scrutinize his work. For a man over sixty, he sure was flexible. "Mr. Dehive doesn't trust easily, with good reason, but he trusts you." Sparks flew at the tip of Mr. Quint's instrument. "Things might get rough, or rougher, should I say, but no matter what—you can't betray that trust."

Somehow, Alias felt more insulted now than he had last week when Ms. Angelius had talked with him about trust over glasses of mead. He more or less knew the role Ms. Angelius played in Deon's life and could understand, and accept, that her warning came from a good place. What was Mr. Quint's stake?

Watching the concern turn to sorrow in Mr. Quint's eyes, Alias changed his reply.

"I won't," he promised.

Mr. Quint flashed him a smile, and just like that, everything was right between them again. "You need help getting this stubborn fool into bed?"

Alias shook his head. "I can manage."

Deon didn't want to get up and made it known quite plainly by pushing himself deeper into the chair. Alias showed no mercy.

"You need to rest in an actual bed," he said, tugging on Deon's arm. "You're going to hurt your back like that."

"Already hurts," Deon mumbled, but he clasped Alias's hand.

He didn't release it on their walk back to their quarters. Alias felt a little self-conscious, and that was before Deon started nuzzling at his neck. Deon was practically draped over his side. It made it complicated to walk, but Alias didn't want him to move. Was Deon always so deliciously warm?

"You're so warm," Deon groaned, echoing his thought.

Pleasantly aroused and sleepy, Alias needed a solid two seconds to remember that the door in front of him wouldn't open on its own. He reached for the scanner. A sloppy kiss under his left ear startled a gasp out of him and caused his hand to slip. With a low chuckle, Deon picked it up and set it back on the glassy surface, long enough for the door to slide open. The screen panels making up the walls showed the woods, a few bright stars peeking out between tree branches.

Deon hummed in approval. "'S nice to have you here at night."

"I'm warm, I suppose."

"Among other things."

Deon's cock stiffened against his hip.

Alias chuckled. "You're going straight to bed," he said in his best authoritarian voice. "Passing out in the BotHouse hardly counts as proper rest."

Deon ruffled his hair and didn't argue, merely requesting that Alias do the same. They took off their shoes, and Alias hurried out of his clothes before helping out Deon. They tumbled into bed together. With a low groan, Deon wrapped himself around him, soft and hard in all the right places. Alias settled into that embrace with unbounded satisfaction. The tantalizing line of Deon's body, the steady beat of his heart . . . It felt like home, more so than his old apartment ever had.

How would it feel to live on his own again in a new place? What kind of place would make him feel safe? Alias decided to shelf such thoughts until he was certain that Deon could care for himself and Ben was fully functional again.

Deon went back to nuzzling his neck. "You're good for me, Alias . . ."

In the dark, Alias smiled to the stars. "We're good for each other."

In a matter of minutes, Deon was out cold. Alias didn't dare move, and not only because Deon was a light sleeper. He felt like he had earlier in the BotHouse. Tingling, except now the sensation extended to his entire body. A thought was nagging at him, the outlines of something rectangular emerging from his subconscious. A door. He'd sensed it before.

All the locks were gone now.

The door rattled violently before opening. An inch at most, but it was enough to send his heart into overdrive. With difficulty, he shifted his focus outward, to the woods on display. The very real woods.

As real as the incoming danger.

Closing his eyes didn't erase the accursed door. If he reached for it now, what would happen? Could he close it after peeking at the other side, or would such indulgence wipe out the door for good and force him to deal with whatever lay beyond?

He pressed a fist against his mouth and shivered, anxiety and excitation intertwined so intimately he couldn't tell where one ended and the other began. Deon shifted in his sleep, fingers digging into Alias's belly, holding him in place.

Sleep was long in coming.

The next day, Alias fully expected to fall asleep in front of his computer despite the caffeine, but he need not have worried: the worldwide increase in number of severe LBV cases, especially those where people died within days, kept him more alert than the coffee. There was no statement from McCarthy, which came as a surprise considering that the overwhelming majority of the new cases were people on Avida or on no antiviral at all.

As far as Alias was concerned, McCarthy's silence was a blessing in disguise. Deon was on his way to Mumbai, in over his head with work already. So was Alias. Doses of LX were finally being shipped overseas, and he spent quite a while making sure the three flight delays were only meteorological. He was preparing for a meeting with Ms. Angelius, wolfing down a slice of apple pie to calm his empty stomach, when his watchphone beeped.

The number on the screen was familiar, but not one he'd expected.

"Alias Novar speaking."

The hospital was probably calling to let him know the price of his mother's care had changed. Maybe she had to be moved into another room? At least credit wasn't an issue anymore.

"Mr. Novar," a gravelly voice asked, "is this a good time?"

"Y-yes." Alias dropped his fork and clutched the edge of the desk until his knuckles turned white. An actual person was talking to him, and it was always a bot that called. *No, no, no, please*—

"Your mother— It happened quite suddenly a few minutes ago," the man said, and his voice seemed to come from far, far away. ". . . into an LBV-typical coma . . . might come as a shock after how long she . . ."

Alias couldn't tell how that conversation had ended. He left his office in a daze. His left hand hurt something fierce, and it only occurred to him later, in the taxi he'd apparently called, that he must have knocked his coffee over.

Ms. Angelius picked up on the first ring.

"Family is the most important thing there is," she told him once he managed to string words together. "I'll hold the fort. Go see your mother, Alias."

The taxi dropped him in front of Mortella General. Alias headed for the entrance, surprised that his legs cooperated. The doors moved constantly: as soon as someone walked out, someone else came in. Patients, doctors, and visitors all wore the same stricken expression, as if every face was a copy of some primordial grief rendered over and over.

Alias didn't care about any of them and bumped into bots and people alike. Guilt clawed at him as he navigated the loud corridors reeking of disinfectant. How could he have thought there was enough time? How could he have let his dislike of hospitals and doctors stop him from visiting his mother more often? She'd always been a moment away from—

"Watch out!"

The harried-looking doctor he'd crashed into only failed to shove him out of the way because Alias was already moving past him. His watchphone buzzed with an incoming call, but he ignored it. Access to Wing D required a stricter screening, and Alias submitted himself to it with little grace. When he reached his destination, he was out of breath, despite not running. The door slid open with the faintest hiss, revealing a single bed and the still shape of Kira Novar.

She was hooked to a disquieting number of machines, at least two more than before. Alias stumbled forward. The room seemed to tilt on its axis. The ringing in his ears registered, but dimly, as if his body was being disconnected, taken apart to be rearranged in the stillness of this new space closer to death.

He sank down in the chair and wrung his hands together. He wanted nothing more than to reach out, but he didn't allow himself this. What comfort had he offered his mother in her last moments of consciousness? He hung his head, breathing shallowly through his mouth. He didn't believe in karma or faith, but he felt like he was being punished for not spending all of his free time at his mother's side. He knew, deep down, that he probably couldn't have done anything to prevent this, but he could have been there more often. Helping in the only way he could, rather than exploring new layers of happiness by himself.

How could he be so selfish as to fight his fear of the virus but not that of hospitals? He might have had a few bruises, but surely he could have found a way to conceal them?

He inched closer, eyes stinging with tears. His mother didn't look asleep. He'd watched her drift in and out of it for years, and he could tell she wasn't sleeping. Her face was gray, her features still. Intravenous fluids poured into her frail body through various entry points on her arms and hands, and more tubes disappeared under the blanket. She was *right here*, but she wasn't there at all.

Her left hand lay close, palm up, as though she'd been waiting for him.

Alias let out a sob and dug his nails into his palms, focusing on the pain. He'd refused to anticipate the worst—the only probable conclusion with the aggressive virus mutation. He'd held on to the miracle that was his mother's stable condition. But even miracles could be used up.

There were other people like his mother, sick people who'd somehow survived a long time with the virus reactivated in their system.

But in the end, they all died.

"I'm s-so sorry, Mother."

Alias squeezed his eyes shut, trying to trap the tears that kept falling. This wasn't about him.

He remained like that for some time, shoulders hunched and hands trapped between his thighs. The room darkened as the sun set. At some point, his neck began to hurt, but he didn't move. He would remain here, by his mother's side, until she didn't need him anymore. *This* was his end of the world. Not the world going mad. Not the virus killing him.

Unbidden, memories of himself as a child surfaced. Bits and pieces. The shape and texture of snowballs in his smaller hands. The scent of flowers in the hollow of his mother's throat. The taste of gingerbread cookies in the fall, a special treat that his mother baked in memory of her own mother.

His mother had loved the outside. Whenever she could, she'd taken her computer out on the balcony and worked there. They'd taken long walks together. An abandoned park two blocks away eventually became one of his favorite spots. Only one of the swings worked, and his mother laughed while she pushed him up and into the air, higher and higher until he, too, would laugh with unbridled joy, sure that he could reach the sky with his toes.

"Love can be a good thing," she'd told him.

"Then why has Father left?"

He'd been seven, at the time. Or maybe eight. His mother had answered him seriously. She'd never shied away from a difficult question, and Alias had been full of them.

"He thought it was the best thing to do. For us. For him. It hurt him too. But I can tell you this: I never regretted meeting him. The link we had together, I will cherish it all my life."

"Even if it hurt?"

"Even then."

Alias couldn't squeeze any comfort from those memories, not when he'd failed her by spending so much time with Deon instead of her. She'd teased him a lot about what she'd called his "crush," encouraging him to explore this avenue of happiness, and he had . . .

And now she was fading away, like the doctors kept predicting she would.

Looking at his mother's relaxed features, he thought of her staying like this, unaware of the world, until the virus sank its claws so deep her lungs gave out.

What was the point of being able to afford the best symptom-alleviating medications if there was no treatment? What was the point of doing this job if he couldn't help her?

What was the point of anything?

"Alias Novar?"

Alias offered no reply. The monotone, genderless voice of the hubot spoke again, slightly louder.

"You need to take that call."

The door closed, and the room was plunged into darkness once more. Alias blinked owlishly. What call?

His watchphone lit up with an incoming call.

Ah. That call.

Alias shifted in his chair, and untucked one hand from under his thighs, flexing his fingers one by one. His skin tingled with the return of blood circulation. He reached for his earpiece, surprised to find it in place.

"Alias Novar speaking," he said in a scratchy voice.

"Hey."

Deon. There were voices in the background, an agitated mishmash of syllables Alias couldn't understand. It was probably Marathi or Hindi, but given his current state of mind, it might very well have been English.

"Everything okay?" That seemed like the thing he was expected to say.

"I should be the one asking that."

"My mother . . ." Alias did what he'd wanted to do since he'd stepped into the room: held his mother's hand. "She's in a coma."

Someone was clearly trying to get Deon's attention in the background, but the CEO ignored them. "I'm very sorry, Alias."

Alias didn't know what to say to that. He supposed he should ask about the negotiations. India played an important role on the international board, and should their president agree to a bulk importation of LX, other countries might follow their example. People that would otherwise become sick because of the flawed protection Avida offered would be safer thanks to the injection.

But none of those people were his mother, whom no antivirals could help, and right now, Alias just didn't care about anything else. If the Earth was swallowed in a giant black hole in the next minute, he wouldn't blink. This level of detachment was new. He liked the numbness.

"Alias? You still there?"

The words weren't harsh or loud, but they pierced Alias's bubble of feigned indifference with devastating efficiency. Alias broke into tears—and not quietly either. He ached for Deon's presence at his side, for Deon's hand in the one still trapped under his thigh, and he knew he was an egoist, but the more he tried to shake that need, the harder he cried.

"Sweetheart." Deon sounded wrecked. "I'm sorry I can't be there."

"N-not your f-fault." Alias hiccupped. Shoulders hunched, he inched the chair closer to the bed. "I can't lose her."

"I know."

"She's the only one I have."

"I know," Deon said again.

The comfort embedded in the words felt automatic, like a hubot's touch. Alias's throat closed as the silence grew heavy, uncomfortable.

"I have to go. I'm sorry."

The call ended before Alias could think of anything else to say.

At first, he thought he wouldn't be able to sleep, but he passed out in the rigid chair late that night. When he woke up, his first impression was one of deep physical discomfort, and it became worse as he took in the still form of his mother. His stomach rumbled, but food was out of the question. As he stared outside at the lightening sky, he decided he could stomach coffee.

"I won't be long," he whispered out of habit, and bit back a sob.

The first machine he found didn't work, but another one a few corridors over provided coffee with minimal mechanical noises of protest. The scalding liquid burned his tongue on the first sip, so he barely tasted it after that, which was probably for the best. Someone in a hurry elbowed him, and Alias was tempted to throw the disgusting coffee at him. Instead, he kept close to the walls, away from all the patients snapping at their doctors and the doctors snapping at their patients. His heart clenched as he spotted a boy, no more than five, being rushed toward Wing B. His little face was streaked with tears. The doctor escorting him looked almost as distraught as the mother.

Back in the silent room, Alias set the coffee aside. The urge to start pacing was so obviously something he'd picked from Deon that he refused to indulge in it. He sank back in the chair . . . and waited.

It was the middle of the afternoon when he dared to climb into the bed. He did so slowly, overly cautious, terrified that a wrong move might disrupt the network of tubes keeping his mother breathing.

"Mother."

The affectionate word came out as an apology.

"I'm sorry I wasn't here when you needed me." He arranged the sheets around her shoulders, aware that warmth wouldn't pull her from the coma but unable to help himself. Looking at her pale face hurt, but not looking hurt more. He brushed a strand of blond hair away from her cheek. "I should have been there. I'm sorry."

If she were awake, she would ask why he apologized.

"Because I've been . . . distracted." That was one word for it. "By someone who . . . But never mind that. I should have come more often to see you."

As observant as she was, she might remark on the lingering color around his left eye.

"Don't worry about me," he said, throat tight. "I certainly don't." He had to remind himself not to grip her hand too tight. Frustration bubbled up—toward himself, toward the virus, toward McCarthy, toward the whole universe. The last time he'd felt this way, Ben had been thrown over the railing of the fire exit at his old apartment building. "I'm so sorry I haven't . . ."

He trailed off, examining his mother's face. For a second there, he thought he'd heard a sigh, but that had to be wishful thinking. The ECG still read the same, and the multiple machines surrounding the bed remained quiet. Alias heaved a sigh and stretched into a sitting position, still holding his mother's hand. His back hurt. Everything hurt. It was fitting and strangely satisfying.

"Do you remember when—"

Another faint noise reached his ears. He went completely still. The lack of restful sleep must have been playing tricks on him. What else could it be? Patients in an LBV coma didn't usually wake up—there were only a dozen documented cases of such miracles, and all a decade old, at least. Holding his breath wouldn't bring his mother back.

It was only because he was watching her so closely that he saw her eyelashes flutter.

"Mother?" Disbelief—and raw hope—filled his voice.

Another flutter. Alias didn't bare blink. He waited, tightening his grip on his mother's hand . . . and against all odds, those delicate eyelashes parted again, enough to reveal brown eyes.

"Mother!"

The doctor took longer than Alias would have liked, but when the man in a white lab coat hurried into the room with two hubots trailing after him, Alias wisely kept his mouth shut and left him room to work. His smile was so wide it hurt. When more doctors came in—four more, which had to be a statistical record—Alias just stepped further into the shadows, for once not distrustful but merely concerned that he would stand in their way. The crowd made it difficult to see his mother, but the doctors' excited voices kept him in the loop.

"Yes, slowly."

"You noted that already? We can't afford to—"

"I'm going to ring my contact at WHO as soon as we're done with her to let them know we've got another case they'll want to check."

"If only we actually knew why these terminal patients wake up again, it might be key to—"

"Hey, you, bring her some water, will you?"

The last question wasn't addressed to Alias, but space appeared near his mother's bed, so Alias hurried to fill it. A hubot offered a glass of water to the doctor who'd made the request, but Alias grabbed it first.

"You shouldn't be in the room right now," the doctor said.

"If I help her drink, that means you can do your actual job," Alias snapped back, his dislike for doctors returning with a vengeance.

He didn't lose his smile, but only because his mother was looking up at him. When she lifted one hand, he directed it to the glass and held it there before bringing the straw to her lips.

"Drink, Mother. You must be parched."

He tuned out the excited chatter until he heard his full name.

"Your mother can't have visitors right now," said the only doctor left in the room. "I'll give you two more minutes with her, and then you have to leave. She needs to rest."

His mother tried to speak. Alias pulled the straw away from her face before it could poke her in the eye.

"Don't overexert yourself, Mother." How was he still crying? He didn't think he had any more tears in him.

"A . . . lias."

"I'm right here."

With as delicate a touch as possible, he ran a hand through her lackluster blond hair, picturing the golden ringlets from his childhood. Back then, she'd looked a lot like Lady Love. Once upon a time, he'd even believed that she *was* the woman the tall statue was modeled after.

"I'm so happy you're back; I don't know how I would . . ." His vision was so blurry he couldn't make out his mother's face anymore, but her hand on his arm was proof that he hadn't dreamed her recovery. "I love you, Mother."

No sooner were the words out of his mouth than he was ushered out of the room without ceremony. He didn't argue. Relief gave him wings. All those strangers he'd dismissed this morning, he wanted to hug them now. Promise everyone that it would be okay. Miracles still happened.

And there were people out there who actively performed them.

He dialed Deon's number, but there was no answer.

Once he left his mother's room, Alias couldn't get in again. She needed rest, the doctors said, but Alias knew how to read between the lines: they were going to do even more tests to try to solve the mystery that was her resistance to the virus. As much as he wanted to put up a fight out of concern for her, Alias didn't—such research was paramount. Maybe, just maybe, more testing would yield answers for the scientific community, explain why some people died within days of a viral reactivation, whereas a handful lived on for years.

Back at the Hive, Alias tried to reach Deon again, only to get his voice mail once more. He refused to let his twinge of concern dampen the optimism sparked by his mother's unexpected awakening—but he did snap at a few callers.

"No, you can't talk to Mr. Dehive right now."

"Is there something unclear about the word 'no?'"

"How about you call back never?"

He had blanket permission to scare McCarthy's people away, and since he wasn't quite there yet, he contented with sarcasm. A few hours into the game, wolfing down his first meal in much too long, it dawned on him that giving a piece of his mind to the doctor back at Mortella might have unlocked a side of him previously unbeknownst to himself. No call could burst his bubble of newfound confidence, no matter how important or quarrelsome the caller was.

Ms. Angelius was in charge, tackling urgent meetings and interviews in the CEO's stead, keeping Alias in the loop just as much as Alias kept her posted. She was overjoyed to learn about his mother's recovery and approved of him hiring a security detail to keep journalists out of her room. A few reporters had called the Hive already, having discovered the connection between Mortella's special patient and Deon Dehive's PA.

Ms. Angelius laughed when Alias confessed to hanging up on a fair number of those.

"I would do exactly the same in your place," she told him. "Did you get any calls worth mentioning?"

Alias's mind went to the one he was still waiting for, but he wouldn't get distracted by Deon's lack of reply. "A couple," he replied after a moment. "Which is more than . . ." He frowned at the pop up on his screen. "There's something else I'd like to address first."

The logistics algorithm he'd refined was alerting him to a discrepancy in production numbers for the LX injection, and it took two calls to Mr. Arvin and several more to the firm Dehive had hired to distribute LX overseas to clear up one big misunderstanding and verify that McCarthy wasn't involved in any way. Alias spearheaded the inquiry; these days, Ms. Angelius wasn't tugging the strings, but rather trusted him to pull. Alias appreciated that shift in their dynamic. He was still no expert, but he was beginning to fill her shoes. He was becoming an agent of change, half a wasp, half a bee, and that gave him some much-needed buoyancy.

The first dent to his confidence came when Deon remained unreachable past his second day in India. By then, half of the people calling Dehive's offices wanted to discuss Kira Novar, and more than one nosy journalist posited a correlation between her waking up from a coma and her son's employment with the creator of LX.

"LX doesn't help people who've already undergone viral reactivation," he hissed for what had to be the hundredth time.

"So what you're saying, Mr. Novar, is that the LX injection isn't derived from your mother's—"

Alias hung up and rubbed at his eyes with a weary sigh. The only upside of his mother getting too much media coverage was that McCarthy's slander was fading into background noise.

He tried not to let Deon's silence faze him. The man was even busier than he was, and Alias would know: he'd dedicated one of his screens to Deon's public appearances in India. In the forty hours since he'd landed in Mumbai, the CEO had given five public press conferences. Alias had watched each of them twice. Deon looked so confident, despite the size of the crowds—or perhaps *because* of it, since it was Deon.

Alias had a different reaction. Despite his best attempts, he couldn't stop thinking about how the massive protest in Texas had ended in a bloodbath not too long ago.

Deon didn't share his concerns. When Alias had tackled the subject before the trip, Deon had insisted that his presence among the people would make a difference. He refused to hide behind a screen or in a locked room because crowds were unpredictable.

Alias had seen first-hand how unpredictable crowds could get.

Ms. Angelius—or Jaden, as she'd insisted he call her—barged into his office around eleven on Friday night to drag him from his desk. Alias mumbled something about not being done, but it was a token protest. Coffee could only power him through so many hours before his body crashed, no matter how many times he tried to prove himself wrong. Case in point: his accidental nap on the keyboard yesterday. Or was it last night? He'd tuned into Mumbai time and couldn't tell anymore.

Jaden shut down his workstation herself and gave him a critical once-over.

"You're just like him," she huffed.

For all that she meant the words as a critique, Alias preened. "Well, thank you, Ms. Angelius . . . I mean, Jaden."

"Well, you shouldn't."

Alias stifled a yawn. "Call you Jaden?"

"You're getting cheeky, hanging up on so many people. Now out with you. I don't want to see you back in that office before eight in the morning . . . local time."

Jaden escorted him out of the office and gave him a pointed look before heading for her own quarters.

After a quick shower and an even more expedient meal, Alias tried to talk to his mother, to no avail. The call to the security detail reassured him to some extent: his mother had been awake part of the day, and the few journalists who'd tried to impersonate doctors had been stopped at the door. The actual doctors weren't happy about being screened every time they visited their patient's room, but since the hospital director was backing Alias's decision to hire bodyguards, there was nothing they could do about it.

And there was nothing Alias could do about Deon's silence. While scrolling news updates on his tablet, he reached Deon's voice mail for the third time that day. Should he leave a message this time? He decided against it—Deon had far better things to do than reassure him.

When his watchphone lit up with a notification a few minutes later, he almost dropped the tablet.

The message was from Mr. Quint.

Don't show up right now, but I'm getting some more work done on your pal.

Alias's excitement turned sour. The first half of the message made it clear that Mr. Quint had talked to Jaden.

I really appreciate it, he replied, because he was polite, and he really missed Ben. Missing Ben wasn't familiar, but it was easy. Missing his mother was familiar, but harder. Missing Deon . . . It was with a heavy heart that he climbed into bed with his tablet and a glass of mead. It wasn't as practical to work from here, and his vision was getting blurry, but Jaden had given him no choice but to bring the office home.

Home. Was that really how he saw Deon's living quarters?

What happened to this arrangement being *temporary?*

Alias rubbed his knuckles over the tension in his chest and checked his favorite news channel to distract himself. The first video he watched was brief, and the sight of a mother in tears clutching the still body of her daughter to her chest was all the more heart-wrenching for it.

"And this is yet another alarming case of fast-acting LBV reactivation in children," a man's voice announced as the grieving woman fighting the doctors and hubots was replaced by a graph. "Children under the age of ten are once again vulnerable to the Loveborne virus, and members of the scientific community have hypothesized that Avida may still be the best—"

Alias swiped his thumb over the grim figures with a scowl, silencing more evidence of McCarthy's scheming. Both Dr. Lentz and Deon had been clear on this: LX offered as good of a protection to children as it did to adults. The whole world should know that. But manipulating the public's opinion was easier when children were involved, and McCarthy showed no qualm in using this to her advantage, advertising the death of every child who happened to be on LX even if they didn't die of LBV.

The NID's inherent paranoia about antivirals that weren't Avida didn't help matters.

Alias knocked back his glass, relishing the burn of alcohol. The sad truth was that children died every day—on antivirals or not, because of LBV or not. McCarthy claimed causality when there was only correlation, and that didn't sit right with Alias.

But what could he do about it, except offer the correct information to as many people as possible?

The next video was of amateur quality. At first, Alias couldn't make heads or tails of what he was seeing. Everything moved too fast, the people blurry shapes highlighted by flying bots, the voices a mess of screams and shouts.

It was a mob. A protest. The local authorities closed in on the participants. The decibel level crept up. Comments flooded the space under the video at increasing speed, each translated from Hindi, Marathi, and Gujarati into English in a matter of seconds.

Alias set his empty glass aside and gripped the tablet with both hands, trying to reason with himself. This protest could be happening anywhere in India. It didn't even have to be about LBV. He was jumping to conclusions.

His hope turned to dust as more and more videos of the same event were uploaded, from different standpoints. A few of them were of excellent quality, and a familiar figure emerged, the blond hair easy to spot amidst the dark-headed majority. Unlike the eye of a storm, there was nothing calm about the heart of this fight. People pushed each other. Fists flew.

And there was nothing gentle about the way Deon went down, elbowed in the face and punched in the side. Protesters gathered around him, kicking him where he lay.

The tablet fell from Alias's numb fingers. The timestamp on the bottom right corner of the video couldn't lie. Two hours and sixteen minutes ago, Deon had been trampled by a crowd.

Why was Alias only learning of this now? Was India putting a lid over the whole thing, was . . .

Was Deon dead?

He dialed Deon's phone, not really expecting an answer, but his stomach sank nonetheless when no one picked up. He scrambled out of bed to get dressed, going through a mental list of people to call.

It took a dozen attempts and three different numbers before he reached someone from the group that had been accompanying Deon on the trip.

"Arvin speaking," said Dr. Lentz's assistant in the tone of voice that implied he almost hadn't picked up.

Alias flung his empty glass, and it shattered against a wall. He took a few seconds to find his words. "This is Alias Novar. *What the hell is going on?*"

He'd never screamed on the phone before, but he certainly did now, demanding answers and reassurances. Mr. Arvin had little good news to share. Apparently Deon had been admitted to a local hospital, but he'd insisted on leaving quickly, drugged to the eyes. He'd since been given more painkillers and was asleep on the jet.

"He really doesn't look good," Mr. Arvin concluded, showing his first hint of concern.

After a quick call to Dr. Lentz, who agreed with reluctance to check on the CEO upon his return, Alias staggered to the pond and leaned over it. His stomach churned from the rush of adrenaline, and he struggled to suck in air. He plunged both hands into the pond and splashed his face, watching his wobbly reflection shatter. The fish scurried away.

"Alias!"

Alias swirled and found Jaden standing in the doorway. He didn't need to see the display of her tablet to know why she'd come—the look in her eyes said it all.

She hurried into the room, the tablet clutched to her hip. "You've seen the video, haven't you?"

Alias gave a slow nod.

"He's going to be okay."

She said the words with such conviction that Alias almost believed her. She walked up to him and held on to his shivering frame as though she gathered strength from him and not the other way around. Alias's throat tightened around a sob.

"He has to be," he whispered, and then said it again, and again, the prayer muffled in the high collar of Jaden's black velvet jacket.

Jaden's only answer was to pull him more tightly into her arms.

They waited in the hangar.

Alias couldn't remember when he'd last slept or ate. He felt sick, the nausea made worse by a throbbing headache that no pills seemed able to tame. If he'd thought his first day of work had been hard, he'd been wrong. This was what hell truly was: the constant back and forth between hope and disappointment whenever his watchphone flashed with a new call, the burning sensation in his chest, the certainty that time had slowed down. Journalists had apparently gotten hold of his private number, because every voice in his ear was an inquiry about his mother's recovery. His lip was bleeding from biting it so much, trying to stop himself from screaming. After a while, the sting didn't register. He stopped taking calls.

He couldn't focus on anything else for long, so he didn't even try. Whenever a hubot came by, he extended his mug and drank the scalding coffee like it was water and he'd been parched. Jaden drank her fair share of it as well. She was constantly on the phone, switching back and forth between English and broken Marathi as she tried to get a complete picture of what had happened. The reason behind her brief, periodic absences was anyone's guess. Alias felt no curiosity whatsoever, but he did notice she grew more haggard and frantic whenever she returned. He began to consider time in relation to her reappearances.

Forty-four minutes since she'd last left. Twenty-three minutes since she'd been gone.

His shirt's buttons were misaligned, and he left it alone. Jaden hadn't bothered changing clothes. Her blue pencil skirt and matching sleeveless blouse remained creased, no matter how often she smoothed the fabric down. Alias had never witnessed her in such a state. He would have remembered seeing her hands shake.

He paced to disguise his own fretfulness. Mr. Quint popped in at regular intervals. They didn't exchange words, but Alias got his shoulder squeezed once.

Jaden came to stand at his side sixteen minutes after her latest return. A strand of hair had gotten loose from her otherwise perfect ponytail.

"I'm so worried for him. And angry at *them*."

Alias agreed silently. He knew exactly who she was angry at: Deon's team for the trip, who should have called as soon as the incident had happened, or at least when Deon had discharged himself from the hospital.

And at himself as well.

"I should have gone with him," he said at last, voice small yet brimming with self-recrimination. "This whole trip was my idea."

"You're not to blame for other people's stupidity," Jaden replied quickly. "And this trip was a good idea, as was you staying here."

Why didn't you go with him? He bit back the words just in time. What would be the point? One more person at Deon's side wouldn't have made a difference.

"He's going to be fine," Jaden whispered. "He is. He walked out of that hospital on his own, which is encouraging. And Dr. Lentz will take over from here."

She sniffed and squared her shoulders, looking straight ahead at the wide, tall doors, still closed. Twenty minutes since her last return, an annoying voice noted at the back of Alias's mind. If he hadn't been holding on to the mug for dear life, he might have been tempted to give her hand a squeeze.

The clanking of the locks retreating startled him so badly he dropped his mug. He paid the shattered porcelain no mind and stepped forward, his trepidation and irritation washed away by relief. Here it came at last: the sleek black jet with Dehive's logo stamped on its side. By the time it came to a full stop and the engines went silent, Alias was surprised his pacing hadn't scraped away the concrete. The side door of the jet rose, and why, *why* was it so slow when every door in the Hive moved so fast?

The sharp pain in his left hand grounded him. It seemed as though he'd gone for Jaden's hand after all—and she was crushing his. He relaxed his grip. Sometime over the last three days, she'd become one of very few people whose touch he welcomed.

He returned his attention where it belonged and found blue eyes already on him.

"Deon!"

He let go of Jaden's hand and ran, heart pounding. A hundred feet separated them, but it seemed like miles—an imaginary distance that, despite his weariness, he covered in record time.

"Hey," Deon said.

His voice sounded hoarse, but he was here, real, tangible. Alias wanted nothing more than to fling himself into Deon's arms, but he held back.

Deon held himself like a man twice his age, stiff and obviously in pain. His face was a mess: purple and red predominated, darker around his mouth and eyes. A white bandage showed from under his hairline and another covered a wide patch of skin at his throat. Bruises littered the skin around the collar of his shirt, and there were more on his wrists, peeking from the sleeves.

Given what that video had shown, Alias couldn't believe Deon was standing.

"Hey," Alias croaked back. His lip had started bleeding again, and he wiped it clean. "Are you—" *okay?* A stupid question, no doubt. He started over. "Do you— Do you need to sit down? Should you even be walking? What can I do? Dr. Lentz has been notified, they . . ."

Deon didn't look at him, or even nod, and that degree of distraction gave Alias pause. When he glanced over Alias's shoulder and appeared relieved by what he saw—or by whom— Alias's heart sank. He told himself it didn't matter and brushed Deon's hand to seek comfort and offer his own.

"You're back," he murmured, as if Deon were a dream that too loud a noise, or too strong a pressure, might banish. His relief was too big to be contained, too powerful to be conveyed by words alone. He wrapped his arms around Deon's tense shoulders instead, slow and careful, needy and trying not to be. "You're back," he said again, the words laced with amazement rather than disbelief.

Deon said his name, a whisper lost in the rapid-fire conversations of his colleagues gathering around them. Blinking away tears, Alias pressed his nose against Deon's throat, breathing in the smell of harsh chemicals, coffee, and sweat, and beneath it all, the unique scent that still lingered in their bed. The warm breath against his cheek tugged at his heartstrings. When a tentative hand found the small of his back at last, he shook with the restraint it took not to cling.

"Thanks for holding the fort." Deon's hand drifted to Alias's hip and gave a gentle push. "You've done great. I needed you here taking care of things."

With some reluctance, and a fair amount of guilt, Alias pulled back. "I should—"

"Mr. Dehive, we need to reconvene and discuss the recent events further." He'd been interrupted by the WHO representative at Deon's elbow. Her white outfit was as strict in cut as her expression. "If we can—"

"Excuse you," Alias cut her off in turn, and didn't falter as nine pairs of eyes zeroed in on him. "Whatever you want will have to wait," he added, infusing his voice with all the authority he could muster, which was a lot more than usual. "Mr. Dehive needs a doctor."

"Mr. Novar—"

"Work can wait. What Dehive needs right now is for the CEO to get what he needs, and I'm here to ensure precisely that." Alias jerked his chin toward the exit and glanced at Deon. "Can you walk, or do you need help?"

They exited the hangar to the sound of complaints, but no one tried to stop them, perhaps because Alias held Deon's suitcase like a weapon.

"When did you wake up?" he asked as soon as they were out of earshot.

"The painkillers they gave me at the hospital only knocked me out for a few hours . . . It's really not as dramatic as the news painted it," Deon said after getting a good look at Alias's expression. "I'm not going to collapse, Alias."

"Then—"

"Stop worrying so much, will you? I'm fine," Deon told him, but it sounded automatic, halfway between a truth and a lie.

"Why wasn't I told . . ." Nostrils flaring, Alias bit his lip and didn't even wince at the sting. The weight of Deon's hand pulling at the crook of his elbow called attention to their pace. He slowed down. "Your team—"

"Alias." Deon came to a stop. He cupped Alias's cheek and lingered there, despite the obvious strain on his shoulder. "We will talk later, I promise. And I swear I'm going to rest soon, but there's some— something I have to do."

Without me? Alias shook his head. "Beside going to see Dr. Lentz, you mean?"

"Yes."

"Is there anything I can do to help?"

Deon's tormented expression closed off entirely. "Not with this, no. You look dead on your feet, sweetheart. Go to bed. Please. For me."

"You need to—"

"I promise I'll go down to see Lentz within the hour."

Alias stared at Deon's figure getting smaller and smaller in the dimly lit corridor, pressing one hand to his cheek in a pathetic attempt to trap the warmth from Deon's hand there. And then it was just him, alone with his questions, overwhelmed by worry and relief, anger and sadness, and something stronger and all-encompassing, something that made him dizzier the longer he focused on it.

He walked the rest of the way to their quarters, dragging the suitcase that seemed a lot heavier now. The door opened at the press of his palm. He dropped the suitcase and toed off his shoes with a huff of disbelief. Why all the secrecy? He could already come and go in the Hive's most private areas as he pleased and had unlimited access to Deon's private rooms. They shared a bed. He even knew where Deon kept his personal safe. What else was there?

It hurt that Jaden probably knew.

Alias leaned against the marble basin of the pond and sank to the ground with a heavy heart and a groan. The headache was fading, and yet he could swear that the pain was spreading, diluted, to the rest of his body, bruising his limbs from the inside out. On the display panels surrounding him, the sea barely moved. Night hadn't quite fallen there, and Alias tracked an odd crab peeking around the smooth trunks of palm trees. The distraction worked for a while, until the scenery brought back the memory of that video. He pictured Deon walking away from the sea, gaze heated . . . except that the water glistening on his chest was blood. Suddenly, all Alias could see was Deon curled up into a ball as the crowd unleashed its wrath on this too-confident man.

Alias hugged his knees to his chest and tossed his head back. It thudded against the marble, but he was too tired to acknowledge the pain. His right cheek still felt warmer than the left, and he covered it with his palm again, focusing on the fact that Deon was back at the Hive—if unattainable for now.

He meant to wait for him, but he must have fallen asleep, because hushed voices roused him.

". . . not yet. But I'm thinking about it."

"Be careful, okay? I know you . . ."

The first voice was Deon's, and the second was just as easy to identify as Jaden. Alias woke fully and straightened, shoulders and back protesting the brusque shift from a slouching position. Deon stood not ten feet away, his back to Alias. Alias's attention shifted to the figure near the bed: Jaden. His head pounded, but he managed to get to his feet with exaggerated care, bracing himself against the edge of the marble basin. He peered down at the pond and focused on keeping his balance. Everything spun, as though he'd just downed the bottle of mead on the nightstand.

"Okay," Deon said. "I will."

"Sleep, Deon."

Jaden left. At least, Alias assumed she did, because her heels clicked as she retreated. Alias dipped his pointer into the water and watched as one fish gave it a cautious lick.

Deon's face appeared in the water.

"Alias, why are you crying?"

They stood so close that their reflections almost merged as the fish swam away in a hasty flick of tail. Alias withdrew his finger from the water and wiped both cheeks with the back of his hand. Deon remained still, watching Alias with the kind of focus he hadn't shown earlier. The dual lighting from the ceiling and the sunset on the replicated beach spelled out his wounds in achingly clear detail. Every bruise and cut on his face. His throat hadn't been spared. Alias stared at the dark blue tie at Deon's neck.

In a moment of madness, he wanted to strangle Deon with it.

"Would you like to hear what Lentz had to say?" Deon asked in a strangely sheepish voice.

Alias shoved both hands into his pockets and nodded, listening with growing dismay as Deon listed his wounds: three bruised ribs, multiple flesh wounds, a sprained ankle, and a bloody knife wound on the right side, an inch below the last floating rib.

"Nothing life-threatening," Deon concluded with a small smile.

Alias sank to his knees.

"Hey, what are you— Oh."

Alias's fingers shook, but he wanted to do this, so he did, jerking at the tight knots of Deon's shoes. A warm hand came to rest on his shoulder. His eyes burned with more tears.

"I'm okay, Alias."

"The hell you are!"

Alias didn't shout, but it was a close thing. He pulled too hard at the laces, and Deon stumbled. An apology rushed to the tip of his tongue and remained there, unsaid. Alias kept his face down as he eased Deon's feet out of his shoes. His skin buzzed where Deon was touching him, holding on to his shoulders for balance.

"Alias."

He set the shoes to the side and spent several seconds making sure they were parallel to each other. Above him, Deon sighed and pulled back.

"Have you been able to visit your mother? I heard she woke up, and I'm so very glad for you."

If Deon thought this would calm him down, he had another think coming. Alias shot to his feet, hands itching to do something about that creased tie, about this maddening situation, but there had been genuine concern and amazement in Deon's voice. The fight fled from Alias.

"I tried to see her, but they wouldn't let me, and . . ."

I was worried sick about you.

The words floated there in the silence.

"I'm sorry to hear this," Deon said, sounding pained. "If there's anything I can do . . ."

Alias blinked. Actually yes, there was something Deon could do. He cleared his throat. "Do you think Dr. Lentz could take over my mother's case? I know that they're not very keen on medicine these days and it would be favoritism, but they used to work at Mortella as an LBV specialist, didn't they? And as much as I don't like doctors, I trust them more than most."

Deon frowned. "I'm not sure—"

"This is research, and isn't that what Lentz and Arvin and the rest of your team in the Lab are doing? Other doctors and scientists have tried for more than a decade to find something helpful in my mother's blood and immune system, even in her genetic code, but maybe Dr. Lentz would see something that others didn't? She would stay at Mortella, obviously, but . . . why are you looking at me like that?"

"Like I'm annoyed?" Deon shook his head and winced. "Because I should have thought of this myself. It *is* a good idea, and I'm sure Lentz will agree, precisely because of the research aspect. The technology they've been working on could come in handy. There will certainly be some minor issues considering the relationship between all parties involved, but Dehive can handle it." He cocked his head to the side. "I have to admit I was shocked not to hear the news of your mother waking up from you."

Alias frowned. "I did call you. Several times."

Deon frowned at him. Alias glared at the bruise on the soft patch of skin between Deon's left thumb and forefinger.

"There must be some issue with my phone," Deon mumbled, the annoyance creeping back into his voice. He fumbled with the creased fabric of his tie. "I'm sorry I wasn't here for you. I'll have my phone checked out imm—"

"As soon as you've rested," Alias cut in, voice firm. "And this isn't a suggestion. As for you not being here . . ." He floundered and allowed himself to enter Deon's space and brush a thumb across his cheek, skirting around the ugly violet bump on his cheekbone. There were so many bruises, so many tangible proofs that Deon was in dire need of someone to care for him.

Someone like Alias.

"I understand you were busy and halfway across the world," he continued, voice trembling. "I do. I really do. But you almost got yourself killed mingling with an aggressive crowd against my advice, and I couldn't reach you; no one on the team that accompanied you could be bothered to— *Fuck*, Deon!" The room was spinning again. He could feel the soft silk of Deon's tie in his grip. Was that why Deon was speechless? Or could it be the screaming?

"At first, I thought you were dead," he confessed in a half whisper. "When I saw the video—" His voice cracked. He patted the silky tie. "I couldn't bear the thought of you never coming back. I'm the one who suggested you should—"

"Alias."

"It was my fault you were there in the first pla—"

"*Alias.*"

The steel in Deon's voice stopped Alias mid-word. He caught the hand splayed on his chest and squeezed it, gaze softening. "You don't get to take so much credit for my own decisions or anyone's else. You're doing such a good job helping me out. I did call you as well, and I did find it odd that I could never reach you or Jaden, as you both answer your phone with such alacrity.

There really must be something wrong with my watchphone." The grip he had on Alias's hand relaxed and morphed into a caress. "I wanted to tell you earlier, but better late than never: I secured the deal with India. Thank you for your wonderful idea."

When Alias yanked at the tie this time, he wasn't following any violent fantasy. Deon's lips parted on a soft groan.

"Alias," he said, and the steel in his voice melted down, the firm grip around his tie reshaping the order into a plea.

Alias breathed the next words against Deon's mouth. "I'm sorry I screamed at you."

Deon's tongue peeked out from between his chapped lips. "I'm sorry I worried you so much."

"Just don't let it happen again." Alias tugged at the tie, drinking in Deon's eager expression, drowning in it. "The next time you put yourself on the line like this, I'm coming with you. I don't care if my staying at the Hive is more practical, I will not—"

"Yes," Deon panted, pupils blown wide. "Anything you want."

Alias caught Deon's mouth in a wild, ravenous kiss. One of his hands found purchase in blond hair, not to pull, just to touch and soak in the warmth beneath. The other caressed Deon through his shirt, a little too fast to be gentle, but Deon didn't protest, only kissed him back with alluring fierceness. Alias swallowed his moans eagerly, relishing the bruising force of Deon's grip on his shoulders. He stumbled back, and Deon followed. For the first time in more than seventy-two hours, Alias felt whole again, as though his senses had been decaying without Deon and were only now re-establishing his connection to the world.

He didn't want to let Deon go, but he needed him naked, all of his wounds exposed for Alias to see. The protesting noise Deon made when he broke the kiss comforted him.

"I'm so glad you're back," Alias said, even though such a one-dimensional emotion hardly encompassed all that he was feeling. "I need— Will you show me . . ." At a loss for words, he tugged at Deon's shirt.

Deon directed his hand to the hem. "Of course."

Getting a wounded man undressed called for some basic precautions, which Alias knew from personal experience. He stood behind Deon to remove his jacket, careful with the sleeves. Next was the tie, which fell at their feet. The shirt followed suit. Deon sat down on the edge of the bed willingly, and let Alias take off his pants, socks, and underwear. Alias cursed at the sight of an awful hand-sized bruise across Deon's inner thigh.

"Lie down," he instructed, barely recognizing the edge of steel in his voice as he stripped down to his boxers.

Deon did as he was told. Alias didn't know what to make of such easy obedience and even less of the satisfaction unfurling in his belly. Action, reaction. A growl vibrated in his chest and made its way out, the feral sound surprising the hell out of himself.

Deon stared at him as though Alias could do anything to him, and he would let it happen and welcome it. Never before had Alias considered himself a man of power, but he sensed a new edge to his adrenaline.

"Fuck, I missed you," Deon rasped.

The rainbow of bruises on his face was barely smoothed out by the dim lights. So much violence carved into his flesh. It reminded Alias of a fight and a fall, a mangled body on the concrete. He recalled all too clearly how much he'd wanted to rip Ben's assailants limb from limb. He'd wanted to avenge Ben, and he wanted to avenge Deon even more.

Crawling over Deon's naked form, Alias cupped Deon's chin where it wouldn't hurt and stared down at him, drunk on the acceptance in those darkening eyes, high on his relief tinged with power, but it was more than simple power, of course—where Deon was concerned, every feeling was layered in nuance. "I missed you more."

Deon melted into the kiss, eager lips parting at the first hint of a probing tongue. The act was still new to Alias, still too enjoyable by far, and he had to rein in his enthusiasm, slow down for both their sakes. He moved down to Deon's shoulders. There were marks there, lines in purple and red crisscrossing, hints of fingers that weren't his own. He pressed his mouth in between those, heartbeat quickening. Deon made a soft noise at the first lick under his collarbone, hands clenching and unclenching in the sheets.

Covering Deon's hands with his own, Alias pressed open-mouthed kisses in between his ribs, mapping out the array of wounds as he went lower and lower still, unable to wipe out the pain dealt to the flesh but intent on adding his own seal to it, infusing every drop of care his heart contained. He wanted to drape himself over Deon like a safety blanket and never let go.

"Ah . . . Alias, sweetheart, you're killing me."

Alias stopped nuzzling the bruise right under Deon's belly button and pulled back, staring at Deon's semi-erect cock with a twinge of guilt. He should have steered clear of that area. He didn't wish Deon to get the wrong idea, to think that this was about sex. Because it wasn't.

"Deon, you need to rest—"

"What I need is you," Deon whispered, eyes a little wide, a little wild. "And I need you now."

A wounded sound broke free from Alias's throat. He bent low to flicker his tongue just below that bruise, soothing goose bumps as they appeared. Deon petted his hair once, eyelids dropping.

"I can lie perfectly still," Deon promised, reaching out to tangle his fingers in Alias's hair. "That is . . . if you want to— We don't have to do . . . anything . . . if you don't— *Oh!*"

Alias had traded tongue for lips, kissing every inch of skin in between the bruises and cuts marring Deon's legs. His cock throbbed at the memory of Deon's mouth on him, but he wasn't done yet—never mind that he didn't know where this was heading. He kept going lower, lavishing those strong legs with attention, mouthing at the soft skin on the underside of Deon's knees, nibbling at the enticing curve of his calves.

"Alias, please."

The raw yearning in Deon's voice slammed through Alias. He placed one last kiss on Deon's ankle before moving back to where he was wanted. An appreciative groan welcomed the first touch to his cock. Alias started pumping it, his strokes even and slow. The angle was awkward, but he didn't mind. The skin was so warm and soft, and it shouldn't have surprised him, but it did. He tightened his fist under the glans and watched the foreskin slide over a wet, pink slit.

Saliva pooled in his mouth as some of his most erotic fantasies floated to the forefront of his mind. He felt fuzzy and light-headed, so very tired. The headache was back as well, but he couldn't care about any of that right now.

"Does it feel good?"

"Amazing," Deon rasped.

The cock twitched in Alias's hand, and more liquid pearled at the tip. With a low groan, Alias pressed his face against Deon's groin, nuzzling the patch of trimmed hair, and then the underside of his cock. The heady scent wafting to his nostrils aroused him to the point of discomfort. Transfixed by the velvety skin slicking up his fingers, he did the first thing that came to mind and darted out his tongue, swiping a broad stroke across the tip.

"Fuck!"

Deon's hips came off the mattress and his left leg seized, prompting another curse that had nothing to do with pleasure. Alias hurried to throw one leg over Deon's and splayed a hand on his least damaged hip for good measure.

"Don't move," he said, lips an inch away from temptation. "Please. You should rest . . ."

Deon went still—except for the hand in Alias's hair. Alias shuddered all over, strangely aroused by the burst of pain at his nape. He inhaled deeply and then swirled his tongue around the head of Deon's cock, languid in his exploration. The taste was strange and not entirely pleasant, but the more he lapped at the hardened flesh, the more Deon seemed to enjoy himself, and the more Alias found satisfaction in the act. He wrapped his lips around the tip and sucked.

"Ah . . ."

The sound was halfway between pleasure and pain. Face flushing, Alias covered his teeth with his lips and hollowed his cheeks, pressing a little more of Deon's cock into his mouth. He remembered the fiery drag of Deon's facial hair on his inner thighs, but he couldn't do that, so he focused on bobbing his head in a slow but steady rhythm, spurred on by Deon's whimpers. The warm weight on his tongue became alluring rather than restrictive. He sucked with renewed vigor. The moisture leaking from the tip was a reward and began to taste like one too.

"Oh, yes, sweetheart, Christ, that feels so good . . ."

The steady stream of praise was well worth the growing wet patch on his boxers. Alias lost himself to the sounds he coaxed from Deon and to the taste of him, more and more pronounced on his tongue, and even started to enjoy the stretch in his jaw.

"That's it. Fuck, you're amazing . . ."

Tears prickled at the corners of Alias's eyes. Deon had both hands buried in his hair, and sharp nails dragged across his skull. With a timid smile, Alias pulled back for air and wiped at his mouth with a trembling hand. Deon's eyes were all pupils, and Alias's cock twitched in response. He dove back in for more, bypassing Deon's cock and craning his neck to give those soft balls some attention. The musk was sharp there too. Alias massaged the sack with extra care. The muscles in Deon's thighs flexed as Alias tongued at the sensitive skin between his fingers.

"Such a good boy, fuck, so good, go on, fuck, you're so good for me . . ."

Alias was so intent on making Deon feel good that he hadn't noticed what he was doing. He froze, groin pressed to Deon's leg, embarrassed. How long had he been rutting against Deon like that? This wasn't about him.

Deon disabused him of that notion.

"Let me feel you, Alias." He propped himself up just enough to brush a thumb across Alias's lips. "You're— Christ, you're the only thing that feels good right now. I want—" With a grimace, he lowered himself back onto the mattress. "Want you to feel good too. Rub yourself on me, come on."

Desire shot up Alias's spine. The strain in Deon's voice might stem from exhaustion rather than desire, but that didn't belie the words. Alias made quick work of his underwear, hot and needy under Deon's expectant gaze. As soon as his cock pressed against Deon's warm thigh, he got back to sucking on Deon's hard flesh with increasing desperation, his hips jerking with little finesse.

"That's it, good boy . . ."

Seeking and giving pleasure at the same time required a higher degree of coordination, but Alias did his best, slurping and gagging, dizzy from the lack of oxygen but also from the praise. When Deon's moans gained volume, Alias used more tongue, delirious with a flavor of pride he'd never experienced before. *He* was the reason Deon was losing coherence. *He* was the cause of Deon losing control.

"I'm— Fuck, I'm close. You should . . . back off."

Alias took the warning as encouragement and bobbed his head faster, the hand that wasn't at the base of Deon's cock flying to the soft balls nestled behind. They felt like velvet and were sticky with his saliva. He linked eyes with Deon, and his pleasure mounted under the onslaught of want swirling in that gaze. He tilted his pelvis and pressed harder against Deon's thigh.

Deon dug his thumb into Alias's jaw. "Come for me, sweetheart."

With a high keen, Alias came all over Deon's thigh. A few seconds later, it was Deon's turn, and Alias released Deon's cock in time to get splashed on his chin and throat. The last drop hit him just above the collarbone.

Deon blinked at him and groaned appreciatively but didn't try to move. Alias darted out his tongue and licked his chin. Like expected, it didn't taste better than it smelled, but the fact that it was Deon, that he'd given him pleasure, sweetened the bitter notes.

"Deon?" he asked, wiping the white fluid in the hollow of his throat.

For a wounded, weary man, Deon reeled him in for a kiss with impressive strength. Alias felt Deon's arm spasm as he reached for the back of his head, but he didn't dare move in case it made things worse.

"I really, really missed you," Deon said when he pulled back.

Alias cradled one bruised cheek, unable to talk, full to bursting with every feeling Deon inspired him.

Deon's eyelids fluttered closed. "And I'm really, really glad your mother woke up. I'll talk to Lentz tomorrow. They've got a gruff manner, but they'll take good care of her."

Alias fluffed a pillow and slid it under Deon's head. "I'm going to take a quick shower."

"Why? You smell good. Come here."

Alias kissed his brow. He felt wide-awake, poised on a line so thin he could barely feel it. The tingling sensation in his chest reminded him of when he'd watched Deon sleep in the BotHouse just a few days ago—of a door ajar at the back of his mind. "I'll be right back."

"Promise?"

Alias's heart hammered in his chest. "Promise."

In the shower, Alias stood under the hot jet, one hand clutched to his chest, soapy bubbles drifting down to his feet. The stall smelled like Deon's soap, like Deon himself, and even with his eyes wide open, Alias could see him standing in front of him, a superposition of crooked smiles and hopeful glances seared into his memory.

He didn't know why he was so wound up, but the more he tried to dismiss the tingling sensation in his chest, the more it felt like a physical ache. He toweled himself with jerky motions. The mirror remained blurry no matter how hard he wiped at it. He wondered what he might have seen, otherwise. If the rush of adrenaline would show on the outside, if the look in his eyes would help him make sense of the tangled emotions inside.

The guilt was easiest to recognize, all thorns and spikes. A part of him regretted not having followed Deon to India—even at the cost of leaving his mother alone. If he'd been there, he might have been able to stop Deon from leaving the secure compound to address the crowd. Deon would still be asleep in the next room, but he wouldn't be hurt. Deon meant so much to him, more than Alias had ever expected anyone could or would. Deon's importance was a weight in the center of his chest, but also in his mind, pushing back every limit he'd ever had.

A frightening, thrilling weight.

When he returned to the bedroom, he was convinced he was about to pass out from nerves. Whatever lay beyond that door in his mind, he had no wish to hide from it. Running away from the things that could hurt him wasn't how he lived his life anymore.

Now, he was running *toward* them—whatever they might be.

He draped the wet towel on the back of a chair and padded to the bed. Deon was sprawled across it, taking up most of the space. His head rolled to the side as Alias leaned closer, exposing a wide column of neck. A moment later, his left hand flexed, turning around, palm up. Reaching out in his dreams, perhaps.

In Alias's mind, the door's outline became sharper than ever before. His heart pounded so hard it should make him sick, but his perception of himself was shifting. Something akin to a sixth sense burgeoned inside him, a new awareness of the world defined by Deon's smiles and dreams.

He yanked the door open.

Look, he told himself, and stared at the bed that was theirs, yielding to the emotion that now had a name. *Feel everything*.

The knots in his belly loosened, granting that emotion freedom to expand until there was no more space to conquer. The remains of his fear turned to ashes, fertile grounds for a fortress of want and will to grow and protect the flame burning strong in his heart. A treasure that not so long ago he would have deemed a curse. A risk much higher than the one he'd signed for, but one he was taking nonetheless.

Love.

He'd fallen in love with Deon Dehive.

CHAPTER TEN
SECRETS AND SUSPICIONS

"The only thing more dependable than change is love."

His mother was smiling. Fading. The dream shrunk back until only her words remained—and a pearly laugh that didn't belong to Kira Novar.

Deon nuzzled his neck and pulled him in tighter. Alias blinked awake with a frown. Hadn't he started the night curled around Deon, not the other way around? Then the rest came back, and warmth flooded him from head to toe. *I love you*, he thought, his body tingling, his chest too tight. He waited for the panic to crash down on him.

It didn't come.

His heart was set.

Painstakingly slowly, Alias extricated himself from Deon's embrace. As soon as he sat up, Deon mumbled something, squeezing the sheet where Alias had been, as though he could sense the distance. As though he needed Alias back with him.

I love you, Alias thought again. He'd never have suspected that coming to terms with a feeling that had terrified him for so long would be effortless. Satisfying. Lust and love were never entirely safe, but he could afford both and be happier. Wasn't that precisely what Deon had been trying to teach him?

I love you.

He rubbed at his chest, humbled by how much love could be contained in so small a space. It left no room for fear, only the urge to smooth the lines of worry at the corner of Deon's eyes and uproot the nightmares. And he would gladly have given both a try, too, had the laughter not rung out again, dismissing any notion that he might have imagined it before.

The sound of footsteps followed, barely audible. Alias surveyed the room, not awake enough to pinpoint the origin of the noise. The daycare center was closed at night, so an employee must be working late and keeping their child close. Alias consulted his mental map of the Hive and frowned: Deon's living quarters were isolated, unlike their centrally located offices. What would a child be doing nearby?

The next bout of laugher was faint, but Alias had been looking in the right direction. He stared dumbly at a palm tree. Perhaps this was a dream within a dream, and he had yet to wake up? As far as he knew, there was only solid rock on the other side of that wall.

His temples throbbed anew, but he supposed the massive headache he'd had yesterday, and the need to sleep for a decade, weren't going to go away after a few hours in bed. Curiosity had him push back the sheets and stand. He was about to get dressed and go investigate when a hand locked onto his wrist, startling the living daylights out of him. "Deon!"

"Where do you think you're going?"

If Alias had been any sleepier, he might not have picked up on the edge in Deon's voice. As it was, he sensed the tension thrumming through Deon's body like it was his own. And if that didn't heighten his curiosity . . .

"There's a child close by. A girl, I think. They're probably lost. I should go and—"

"There's no need." Deon yawned, but there was something strange about his expression—the tightening of his jaw, at odds with his casual tone. "All my employees who have children take very good care of them."

Alias bit his lip. A child from the daycare had died recently. Given that they were indeed well cared for, the death had been alarming. Hopefully, the source of this voice was faring better.

"I never doubted that," he said slowly. "But the sound seemed to come from, er, outside, which is weird—"

"You love running in those woods, you even slept there once, and you find it weird that someone would take their child out for a walk?"

Alias scratched the back of his head with a sheepish smile. "Well, when you put it like that . . ."

Fondness crept into Deon's voice. "Come on, get back here. It's Sunday morning, you can sleep in." He tugged at Alias's arm. "And I sleep better with you in my arms."

The way Deon said it, he was stating a fact, but to Alias, it was so much more than that. He knelt on the mattress. Looking down at Deon's tousled hair and bleary eyes, he was struck with an emotion he could now put into words. But he wouldn't. Even if love was mostly safe, he shouldn't encourage Deon to develop corresponding feelings of affection by exposing his.

If LBV hadn't threatened the one person he knew for sure loved him, he might think differently.

"Shouldn't we apply some ointment on your wounds?" he asked, feeling stupid for not having considered it the night before.

Deon wiggled his fingers at him. "I just need you."

The words tugged at Alias's heartstrings so hard it was painful, but it wasn't an entirely bad pain. Deon caught his hand and pulled. Alias followed the motion but resisted when Deon directed him to lie down on top of him.

"I can't put weight on you, remember?" he said, and traced the outline of a bruise on Deon's shoulder. "As much as I'd like to—"

"I want that weight on me," Deon said, "and if this were a dream, I'd say I want you in me too."

Alias, who was doing his best not to add to the canvas of bruises, went completely still. Deon used the opportunity to nuzzle his throat, which Alias bared without prompt, earning himself a deep groan and the hint of teeth.

"Scratch that." Deon reached for the back of Alias's head with his other hand and tugged at the short hair there. His breath came out in hot puffs as he spoke. "If I wasn't about to break something the moment I started to stretch myself, I'd *beg* you to fuck me right now."

He sounded desperate, and Alias found himself equally desperate to enact the fantasy. Deon would give directions as Alias caressed every inch of his body with care. It would be intimate and overwhelming to bury himself inside this man, to forget everything that wasn't *them*, while Deon guided his hips and told him he loved him back— No, *no*.

"I'm here. I'm right here, sweetheart."

The hand on his cheek migrated to his mouth, and a thumb slid between his lips, coaxing them open. Alias exhaled sharply. His eyes stung with unshed tears.

"I'm sorry."

Alias caught Deon's hand before it got out of reach. "W-why are you apologizing?"

"Because sometimes I forget your fear," Deon said gently, lacing their fingers before tracing Alias's jaw and chin, perhaps seeking some reassurance for himself. "Even though it doesn't drive your life anymore, it remains there." He tapped Alias's temple with a finger.

Alias shuddered all over. "There's no need to apologize, I'm not—"

"Really?" Both of Deon's eyebrows jumped toward his hairline. "Your lies need some work, sweetheart."

Alias hesitated. He could correct Deon, explain that he wasn't afraid for *himself*, but that would mean admitting to feelings he'd rather keep to himself, at least for now.

"You're right," he said at last. "The sex is . . . I enjoy it, more than I ever thought I would, but it still frightens me." Lies were easier to tell with a kernel of truth in them, apparently. He pressed their linked hands to his belly. "There's still no reason for you to apologize."

Deon remained quiet for so long Alias thought the conversation would end there.

It didn't.

"I have this recurring nightmare." Deon kissed their linked hands. "In it, I wake up from a deep slumber convinced that you're a fantasy designed to drive me mad." He shrugged and then grimaced. "There's one thing I can do to calm myself down, when I wake up for real."

"What is it?"

"Touch you." He turned his hand around and squeezed Alias's. "Be reminded that you're right here, with me."

Alias had no idea how to reply without giving away the extent of his feelings, so he settled for a peck to Deon's shoulder.

I love you, he thought, lulled to sleep by Deon's steady heartbeat. Perhaps a few more hours of rest would make the headache go away for good and give him the necessary energy to face the next few days. He felt weary to the bone, and he wasn't the one who'd been beaten within an inch of his life.

He curled himself around Deon's sleepy form.

I love you so much.

Beyond the walls that offered different worldviews, the child had gone quiet.

By the time Saturday rolled around, Alias wasn't feeling any better, but he blamed the lingering fatigue and headaches on the lack of sleep. Managing the worldwide distribution of a life-altering product and polishing the Dehive image McCarthy had torn through amounted to a titan's task, a fact that Deon reminded him of whenever they found themselves in bed at the same time, too tired to do much past cuddling. Deon hadn't slept enough in the past week either, but at least his wounds were healing well.

Alias got up bright and early, despite the possibility of lingering in bed. The other side of the mattress was cold. Hoping that Deon was resting somewhere else, be it the small cabin in the woods or in a dark corner of the BotHouse, Alias got dressed for his morning run.

He only managed half his usual circuit, too exhausted for more, and spent a while in the shower trying to brace himself for another day. After his second cup of coffee, he felt alert enough to go through the most urgent emails and return some calls. The Ice Lady might have gone quiet over the last couple of days, but no one felt reassured, least of all him. She hadn't taken a vacation in eight years, as she'd reminded the press when Deon had taken last Sunday off to heal.

In the middle of the afternoon, when the first snow of the year drifted past his window, Alias allowed himself the treat of a video call from his office.

"You look rested."

Alias could hear the sarcasm in his mother's voice and couldn't disagree. A faint smile floated on his lips despite the throbbing headache making itself at home in his skull. "I'm glad you're awake. And sitting. Can you leave your bed at all yet?"

"I don't have that much energy, but at least the doctor you got me has a fantastic bedside manner."

Alias had to arch an eyebrow at that. Dr. Lentz's bedside manner certainly wasn't why he'd insisted on them. He studied his mother, fully aware that she was still on borrowed time. The feverish glaze in her eyes was still there, and her face hadn't lost its ashen quality, but she was awake and talking, sitting and taking sips from a glass.

It could be a lot worse.

His mother's voice shook him from his thoughts. "I miss you, Alias." The concern in her expression was unmistakable.

Alias's chest clenched. He'd only been able to see her in person once, even though Dr. Lentz—who'd jumped at the opportunity to become her primary physician—had made sure their patient's son could visit. "I miss you too, Mother."

She tutted. "Why does it look like you're not getting a wink of sleep? Surely with LX getting a mostly positive response, you can afford to rest. Are you well?"

"I'm . . . just very tired," Alias replied, slouching. "I try to sleep, but there's . . . so much to think about."

Her eyes narrowed at him. "Is anxiety keeping you awake?"

Alias shook his head. He was concerned about his mother, and Deon, and McCarthy's silence, but that wasn't why he spent half his time in bed wide awake: the root of that problem was the feeling burgeoning in his chest. Love made his body *sing*. It was exhilarating, invigorating, akin to poetry in a foreign language he was learning to speak by instinct alone.

His mother set aside her glass of water, now empty. "How is Mr. Dehive doing?"

When had he started rubbing his chest? He stilled his hand—his shaking hand, apparently. He vowed to not drink any more coffee today. "He's not sleeping much either," he replied in as level a voice as he could manage, "but yes, he is . . . better."

"That's good to hear."

She leaned forward with a kind smile. Alias wished there was no screen between them, no miles that kept them apart. He wanted to hug her so badly.

"Why aren't you at home today? Did Mr. Quint fix Ben faster than expected?"

Taken aback by the non sequitur, Alias opened his mouth, then closed it again. "No? I mean, Ben isn't out of the BotHouse yet; it just . . . makes sense to sleep at the Hive with my schedule." It wasn't technically a lie, and it was better than the whole truth. His mother didn't need to know about the attack and his trashed apartment.

Or the nature of his feelings for Deon.

"Oh, I see," his mother said.

"What?"

"You're living with Mr. Dehive at the Hive now, aren't you? I know you have new clothes, but these look . . . borrowed."

With a sense of dread, Alias looked down. The dark blue silk pants—the first pair he'd put on in the dark this morning—definitely belonged to Deon. Alias could've smacked himself for overlooking *this* part of the presentation.

"He must like you very much."

Alias's heart jumped into his throat.

"I love him."

He slammed a hand over his mouth. He hadn't meant to say anything, to anyone, but the lack of sleep wasn't helping his brain-to-mouth filter. He tried to school his expression into something neutral, but he'd never been good at lying.

His mother lay down on her side, giving Alias a view of the window as she shifted the tablet. When her face appeared again, she seemed surprised. A little sad, but not shocked.

"I would be happy for you—" She flicked a hand toward the screen, as if pretending she could touch his shoulder and hold him. "—if you looked happy about it."

"I am happy . . ." Alias sighed. The headache was getting worse. "I'm just too tired to look the part."

"You should be in bed right now, then . . . unless *that*'s why you're not getting any sleep?"

"Mother!" Alias was sorely tempted to hide his face, but that wouldn't make the blush go away. "That's not . . . I'm just . . . It's all so new." The tips of his ears burned. "And complicated."

"After this whole thing with McCarthy blows over and Mr. Dehive—or Deon, I suppose—has some time in his schedule again, I'd like to meet him, my dear boy. Face to face."

"Mother, I don't need you to intervene."

"Who said anything about intervening?" She poked the screen and smiled gently. "Your happiness is important to me, and if he plays any role in it . . . Have you told him how you feel?"

"No."

His face must be giving his mother more information than his answer had, because her brow furrowed. "Oh, Alias . . . What if he's already in love with you?" she asked with too much understanding.

Alias gripped the arms of his chair. "I almost lost him in India, Mother. I know it's not the same, but I . . . I need more time."

"You don't have to explain yourself to me." His mother's voice was getting raspy. Her eyelids drooped, but still she smiled. "You have come so far, and I'm so . . . proud . . ."

Her head lolled, eyes rolling backward before fluttering shut.

"Mother!"

Alias reached for her, but his hand hit glass. Pain lanced through his chest. Dr. Lentz had warned him that a second coma was to be expected at any time—one that his patient had even fewer chances to wake up from.

"Just prepare yourself," Dr. Lentz had told him before going through the rationale of their prognosis, as blunt as ever. *"Miracles are few and far between, and your mother already used hers."*

Just as Alias convinced his body to move, the screen turned black, and the office was swallowed by darkness. He shot to his feet and selected Dr. Lentz's number on his watchphone, pacing as he waited anxiously for the annoyed drawl in his ear. An orange glow, one quite different from the usual artificial daylight, flooded the office at the precise moment Dr. Lentz's voice mail message started.

"Don't leave a message, unless I asked you to."

Numbly, Alias hung up. Panic returned with a vengeance when he caught sight of the computer screen.

LOCKDOWN.

And then: *The Hive is in lockdown. Please remain calm.*

Alias rushed out of the office, mind spinning with increasingly apocalyptical scenarios. He felt many things, but calm was not one of them. Deon didn't answer his phone. Jaden didn't pick up either. Alias tried Dr. Lentz again, to no avail. He checked the news on his watchphone, hoping to trade panic for knowledge.

Instead, he got both.

How Deon Dehive Tricked the World

Alias had never read an article and double-checked the sources so quickly.

"That can't be true," he gasped in the eerily quiet corridor.

Dr. Lentz's number blinked on his watchphone.

Alias tapped to answer. "Tell me it isn't true."

"We wouldn't be in fucking lockdown if it wasn't," Dr. Lentz snapped back. There was shouting in the background. They did some shouting of their own before getting back to Alias. "A variant like this has always been a possibility. Everything's possible with that damn virus and its damn variants, and as much as I'd like to refute McCarthy's findings, we've just confirmed them in the Lab."

The text of the article blurred, but the words were already carved into Alias's mind.

LX offers barely any protection against the new LBV variant, which is more aggressive in cases of love than lust.

"So those studies she shared on the first day LX started being distributed about children being more vulnerable—"

"The virus mutated just enough in a matter of days for her old lies to become the new truth," Dr. Lentz hissed. "LX has never been a threat to children, obviously, but platonic and romantic love is about to get a lot of people killed no matter which antiviral they're on. Avida is more useless than ever, even if McCarthy likes to pretend only LX is concerned here. Have you seen this article about LX causing what people are calling the L-variant? I know that LBV has mutated unusually quickly recently, but I swear to God—" A metallic *clang* sounded in the background. "Do people simply forget that Avida had been getting steadily less effective before LX even started getting distributed?"

"LX—LX was always going to fail against one variant or another," Alias mumbled.

"That's the fate of any antiviral when the virus it works against mutates too much, and as our luck would have it, this latest variant is different enough for LX to be just as useless as Avida."

The wall at Alias's back was the only reason he didn't collapse on the floor.

". . . you reached Mr. Dehive? Novar, talk to me."

Alias shook himself. There was now a pain in his chest matching the one in his head. "No, I— He isn't answering," he gasped. "I'll look for him, Dr. Lentz, but please, you need to check on—"

Dr. Lentz ended the call before Alias could beg them to look in on his mother. Alias stared at his watchphone as a wave of nausea threatened to engulf him. For a moment, he was sure he was going to throw up or pass out, but then he started to move, one foot at a time. He wasn't completely useless—he refused to be controlled by panic ever again.

But the idea that he could be happy, truly happy, and embrace the feelings he'd feared all his life, was gone.

He slammed the lid shut on his concern for his mother after placing a call to her security detail. There was nothing else he could do, and he hated it, but it was the truth.

Now, what about the lockdown?

Alias raced down the darkened corridors. The few people who crossed his path attempted to stop him to get answers, but he had none to offer, only suspicions—and questions—of his own. Was the lockdown in place because of the NID? If so, were they going to arrest Deon, even though the virus was hardly his fault, and he'd never promised LX would protect against all variants? He checked his watchphone for clues, but the internal notifications amounted to general advice for all staff:

Stay calm. Stay inside.

He only understood the latter after he barreled into the main hall, where apparently half the staff had gathered to panic as a single unit.

A crowd was also growing outside the Hive, and it was much more agitated than the one Alias had spotted from Mortella's rooftop a few weeks ago. Were any of these people impatient to get LX, or had they all gathered here to protest its very existence?

The first rock thrown against the glass doors startled him. Alias watched a second person pick up a rock and gaped in disbelief as a tall, *pregnant* woman drew a *gun*. The bullet hit the glass doors with a ping that echoed in the suddenly quiet hall.

The chanting from the fifty or so people outside became clear. "Dehive is death, down with Dehive!"

Alias took a reflexive step back when another bullet struck. The glass was apparently reinforced because it didn't crack, not even when several more bullets connected with the door in the same area. Alias couldn't help but notice that they were aimed at chest level. Most of the staff had fled the area, and he found himself standing alone in front of the angry mob, ears ringing as the woman sheathed her gun. Several fists started pounding on the glass.

He stumbled back like those fists were punching him instead.

Like he was back at his apartment being attacked.

Don't be afraid. Deon needs you.

He repeated the mantra in his head until the spell broke, and he could think again. He glanced past the throng of rioters. Vehicles were emerging from behind the closest line of trees, mangling bushes. Black shapes adorned with aggressive, blinking red lights replaced the usual greenery. A compact row of officers exited the vehicles and marched toward the mob. The thin layer of snow didn't slow them down.

Alias spun on his heels, trying not to think of his mother, or the attack, or the many things that made it impossible for his breathing to even out. His hand felt clammy when he pressed it to his earpiece, willing Deon to pick up.

"Come on, come on . . ."

There was a click as Alias was sent to voicemail. He almost threw the earpiece at the wall. "Damn it, Deon, tell me what's going on. I spoke to Dr. Lentz, but there has to be more to the lockdown than the L-variant and it's aggressivity in cases of—" His voice broke on the next word: *love*. He gripped the earpiece until his knuckles turned white. "Deon." He infused his voice with as much confidence as he could muster. "The NID's already here. If it's about the mob, good, but I get the feeling you're not telling me everything. You can have your secrets, but I need to be kept in the loop, or I won't be able to help you. Let me help you. Call me. *Please*. Message end."

Deon wasn't in the Lab. No sign of him in the BotHouse either. Alias couldn't check outside in person, as even his biometrics failed to let him out while the Hive was in lockdown— not that he was keen on getting up close and personal with the rioters or the NID officers. He stalked toward his and Deon's quarters, but he didn't run. Paradoxically, the unrest in the Hive infused him with calm. He had to be. The other employees needed reassurance. When Deon reached out for him, he would need Alias clear-headed.

Hailed as he was at irregular intervals, it took him a while to notice that his body struggled more and more to follow his mind. He wiped sweat from his brow and frowned at his trembling hand, slowing to catch his breath. All that adrenaline should grant him at least the illusion of limitless energy, and yet, it didn't.

He leaned against the wall, just around the corner from his and Deon's quarters, biting back a bout of hysterical laugher. What was the saying again? Bad things come in three?

He flinched as the only door nearby opened.

"You will do nothing of the sort, do you hear me!"

Jaden. Alias peeked around the corner. He'd never heard her sound or look so angry. She stood in front of Deon, who had his back to Alias. Neither seemed to have noticed him. Jaden's arms were looped around Deon's neck, and her hair was all mussed, her beautiful face streaked with tears. The muscles in Deon's shoulders flexed as he returned the embrace.

"I can't wait any longer, and you know it."

"The mess McCarthy has made won't go away because you will it!" Jaden hissed. "The NID—"

"The NID isn't here *only* because McCarthy made more outrageous claims, and this mess has existed long before she was born." Deon's voice rose, but the pacifying tone remained. "Avida, LX . . . The virus was always going to win because neither of these antivirals help people like her, but now we might finally have a way to save those who are otherwise condemned. LX was just a preventive measure, but this . . . You know how long I've been at it, how hopeful we've all been. It's different from the previous—"

"You can't expect this argument to convince me—"

"The basis for this technology has been in development for a very long time, and our specific application doesn't change that fact. The L-variant doesn't change that. It's ready for human trial. Just talk to Lentz—"

Jaden's hands moved from around Deon's neck to his face. "I'm talking to you. About the risk that still exists, about the necessity to wait and consider what may need to be adjusted now that the L-variant—"

"This new variant is exactly why I need to do something!"

"You mean because of Bee?"

"Of course, it's about Bee! But it's about everyone else too; it's a gamble to save humanity, and that means the time for theory is over."

Their voices dropped to whispers, intimate and urgent.

"Even if that was true, Deon, now is hardly the time to—"

"I know, I know. We'll deal with this mess first. But after . . . I need to fix this, Jaden. For Bee. For us."

Alias's head throbbed at the gentleness in Deon's voice. Those hands he'd held a hundred times disappeared from view, only to reappear on Jaden's face, mirroring her posture.

"I could do it, later," Jaden whispered. "It doesn't have to be you. The world needs you a lot more than—"

"The world needs you just as much as it needs me." Deon's voice was fiercer, strong. "She certainly does. She loves you, Jaden. We both do. So much."

Alias retraced his steps in a daze and stumbled into the nearest bathroom. His knees hit the ground and he threw up, half in the toilet, half on the tile. He gripped the porcelain so hard his hands hurt. Nausea swam in his gut, thick and hot, and he retched until there was nothing left in his stomach. He curled up on the floor, the taste of bile layering with tears at the back of his throat.

Why did it hurt so much? Deon deserved to be happy, and so did Jaden. The love Alias had been nursing in secret didn't have to be reciprocated to flourish, even though holding on to it might end up killing him after all. But he couldn't uproot it. Despite the mounting pain in his constricted chest, love was slithering through the cracks in his heart to better hold it together. Only last night, he'd wished to hear those three words from Deon, *I love you's* that belonged to him alone.

Not anymore. Not when Deon was already at risk from loving *one* person.

Alias wrapped his arms around himself and tried to regulate his breathing, seeking memories of Ben's soothing, mechanical voice. It was better that Deon didn't return his feelings, he told himself. And there was no point in jealousy. He didn't want to feel torn up inside while there was a real mess outside, but the burning sensation in his throat was spreading with every shallow breath he took, the pain in his skull so fierce he thought he was going to pass out.

Move.

He repeated the word until his muscles obeyed and he left the cubicle. The corridor was empty, but not quiet, faraway shouts and screams spreading through the Hive. Alias reached Deon's quarters—he couldn't consider them *theirs* right now—without a plan, only a few ideas that felt like dead ends. But he wasn't going to break down again. Deon's feelings for Jaden weren't nearly as important as his mother's unknown state, the L-variant, or the mob outside.

Or the pain that sent him collapsing against the door as soon as it slid closed behind him. He doubled over with a gasp and braced his hands on his knees, vision swimming.

What if the way he felt had nothing to do with heartbreak? He checked the symptoms: shortness of breath, chest pain, migraines, extreme weariness, nausea, fever. He'd been experiencing them for days, but they'd come and gone, and he'd chalked them up to too much work and not enough sleep, because he'd spent too long living in paranoia. After all, none of those symptoms were unique to LBV.

Not individually, anyway.

The rush of terror and despair he'd anticipated for most of his life didn't come. Instead, relief washed over him, obliterating everything else, if only for a moment. The threat was right here, it was real and immediate, the virus multiplying in his cells, causing the symptoms and beckoning death. There was no cure, but maybe like his mother, he would be extremely lucky—until he wasn't.

"Alias."

"Ben?" Alias stepped away from the door and gaped at the hubot standing in front of the pond. His right foot got caught in a piece of clothing, and he hopped on his other foot like a lunatic, trying to disentangle his shoe from the collar of a shirt. "What are you doing here?"

Ben navigated the discarded clothes and machine parts with unusual slowness. Its big eyes blazed red. Alias kicked the shirt away and met Ben, halting its wobbly steps.

"You're sick," the bot remarked, the syllables intermittent, mechanical. "You should see a doctor."

Alias barked out a laugh. His chest ached. "I'm pretty sure I'm sick with LBV."

"Your temperature is high," Ben agreed. "Perhaps I am malfunctioning still, but you do not seem worried."

"I'm not."

"What changed?"

Alias didn't answer, just rested his shoulder against Ben's arm. The hubot's torso retained bumps on the right side, and a scorching black scar ran in a zigzag across half of its left leg. Its arm was shiny but still marred from its fall. The multifunction hand twitched. Why had Mr. Quint brought the hubot to his— Deon's—quarters if it wasn't fully fixed? Alias curled his hand around Ben's and exhaled slowly. His body begged him to lie down, but there would be enough time for that soon. He had to do something. Had to do this job and help people.

Like Deon did.

He thought he heard his watchphone ringing, and Ben confirming that someone was attempting to reach him, but the present faded as the scene he'd witnessed earlier replayed in his mind. The parts he'd overlooked, sidetracked as he'd been by his hurt feelings, were now loaded with meaning.

Deon had another means to fight the virus, one that might help people who were already suffering from LBV.

And he planned to test the current version, which could prove lethal, on himself. Perhaps not today, but soon. Because . . .

"You should answer." Ben's voice seemed to come from far, far away. "It's probably important if he keeps calling."

Alias ignored the ringing in his ear. Deon wouldn't change his mind if Alias asked. Jaden had tried, and she'd failed.

There was only one alternative—one borne out of emotions, but entirely rational as well.

"What are you doing?" Ben asked, trailing after him.

The red book appeared as meaningless as it had the day Deon first revealed the safe. Alias ran a finger over the cover's embossed fancy script. There was no telling where this secret injection was kept, but he was willing to bet that Deon wouldn't keep all of them in the Lab with the traitor's identity unclear. Everything that mattered to him, he kept close.

"I have no idea what I'm supposed to do," Alias whispered. "There's a riot outside, the NID arrived, Deon's in trouble through no fault of his own, and going by how bad my symptoms already are, I have to assume I don't have much time left . . ."

The sound of the door opening silenced him. Without being prompted, Ben moved between him and the door. Alias held his breath, not daring to move.

"Alias!" Deon's eyes flickered to Ben, then to him. The pinch of his eyebrows eased. "You weren't answering, and I was concerned you might be outside." He hurried across the room. "I'm glad I found you; things are going pear-shaped and— What's wrong?"

Alias shoved his hands into his pockets before he could be tempted to pull Deon into his arms. "What's going on, Deon?" The urge to throw up was back. He took a deep breath and tried to convince himself that this was just nerves. "You've put the Hive into lockdown to contain the mob, right? The L-variant isn't your fault. Surely the NID gets that?" he continued, trying to be as useful as he could, while he was still able to stand. "Surely there's a limit to how believable McCarthy—"

"The problem with her is not the lies but the truths." Deon's jaw clenched visibly. "Old truths she holds onto until the time comes to wield them like weapons. I just never expected her to . . ."

A booming noise shook the room. Deon steadied Alias with one hand, barking orders into his earpiece while he consulted his tablet. Incredulous, Alias watched cracks tear through the screen panels making up the ceiling and walls. The next tremor cut a palm tree in half. A portion of the ocean vanished in pixels. More illusions gone. A hysterical chuckle bubbled up in Alias's chest. Deon ended his call with a series of curses.

Alias gripped Deon's wrist, pretending he didn't need the support. Deon's dark blue eyes were reminiscent of the sky just before a storm.

Alias felt like a storm already unleashed.

"Then what is her endgame?"

Deon grabbed his other shoulder, bringing them face to face, uncomfortably close. Alias felt warm skin under his hands. He'd reached for Deon despite his resolution. He couldn't help but wish once more—one last time—that Deon's heart could be his.

"You're not well."

"You expect anyone to be well today?" Alias squeezed Deon's wrist. "Deon. What's really going on? You had only *one* officer visiting on the day that child got sick, and everyone knew that McCarthy's explanation was a lie. There are *dozens* of officers outside now. What kind of truth can bring the full wrath of the NID down upon you? Surely not the fact that LX and Avida are *both* useless?"

Deon bit his lip. "Can I trust you with a secret?"

A shiver jolted up Alias's spine, and it wasn't caused by a tremor. Deon tightened his grip, eyes searching, seemingly unconcerned by the chaos unraveling around them. Alias wasn't either. The beach might vanish, the walls might crumble, but as long as Deon needed him, Alias would be strong.

"Of course, you can trust me," he said, and meant every word. He didn't wince, even though Deon's fingers dug harder into his shoulders. The pain sharpened his focus and kept it away from the other pain. "I'm listening."

Deon's breath was warm and quick on Alias's cheek as he leaned in.

"There's someone I want you to meet."

CHAPTER ELEVEN
DUEL FOR A BILLION EYES

D eon did something to the wall near the splintered palm tree, and a small section of the pixelated beach retreated behind cracked displays to reveal a narrow black door. A biometric scanner awaited input. It was nowhere near as flashy as the model replicated through the Hive, and at thigh level to boot. Alias wouldn't have spotted it if Deon hadn't awkwardly crouched to press his palm to it.

"You didn't know about this door."

"I didn't know about this door," Alias confirmed, and pretended that the suspicious tone didn't hurt. And it didn't—not nearly as much as the migraine drilling into his skull and the phantom fist squeezing his lungs. At least he wasn't coughing blood yet. Or passing out in exhaustion. Either would be harder to conceal, and Alias begged his body to hold on for a while longer. Preferably, until after he met whomever Deon had gone to great lengths to hide.

Until after he tested Deon's secret weapon.

He had nothing left to lose, after all.

Deon gestured toward the entrance. "Come on."

The tunnel was too narrow for them to walk side by side, so Deon led, with Alias one step behind. Deon's quarters were carved into rock, but no effort had been made to fill the chasm between nature and technology in this section, so the other two doors they passed stood out. The ground was rough concrete sprinkled with sand. Spiderwebs hung in the corners. The dim lighting was yellow, not orange—this place must have its own emergency electricity network.

A distant groan reverberated through the rocks. Though the vibrations lacked the strength from before, the floor was dotted with roots, and Alias tripped. He would have cracked his skull open on the rocks if not for Deon's reflexes. His grip hurt, but Alias let it happen as he was brought back to the day they'd met. Back then, his reaction to Deon steadying him had been to shy away, even though he'd *needed* their connection.

He still did.

"Careful," Deon said, voice rough, and released him. "We don't have much time."

On cue, another tremor shook the tunnel. Dust drifted down, and Alias pressed a hand to his brow to keep it from his eyes.

"What is this place? Who is it you want me to meet?" He tried to match Deon's pace without making it obvious how difficult it was. "Shouldn't we be talking to the NID and clearing things up rather than letting McCarthy have monopoly over the narrative—"

Deon halted so abruptly that Alias stumbled into him.

"I'll be dealing with that mess soon enough," Deon said, catching Alias again, keeping him upward. Always.

Alias swallowed hard. There were several questions in Deon's gaze, and no answers. A warning, too, tinged with guilt. And a lot more that Alias wasn't able to decipher because he was too busy pretending that his lungs weren't on fire.

"I need someone I trust to keep an eye on Betty."

"Betty?" Alias rasped.

Deon crouched. They'd reached another door with a similar scanner.

"Betty. My daughter."

Alias heard the words, but their meaning didn't register. Overwhelmed by the unexpected perfume of flowers, he followed Deon into a vast room adorned in shades of blue and green. It was half the size of the quarters they'd left behind, with a low ceiling and no window. Were he an inch taller, Alias would have had to duck his head. He took in the wooden bookcases, the matching desk and chair, and gasped as his eyes landed on the bed.

And the child lying in a sea of colorful pillows.

"Betty," he said, whispering the word, trying out the two syllables.

Deon didn't speak. When Alias stepped forward, Deon made no move to stop him. Alias stood at the foot of the bed and exhaled sharply, chest tightening for reasons unrelated to his illness. The little girl could not have been more than six years old. Alias hadn't met many kids until he started working at the Hive with its daycare center, but this one struck him as too thin. Her breathing was weak. She breathed on her own, but the mask and tubes on the nightstand and the machines surrounding the bed made it clear that this wasn't always the case.

Beyond her illness, she was like any other child—a child who was loved. Her twin braids, neatly done, spoke of care. The red highlights gave the blond hair a fiery strike. Her heart-shaped face was dusted with freckles, including her pointy chin and nose. The overall sharp bone structure must have lent her a fierce look when she was awake. But she wasn't awake, and everything about her appearance tugged at his need to help. It was no wonder Deon felt so protective of her.

His daughter.

Alias braced himself against the headboard. He'd inherited his father's jaw, but he didn't even know his name. Since artificial insemination had become the norm half a century ago, children had been raised by only one parent. Why put more lives at risk when society needed every person it could get to help rebuild? At that time, there were nuclear plants to handle and shut down, hospitals and factories to staff, planes to fly, and crops to grow and harvest. Potential child-bearing adults had been dwindling by the thousands, and the children who were born rarely survived past ten. By the time the first Avida pills were issued and the NID relaxed its iron-clad rules enough for people to wander the streets again, the population had been cut in half.

"She's strong," Deon said, voice barely audible. "She's always been strong, my little bee, even though . . ."

Deon choked on the word and fell silent. Alias didn't dare turn toward him. As much as he wanted to offer comfort, he didn't think he could. Or should. Where was Jaden?

"My little bee."

It clicked.

Oh.

All those quick exits for personal reasons, all those mentions of *bees*, or rather, *bee*, singular . . . When Alias had called Deon and found himself speaking to Jaden instead, Deon must have been here. When neither of them had been reachable, they'd probably both been taking care of the girl. The conversation Alias had overheard earlier had been about her too. Deon, Jaden, and Betty were a rare miracle, the original family unit: two parents and their child.

Of course Deon was willing to risk his life if it meant there was a chance he could save his little girl! Betty's existence explained why Deon had been so angry about McCarthy claiming he didn't care about children—and so angry at himself, at his own helplessness. Jaden's decision to hand the mantle of personal assistant over to someone else when she was so well suited to the position was a no-brainer.

Any mother would do the same to take care of her child.

However, two mysteries remained: Deon's decision to pursue a practical stranger when he already had a family . . . and how the existence of his daughter served McCarthy.

"I can't leave her alone right now," Deon admitted.

Alias shook himself. "Of course," he hurried to say, silently berating himself for getting distracted by his feelings again. "I can watch over her. Is that— Is that why McCarthy is here?"

"Among other things."

There was something odd about the tone, if not the words, but Alias didn't have the mental wherewithal to read between the lines.

"How long has your . . . daughter been sick?" he asked instead, keeping his voice low so as not to wake up Betty.

"All her life." Wistfulness cut through the anger in Deon's equally low voice. "A rare case, not unlike your mother's. And . . . there's something else I have to tell you."

The slideshow of emotions that crossed Deon's face made it clear that what he was about to say held significant importance.

"The LX injection is quite recent compared to the other project I've been working on."

"Another injection?"

"Not quite. Well . . . it is injected, but it's not a standard antiviral. This technology . . . it's still in its infancy, despite many an engineer claiming a breakthrough over the last two centuries. Lentz and a number of select bioroboticists sworn to secrecy have worked very hard on this. It's still not ready, technically, but if it works, if these little bots can help Betty and your mother—"

Alias gaped. "You mean . . . *nanites?*"

He must have sounded a little angry, on top of surprised, because Deon raised both hands in surrender.

"Like I said, it's still a work in progress. That's why I was waiting to tell you." The desperation in Deon's voice tugged at his heartstrings. "I'm just . . . so fucking tired of giving false hopes, to you, to myself, to *Betty*, to the whole world. I want to help and I never seem to get it right." He let out a shuddering breath. "There aren't many people who know about the nanites, and most of them are the ones who have been developing what we call the Bot-injection, or B-injection for short."

Deon spoke faster now, as though the words had been piling up inside him. "You asked me once why I went into virology. It was for my daughter. It's always been about my daughter. I would give my life for her, and McCarthy knows that, and all her efforts to make it look like I don't care about children . . ." His hands balled into fists. "Both Avida and LX are failing, and maybe, just maybe, if she wasn't spending so much time painting me as an imposter, we could work together against our common enemy to save . . ." His eyes shone with unshed tears. "There are days I manage not to hate her, but the day she comes kicking down my door with NID support and bogus claims, the day she threatens to take Betty away from me . . ." He shook his head and let out a disbelieving, dark chuckle. "Today isn't one of those days."

Alias recoiled, which brought him closer to the bed—in an instinctive, protective stance. "Why does she hate you so much?" He'd thought McCarthy was shallow and cold, but dragging a child into her little competition with Deon?

"She has . . . issues."

Deon made it sound obvious. It wasn't. Not to Alias.

"Issues with what? Can this really be about your old professional disagreements?" No answer was forthcoming, so he shifted gears. "Does she know about the B-injection?"

A shadow fell across Deon's face. "My suspects for McCarthy's spy have been narrowed down to employees of the Lab, so I will prepare for the worst and hope for the best."

Alias's voice shook. "Dr. Lentz?"

"No. They and I go way back, and I would never have entrusted your mother's care to someone I couldn't trust with my life." Deon's shoulders sagged. "If McCarthy does know about the B-injection, then she will seek to destroy it."

"Destroy . . ." Alias couldn't believe what he was hearing. "She can't do that."

Deon let out a derisive chuckle. "Antiviral nanites are highly experimental, and with how things are going with LX, she might be able to pull it off with the NID on her side. I can't believe she's ignored—"

"And I can't believe you didn't tell me about the B-injection and your daughter before."

The temperature in the room seemed to drop. Alias let himself be backed against the wall, too weak to resist the push. Deon's body pressed to his own, the whole line of it hot iron, but the normal resulting arousal was notably absent. The room shook again, but being pinned to the wall kept him from falling.

"I don't owe you anything, least of all my daughter."

There was nothing tender about the way Deon held Alias's chin, but the ice-cold tone hurt more. Alias let out a pained sound as Deon's fingers dug harder into his jaw. Sweat trailed down his back, and for once, the cause wasn't fear. He wished it was.

"You don't owe me anything." His voice shook. "I know that. But I work for you, and I can't do my job properly, I can't help you if I'm missing half the pieces. Your daughter is your secret, but the B-injection should have been ours . . . Unless you don't trust me after all?"

The cold anger bled from Deon's eyes, and his hand drifted to Alias's throat, the touch light and apologetic. He looked away. "I didn't want to give you false hopes."

"You already said that, but you should know that I'm not as easily frightened as I once was. Besides, we're talking about *bots*, Deon." Alias took a deep breath. "Go. I'll stay here and make sure no one gets to her." The urge to kiss Deon one last time was almost as strong as the need to lie down. He shoved his hands into his pockets. "You think McCarthy might find us here?"

"No. Almost everyone who knows about this room is currently in it. She ought to be safe. Jaden would have preferred to be here, but with the NID ready to take the place apart searching for Betty, and that riot making things even more tense, we thought it would be best if she tried to talk things through with the NID first. I'm not—" He racked a hand through his hair. "—in the right frame of mind for polite conversation. I can deal with them closing the daycare center and sitting me down for yet another fucking useless discussion, but they're also here to steal my daughter from me, and—"

"Can they even do that? She's your daughter."

Something akin to pain flickered in Deon's eyes. He squeezed Alias's shoulder. "That may not be enough."

Alias covered Deon's hand with his, blinking back tears of pain. "You can trust me. I'll protect her."

"Thank you."

Warmth infused Deon's voice, and the intensity of it suffocated Alias. Words bubbled at his lips, but they weren't meant to be said out loud. "Go," he hissed through his teeth. "I won't leave her side."

"Alias . . ."

Alias remained silent. Stiff. And he waited. Deon kissed his daughter on the forehead and whispered something. Afterward, he reached toward Alias, who stepped back in time to avoid a parting touch.

Deon left.

The moment the door closed, Alias's legs gave out. The plush green carpet cushioned his knees, but they still ached. Every joint in his body felt fragile. He rested his head on the bed. How was he supposed to protect the little girl in his current state? Betty. Bee. Was Deon so fond of bees because of the one he kept hidden, safe from every harm except the one he hadn't vanquished yet?

He couldn't shake the feeling that Deon was still hiding something huge from him.

"Daddy?"

Betty shifted in the bed. Alias froze, not having expected her to wake up so soon. She yawned and rubbed her small fists over her eyes. Her pout had Deon written all over it—and her frown was an exact copy of Jaden's.

"What are you doing here?"

She didn't seem concerned—unlike Alias, who was terrified of saying the wrong thing.

"I . . ." Had Deon mentioned him? It would explain why she didn't ask his name or try to call for help. Did she spend all her time here? He dreaded the answer, and he had to fight the urge to wrap her in his arms and tell her everything would be all right. "I'm here to . . ."

"Daddy asked you to keep an eye on me?" The shrewd look she gave him wasn't one he'd expected from a child. "Is that why you're sad?"

Alias squirmed under her watchful gaze and lifted a corner of his shirt to wipe at his cheeks. Those were definitely tears. "Not at all. I'm just . . ." He was ridiculously underprepared for this. For her. "Tired," he said, the understatement tasting sour in his mouth. "How do you feel?"

Betty checked the readings on the machine closest to her and nodded before returning her attention to him. "Tired too. I am most days. It's annoying as it makes it hard to get up and make new friends. Where is Jay?"

"Jay?"

"Jaden," she clarified.

She called her father daddy, but her mother by her given name? Alias dismissed the thought. It wasn't his place—or the time—to ask. "Your father's getting her," he said, stretching the truth. "I'm sure they'll be back soon."

That seemed to settle it for her. She leaned back into her mountain of pillows and gave him an expectant look. "Are you going to tell me a story, then? I have lots of books you can choose from—"

The next tremor was followed by a deafening roar. Alias shot to his feet.

"What's going on?" Betty was hugging a pillow. Her arms were thin and the wrists bony. Fragile. Watching the distress widening her blue eyes—Deon's eyes—he found the words he needed.

"Some people believe lies about your father. And they shouldn't."

"What do they want?" Betty sat straighter as the next quake shook the room. Dust fell from the ceiling. She sneezed, and then coughed. It sounded like it hurt.

Alias hurt for her. "It doesn't matter. You're safe here."

"Is my daddy safe too?"

"Of course. Nothing's going to happen to—"

A booming crash drowned his voice, and a second later, a giant crack appeared in the ceiling.

"Betty!"

Later, Alias would be hard-pressed to explain how he pulled it off. One moment, he stood frozen in horror, and the next, he exploded into motion, grabbing Betty and pulling her to the ground with him, using his own body as a shield while half the ceiling collapsed around them. There was no thought process involved in the act, only instinct, and when something heavy landed on his right leg, it didn't hurt.

Through it all, Betty didn't scream, not even when the wires connecting her to the various machines were ripped free from her arms and chest—she just held on to his shirt with her tiny fists. Alias didn't dare move, intent on staying there until the whole ceiling crashed down on him or the tremors stopped, whichever came first. His heart galloped as he awaited the next quake. The taste of blood was familiar, grounding. Had he bitten his tongue? He adjusted his position, not wanting to crush Betty by mistake. Soft sobbing reached his ears.

"Hey, it's okay," he croaked, and pulled back, wincing at the pain shooting up his spine. "Betty. It's over. You're okay. You're okay, right?"

She gave a little nod, eyes wet with tears. She was so small under him. He tried to smile as he said the words again.

"It's over. You're okay." He hadn't used we for obvious reasons, but he tested his limbs and nothing was broken. He probably sported impressive bruises, and his neck and right shin ached something fierce, but he was still mobile and able, which was all that mattered.

Unfortunately, the room was devastated.

"I don't think we should stay here."

Betty followed Alias's gaze to where the ceiling had caved, wiping away her tears and smearing dust over her cheeks in the process. The hole was big, with uneven edges cut in the sharp rock that had previously shielded this room. An uprooted tree lay precariously close to the edge, the network of roots hit by a ray of artificial light. The sky was dark, and the air was filled with distant shouts and roars.

"Is m-my dad going to be okay?"

Alias's throat clenched shut. He grabbed Betty's sweater off the top of the end table and her slippers from under the bed, and helped her put them on. The end of her right braid had come loose, and blond hair spilled over her delicate shoulder. He tucked the loose strands behind her ear and offered a reassuring smile.

"Your father can take care of himself. Both your parents can," he amended, because of course Betty would be concerned about her mother as well. "We should find some place safe. Do you need me to carry you?"

"No."

That ended up being for the best. When the adrenaline rush ended, the pain in his back and leg heightened his earlier weariness. Betty wasn't doing much better, and Alias had to slow down for her sake.

"I can walk faster," she insisted.

Her pinched expression was such a perfect mirror of Deon's earlier that Alias stumbled, another kind of pain searing through his chest. They passed one of the doors he'd noticed earlier, and it occurred to him that it might lead to Jaden's quarters.

"You don't look like you can protect me," Betty said, her no-nonsense a throwback to both her parents. "Are you okay, Mr. Alias?"

Alias considered lying some more, but what would be the point? He probably looked just as bad as he felt.

"No."

Betty was already reaching for his hand, the weariness in her wide blue eyes tempered by a trust Alias didn't remember earning. What had Deon told his daughter, for the name to stick? A surge of protectiveness washed over him as her hand wrapped around his own. It felt cold against his clammy palm.

"But you will be okay?"

Tears pricked at the back of his eyes. He nodded once and shifted his focus to his feet. One step. Two. Right, left, right again. Slow and steady. The uneven ground of the tunnel was even harder to navigate now. At least the narrow space meant that walls were always close enough for Alias and Betty to brace against. He was afraid all over again—that he was going to pass out and fail Deon. Betty.

They entered the bedroom with cautious steps. To Alias's amazement, the place was mostly intact, with only a few cracks running through the disfigured beach and debris littering the floor. A slice of the sea flashed bright blue before turning to black in a shower of sparks. One of the displays hung from the wall, putting a hole in a patch of sand thousands of miles away.

Ben walked up to him, eyes still blazing red. "I was concerned for you, Alias."

"There's no need." Alias forced a smile. "Betty, this is Ben."

Betty reached for one of the hubot's hands and shook it before glancing around.

"I'm not supposed to leave my room without a friend to make sure I'm okay, but I suppose you're both my friends now. If I pass out, you'll look after me." Although her expression spelled out curiosity, insecurity colored her voice. "Where are we going now, Mr. Alias? You're not . . ." She huddled closer to him, gaze flitting between him and the main door. "You're not leaving me here alone, are you?"

"Of course not!"

Another tremor hit, but it was fainter than before, farther away. The rioters? The NID? What kind of formidable truths was McCarthy wielding to spur such violence? Deon having a daughter must be one of them, but what other leverage did she have? Deon had spoken of old truths using the plural.

Could Alias afford to wait for all the puzzle pieces to slot into place? He was probably going to pass out before Betty, and then he wouldn't be able to help. He had no wish to become even more incapacitated if there were severe side effects, but what if taking the B-injection was his only option for keeping it safe—and maybe, hopefully, ensure the survival of his mother and countless others?

Alias tugged at Betty's hand, and she followed him to the bookcase, Ben trailing after them. He leaned there, focusing as best he could on breathing. Was this how his mother felt before falling into a coma? What if he skipped that stage entirely and died right here, leaving Betty to fend for herself, with only Ben as protection?

He couldn't die now. He couldn't—

A hand tugged weakly at the hem of his shirt. "What are you doing?"

"There's something . . ." Alias exhaled sharply as he pushed and pulled at the book, trying to figure out how the safe worked. He sagged in relief when his finger connected with the tiny nub of a switch. Flicking it caused the book cover to slide back, exposing a metallic safe. The scanner on it seemed to undulate. Alias gripped the safe with both hands, waiting for the room to stop spinning. "I—I think there's something I can do to help your father." He put his right palm on the scanner and swore under his breath when nothing happened. "But I may not be able to."

"What's in there?"

Alias wiped at his forehead and blinked down at her. His head pounded. "What do you know about your father's work?"

With a groan, he gave in to the urge he'd been fighting for the last half hour and sank to the floor. A spasm shot through his right leg, but thankfully, he was almost sitting and didn't make a spectacle of himself. The certainty that he was about to pass out persisted, and he fought it, eyes intent on the girl who mirrored his posture.

"I know a whole lot," she said. "He is a very intelligent businessman, and his company makes bots. He also tries to save the world because I'm sick and he doesn't want me to die. That's what Jay explained, anyway." She shrugged. "I'm not sure that's how things work, though. But I trust him. And he trusts you, so I do too."

They both glanced up at the safe.

"So you know about the LX injection?" Alias asked.

Betty nodded. "It helps people, but doesn't work on those who are already sick, which makes him very sad, because he wants to help people like me." She cocked her head to the side. "People like you?"

Alias pondered the consequences of what he was about to say and decided that Deon wouldn't have entrusted his daughter to him if he didn't trust Alias's judgment. "He's been developing a new . . . injection of sorts to help people like us, but it isn't ready yet."

Betty's frown reminded Alias so much of Jaden that he felt like an intruder. When she spoke, it was with Deon's determination peeking through her obvious weariness.

"I need to test it, then."

"I do," Alias was quick to correct her, horrified to learn that self-sacrifice ran in the family. "We're not risking your life."

Betty's eyes gleamed with fury and understanding that would have befitted someone twice her age. "Then why are you risking yours?"

Alias could try to explain that the person who made up the lies about her father meant to have it destroyed. Or tell her about his mother and how this might be her only chance—and Betty's. He didn't want to worry her by mentioning how sick he was, even though the increasing weakness was the main reason he was considering injecting himself with experimental nanites.

Ben took a step closer. "Alias, you should reconsider. There is still time—"

"No, there isn't." He glanced down at Betty. "I need to do this because it's the only way to keep your father from trying it himself." Not the truest answer he could give, considering Deon's current preoccupations, but one that Betty might understand. "And there might be a copy in here. In this safe I can't open."

Betty struggled to her feet and thrust her face into his. "Is my dad sick?" she asked, half-shaking him, half-holding on to him.

"Don't cry." Alias fought the tears that threatened to spill in sympathy. The panic in Betty's voice would have broken his heart all over again had it not been in pieces already. "No one is going to die."

"Promise?"

"Promise." It wasn't a lie, not when it could still be the truth.

"Okay. So how do we open the safe?"

"We can't." Alias sighed, and then paused. He couldn't open it, but the safe lock was a DNA-coded model he recognized from his virtual PA days. These safes kept out everyone but the person whose DNA was keyed into it . . . and anyone who shared enough of that DNA.

The flaw was a closely kept secret, one that Deon might not be aware of.

"Maybe you can," he rasped.

The safe was too high for Betty to reach on her own, so Alias lifted her off the ground. His arms shook from the strain of holding it.

"It works!" Betty pulled the metal door with both hands to expose the content of the safe. "Look!"

The safe was empty, save for the one thing Alias had hoped to find.

Betty wiggled her fingers. "Let me—"

"No." Alias put a squirming Betty back on the ground, out of the way of temptation. "It has to be me."

"What if it doesn't work?"

"That's why it has to be me."

"Alias, this isn't safe," Ben tried again. "What would your mother say?"

"My mother—" Alias gritted his teeth. "—is in a coma. Again."

His hand shook as he picked up the hypospray, but he didn't dread what was to come—he trusted bots a lot more easily than people. He peered at the small metallic device. It looked like nothing. It might do nothing. But on the off chance that the little bots inside could beat the virus, or at least keep him alive long enough to keep his promise to Deon . . .

Dizzier than ever, Alias rested most of his weight against the bookcase, holding on to the hypospray like the literal lifeline it was. For so long, a part of him had been missing. He'd found it without searching, almost by accident. Deon's smiles and kisses had filled the empty space inside him with warmth, with trust and affection, until there was so much of it his own body betrayed him. Deon might not love him, but love was about giving, not receiving. It was about protecting those who refused help and making the hard decisions despite a hundred distractions. Love didn't require permission and didn't bow to reason.

And being in love breathed color into the gray landscape of his life, freed him from the shackles of fear. It was worth every twinge of pain in his chest right now, every moment he'd worried, and the looming threat of death.

Because love was life.

Slow and steady, he reminded himself, and positioned the tip of the hypospray against his arm. Deon's smiling face flashed before his eyes, causing his breath to stutter. He gritted his teeth again. Yes, he was doing it for Deon, and Betty, and his mother, but also for those who didn't know that a solution might exist. He would prove wrong the people who wished to bring Dehive to its knees.

He would remain alive long enough to do that and much more.

Breathe in.

Out.

Slow and steady.

"You must like my father very much," Betty whispered.

Alias's heart clenched.

Come on. One, two—

BANG!

The explosion knocked Alias off his feet. His knees hit the ground hard, and he hunched over as every pain sensor in his body flared to life. Betty curled into him with a shriek. Alias held on to her with one hand, the other wrapped around the hypospray, thankfully intact. He put it in his back pocket to free his hand.

Movement drew his eyes to the door, or rather, the space where it used to be. The door had been blown inward with chunks of the wall and now lay on the floor, its edges sharp and smoky.

On it stood a woman wielding a fierce-looking gun. Her skin was alabaster, and she was startlingly beautiful—in the way dangerous things often were. Her straight blond hair hit her jaw. The sharp blue of her skirt and shirt brought out her eyes. Alias couldn't decide if the prefect symmetry of her features contributed to her beauty or to the aura of danger that made his hackles rise.

"You're the assistant," the Ice Lady said, and stepped off the door, her dark heels clicking. "Alias Novar, is it?"

Alias climbed to his feet on wobbly legs. The gun should frighten him, but the truth was, Lyra McCarthy's mere physical presence conveyed a threat that all those videos he'd seen of her hadn't prepared him for. Sensing Betty at his back, he gestured for her to retreat farther into the room, away from McCarthy.

"Why are you doing this?" he rasped.

"Why would I not do everything in my power to protect my daughter?"

Alias stumbled. He must have misheard. Betty was Jaden's daughter? She looked . . .

A lot more like McCarthy than Jaden. And it made so much sense too. Deon had worked for McCarthy for years, before they'd parted ways not so amicably—just after McCarthy had taken a mysterious two-month vacation. How long ago was that? Seven, eight years? The timing would fit if Betty's illness made her look younger. Wouldn't that explain Betty's confusion at the mention of her *parents*, plural? And then there was the fact that Betty called Deon *daddy*, but Jaden by her given name.

And, of course, the physical resemblance. Now that he knew what to look for, he could see Lyra McCarthy's features reflected in Betty's, in the pouty lips, the curve of her jaw, the slightly upward tilt of her nose, the pointy chin. Genetics. It was hard to believe but harder to deny.

Did Betty know? With the way she'd gone silent, it was impossible to tell.

"I haven't seen her in eight years, Mr. Novar." McCarthy inched closer. "Why do you think I am so intent on taking down Dehive? For years, he kept Elizabeth away from me, my own daughter, and I will not have him experiment on her any longer."

The bookcase dug into his back. Could McCarthy's determination to drag Dehive into the ground really be nothing more than a mother's desperate attempt to free her daughter—a daughter who had been kept from her? Was this the root of McCarthy's issues? It sure sounded like the kind of old truth that could be weaponized to push NID to extremes.

"He didn't— He must have had his reasons—"

"What good reason could a man possibly have to deny a daughter her mother, and a mother her only child?" McCarthy cut in sharply. "How can you justify this? How can you even pretend to understand a mother's pain?"

Coming out of her mouth, the word *mother* sounded like more of a weapon than the gun she held, and Alias felt riddled with bullets. He didn't know what having a child felt like, but he suspected that his mother would have moved heaven and earth had she been denied him.

McCarthy lowered her gun and dropped to one knee, clutching her chest.

"Elizabeth . . ."

The scar on her cheek stood out as her jaw tightened, a sharp line parallel to her hair. White on white. Layers of ice, melting. She spoke Betty's name again, louder. No answer came.

"You have to help me," she said in a strangled voice, turning her focus toward Alias.

What was he supposed to think? He didn't want to believe her, because if he did, it meant Deon had lied to him all this time. And he trusted Deon, despite the secrets.

McCarthy's shoulders hunched forward. "You care for her, don't you?"

"Of course, she's—"

"Then you understand why she can't stay here. He will keep experimenting on her—"

"He would never do that!"

"Had he told you she was mine, or was that yet another thing he lied about?" McCarthy shook her head, a pitying expression on her face. "Deon Dehive would spin any number of lies to get what he wants. That's why this dangerous injection he's been developing is being confiscated right now by the NID to be destroyed."

The hypospray in Alias's pocket felt like it was melting, burning his skin through two layers of fabric. "You're wrong."

McCarthy stood up, nostrils flaring in a display of anger she'd never shown on screen. "I've never been wrong about him. How could you help him keep my daughter away from me?" She sneered, mirroring the hate that had filled Deon's tone. "How would your mother feel if you were kept away from her?"

"Shut up!"

In a heartbeat, McCarthy was in his face, her eyes alit with cold fury. Alias tried to push Betty toward the bathroom again, but she was gripping his shirt with both hands, muffling sounds into the fabric. Ben stepped closer, but its programming made intervention complicated.

"Deon is using you." McCarthy gripped the front of his shirt. "He's using all of us. You think he cares for you? He's the best liar there is, Mr. Novar. Has he told you already that you're the only one for him, like he told me once, before taking my daughter away from me? I lost eight years of her life!"

"He's never—"

A single tear trailed down McCarthy's cheek, crossing a scar. "He has a gift for making other people feel special. To make you trust him. But he lies. He lies all the time, to everyone, even to himself. The only thing you can trust is his ambition, because that's what gives him purpose. He takes and takes and *takes* without end."

McCarthy's voice had gone soft. Alias didn't know what to believe. Truths and lies blurred together, making his head spin. He hurt, and he couldn't tell where it started and where it ended, or why he was rooted to the spot like he was the one made of ice.

"You see, don't you?" McCarthy hid the gun behind her back and extended a hand to the trembling girl. "Elizabeth, come with your mother."

Finally, Betty let go of his shirt and took a step back. And another. "You're not my mother."

"Of course, I am."

"I'm not coming with you!" Betty cried.

She ran.

McCarthy tried to push past Alias, but he wasn't about to break his promise to Deon. There were so many things Alias didn't know about the man, barely understood, but he knew, he just did, that Deon cared. For his daughter, for Jaden, for Mr. Quint, for the people, for *him*. Secrets were stitched into that embroidery, but it was an embroidery Alias *loved*.

"Get out of my way."

McCarthy shoved him with impressive strength. He spun and cracked his brow against the wall. He gripped the shelf, but his legs gave out anyway. McCarthy holstered her gun and darted past him. Alias lifted a hand to stop her, but she was too fast.

A metallic hand caught his shoulder.

"Alias."

Ben helped him back to his feet. It had fresh scratch marks on its face from the explosion, but it moved with minimal awkwardness. Alias jerked his chin at the intruder. McCarthy was standing in front of the bathroom door, pleading voice growing harder with every word that Betty ignored.

"Ben, we have to—"

"Give it to me."

McCarthy had swirled around, glaring at Alias. There was nothing motherly about her expression.

"What?" With both hands wrapped around one of Ben's large arms, Alias stepped back.

McCarthy followed. "The injection," she said, cold voice matching her nickname. "Deon would have kept at least one vial outside of his lab, close by, and you . . ." Her eyes narrowed. "You either have it, or you know where it is. Give it to me right now."

"Or what?" Alias felt strangely light-headed and daring. "You have no leverage against me."

"Is that what you think?"

She drew her gun and pointed it at him.

Alias laughed. "I don't care—"

"Okay, then."

She trained it on Ben.

Alias meant to step between Ben and McCarthy, but froze. If both he and Ben went down, Betty would be undefended. But Ben . . .

"Do you think them alive, Mr. Novar? Are you fond of these despicable pieces of metal?" She spat the last word.

Alias tightened his grip on Ben's arm until every joint in his hand hurt. "At least they have a heart."

What was left of McCarthy's carefully crafted mask of a concerned mother crumbled. "You naïve little whore."

She fired.

Screens exploded in a shower of glass and sparks. Betty shouted his name, but Alias couldn't get his vocal cords to function.

"I will come for you shortly, Elizabeth," McCarthy called back, without glancing at the bathroom door. "There's no need to be afraid."

Ben was perfectly still, like only bots could be. Alias startled as something hit the floor at his back with a *crack*. Probably one of the screens. McCarthy cocked the butt of the gun against her hip.

"I won't miss next time."

Alias reached for his back pocket with a trembling hand and took his time retrieving the hypospray. He didn't need to fake the pain and dizziness—he ached everywhere. But the hope within him was bright. He revealed the hypospray from behind his back, keeping it close to his body.

"Hand it over." She shifted the gun. "Now, before someone gets hurt."

Alias adjusted his grip on the injection. *Please*, he told his body. *Don't let me down.* He met McCarthy's eyes. "I love him, you know."

She tossed her head back and laughed.

There.

The distraction he needed.

He pressed the hypospray to his bicep and squeezed. Despite it being the same delivery system as the one used for the LX compound, there was pain this time as the tiny bots flooded his veins in one scorching wave of agony. He hunched forward with a gasp. The empty hypospray fell from his limp fingers and hit the floor with a *click*, cracking but not breaking.

"What have you done!" McCarthy screamed.

"Been not as naïve as you think." Alias kicked the hypospray away as McCarthy lunged for it. The pain from the injection was gone, and he felt . . . about the same as before. Strong, despite his weakness. Alive, despite death's whisper in his ear. "Doing the right thing. But of course, you wouldn't know what that means."

"You little shit—"

The walls shook again, and McCarthy lost her footing, her grip on the gun slipping. Several screens dropped to the ground in a shower of sparks. Bits of ceiling fell on the bed, and more turned the pond murky. The ground wouldn't stop trembling. What was going on outside?

The ceiling just above Alias's head caved.

Ben pushed him to the floor. With a strong sense of déjà vu, Alias hit the ground. A scream rose, sharp and shrill. His mouth was flooded with blood, and his tongue stung. He heard, *felt* rock and concrete cracking down Ben's supine form.

But Betty didn't have anyone to protect her.

"We need to . . ." Though the push might have saved his life, it had knocked the breath out of him. "Betty. In the . . . bathroom." His lungs burned. "Can you stand?"

"I am in working order," Ben assured him, its voice as steady as ever despite a chunk of rock the size of Alias's head hitting its back and rolling off and to the side. "But we have to wait. It is not safe for us to move yet."

"Betty . . ."

Alias trailed off. It was no use. Hubots were programed to protect humans, but they also tended to display loyalty to their owner, much like a dog would. And Ben might have eyes stuck on red, motor problems, and all kinds of other issues, but it would have to be crushed to a pulp for the rules underlying its AI core to be wiped out.

For Ben to protect anyone else while Alias wasn't safe.

So, he waited.

It took almost a full minute before the rumbling stopped and Ben deemed it safe to help its owner to his feet. Alias scanned the room, trying to ignore the constant shivering and bile flooding his throat. McCarthy lay close by, lower body twisted to one side, eyes closed. Blood trickled down her scarred cheek, but she was breathing, according to Ben.

"I will call the emergency services," the hubot added.

"That's not necessary." Alias could hear several pairs of boots getting closer—no doubt officers of the NID, perhaps looking for McCarthy.

He moved toward the bathroom. The door was cracked open, and wide blue eyes peered around.

"We have to go."

Up to that point, Alias's vision of the apocalypse had been limited, in a way, to what he knew to fear. The permanent absence of motion. Light fading away as his body shut down. Distant screams beyond walls that closed in.

Fire hadn't been part of this vision, but that mistake was rectified the moment he stepped out of a hole blasted in the side of the Hive. The woods were on fire. Bright flames in orange and red latched on to trees and bushes, devouring branches and bark until the fifty-foot-tall giants Alias used as landmarks for his daily run were nothing more than blackened statues of ash. Thick smoke spiraled around the carnage. There was so much of it that it blotted out the sky.

To make things worse, it was freezing, the light snow a constant reminder that there were several explanations for his shivering.

"I'm s-scared, Mr. Alias."

"It's okay." Alias caught the small hand digging into his collarbone and gave it a reassuring squeeze. "We're going to be fine."

Ben steadied him when he caught his foot in a root, the multifunction hand a welcome grip on his shoulder. Alias leaned against the hubot with a whisper of thanks. He'd run so often in these woods, and yet he could hardly carve himself a path now, stumbling under the weight of the child curled on his back. The screaming seemed to come from everywhere at once. He didn't need to see the NID trying to contain the rioters to know that people were getting hurt.

Because McCarthy was adept at twisting the truth—and choosing the best moment to reveal secrets—for maximum impact.

Alias squeezed Betty's hand harder, heart pounding. If McCarthy wanted her, it would be over his dead body.

You're not going to die today, he told himself firmly.

"This way, Alias."

It was better to let Ben lead the way. Sweat ran down his face and into his eyes, joining black spots in obscuring his vision. He swiped a trembling hand across his eyes. His lungs were on fire. His whole body was on fire, but his skin was the same white as usual, untouched by flames.

The fever was getting worse. His world was collapsing, inside and outside, but he had to keep going. He had to have faith in these bots, as tiny and experimental as they were.

"Careful, Alias."

Ben nudged him with its mitt hand, steering him away from a root that would probably have tripped him. Alias followed his guide away from the chaos. Powerful spotlights had been turned on, miniature suns that lit up a line of twelve-foot-tall crowd-containing NID bots. Smaller bots of various forms plugged the holes in the wall, trying to prevent the rioters from escaping into the forest. Some of those bots might have been Dehive's, but the line was too far off for Alias to tell them apart. The shouting was getting louder over the alarms blaring and the weapons firing. Even the roaring of the fire couldn't drown out the crowd.

The screams of pain.

Despite the heat closing on him, Alias felt like he was freezing over. But he couldn't stop moving. Betty needed his protection, and he needed . . . to keep doing what he was doing, helping in every way he could. Gunfire and explosions filled the air, but none of it motivated him as much as the occasional whimper from the girl he was carrying. He wanted to reassure her and, sometimes, the sounds that left his mouth even resembled words of comfort.

If he hadn't felt so weak, he would have been terrified too.

He wiped his brow again and almost poked himself in the eye with a glass shard embedded in his forearm. His fingers shook as he took it out, and when he looked at his hand, it was sticky with blood. Like honey.

Bees.

"The cabin," he rasped. "We could get there."

"What cabin?" Ben asked. "Where is it?"

Betty tightened her hold around his neck, and Alias coughed as he tried to orient himself. With the fire gaining ground and the smoke obliterating his usual markers, he couldn't tell which way to go. His cough turned into a snarl of frustration.

"I . . . d-don't know," he admitted, but described it as best as he could.

"I can find it," Ben promised.

With his bloodied hand—he was holding on to Ben with the other—Alias pulled up the collar of his shirt to try to keep the smoke away. It was a mitigated success. Ben did its best to keep them away from people and smoke alike, but both were gaining ground.

"We have . . . to . . . hurry," Alias said, and got no reaction. Maybe he'd merely thought the words? His vision tunneled, fogged with black at the sides, and the tremors in his upper body were now affecting his legs as well. He barely protested as Ben transferred Betty onto its back.

"Is the cabin still far, Mr. Hubot?"

"According to what Alias had told me of its location, it should not be more than a ten-minute walk eastward, Betty."

"Not . . . far, then," Alias rasped, and tried to smile. "And w-well hidden, which . . . is good."

Betty wound her arms around the base of Ben's head and surveyed him with worried eyes. At least she wasn't asking about her father and Jaden anymore. Not that Alias needed her reminder to worry about Deon or his mother. He just had to listen to the screams cutting through the weapons' fire to picture Deon beaten up and unconscious, and his mother asleep for the rest of eternity. Unfortunately, he couldn't do anything for either of them . . . but he could get Betty to safety.

For a while, he even thought he would succeed.

"Don't move!"

An NID officer appeared in front of them. She didn't have her weapon drawn despite the general chaos sparked by the rioters, possibly because of Betty's proximity, but her stance evoked a threat nonetheless. Alias and Ben moved at the same time, the former to shield Betty and the latter to shield him. Alias ended up at the hubot's back. He covered as much of Betty's shivering form as he could and begged his body to hold on a little longer.

"Hand her over!" the officer barked. "No brusque motion. You, behind the bot, you'd better do as I say, or you'll be found guilty of aiding and abetting in the kidnapping of a child." She raised her left wrist and spoke into her watchphone. "Hey, I found the little girl. She looks sick but unharmed."

"Is she one of the bad people?" Betty whispered, and reached blindly for him.

Alias clasped her shoulder. He wanted to talk but dreaded that the moment he opened his mouth he would throw up instead.

"Show your hands or I'll have to subdue you!" the officer ordered, hand moving to her holster.

Alias rested his brow against Betty's head, just for a second. He doubted the woman would draw a lethal weapon, but he wasn't about to take the risk with Betty under his care.

"Step down, Ben."

"Alias, you are—"

"I said, show your hands!"

Alias stepped away from Ben and lifted both hands. The officer's face was half-hidden by a helmet.

"Don't bring her to McCarthy," Alias begged. "She needs her father—"

"On your knees!"

"I'm—" *trying*, Alias meant to say, but the word devolved into a coughing fit.

The officer had yet to draw her weapon, but more officers had approached from behind, barking orders. One of them addressed Betty in hushed tones, trying to coax her into letting go of Alias.

"It's dangerous out there, Elizabeth," the officer insisted. "Please let us bring you to safety."

Betty only clung harder to Alias. She was crying and coughing, whimpering his name like she was worried *for him*. Alias tried to do as he was told, but his body had gone stiff and refused to obey. An argument erupted when the officer who'd first approached Alias told one of her colleagues to keep his weapon sheathed. Alias knew there was shouting, but the sound of his heartbeat picking up speed was deafening.

"Don't shoot!" someone screamed. "You're going to hurt the girl!"

It might have been him. He was so afraid. For Betty, Ben, his mother, and Deon. For what was possibly the last dose of the B-injection, of which he'd made himself a vessel.

"No one is hurting this child," a voice rose from behind him. "Dehive won't get to hurt any more children after today."

Pain exploded at the back of his head.

The world was gray. Green crept in, and then hints of red, hot and blinding. *Fire*. It lit up the corners of his vision, and yet it felt much closer, licking at his bones. A loud *crack* reverberated inside his skull, devolving in a cacophony of arguing voices. He twisted his head just in time to throw up.

His hands were bound at his back and he hurt all over, every inch of his skin aflame. He remained prostrate, dry-heaving in what appeared to be grass, breathing through his mouth to avoid the stench of his own vomit. The coppery taste of blood was mingling with the bile on his tongue. His head felt like one giant ball of nothingness, his thoughts wandering too far off each other to connect in any semblance of sensible reflection.

A rough hand pulled him up onto his knees. Sitting back on his haunches with a pained gasp, Alias blinked past the tears. No, not tears: rain. The drizzle was faint, almost as light as the snow before, but the wind was strong and pushed smoke into his nose and mouth, burning air down to his lungs. He coughed and almost threw up all over again. How long had he been unconscious? The sky amounted to a gray blot of watery ink and didn't offer a clue.

"Let him go, you bunch of— Fuck you!"

It took a few seconds for Alias to connect the voice to Mr. Quint. When the pressure at his shoulder vanished, he found the strength to lift his chin and take stock of his surroundings.

Feet. Grass. Ashes. The Hive nearby. It would seem that he'd been dragged closer to the riot while he'd been unconscious. There were at least twenty people surrounding him, but only a few had eyes on him. The rest were watching Mr. Quint, who managed to land exactly one punch before a bulky officer threw him to the ground and held him down with his arms behind his back. Another officer moved in front of the duo, dragging a cuffed rioter who screamed at the top of her lungs.

Alias's own wrists were chaffed, and he shuddered in sympathy until his eyes landed on a familiar figure near a line of trees untouched by the fire, about a hundred feet away.

"Deon."

The word came out as a croak. It was raining harder now, and there was no way Alias could have been heard, even if the shouting had diminished. A dozen officers flanked Deon, escorted by two crowd-controlling bots. Deon's wet hair was plastered to his skull, and his shirt hung to his frame. He stood stock-still, which made sense considering his armed entourage and the bruises blossoming on his face. Alias could sense the despair and fury rolling off of him and shared his anguish. He strained to see past the wall of people around him, seeking out a little bee.

"Don't move."

Alias recognized the authoritarian voice from before, in the woods. The man was probably the same who'd knocked him unconscious. Alias had no energy left for righteous anger. Not when Deon looked eager to keep fighting a battle he was bound to lose.

Following the man's gaze, it was easy to understand why.

In front of what used to be the main entrance of the Hive, McCarthy stood with an owner's arrogance, her heels steady on a carpet of glass shards. At her left shoulder a smaller woman cowered, extending an umbrella to keep McCarthy dry, and at her right side was a high-ranking officer of the NID. His helmet was pulled up, exposing a stern expression.

Betty was nowhere to be seen, and Ben seemed to have vanished as well. Alias anxiously searched the rows of rioters still fighting off NID officers.

"If you move again, I'm going to stun you," the officer at Alias's back warned.

Alias stopped trying to stand up. McCarthy wasn't paying attention to either him or Deon, for she was too busy looking in approval at the NID officer addressing everyone in attendance, and the countless dragonbots buzzing in the air.

"People, please. We agree with you. Deon Dehive released an injection that would have benefited from more testing," he said, brow furrowed.

Do they actually believe such nonsense? Alias thought. *The problem is the L-variant!*

"Is LX really why the NID's here?" one the rioters currently being handcuffed shouted.

"Why are *you* here?" a journalist inquired through their dragonbot.

The rioter's expression turned stormy, matching their surroundings. "Because Dehive's experimenting on children."

"Including my own daughter," McCarthy chimed in like she'd been waiting for exactly that opening.

The officer at her side shot her a disapproving glance as the crowd of rioters and the journalists went wild with questions.

"You have a daughter?" asked a hundred voices at once.

"Yes, I have a daughter. One that Deon Dehive has kept away from me, and one of the many children whom he plans on testing another injection on."

To Alias's mounting frustration, McCarthy's expression morphed into the mask of the tearful mother she'd worn earlier, and everyone except himself, Mr. Quint, and Deon seemed to buy those lies hook, line, and sinker.

"That isn't true!" Deon screamed.

"Really?" Triumph flashed on McCarthy's face. "So you haven't been developing an antiviral that's more dangerous than LX? I haven't been missing my daughter for *eight years?*"

The NID officer who'd been trying to get her to stop talking relented, and Alias could see the despair etched in Deon's features even from a distance—could feel the uncomfortable twisting in his own gut at McCarthy's clever manipulation. She didn't have to say much, just twist the truth in a way that gave everyone pause. These people didn't know Deon or understand how viruses worked, they merely had fears that McCarthy was more than happy to fuel.

Alias saw Deon's lips move, but he couldn't hear him anymore, only feel an echo of hopelessness as Deon defended himself with words no one was willing to hear. Alias's chest tightened at the sight of the man he loved getting red in the cheeks from how much he was screaming. He wasn't in cuffs yet, probably because there was still confusion—just enough doubt—for the NID to hesitate on the procedure to be followed in such a unique case. But the officers at Deon's side all had their weapons trained on him.

"Elizabeth!" McCarthy exclaimed, and stepped away from the umbrella.

Alias whipped his head so fast his neck popped, but he couldn't care less: Ben had just emerged from the woods. Holding its mitt was a snot-faced and drenched Betty Dehive, who called out to her father in between coughing fits. Deon told her to stay put, stay safe, focus on breathing, but stubbornness clearly ran in the family.

Whispers rippled through the crowd, tension mounting with every tentative step the child took toward her father, a heavily damaged hubot in tow. Alias's heart sank as he took in Ben's state: a barely glowing red left eye, a missing arm . . .

Betty stumbled and fell to her knees.

Three things happened in short order.

Ben reached for Betty, and Betty, trembling, reached back.

Someone shot Ben in the head, missing Betty by inches. Ben collapsed in a heap on top of her.

Alias leaped to his feet and ran.

"Stop!" bellowed several voices at his back.

Alias kept running. He should have been too weak to walk, but his feet pounded the ground with a metronome's regularity. He'd run for so long it was the most natural thing in the world.

"Stop!" called out more voices, louder.

He didn't try to duck as several weapons went off. He was a fast runner, even on wet grass. The weakness and pain couldn't take that away. If anything, it boosted the panic that gave him wings. He picked up speed as the sound of pursuit grew closer. More bullets were fired, sizzling inches away on either side of him, tearing through the soft pattering of rain and the crackling noise of the fire still going strong.

He didn't stumble or hesitate. His shoulders ached, but he was too caught up in his objective to worry if it was caused by the cuffs or a bullet. It didn't matter either way. He couldn't stop. He had to get to Ben and Betty before the NID officers. They were fast too. Healthier.

But he was infinitely more motivated.

An officer ordered a cease fire when he got within ten feet of where Betty lay crushed under Ben. Alias skidded to a stop and sank to his knees in front of them. His throat closed up as he spied a lock of blond hair in the grass, cut clean by Ben's multitool hand. Shuffling forward, he tried to figure out a way to help them.

"Betty? Ben? Can you hear me?"

There came no answer from Ben.

"Mi-Mister A . . ."

"Betty!"

Alias braced one shoulder against Ben's torso and started to push. The metal heap budged a few inches. He strained on his knees, gathering what little strength he had left. When an officer appeared beside him and started helping, he tensed but couldn't allow anything to distract him. Agony spread down his spine as they pushed upward to lift enough of Ben for Betty to crawl out. The shoulder supporting Ben screamed at him, the bullet digging further into muscle, but Alias didn't let go until Betty was in the clear. When she hugged him, he was forced to drop Ben, and it was one of the hardest things he'd ever done.

Ben might not be alive, but he'd taken care of Alias for so long it had become a part of Alias's life. A part of *him*.

"Mr. Alias."

Betty was shivering hard. It was cold, despite the fire. Colder than it had been—except for his arm. The thick and viscous blood running in rivulets down its length should have been more alarming than it was. He'd been shot, after all.

"Please help my father," Betty croaked.

A half circle of armed officers closed in on them. The woman who'd helped him move Ben—the same woman who'd found him in the woods earlier—spoke in a soft voice.

"Hand the child over, Mr. Novar."

Alias tried to stand, but it proved impossible with his hands still cuffed at his back and Betty clinging to him.

"P-Please," she wheezed.

Her pull turned into a push, into support, just enough for Alias to find his balance and climb back to his feet. She wrapped trembling arms around his waist afterward, making Alias wish he could return the hug as he gave the officers the most challenging look he could muster.

"She doesn't want to be handed over. And with reason: for her whole life, it's her father who has protected her."

It had been the right thing to say: the woman faltered, and so did her colleagues, trading uncertain looks between them.

Maybe not all the NID officers were of one mind about this. Maybe there was hope.

Maybe he could speak his mind and help tip the balance in Deon's favor. This wasn't something he could have done before, but he'd changed a lot. If seeking the limelight to shift public opinion was the best thing he could do to help, then he would do it. In his veins flowed a scientific gamble, and if it wasn't good enough, then nothing would be, not in time for him anyway.

"That man is dangerous!" McCarthy shouted, coming closer, sowing more lies with each step, the rain drops hitting her cheeks forming the only tears Alias could ever believe. "He's Deon Dehive's assistant and lover and helped keep my daughter away from—"

"I'm just someone who would protect a child who isn't mine with my own life."

Alias glanced up at the swarm of dragonbots hovering in the air above his head, big lenses pointing down in his direction, voices pipping through the speakers while they got close-ups of whatever expression he was wearing right now. The barrage of questions heightened the pressure beneath his temples, and the buzzing wasn't helping. It was downright unpleasant, actually, so unlike the bees' smooth, comforting hum, but these bots were listening to him—not McCarthy, not the NID, not the rioters.

Him. Just a person, but one who held someone special and unique in his arms: the only child of the two most significant players in humanity's fight against the Loveborne virus. Two behemoths who'd been at odds for so long it defied reason that they used to get along enough to have a child together.

Maybe that was one reason he got to be heard. Handcuffed, but free to use this small window of opportunity to speak his mind while the NID tried to decide how to deal with the situation.

"I . . ."

He trailed off as the scenery in front of him shifted, morphing into the park he used to visit daily, back when running was the only thing he enjoyed. He was standing as tall as any dream, his attention not on the plaque commemorating death but on the sculpted figure and the meaning she held. Impossibly, the statue bent at the waist, the woman's mysterious smile one of approval. The light at her back was growing brighter. He could sense its warmth on his skin, like a wildfire about to consume his body. Large bees the size of dragonflies dangled from the long mane of copper, replacing the still cogs that had lost their purpose.

Alias dug his thumbnail into the meat of his other palm, using the jolt of pain to shake off the hallucination. The statue vanished, replaced by a cloud of wide lenses. How many people were hanging on to his every word? Thousands? Millions?

"Mr. Dehive didn't do any testing on his daughter," he said in a whisper recorded for everyone to hear. Betty held on to him like he was her lifeline, and yet he could have sworn she was *his* tether to reality, her shivering form the missing link between his disjointed thoughts. "He's very protective of her, and all of us. This new injection he's been working on is still a work in progress, which is why it's been kept a secret. If you look at my left bicep—"

"It's been kept a secret because he uses it on unsuspecting children!"

Only a few dragonbots turned toward McCarthy while their fellow journalists converged to take a closer peek at the injection site. Alias had to tell himself that he could still breathe, that there was still air.

"The first person Mr. Dehive tests anything on is himself, because he's selfless and refuses to have anyone else take a risk he wouldn't take. He only ever wishes to help others and has been working relentlessly to ensure his daughter's survival. And I'm," he continued, voice breathy, vision swimming, "I'm much the same, which is why I took this injection just a few hours ago. I'm sick with LBV and I . . . want to help in any way I can."

The burning woods had become an intricate tapestry of red against the pitch-dark sky beyond, but there was no heat, only tiny shards of ice growing inside his bones, threatening to silence forever the truth he still had to share. As the words tumbled from his numb lips following the hopeful twirl of the gears slowing down in his head, Lady Love kept watch over him, the bright blue of her eyes revealed at last. She was the sky and the ocean, she was Betty and Deon.

"Mr. Novar?" asked the statue in a thousand voices.

"The B-injection . . ." His lungs strained. He was so cold, and so hot, and it was hard to talk with his teeth clattering. "Whether it works or not at this early stage is irrelevant. Finding a solution requires time. What is important is that Mr. Dehive is doing ground-breaking work and needs to continue to do so because Avida and LX are failing, and maybe it's time to try something different in our fight against LBV." He smiled fondly as he jerked his chin at his shoulder. "Nanites might just be the key to triumph over LBV."

Lady Love changed shapes, became bulkier and taller, stretching far above the Hive.

"I . . ."

There was wetness at his knees again. So much wetness on his arm, on his face, and in his mouth. The taste of honey coated his tongue, mingling with blood and bile. Alias screwed his eyes shut, opened them, and found himself staring at a billion eyes he couldn't see.

"Alias!"

It shouldn't be possible, and it didn't make any sense, but he heard only one voice amidst the chaos: Deon's, calling out his name as the bees closed in on him, so many of them, buzzing in a frenzy, so loud, too loud, as though they lived in his ears, inside his head. His thoughts were sweet, in a way. Hope should be.

Words he hadn't known to plan were right there on the tip of his tongue.

"I'm n-not asking you to trust the word of a stranger. I . . . I'm asking you to trust my will to help. To trust . . . my will to k-keep on living to keep offering hope." Tiny hands were clutching at his shoulder, too small to belong to the statue. A sharp pain radiated from his chest outward, sizzling hot in the icy-cold path of his veins. His tongue felt too big in his mouth, and his mouth too small for the words. The crushing pressure in his skull made him double over, but he wasn't done.

"That's . . . that's the only risk I'm asking you to take."

Darkness descended upon him, drowning everything but the flames devouring him.

CHAPTER TWELVE
THE MIRACLE OF LOVE

He couldn't feel the ground under his feet, and yet everything was moving. The woods were gone, and in their place sprouted fully-formed walls blossoming into hexagonal ceiling tiles. His heart hammered, and the walls reflected its frantic staccato, undulating in a stream of honey-colored waves. The inside of his head felt sticky, like he'd entertained too many sweet thoughts. The rest of him burned as though the fire had relocated into his veins. This fever was unlike any he'd ever had. He frowned at the flashing red lights. That wasn't right either. Honey shouldn't be red. The bees should leave his ears, return to their hive where they belonged.

After a while, words emerged from the buzzing.

". . . you complete lunatic, reckless idiot! Springing something like that on me. Fuck, Alias, why would you not tell me you were sick?"

Alias. Right, that was him. And he did feel sick. About to throw up, actually. Again. Or pass out. It explained why he was being carried. Just holding on to the person carrying him was draining the last of his strength. He turned his head enough to press his face into the wet fabric stretched taut over a muscular chest and heard a sharp intake of breath.

"Stay awake," the voice ordered.

A jarring motion filled the back of Alias's throat with bile, but he managed to hold it. At least the bees were gone.

Bees. Why was this word important?

The arms holding him shifted, one hand covering the back of his neck. Apparently, he'd been nuzzling the wet fabric of the other person's shirt but didn't feel like stopping. The hand on his nape felt solid. Safe. It seemed to reach inside his skull and help him sort through the wandering memories. Images replaced the flashes of red: a child hidden away in a bunker, the pinch of a hypospray, gunshots, Deon—

Was Deon carrying him?

"Alias, can you hear me?"

His eyes rolled back into his head.

It was raining again.

He didn't mind the rain, although it made running trickier. His teeth were clattering, and it was no wonder: the rain was cold. Red dripped down his arms and wrist, washed down by icy water.

Blood. This was blood being washed down the drain. The back of his head hurt fiercely. Maybe that's where the bleeding came from? Something . . . a hand . . . was rubbing him there. Both of his hands lay at his sides, limp and useless, knuckles brushing against the hard tiles as the hand rubbed and kept on rubbing—

Wait.

He wasn't outside. This wasn't rain making him cold, and no tree was keeping him upright: he was sitting with his back to someone else's chest . . . in a shower?

The hand at his nape vanished, and strong arms encircled his shoulders.

"Don't you dare leave me."

He knew that voice. *Deon.* He let his head roll back and felt Deon's warm breath against his temple. Where was Ben? The last time he'd seen it . . .

"C-cold."

"I know." Warm lips found his temple and trailed a series of kisses down one side of his face. "But you're running a high fever, and I have to bring your temperature down. Dr. Lentz is on their way."

Why? Alias didn't ask. He was just so cold. And tired. But he had to stay awake . . .

"Hey."

There was a gentle tap on his cheek. Alias blinked in confusion. Where was he again?

"Stay with me, Alias. Stay awake. Help is on the way."

Help for what? Ah, the fire. The fever. LBV.

A horrible idea took shape in his head: What if Deon was sick as well?

Somehow, he managed to find the strength to lift a hand and grip one of Deon's wrists.

"You . . . s-sick?"

"*You*'re asking *me*?"

Deon shifted at his back, and it occurred to Alias that Deon had kept his clothes on, whereas he was completely naked. Not that it bothered him. He just wanted to make sure . . . something about bees . . .

"B-Betty . . ." Hit by a spell of dizziness, he waited a beat, and then tried again. "She okay?"

The arms around him tightened.

"Betty is fine, and I will be too, once Lentz arrives."

Alias tried to wrap his head around the meaning of the words. "For Betty?"

"For you."

The anger in Deon's tone registered on the same level the water did: something to be endured. Deon freed an arm to press the back of one hand against Alias's brow. Alias tried to bite back a whine at the contact. Light as the pressure was, it turned the dull ache inside his skull to throbbing agony.

"Shh. Here, stand. Come on, brace yourself against me. Careful with that arm, you've been shot."

There was a dangerous undercurrent to those words, one Alias was too exhausted to decipher. He managed a vague noise of agreement.

"That's it," Deon praised, voice warm again. "Nice and easy."

Alias couldn't stand on his own. His feet skidded on the tiles, but Deon's grip on his arms was iron. The water was turned off, and the world shifted as Deon picked him up. He was dripping and shivering, and so was Deon.

"W-wet clothes," he rasped, tugging at the shirt against his cheek. "C-cold."

"Don't concern yourself with me." Deon kicked the door of the shower stall outward and strode toward the door. "Damn it, Alias, these nanites were in my safe for a fucking good reason."

"Am I . . . dying?"

He felt no concern at all, but Deon sounded afraid when he replied.

"You are not dying. You're not, Alias, do you hear me?"

But you're not sure it works. No one knows.

Deon's face was losing color and growing dimmer. Blurry.

"I'm—"

"Don't. You're not. You can't. Stay awake, Alias!"

Alias's head rolled back. Deon cradled it in one hand and looked down at him. He'd never looked fiercer, surer, than in that instant, eyes blazing with a fury just short of madness.

"My mother . . . She . . ."

"Stay with me, Alias." Desperation crept into Deon's voice. "I'm taking care of everything, just stay with me—"

His grip slackened on Deon's shirt as the darkness returned.

The swarm of bees made no noise, but they surrounded him, filled him. He should suffocate, but he didn't. In a way, he was part of the hive.

Alias!

On his tongue, the sweetness of honey was strong. He was falling, alongside a million bees, but he wasn't afraid. The more he fell, the more distance there was between him and the pain. He was exhausted, and it was easier to let the current carry him. To go down, to fly away and leave it all behind—

ALIAS!

The light was too bright, but at least it wasn't red anymore. His mouth tasted of vomit, rather than honey. The sensation of freefall was gone, but there was a new lightness to his limbs, and the pain was but a memory. Sure, he felt sore and weary, but the mind was easy to fool. Maybe he *was* dead?

He closed his eyes and opened them again.

The light was still too bright. And so very white. Where was this? Turning his head hurt, but he managed. The room was unfamiliar, but the strangely organic-looking walls and ceiling indicated he was in the Lab.

A vast array of machines surrounded him—familiar machines he'd seen all too often at the hospital. The two IV drips shed some light on the cottony sensation in his head and the lack of pain. He was glad. If he was drugged, he was alive. Awake.

Deon was sitting next to him on an office chair with his shoulders hunched and lips bloodied. His right eye was purple and swollen. It widened, and so did the other.

"Alias."

A straw was pressed to his lips, and cool water trickled down his throat. It felt divine.

The only door in the room opened on a disheveled, sour-looking Dr. Lentz. Deon jumped to his feet.

"It's about time you showed up."

"Well, I did the fucking best I could considering the storm both of you unleashed. The NID's everywhere in the Hive and the ten officers at the door of my own office—thank you for taking over my space by the way—felt the need to question me for a very long time. As if you and I are not currently allowed some latitude because *someone* went behind our backs to make themselves into a live petri dish."

Alias wondered why he'd ever disliked doctors when this one was so funny. He opened his mouth to argue that it made sense to try the B-injection because he was dying, but the twin glares directed his way silenced him. It was probably for the best, anyway. He felt about to pass out, again. At least the painkillers were working well.

Dr. Lentz got to work, mumbling about how his mother looked a lot better than he did.

"So she . . ." Alias's eyes stung with unshed tears. "She's fine."

"She's more stable than you are, that's for sure. *Fine* remains to be seen, for her and you."

Deon's scowl remained. Alias didn't get why. He felt fine. Mostly. He couldn't move much, but breathing was easier now, and the horrible pain in his skull and, well, everywhere, had decreased a lot. He still felt overheated despite the chills, but the word *fever* was thrown around enough for him to remember why.

At some point, he was moved to his side.

"Dr. Lentz is changing your bandage," Deon said. "You've got an awful wound at the back of your head."

"There's a bullet wound on my shoulder," Alias pointed out helpfully.

Deon mumbled something under his breath. "Well, the good doctor will check that one too, won't he?"

Alias caught Deon's gaze and read concern there. Worry. Why was he so worried? Couldn't he see that Alias was fine? Hadn't he himself told Alias that he wouldn't, *couldn't*, die?

He fell asleep before he could ask.

The next time Alias saw Deon, it was through the filter of a screen, with a distance of several hundred miles between them. The volume was off, but subtitles reflected the discussions, little black letters moving from one end of the screen to the other at crawling speed. His tired eyes struggled to follow. Every now and then, though, an important word would stand out, Deon's expression would change, and puzzle pieces would slot together.

A hard-set jaw. *Negotiations.*

The flash of a proud smile. *Hard work.*

A furrowed brow. *Terminal patients. Children.*

Deon was frowning a lot, and small lines of tension appeared at the corners of his eyes whenever the word *injection* was mentioned off screen.

The first time *injection* and *Novar* were mentioned in the same sentence, Deon stood up.

He didn't sit down again.

At least, not until after Alias fell asleep, the word *hope* branded on his eyelids.

A lot had happened while Alias was out, and Dr. Lentz— not Deon—had caught him up. Apparently, the man he loved had been arrested and released in the same day, and the NID had pivoted to McCarthy and her lies. The nanites were working, another bit of news Dr. Lentz had broken to him. Mr. Arvin, the mole within Dehive, had been arrested.

Alias tried to be happy about it all. Deon seemed to be okay, although he hadn't visited in days. Alias missed him. Greatly. And now that love wasn't life-threatening anymore, he wanted to let Deon know how he felt.

And ask how Deon felt about him. Deon obviously liked him, but there was a difference between *liking* and *loving*—a difference between Alias and Jaden. Unless Deon loved them both and just hadn't found an opportunity to tell him?

Alias wouldn't know unless he asked.

He took some comfort from an interview later that night, long after Dr. Lentz had left their office to check on their other patient.

Deon talked almost exclusively about him in this one.

"I never wanted Mr. Novar to try the B-injection, but he did."

"Mr. Novar is the most courageous person I know."

"I trust implicitly very few people these days, but I trust Mr. Novar with my daughter's well-being."

"Of course I care about Mr. Novar."

McCarthy's former supporters were few and far between, and the interviewer wasn't among them. Alias's name was thrown around a lot, and the interview was concluded with statements from specialists around the world sharing their enthusiasm that a nanite-based antiviral was the miracle they'd been waiting for.

To say that his mother had been worrying would be an understatement. Alias couldn't hold it against her. He'd watched the statement he'd given a week ago, and the young man on the video looked dreadfully pale. The close-ups of his bloodied shoulder and red-shot eyes certainly added to the general picture.

Alias's confession that he'd made a test subject out of himself hadn't helped, and neither had his justification.

"The world needs Mr. Dehive, not me."

This statement—which he couldn't remember making—had made a lot of headlines. Alias's voice had been a hoarse whisper, but the mics of the bots had picked it up without issue, turning it up for the world to hear. And the world wanted to hear it, again and again—the whole speech. It was surprisingly coherent, a miracle considering how delirious Alias had been, high with fever and hallucinating half the time. And not only had he made sense, but he'd been convincing too.

"I'm feeling much better now," he told his mother for at least the hundredth time.

His mother's expression made it clear that she would have jumped through the screen and shaken some sense into him if it had been possible.

"And where is Mr. Dehive now?"

"He's working." Alias reclined against the mountain of pillows with a wince. "He's got a lot to do, what with the B-injection and the betrayal of his chief virologist's assistant."

His mother scoffed, brow pinched in disapproval.

"You saved his company, my dear boy. You saved *the world*. He should be with you."

The words weren't new, but the ECG scanning his heartbeat beeped faster. He picked up the glass from the bedside table and took a quick drag of water to win some time.

"You can tell him now," his mother said, voice softer. "You should."

"I will," he said, with only the slightest hint of disquiet. "We need to talk about a lot of things."

The door slid open, preventing his mother from asking about the specifics.

"Mr. Alias!"

Alias had expected Dr. Lentz, but it was Deon, accompanied by an energetic whirlwind of a child who launched herself into Alias's arms, knocking the tablet aside in her enthusiasm.

"Take care of yourself," his mother said, voice muffled by the bedsheets. "I love you, Alias."

"Love you too," Alias managed through a curtain of blond hair.

The screen turned off. As discreetly as possible, Alias got the hair away from his face and tossed the tablet aside.

"Who was that?" Betty inquired, just short of bouncing in his lap. "Do you feel better? You look better." She tucked the strand he'd just freed into the bun at her nape, or at least tried to, obviously more interested in all the answers she wasn't waiting for. "Did you see my first speech? I was nervous but Dad told me it didn't show."

"What did I tell you, Bee? No overwhelming your new friend while he's recovering."

For all that Alias had heard Deon's voice often over the past few days, that deep rumble, and the hint of a smile in it, got to him like a new dose of the B-injection. He would have liked to keep the tide of relief and longing to himself, but the ECG sold him out, and Alias found himself fighting his body's reactions while Deon's attention darted to the obnoxious machine.

"Sorry," Betty said, her cute little face scrunching up in contrition.

Alias took a fortifying breath and pasted on a reassuring smile. Betty wouldn't understand why he was so worked up. He just had to be patient for a little while longer. "I'm feeling much better now, I assure you. You're not overwhelming me."

Betty whipped her head around. "You heard, Dad? I'm not doing the overwhelming thing!"

"I can see that."

The door opened again.

"Hello, there."

Jaden waved at him from the doorway.

"You look much better," she said, clear approval lacing the words. Her hair was braided tightly, not a strand out of place, but her pearl shirt was wrinkled, and she held her matching three-inch-tall shoes in one hand. "I can't stay long. I just came to see how you were doing with my own eyes and take that little bee out of your hair."

"More like her hair away from him," Deon quipped.

"Come here, Bee." Jaden extended a manicured hand. "Alias needs his rest."

"But—"

"And your dad needs to talk to him."

That argument seemed to work better. After a brief but overly tight hug, Betty hopped to the ground, her pout transforming into a grin she relocated into Jaden's arms. Alias waved back as she was whisked away, the ache in his chest growing to unbearable proportions.

The soft sound of the door closing caused his gut to tighten in anticipation.

"So." Deon unbuttoned his jacket and shouldered it off with a jerky motion, tossing it on the back of the only chair in the room. He was dressed in full business attire, his black slacks and waistcoat sharp against the crisp white of his shirt. His blood-red tie sat askew at his throat, the knot loose. He untied it with a practiced gesture, his hands quick and sure, so unlike Alias's own, twitchy in his lap. "You look better."

Alias's eyes jumped to the dark purple of a healing bruise at the corner of Deon's mouth, and then higher, to the star-shaped wound at the very edge of the swollen skin around a blue eye.

"I feel better." The truth, with a small lie embedded in it. "You look worse."

"Why, thank you."

Alias flushed. "Er, I mean—"

"I know what you mean." Deon chuckled, but it sounded wry and self-deprecating. He looked exhausted, hurt, and somehow, more beseeching than ever. He pushed away from the door and tossed his bunched-up tie on the chair. "May I?" He jerked his chin at the bed.

Alias scooted over hastily.

"Thanks." Deon plopped down on the mattress beside him. "I thought this day would never end." The bed creaked as he curled a leg sideways and pressed a hand onto the bed, bracing himself against it. "You know that Betty kept asking after you?"

Alias had to bite the inside of his cheek to not reach for the new marks on Deon's face and explore them like he'd explored the rest of him. He shook himself, wishing he could unplug that ECG. They really had to talk first.

"I'm . . . I'm glad she's better at last. And my mother. Even Ben—"

Deon's lips thinned in anger. Alias sat straighter on the bed. He knew why Deon was angry, of course. But he wasn't about to accept a second tongue-lashing today.

"You know why it had to be me."

"No, I don't."

"Like hell you don't. I was sick, not you."

"That's not—"

"The responsibility fell to me," Alias said, speaking louder to prevent another interruption. "It's simple math, Deon. And besides, you said I was going to be fine, so which is it?" The ECG's beeps sped up yet again. "Did you lie to me?"

"I thought I was going to lose you!" Deon roared.

Alias's heart skipped a beat. "You said I was going to be fine . . ."

"Fear isn't rational, remember?"

The look on his face was familiar. When Alias had passed out, Deon had raced to Betty and Alias. But the close-ups from the dragonbots had made it clear that the name on his lips hadn't been his daughter's but that of the young man who'd collapsed. Deon had picked up Betty first, but only long enough to make sure she wasn't hurt before handing her over to Mr. Quint of all people. There had been several minutes of heated discussion before Deon was allowed to carry Alias back inside the Hive, but there had been no denying how concerned he'd been.

"Fear isn't rational at all," Alias said slowly. "But taking the injection was."

Deon's nostrils flared. "No, it wasn't. I cannot protect you if—"

"How is that fair?" Alias protested, tears gathering at the back of his eyes. He didn't want to cry, everything was fine, but . . . "Why should you have the monopoly on protection? I would do anything for you! You don't get to tell me—"

"Alias."

Deon pulled apart the hands he'd been wringing together, but Alias didn't protest, too busy trying to keep a lid on his emotions. The soft back and forth of Deon's thumb over the new scar at the back of his right hand didn't help him calm down.

"Alias," Deon repeated, voice so much softer, pleading.

The bright light of the lamps caught the side of Deon's face, painting the taut features and faint new scar in chiaroscuro. Those blue eyes never failed to act on him like a magnet, and right now, they connected to his heart, every second of scrutiny tightening the vice around it. Blood roared in his ears as the gleam of affection seemed to expand in Deon's gaze, closer to hunger in some inexplicable way and yet much more tender than lust.

The hope in Alias's chest expanded. His eyes stung. He didn't know why he wanted to cry, and when a horrifying sniffling sound tore from his lips, he cringed. A tear fell down his cheek, quickly followed by another.

"Are you in pain?" Deon reached for his earpiece. "I'll call Lentz right aw—"

"No, I'm fine." Alias smiled through his tears. "I love you."

Deon's eyes widened almost comically, and his jaw dropped.

"I . . ." Heat crept up Alias's throat and cheeks as the silence stretched on, fraught with tension. "I think I might have for longer than I was aware. This is . . . very new to me, and I don't know how—"

"You're doing just fine, and I love you too, you reckless fool."

Every frantic thought swirling in Alias's mind screeched to a halt. "But . . ."

"But what?" Deon pressed the tip of his nose to the straight arch of Alias's and rubbed them together. "You want the monopoly on love? I'm afraid it's too late for that."

Alias's brow furrowed. "How does that work? I overheard you talking with Jaden," he admitted, and spared a glance, or more accurately, a glare, for the ECG that betrayed his nerves. "You were discussing the B-injection. That's how I learned it existed. And then you . . ." His voice broke. "I don't want to make things more complicated for you—"

"Oh, Alias. It's not like that."

Deon pressed a finger under Alias's chin. Alias had half a mind to bite it off, and some of his intent must have shown, because Deon's eyes lit up with a mix of mirth and hesitation, and he pulled his hand back.

"Jaden is Bee's mother in all the ways that matter, but we love each other like the best of friends. We care about each other and Betty deeply, but there's no desire or romantic affection between us."

"The relationship between Mr. Dehive and myself shouldn't be relevant to the one blossoming between you."

It was exactly what Jaden had implied, back in the cabin.

All the agitation that had weighed down on him since Deon had walked into the room lifted from his shoulders. "Oh."

"Yes," Deon agreed, voice soft and hopeful. He framed Alias's face with both hands and smiled as the touch was welcomed this time. "I don't go around telling people I love them on a whim, you know. I love Betty because she's my daughter, and Jaden as a friend, but I love you as a lover, Alias. *I am in love with you.* It's been"—a shadow fell across his face—"killing me to keep it to myself, but I couldn't put you in that position, even if I suspected it was mutual. Not while you had your mother to care for and barely slept because of this job. I wanted to wait, and then . . ." Deon's voice broke. "I thought the variant, and this experimental antidote, was going to take you away from me."

Alias's mind spun. The revelation that it wasn't air but solid ground on either side of the thin wire he traipsed on, floored him.

"What if I'm bad at this?"

"You can't be." Deon sounded so sure. "You really can't." His hands were languid on Alias's cheeks, his gaze patient and curious, *loving*. "The fact that we've told each other how we feel doesn't change those feelings or how we've acted on them so far. You're already good at this, trust me." He brought one of Alias's hands to his chest and pressed it there, over his pounding heart. "I can feel it, right here."

It dawned on Alias that Deon's love for him wasn't new. He'd just been too overwhelmed to recognize it for the mirror it was. A mirror of his own feelings.

He extended his fingers as far as they would go, and Deon's heartbeat quickened, matching the ECG. And why wouldn't it? For all his wealth of carnal experience, Deon might not have been touched like this before—with romantic love. Was he, like Alias, marveling at how good this simple contact felt?

"Alias," Deon whispered.

To Alias's ears, it sounded like yes. More tears spilled and trailed past Deon's thumb.

Deon caught one with his lips. Alias turned his head on instinct, angling his face for a kiss. A sob shook him as Deon tangled both hands into his hair gently, careful of the healing wound at the back of Alias's head. Deon's mouth was gentle as it moved against Alias's, and in between each press of lips, each precious kiss, he put those feelings into words.

"I love you."

Alias shivered, both hands spasming on Deon's chest. Their mouths met again, briefly.

"I love you."

Alias moaned, shivering harder. He doubted there would ever come a day when such words became so commonplace his chest didn't fill with fireworks.

Deon brushed the corner of Alias's mouth with his lips. "We're okay?"

"More than okay." Alias hooked his chin over Deon's shoulders and hugged him tight. After a life of panic attacks and deprivation, it seemed that now there was too much, all at once: too much bliss, too much meaning, too much love.

Alias pulled back to cup Deon's cheek and traced the sculpted jawline with his thumb, back and forth, careful around the healing wounds. Deon brought Alias's wandering hand to his lips and kissed each knuckle with a smile that bordered on shy.

Alias didn't feel shy. He felt bold, empowered by the knowledge that he was good at loving.

He just had to follow his instincts.

With one firm push, he backed Deon up against the headboard, and crashed their mouths together. His lover's taste exploded on his tongue as they devoured each other.

Lover.

"Reckless idiot," Deon gasped in between kisses. "*My* idiot. Testing dangerous compounds that could have killed you."

"That might have killed you if I'd let you." Alias groaned, scraping his teeth over the soft skin covering Deon's frantic pulse.

Deon arched his back, hands moving to Alias's hips. "God, I love you so much."

Alias held on to any part of Deon he could reach while he tried to make sense of his luck. This love really was his, a promise that Deon reiterated to him as he dug a thumb into his jaw, tongue thrusting into his mouth and caressing Alias's own. They moaned into each other's mouth, words turning into senseless gasps and groans. Alias lost himself in Deon's warm embrace, mind going blank as rough hands stroked the skin above the waistband of his sweatpants.

Deon jerked back, eliciting a distressed noise from him. "I'm not going anywhere, but you need to drink. I can tell you're not only flushed because you're turned on."

"I'm not only exhausted either," Alias countered. "I've been in bed all week."

"I know."

Alias drained the last of his water without arguing further, and Deon, true to his word, didn't move from his side.

"I'm baffled by how fast my daughter warmed up to you," he said out of the blue. "Not that you're not very likable, but LBV made it difficult for her to engage in many social activities whether she had the energy to leave her bed or not. She's met health specialists and educators and made a few friends her age, but the only constants in her life are me, Jaden, and her grandfather. So she doesn't exactly trust easily. I guess I'm to blame for that, as I never did either."

The straw popped from between Alias's lips. "Her grandfather? I never . . ." His eyes rounded as he recalled how casually Deon had entrusted Betty to Mr. Quint. "Wait. Is Mr. Quint her grandfather?"

"Why yes, of course." Amusement danced in Deon's eyes. "I mean, isn't the resemblance obvious?"

Alias considered it. There had been an inexplicable bond between the two men he'd never quite been able to explain, as well as the mannerisms they shared. Mr. Quint's protective streak made a lot more sense now. "I guess it is."

Deon removed the empty glass from his hand. "I should let you rest," he said, sounding earnest and regretful. "You need it."

"I've rested enough."

"You're still recovering. *Protecting me* has consequences."

An undercurrent of ire laced his voice, and Alias suspected that they would argue about his unilateral decision to take the injection—and Deon's unilateral intention to test it himself—for a while to come.

"McCarthy would have destroyed it all, and for what, greed? Revenge?" He shook his head. "I'm certain you didn't keep your daughter away from her, so I'm at a loss to explain her behavior. What really happened between you two that McCarthy would go to such extremes?"

"Ah." Deon leaned back against the headboard and sighed. "Well, it's quite a sad story. On many levels."

Alias could practically hear the gears turning in his head.

"We didn't . . . plan that night. I'm still not sure what came upon us." Deon tilted his head back, eyes unfocused, no doubt seeing fragments of the past instead of the ceiling. "We never liked each other that much, even though we worked seamlessly for a while. She's always been ambitious, and I was—still am—more concerned with the human repercussions to . . ."

Deon didn't finish the thought. Alias didn't push him, even though the idea of hate sex raised more questions.

"When she became pregnant, she blamed me." Deon let out a mirthless laugh. "She never wanted children, you see. The responsibility. I wasn't considering kids at the time, but the instant she told me, I knew . . ." His voice broke. "I wanted to make it work. Despite our . . . disagreements, I was willing to be there for her, to support her." He dug the heel of his free hand into his eyes and huffed. "She wanted neither my help nor the child, and for a while, I was sure she was going to get an abortion."

Alias sucked in a breath.

"To this day, I'm not sure why McCarthy made the choice she did," Deon said, sadness lacing the words. "But I'll always be grateful to her for bringing Betty into this world."

"So she hates you because . . ." Alias trailed off, not sure how that sentence was supposed to end.

Deon reached for Alias's hand and squeezed it. "It's complicated."

"More complicated than having a child together?"

"Yes. It's no excuse for what she's done, but she had a . . . rough past. When her mother was killed—"

"The virus?"

"Murdered," Deon corrected. "She made sure it wouldn't be common knowledge."

Alias stared. Sympathy was the last thing he'd expected to feel toward McCarthy. When Deon spoke again, his voice was pitched lower.

"Her mother was killed for two hundred forty-three credits. A ludicrous sum."

Alias wouldn't call half his former rent *ludicrous*, but the amount wasn't important.

"McCarthy didn't come out of this unscathed, and I'm not even talking about losing her mother. That night, she was hurt badly by the man who'd killed her mother. She almost bled out in an alley not far from where you used to live."

"Oh . . . Is that why you wanted so badly for me to move out?"

Every emotion on Deon's face seemed to fade, before returning with renewed intensity. Concern. Regret. Tenderness. Sympathy. *Love.*

"Among other things."

Alias shivered. The attack on him and Ben at his former apartment was still fresh in his mind. "I'm confused," he said slowly, gathering his thoughts. "She was ready to destroy your work and kill *millions* to make one person pay?"

"As hard as they might try, some people never recover from the traumatic events that shaped them." Deon took a deep breath. "She must have grown up isolated and without support."

"I grew up isolated too," Alias remarked.

"Yes, but you had a mother to care for, someone to love who loved you right back and tethered you to your humanity. You also made a friend in Ben. McCarthy disliked to talk about her past a great deal, and I believe that part of the reason is that she never had someone who made the past worth remembering. It doesn't excuse what she did. It didn't make me any less angry. But I can understand why someone who might never have been taught to care for herself and others might have chosen the path of destruction.

Alias shivered at the memory of McCarthy aiming her gun at him. What would have happened if the ceiling hadn't collapsed? If—

No. There was no point dwelling on the past.

"Do you think the world is safe now?" he asked tentatively. "From her, I mean?"

"I sure hope so, with her behind bars for assault and attempted kidnapping. Even if her lawyers get her out, her reputation is ruined. But people tend to be very dramatic when they have nothing left to lose." Deon's expression hardened again, at odds with the tender hold he still had on Alias's hand. "Tell me, Alias . . . How did you get access to my safe?"

"There was a flaw." Alias wasn't ashamed of what he'd done, just of how it had been achieved. He told Deon how he'd enlisted Betty's help and gotten to the hypospray just in time, relating McCarthy's demands next. The gun went unmentioned, but the way Deon pursed his lips and pinched his brow made it clear that this particular detail was known to him.

"You kept my daughter safe through it all."

"Well, I tried my best, but—"

"McCarthy had you at gunpoint and demanded that you hand over my daughter and the B-injection, but you gave her neither."

Alias shivered at the pressure of fingers at his nape and the heat filling Deon's gaze.

"Of course not! Betty is yours, and the nanites were mine."

The last word was barely out of his mouth before Deon's mouth found his throat. Alias looped his arms around Deon's neck, yielding to the passionate embrace, gasping at the drag of teeth over his frantic pulse.

"So brave." Deon's voice was so low it was barely recognizable. "And reckless . . . Do you have any idea how I felt when I saw you collapse with my daughter in your arms?"

Alias gasped as cool fingers snaked under his shirt. His skin buzzed, and he dug his nails into strong shoulders, back arching as Deon mouthed hungrily at the line of his neck. "I— I tried to keep her safe, I—"

"And you did. You and that hubot you claimed and worked on so hard both did. But I was worried about you. *You* were the reason I thought I'd lost my mind."

Alias's heart missed a beat. "Deon." It felt surreal to be the one to pull back. To witness the tears on those bruised cheeks. He didn't think he'd ever seen Deon cry.

"Just hold me . . . please?"

When Deon tried to tuck his head under Alias's chin in an obvious attempt to hide, Alias let him. He wanted Deon to talk to him, but perhaps a minute of silence was what Deon needed. Alias let his fingers skim along Deon's broad back. Could Deon soak in the love Alias was trying to express? He tightened his hold as Deon made to pull back.

A chuckle drifted to his ears, the sound happy, if a little wet and fragile. "Just want to kiss you again. That okay?"

"More than okay."

Their mouths met in a light, sweet kiss. The lingering taste of salt would have tugged at Alias's heartstrings if not for how Deon deepened the kiss almost immediately, his enthusiasm wild and contagious with every stroke of tongue. His hands weren't idle either, and before long Alias's shirt was gone, the heat of fabric replaced by the warmth of eager palms.

"You sure we're—ah—done talking?" Alias managed to get out.

"I believe we've talked enough for today." Deon coaxed Alias into lying down and set about covering his chest with kisses. Especially the spot over his beating heart. "I just . . . Fuck, I thought I'd . . ."

Lost you.

Deon's fingers dug into his sides, too hard, but Alias didn't mind. He could read the fear in Deon's hands and lips. He could hear it in Deon's voice, tinged with desperation, and he could taste it on his tongue as he drew Deon in for a kiss.

"I need you," Alias whispered, tugging at Deon's own shirt, sliding his hands under the fabric and dragging his nails down the broad back.

Need to know that you, too, are safe.

Deon didn't reply with words, but the way he hurried to get them both naked spoke for itself. His kisses turned ravenous, a little too rough, just like his hands, caressing over the narrow width of Alias's stomach, each press of fingers arousing in its familiarity. Alias welcomed it all, his own hands roaming over every inch of skin they could reach. Perhaps he should feel vulnerable, stretched out beneath Deon, hips bucking helplessly, but those blue eyes were so soft, so loving, it wasn't hard to let go and relinquish control. In fact, it was the easiest thing in the world to lose himself in Deon's scent and skin, in his reverent whispers. To drown in the knowledge that Deon was right here, with him. Completing the strange puzzle of his life.

"Beautiful . . . Reckless . . . So precious . . ." Deon sucked Alias's right nipple to a taut peak. "I can't ever lose you, sweetheart."

A blush crept up the back of Alias's neck as his little needy sounds and the beeping of the ECG pierced the fog in his mind. "C-can we turn this thing off, please?"

"I don't think so, no."

"Why not?" The protestation came out as a whine.

The kisses Deon bestowed on his neck and shoulders turned feral, hungrier. "Because it will let me know if you're getting too worked up."

"What about if you—*ah*—are getting worked up?"

"I'm not the one who risked my life."

Alias grabbed a fistful of blond hair and snarled. "Please. As if you wouldn't . . . have . . . n-nh . . ."

"You were saying?"

Deon had taken hold of both their cocks. His palm was dry, but it felt wonderful anyway. Every few strokes, he swiped his thumb over the tips, making the slide smoother. Alias dug his heels into the sheets as pleasure gathered at the base of his spine.

"That's it, sweetheart . . ." Deon latched his mouth onto Alias's throat. "You're amazing, you know that? You drive me mad, but that's because you're fucking incredible, and I never want you to change."

Alias arched up into Deon's fist, helpless not to react to the string of praise.

"That's right," Deon crooned, his hand picking up speed. "So good for me. The *best*."

"D-Deon, I . . ." Alias brushed a trembling finger over the coarse hair on Deon's chin, shivering at the warm, throaty exhale over his knuckles. "I need— I need you . . . inside me."

Deon nipped at Alias's wandering finger with a growl. "You should—"

"If you say 'rest' one more time, I swear I will go for a run."

Deon kissed the protest with a faint chuckle. "God, I can't believe I'm considering this right now. I had plans for your first time, you know, and none of them involved a hospital bed *in which you are recovering*." He pulled back, lips twitching in amusement, pupils blown wide, and started rooting around in the bedside table that Dr. Lentz kept stocked with medical equipment. "There should be . . . ah, here it is."

Watching Deon produce lube from the top drawer, Alias couldn't help but blush.

"Medical grade," Deon purred. "Wasn't put there for sexy reasons, but works perfectly for our purpose."

Deon went back to kissing him while he slicked his fingers. He didn't seek Alias's hole right away, seemingly content to drag the pad of one digit back and forth over Alias's taint while peppering kisses on the inside of his thighs.

"Remember, this isn't supposed to hurt, sweetheart." Deon's voice was low and steady, designed to appease. "If it does hurt and for some reason I can't tell, or if you'd like to stop, or pause, you need to let me know, okay?"

"Okay."

There was a question on the tip of Alias's tongue, but he forgot it as soon as Deon wrapped his lips around the tip of Alias's cock. He sucked gently on the glans, adjusting Alias's legs oh so carefully to his liking. Alias's hands turned to fists in the sheets. He wanted to tell Deon to fill him up right now, because he felt so empty and he needed it, needed him, but he knew Deon wouldn't rush this. Would there come a day when they did this, made love so often that Deon could press into him as soon as their clothes came off?

"Fuck, the mouth you've got, Alias."

Oh God, had he been saying all this out loud? He snapped his mouth shut.

"So pretty," Deon groaned, and gave a slow lick to the underside of Alias's cock. "I came here to check on you and give you a stern talk about risking your life but here I am, making love to you." He circled Alias's rim with a slick, warm digit and grunted as the teasing earned him a whine. "You're exquisite. So deliciously sensitive. So determined. It's no wonder I've fallen for you. I'm so glad you decided to tell me how you feel, because I couldn't hold back anymore."

Alias felt the pinprick of tears at the corners of his eyes, but it was happiness blooming in his chest, a raw delight that kept growing, spreading outward until his extremities tingled. Deon kept the compliments coming as he pressed his finger in, mouth hot on the inside of Alias's thighs, the scratch of facial hair against the tender skin of his sack creating the most delicious contrast. Alias dug his heels into Deon's back in an attempt to get him to hurry, light-headed from all the praise.

"Someone's impatient." Deon chuckled, but he worked a second finger alongside the first. Soon enough, those two fingers were rubbing over that tender spot, stretching him with exquisite care and rewiring his body in lines of mindless pleasure and eager pliability. Alias's belly clenched in anticipation, and he moaned Deon's name again, and again, until it was the only word he remembered.

"Fuck, you're hot." Deon pulled both fingers halfway out and pushed them back in, scissoring them. "You take me so well. There, feels good?"

Alias's answer was to work his muscles, clenching and unclenching around the velvety digits. Deon's free hand curled around Alias's cock, giving it a lazy pull. Alias gasped, unable to decide if he wanted to thrust forward or backward. Deon bit over the pulse in Alias's neck while his fingers sped up, breath warm and ragged. Alias vibrated out of his skin with need. He didn't think when he pulled those thick fingers away, and he sure wasn't thinking as he curled his hand around Deon's hard cock and guided it blindly to his twitching entrance.

"*Alias.*"

His head hit the headboard. It hurt, but that pain was but a drop in the sea of his joy and pleasure. He lifted and pushed his hips in a desperate attempt to sheath that delightful promise of fullness.

"Shh . . ." Deon caught Alias's hand in a vice and lifted it from his cock, kissing every knuckle. "Sweetheart, you make it very hard for me to remain a gentleman."

His cock twitched against Alias's hole, and Alias whimpered, moving his hips in small circles, willing his body to yield to the intrusion.

"Wait, wait." Deon squirted more lube onto his fingers and coated Alias's entrance, massaging the fluttering muscles into submission before lowering Alias's trembling legs off his shoulders. "Okay, let's get you on top." He lay on his back and slicked his cock, encouraging Alias to get up on his knees and straddle him. "It'll be easier this way. You'll be able to control the depth and the angle."

Alias exhaled sharply.

"Take your time," Deon instructed.

Alias held Deon's thick cock in one hand and lowered himself onto it, as slowly as he could bear—as fast as he dared.

"That's it," Deon grunted, hands caressing Alias's flanks. "Slowly."

When the head breached him, Alias braced himself on Deon's shoulders, nails sinking into the tanned skin as the tight muscles of his ass spasmed at the intrusion. He wanted to bury his face in Deon's neck, but the angle was wrong. He bore down further and felt Deon's hands on his ass cheeks, thumbs massaging his rim.

Pain and pleasure shot up his spine, sensations crisscrossing in a complex, beautiful mess of contradictory signals. He sank down the rest of the way, thighs trembling as more and more of Deon filled him. When Deon's balls pressed against his backside, he let out a breathy gasp. They fit so well. They just did.

"Feel full," he rasped, and tapped the tip of Deon's nose playfully. He felt drunk and had to chuckle at the bewildered expression he received. "Feel good."

Deon groaned. Alias pulled back the tinniest bit, relishing the warm heat inside him, the tantalizing pressure stimulating parts of him he'd never touched before. He shifted his hips in slow circles, exploring the new sensations afforded by this position.

"God, you're a vision."

Deon's voice was laden with adoration. It flowed down his spine, sweet and thick like honey, the drops heavy as they touched his loins. Deon's fingers followed the trail, wrapping a hand around his throbbing length. Entranced by the song of skin smacking against skin, Alias braced himself against the headboard, the carved wood digging into his palms as he bounced on Deon's cock. The discomfort faded as the pleasure mounted, heightened by all the praise he'd apparently earned. His ears were ringing as he picked up the pace, seeking out the point of no-return, but something was missing, he needed—

Deon's hips snapped upward, meeting his. The next thrust nailed Alias's prostate, ripping a broken cry from his throat.

"You're perfect, Alias." Deon's breath was ragged. His hair stuck out in every direction, and his cheeks were pink from desire, his mouth red and slick. "Such a good boy, allowing me to love you like this. I love you so. Fucking. Much."

Alias's pleasure ratcheted up another notch the moment Deon's hand sped up on his cock. Alias didn't recognize the sound that left his mouth, and he clawed at Deon's chest as spurt after spurt shot from his cock.

"Alias."

Blue eyes widened. Alias cupped Deon's cheek with a tender hand, heart pounding hard for a whole new reason. He could decipher Deon's complex expression just fine, read the desperation and everything it entailed in between the lines of determination and pleasure.

"I'm here."

He snapped his hips faster, hand caressing Deon's face, thumb catching on his lower lip. It was his turn to say those words over and over, to make sure Deon knew they were real. That *he* was real and not going anywhere.

"I love you."

Deon spilled inside him with an unarticulate noise. Alias bent down for a kiss, but the position didn't allow him that much latitude, especially with wobbly legs. The soft gleam in Deon's eyes was mirrored in his smile as he helped Alias off him and onto his side. After cleaning them perfunctorily with his own shirt, Deon pulled the sheets over them.

"Let's get some rest, okay?" He started to pull Alias against his front and paused. "Do you need water or—"

"Just you," Alias whispered, half-asleep already, and snuggled further into his lover's embrace. *Lover*, he thought, giddy. He hadn't meant to fall for Deon, but he had. And against all odds, Deon loved him back. "Just need you."

EPILOGUE

Alias slowed down as he reached the small clearing. A quick scan of the trees produced the people he'd been looking for. Two women and one little girl were busy tending the garden, kneeling with their hands buried in the soil. A flying bot watched over them. Hovering and small talk was all it could do for now, but Dario Quint was working on a solid humanoid shell when he wasn't tinkering with its core processors.

"Hey, Ben."

"Hello, Alias," Ben replied, its voice slightly distorted.

Alias smiled to himself, taking in the scene before him. His mother's face had a healthy glow, and the blond hair the Loveborne virus used to tarnish now blazed under the sun, the strands dancing at her shoulders as she dug yet another hole into the ground.

Betty selected a seedling and handed it to Jaden, whose hair floated wildly around her face for once. The earnest expressions of everyone involved was endearing. The garden was one of Jaden's many side projects she seldom had time to pursue, one that his mother and Betty, who all but lived in the woods after so many years bedridden, were happy to help with. Both his mother and Betty had recovered entirely—like eight-five percent of the people who'd received the B-injection.

A miracle.

One that McCarthy was still fighting. Last he'd heard, her lawyers had gotten her charges dropped and she'd fled to India. Apparently, there were threadbare strings she could pull from within one of the rare pharmaceutical giants in Asia still opposing the liberal distribution of the B-injection.

"It has such tiny roots!" Betty exclaimed, delicately laying the aforementioned roots against her soiled palm. "The rain won't crush it?"

"They will grow," his mother reassured her. "Would you like to try and put it in the ground yourself?"

Alias's chest swelled with affection as his mother guided the smaller hands. Something hard poked his shoulder, and he might have startled if Ben wasn't right there in his face.

"You still appear tired."

Alias sighed. He'd been among those who'd taken the longest to recover. At least he was back to running. And working, although on a more relaxed schedule per Deon's orders. He'd stood his ground, but it wasn't a fight he could win. Not when Deon fought so *dirty*.

His cheeks heated at the memory of last night, and Deon's latest "argument."

"Alias!" Betty exclaimed.

His mother caught the dropped seedling and watched with fondness as Betty threw herself at him. She couldn't have grown much in three months, but every time Alias held her in his arms, he could swear she'd just undergone a growth spurt. He ruffled her hair with his nose and managed not to get any in his mouth.

"You girls look like you're having fun," he said.

Jaden wiped her brow with the back of her hand, adding more soil to her face, before waving at him. Alias replied to her wave with one of his own, before pointing out the smudge. She rubbed at it with the little frown that Bee often had when puzzling over math.

"Looks like everyone's having fun," an amused voice rose at Alias's back.

Alias spun around, his smile widening further. "Hey."

"Hey yourself."

Even after all these months, the simple act of kissing turned his world upside down. It felt even better now, with the knowledge that this love was shared.

"It's easier than I expected," Deon said, fingers running through Alias's hair.

"What is?"

"To love." He cupped Alias's cheek. "It's not as much of a health risk as it used to be, but it's always going to be . . ."

"A vulnerability?" Alias finished for him.

The faint line between Deon's brow disappeared. "And the most wonderful sensation in the world, when it's shared. I never relish the prospect of being vulnerable, but some people—" He kissed the top of Alias's head. "—are definitely worth it."

"Like you."

Deon's eyes were so bright, so blue, the feelings they harbored stretching wider than the sky. "The first time I saw you, my first thought was to protect you. I didn't know you, then, and this protectiveness I felt, this vulnerability, scared me shitless."

Alias huffed. "I'm sure I was more afraid of you than you were of me."

"I'm glad you're not afraid anymore."

"So am I," Alias said, and smiled up at his lover.

They sat down in the grass, Deon with his back against a tree and Alias cuddled up against him. The sky started to darken, prompting Jaden to choose her own tree to lean against, a yawning Betty in her lap. Alias glanced at his mother, who'd elected to lie down on the grass to better watch the sky, a dreamy expression on her face.

Alias brought Deon's hand to his lips, kissing each knuckle in turn.

"'The day you are born, and every day afterward, brings you closer to your death.'"

Deon snorted. "That's an awfully gloomy mood you're in."

"It's from a poem from the 2200s, not a personal belief."

"It's still kind of sad, even if it's true."

"That isn't how the poem ends." Alias had to think for a moment. "'Every day that you love makes that waiting more bearable,'" he said softly.

Deon pressed a kiss to the corner of Alias's smiling mouth. "I like those words better."

"So do I."

Dear Reader,

Thank you for reading Aurecie Macbeth's *Loveborne*!

We know your time is precious and you have many, many entertainment options, so it means a lot that you've chosen to spend your time reading. We really hope you enjoyed it.

We'd be honored if you'd consider posting a review—good or bad—on sites like Amazon, Barnes & Noble, Kobo, Goodreads, Twitter, Facebook, Tumblr, and your blog or website. We'd also be honored if you told your friends and family about this book. Word of mouth is a book's lifeblood!

For more information on upcoming releases, author interviews, blog tours, contests, giveaways, and more, please sign up for our weekly, spam-free newsletter and visit us around the web:

Newsletter: riptidepublishing.com/newsletter
Twitter: twitter.com/RiptideBooks
Facebook: facebook.com/RiptidePublishing
Goodreads: tinyurl.com/RiptideOnGoodreads
Tumblr: riptidepublishing.tumblr.com

Thank you so much for Reading the Rainbow!

RiptidePublishing.com

ACKNOWLEDGMENTS

I'd like to thank everyone who's supported my writing and been involved in this book, from my family and friends to the whole team at Riptide. Special thanks to A. for encouraging me to keep going when I thought I couldn't.

Last but not least, thank *you* for reading!

ALSO BY
AURECIE MACBETH

Read Me True

ABOUT
THE AUTHOR

Aurecie Macbeth has been crafting romance stories for half her current age and doesn't plan to stop anytime soon. When her writer lair is empty, Aurecie is either rock climbing, learning to be fluent in six languages, or daydreaming about more stories. She doesn't have a teckel (yet), but she loves these dogs so much that most people assume she must have at least twelve. Speaking of twelve: when she's forced to get up before that time, she recoils from sunlight like a newborn vampire—make sure to throw some holy coffee her way.

Twitter: twitter.com/aurecie

Goodreads: www.goodreads.com/author/show/19992547. Aurecie_Macbeth

Enjoy more stories like
Loveborne
at RiptidePublishing.com!

Fall and Rising

Threads of chance and destiny
draw these three together.

ISBN: 978-1-62649-301-8

A Taste of Rebellion

He's ready to fight for his
people, but will he fight for
love?

ISBN: 978-1-62649-948-5

www.ingramcontent.com/pod-product-compliance
Lightning Source LLC
Chambersburg PA
CBHW030640020726
47493CB00006B/1798